weight of a woman

judith jackson-pomeroy

ODYSSEY
BOOKS

Cataloguing-in-Publication entry is available from the National Library of Australia: www.catalogue.nla.gov.au

978-1922311627 (paperback)

978-1922311634 (ebook)

Cover design by 100covers.com

This book is a work of fiction. Names, characters, places, and incidents are either the product of the author's imagination or are used fictitiously, and any resemblance to actual persons, living or dead, business establishments, events, or locales is entirely coincidental.

To my children:
Blythe (who grew up during the writing of this novel) and Bryony "Brin"
(who doesn't remember a time before this story lived).
The two most precious things on earth.

chapter one

The club erupted into applause as Eyva bellowed a final scream into the microphone. It vibrated down Sara's spine and lingered in the space behind her knees. She put her drink down on the bar to applaud, waving away the nuts Marco pushed in her direction.

"They're outrageously political," Sara gushed.

Eyva, her former student, alternated her voice between screams and breathy whispers, leaving the lyrics almost completely unintelligible to Sara. Catching the odd word, and knowing the band was famed for their polemics on class, race, and gender oppression, she guessed that the song had at least *something* to do with sex workers, but who really knew?

Marco shrugged, indifferent. "Not very lyrical."

"They're asking the question: is your life censored?" Sara bellowed as the thunderous cheers died down.

"My life is uncensored; therefore, I am," Marco said, rummaging through Sara's bag, landing on a lip gloss. "Do you have a compact?"

She batted his hand away and dug into her bag to pull out a thick wad of paper. "Read this." She thrust the pages at him. "It's my updated syllabus for the feminist philosophy seminar."

Marco mocked exertion at the heft of its weight. "It's a veritable tome!" He flipped through the dozens of pages. "And you carry it around? To clubs?"

Sara played with her cocktail napkin, suddenly self-conscious of her nerdiness. "I came straight from my office."

"It's Friday tomorrow. Lighten up, Sara." Marco read the course description: "Emphasis on how intersectional philosophy explains women's experience." He handed it back to her. "Sounds exciting."

She shoved him playfully. "It is exciting, and you know it."

"So, get your veritas in there, like, Women's Studies: Explanations on Why Our Lives *Suck*. Crush it with onomatopoeia." He pushed the bowl of nuts closer.

Sara laughed and took a sip of wine to save Marco from force-feeding her. "We're not all award-winning poets like you, Professor Gonzalves."

"Don't you need to soak that up?" He motioned to the fresh glass of wine the waiter put on the bar in front of her.

"From that guy over there, Professor Sara," the waiter told her, pointing across the bar. Recognizing him as one of her students, she lifted the drink and nodded 'cheers', then turned back to Marco. She pushed the nuts back in his direction.

"I forgot you only eat cruciferous vegetables," he said as Eyva screeched into the microphone: "Stay real, dudes! We love you!" to which the crowd erupted into more applause. Marco laughed.

Enthusiastically, Sara joined the laugh, hoping to distract him from his patronizing and increasing therapy-like attention to her chronic dieting, or what he'd taken to calling her eating disorder. Her ire increased as she recalled all Marco's cracks about her eating habits. The other day he had a particularly theatrical reaction to stumbling across her calorie-count notebook while looking for a lip liner in her bag and complaining that her 'cis White woman' tint didn't complement his skin tone. She knew chronic dieting was perhaps not the best way to represent herself at her current gig in the women's studies department at a no-name university—and it would look even worse at Wellesley, the place of her academic dreams, where she'd just applied for a fellowship. She was supposed to be a role model, teaching female students how to liberate themselves from the social pressure to be pretty and thin. *The irony, for god's sake.* After all, she was the expert, the go-to person on campus for all that was known—and even the not-so-well known —about women's issues. Not to mention she was also the lone PhD volunteer at the Women's Resource Center (WRC), where she both counseled rape survivors and lectured on eating disorders. No, the dieting was not an eating disorder; it was just an attempt to get back into her designer jeans. And *this* was what was really troubling her —fashion, or what she called *visual small talk,* the apparel equivalent of small talk. She spent most of her meager wages on designer shoes, belts, and jeans. That and Trader Joe's three-dollar bottles of wine. She got the clothes on consignment or at T.J. Maxx, and just that morning, on eBay, discovered a great deal on some Jimmy Choos. Coveting the anti-fashion look, she wanted to look deliberately dismissive of capitalism and the hegemonic norms regarding feminine appearance. She guessed none of the thought leaders at Wellesley would occupy themselves with the vagaries of fashion. Sinking with the thought, she realized she would never be as good of a scholar as those at Wellesley. Surely they had accumulated enough patriarchy-survivor therapy to become self-actualized, freeing themselves up to focus on solving the real problems like women's oppression, not wasting time on eBay like *this* archetypal cis White woman.

She eyed Eyva with admiration. With her lacy black bra, Catholic-school-girl-style skirt, Doc Martens, and knee socks, the words *rape, incest,* and *slut* were scrawled in black lipstick on various limbs; she was as resplendent in her anti-fashion as she was in her attitude. Sara shot an eye over her own outfit: designer jeans and Hermes belt. She tutted with disgust at her visual small talk problem, then sank still further as she remembered her Jimmy Choo purchase. She'd never get into Wellesley if they knew.

She encouraged Marco to reconsider the music, more to distract from both his badgering about her food intake and her further angst about her fashion problem than trying to convince him. "The Bacchantes are only heralded as the best post-punk feminist band in New England."

"They sound just like the Anoraks." They *were* very similar to the Anoraks, the all-girl band that she'd just spent the past eight months researching. "But louder," Marco added, just as Sara spotted Allyson.

Allyson was one of the most opinionated voices in her class, and a student volunteer at the WRC. She bopped over to the bar, joining

Sara and Marco. Jumping up and down like a pogo stick, Allyson spouted, "Aren't they awesome? I'm in love with the drummer." The drummer, another girl clad similarly to Eyva, but sporting crazy long dreadlocks and heavy, smeared make-up, waved wildly in their direction. Allyson grabbed Sara's hand to drag her toward the stage.

Of course, in usual circumstances, it would be unthinkable for such an interaction to occur between student and professor, but Sara's relationship with her students was unique. Her seminar mandated a rethinking of the professor-student relationship. Something innovative and completely deconstructed, not the pedagogy of the elite that was in place when she went to college. To foster that, they met once a week at the Tin Palace, a popular campus bar, and occasionally she even went to events like this with them.

The Baccantes were made up of Jeff, the bassist (who wore a T-shirt that announced 'dickless loser'); Brad, the guitarist (gender deliberately ambiguous); Z, also known as Deb; Eyva, their singer; and their latest lead guitarist, Poetry Boy. Seeing him there, Sara felt her heart beat a little faster, her breath caught in her throat. He'd been a former student of Marco's and the longest-running member in his group, the Men's Circle, a sort of alternative support group devoted to tearing down and reconstructing cultural scripts about sexuality, fashion, and language to focus on enhancing self-authenticity. Sara tried to pay attention to Deb, who was holding hands with Allyson while she rattled on about a music scout who had apparently come to see Poetry Boy. She watched him curiously as he chatted with Eyva, gesticulating with his hands and face. She hadn't seen him so demonstrative before. Maybe, between the volume of noise and the odors of cigarettes, pot, and alcohol, exaggerated responses were needed in order to appeal to a higher sensory system and get anyone's attention in this place. He went by Seth too, not just Marco's preferred moniker of Poetry Boy. Despite Marco being known for his breathless enthusiasm for guys he liked, this one had completely captured her interest with his fine mind.

Up until two weeks ago, when he enrolled in her seminar, she'd only ever *seen* him. The first time, Marco was visiting her office and began pointing frantically and yelling "Poetry Boy!" as Seth sailed by her office window on a skateboard.

Extricating herself from the gathering on stage, Sara headed back to the bar, chastising herself. What was she thinking? It was ridiculous. After all, she was a professor—well, an adjunct lecturer at a "No-Name University" where she had no firm contract—and applying for a fellowship to Wellesley, although she knew that her application was probably the biggest long shot in the history of academic aspirations. Also, he was a student, notwithstanding at the graduate level and surely barely five years younger than her. Nonetheless, he was her student. And besides, she had a boyfriend. Tom was a professor at the same university, with a proper job, not some poetry-reading gig and a side job playing guitar at local clubs and counseling male students in the DIY culture espoused in the Men's Circle. All right, she *was* turned on by Seth's sexy, unkempt look, his grasp of the books on her curriculum, and his sensitivity and empathy for the girls' voices in the seminar, but Tom was handsome. Classically beautiful with his chiseled jawline and cut body, and smart too. Although, unlike Seth, he hadn't read a single book she liked. She tried to reassure herself that this was all just silliness, almost exclusively alcohol-induced silliness. Despite that, just to be safe, she reminded herself not to drink too much more around Seth because, if she did, she was certain to forget her resolve and flirt.

Poetry Boy joined her at the bar, simultaneously distracting and disarming her with his smile. She felt only aggravation with herself. Aggravation and sudden heat with his close proximity. Seeing him take in her inebriated state, which was impossible to hide next to his obvious sobriety, made her utterly self-conscious. He smirked, steadying her.

"Great set," she said, hoping to redirect from her slightly drunken stupor. While Sara never lost sight that she was the professor, she recognized her approach to pedagogy created a fine line for both her and the students to tread. Sometimes students did become confused about the relationship, pushing and even perforating the boundaries. With experience behind her, Sara made sure that no serious infractions occurred, no lines were irrevocably crossed. However, with her inhibitions discarded in that last glass of wine, she was left clinging to a narrow hope to resist flirting.

She sipped from her glass of wine. "Not drinking tonight?"

"I don't drink very often."

This made her feel even more self-consciously drunk, so she was relieved when Callum and Michael appeared. The three of them together represented the entire contingent of male students in her class. Only the bravest men ever enrolled, making her wonder who would drop out before the semester ended. The two of them toted the largest mugs of draft beer she'd ever seen, plus a glass of wine for her.

"Who's the whore-inscribed babe?" Michael queried Seth, checking out Eyva.

"Fuck off," Sara heard Seth say as she looked around in desperation for a lifeline, or some similarly inebriated female company. Spotting Allyson, she nodded a farewell and snuck away.

The escape was short-lived. Seth joined her at the bar once the band started their second set. She noticed him quickly glance at yet another fresh drink in her hand, and her anxiety over being judged got the best of her.

"Have one. Might loosen you up a bit."

Seth raised his eyebrows and laughed.

Sara held her glass to his lips, insistent. "Seriously. You need this. Please."

After gazing at her for a long moment, he finally placed his hand over hers to steady the glass as he sipped from her drink. Mortified at the effect of his hand on hers, she tore the drink away, spilling most of it on the floor before he barely took a sip. Trembling all over, overcome with shyness, she feigned a casual smile, hoping the dim light of the club would hide her blushing.

"Well, it's a start."

He nodded and dropped his eyes to the floor. "I finished the book," he blurted. "Marxist..." he started, reminding her of the title, but of course she remembered. She routinely loaned books to students, and they were returned months, even years later, usually unread.

"You've only had it four days."

He shrugged. "I thought it was compelling."

Sara laughed so hard she choked on her drink. "You found *Intersectional Theory: Contextualizing Women's Oppression* compelling?"

Seth smirked at her astonishment. "Super tight thesis about women as the first slaves," he said, and started to expound on the theory. He was certainly using all the appropriate words. She caught something about the connection between capitalism and patriarchy, then a reference to the proliferation of gender norms that are necessary to reinforce the legitimacy of hegemony, but since her head was throbbing, the room spinning and becoming a bit hazy, she really couldn't say for certain whether he was talking about philosophy or one of those clever children's programs on PBS.

He cast a penetrative gaze into her eyes, and she held it, considering how sexy he was, and then was vexed to notice that he was yet another person who appeared to have a solid grasp on the anti-fashion look. She was particularly taken with a piece of hemp string that seemed to function as a belt. In contrast to her own look, his resigned her to the knowledge that she might be forever doomed to *visual small talk*—that is, censored, boring. She surveyed her labeled look again and made a silent vow to get herself to one of Eyva's workshops, where she could liberate herself from this problem.

Sara suddenly realized he was awaiting a response to what must have been a question. She scolded herself as she stared blankly back at him, hoping that if she did this long enough, he might repeat himself, move on, or believe she was giving it some deeper, professor-like thought.

When he opted to repeat the question, Sara made sure to pay attention, finally gathering that he was trying to understand the difference between materialist and historical Marxism.

She wanted to scream, "You think in my state I could even say those words?" In hindsight, that response would have been better than the one that spilled from her mouth.

"I don't know." She laughed with a shrug as she rocked back and forth with the music. "Right now, I couldn't tell you the difference between a feminist and a pole dancer, although, in my defense, some pole dancers are feminists." Cringing, racking her brains for where that comparison had come from, Sara buried her nose in her glass, guzzling to keep from saying anything more.

Sara chided herself for skirting so close—so many times—to slicing through the thin veneer of the boundary that stood between their respective roles. She barred herself from opening her mouth again and resisted the urge to bury her face in her hands.

"Maybe you could explain it during office hours?" He slammed the barricade back into place.

"Absolutely," she said, relieved. "I'd like nothing more than to explain it then, when I'm sober."

Luckily, at that moment, before Seth could respond or Sara could dig herself a deeper trough of ignominy, chaos erupted on the stage. Eyva was being mauled by a surge of fans that security was unable to hold back. Seth tore across the room, screaming at the security officers. With the risk of bruising every limb, Sara watched as he dove over the barricade at the exact same moment one of the security team scooped up Eyva like she was a bag of feathers.

Sara's sides suddenly ached severely from hunger, prompting her to consider eating the little snack she had perennially tucked in her bag. Fifty calories. Zero fat. She thought she could spare it. With a hungry purpose, she strode off back to the bar, away from the stage, where Seth hugged Eyva.

Berating herself for having drunk so much that she needed to break her no-food-after-eight rule, a twinge of jealousy stabbed at her.

Marco interrupted her thoughts. "What the fuck is that?" He screwed up his nose at the sight of the snack she produced from her bag.

"Kamut cereal," she told him, delving for a handful before looking back at the chaotic scene on the stage, wondering if Seth and Eyva were *together*. "Don't say anything," she warned Marco, not needing more snarky comments about the weird foods she permitted herself to eat. She was feeling miserable enough already, both about her hunger and the risk of never getting back into her jeans, and because she felt silly caring so much about Seth's status with Eyva. "I know I'm hot-mess professor of the year," she muttered glumly.

In between bites, she shot a sarcastic smile at Marco's raised eyebrows and reflected on her shortcoming. As she looked with longing across the room at Seth, she considered that maybe her chronic dieting and her visual small talk issues were not her only problems.

chapter two

Determined to be the poster child of scholarly decorum after her behavior with Seth the night before, Sara scurried through her office bookshelf, pulling one classic text after another in the hopes of putting together a lecture to redeem herself. With takeout coffees in hand, Marco entered. Mumbling thanks, Sara barely looked at him.

"Why so frantic?"

She flipped through a text. "I was so drunk last night."

"I noticed," he said absently, rifling through her desk, pulling out a pamphlet Sara had written for the WRC on both her professional and personal experience with sexual assault. "You should read this," he said, idly scanning it before flashing her the section on addictions. "Eating disorders, substance abuse, a preoccupation with sex."

Sara shot him a derisive smile, ignoring the bait. She was far too busy (and too hungover) for that conversation. "I think I said some crazy things to Seth," she said, hoping since he was one of Marco's favorite subjects, this would effectively deflect his interest.

He stopped to give her his full attention. "Like what?"

"I don't even remember much. I just know it was guttingly embarrassing, utterly lacking any professorial composure."

"You might be more lucid, or at least more amenable to coherent conversation, *if* you ate a couple hundred handfuls of that gross cereal *before* you go and drink an entire bottle of wine with margarita chasers." Marco returned to rummaging in her desk after tossing the pamphlet at her.

"Not helpful, Marco," Sara said, continuing to scour the book-shelf. "I have to make it all better. He's my student, thanks to you telling him I am the only straight White professor on campus that understands anything about being woke, although he must be doubting that now."

Marco picked up the pamphlet and shoved it into her free hand, then sat back down to resume his perusal of her desk. "Be on your professor-of-the-year game, you mean." He landed on an unopened box of condoms in the top drawer. "Really? Does Tom frequently stop in for an office fuck? Because that seems unlikely, given what I know about Tom." He said his name disparagingly.

He was right. She fell silent and started playing with her hair, curling a strand tighter and tighter around her finger.

"What's up?"

She released her finger from her hair to examine the purplish-red bruising. "I think it's getting serious."

"What was your first clue? Because it should have been the box of condoms he leaves on your nightstand."

Her first clue was that not only did he expect to see her every weekend, but he also expected to stay over regularly. Then, about a month ago, she noticed he was leaving more of his things at her apartment. Even his homemade kimchi supply had started to pile up in her bare fridge, and he'd begun to encourage her to eat better foods. She supposed by "better foods" he meant something other than her staple protein bars and spinach. When he said, "For your health, Sara," she'd almost broken up with him.

"Ugh," she said, throwing her face into her hands, followed by the rest of herself onto her office couch.

"He's so…perfect, with his perfect hair and never-pilled wool sweaters, all his academic awards, and total respect from the univer-sity," she said, as if these were reprehensible character flaws. "I'm messy."

Sara wasn't at all surprised when Tom had asked her out for coffee. She'd caught him looking at her when they would run into each other at her favorite campus spots, including the bagel café, where she would buy her black coffee and hold-everything-but-the-spinach salads while he ordered his whole milk latte and roast beef on rye, or at the natural food store where she bought five-pound bags of carrots to nibble on throughout the day and he bought unnaturally copious amounts of yogurt for an average male. She couldn't understand why this Poster Boy was interested in "messy" Sara. *But, of course, unlike me seeing right through him, maybe he hasn't noticed my choices.*

Marco nodded. "Messy indeed. There's your heavy drinking, your starvation diet," he went on, ignoring her gestures to stop. "Your tenuous status at the university."

She cut him off. "He's visual small talk itself. He's not living authentically at all," she whined. Feeling guilty, she tried to soften it. "Bless him. He must spend a small fortune on dry cleaning all those wool sweaters."

"Those are your objections?" Marco laughed. "He might be the straightest, Whitest man I've ever known, but at least you're getting to screw GQ boy."

Sara's objections were pathetic when it was put like that. Busy enough dealing with her need to redeem herself as a good professor, she decided she could deal with the increasingly uncomfortable feelings about Tom another time. "You're right. If nothing else, it's at least safe, regular sex." This, of course, elicited a lascivious smile from Marco.

Sex was something they talked a lot about. Rather than closing the subject of Tom, she should have known it would be an opening for Marco to talk about his favorite topic: DIY sex—experimental sex, the turning of traditional ideas of sexuality on its head that the Men's Circle promoted. It was Marco's thing. Sara bled feminism, so she should have been more curious to understand, but she couldn't help shrinking away from mentions of S&M or role playing with outfits and scripts. It was a slalom-like discourse, taking one down time-consuming paths, and she had to get to class.

As Sara got up to leave, she kissed Marco on the lips before nodding at the box of condoms. "I picked those up today. I didn't want to leave them in my bag with all my lecture notes." She shoved her syllabus into her bag. "I had visions of them spilling onto the lectern when I pulled out my notes. Be an odd impression of your professor, wouldn't it?"

Marco gave a noncommittal nod, checking his hair in his compact before handing it to Sara. "Check your teeth. Spinach, I think. And I disagree. It wouldn't be an odd impression. You could use it as a teaching point. Force them to situate their shock in the context of their cultural assumptions about professors being asexual beings." He got poetic with his politics. "A Walt Whitman, *Song of Myself*, valved voice moment." It was hard enough to keep her students' attentions on the tomes she assigned, let alone with visions of condoms in their heads.

Finishing her inspection, Sara motioned to the door. "Let's go."

As they prepared to leave each other, Sara on her short walk to her seminar room and Marco to his office across campus, she returned to the subject of her teeth. "By the way, is it gone? Was it spinach?"

Marco inspected and nodded. "What else would it be? You never eat anything else."

Sara exhaled heavily, flustering as she walked off. "I eat lots of things," she said, breaking into a jog as he queried loud enough for passers-by to hear, "How *do you* bend that eating disorder around your role as women's studies professor?"

* * *

More prepared than she'd ever been for a seminar, Sara waved the course text at her students, then turned to the whiteboard to scrawl:

How does Marx conflate gender and class?

Are unexpurgated lives possible within gendered reality?

She wrote speedily, then spun around to slap her hand on her words.

Callum shook his head and cocked one side of his lip in amusement. "*Gendered* what?"

"Page two in the text," she told him. "We'll connect this with the question of female sexual agency."

Intending to address the entire class, her eyes inadvertently landed on Seth. His penetrative gaze immediately gave her goosebumps. Fortunately, she had Allyson to remind her of her mission to be professional.

"Patriarchy prevents women from living authentically," Allyson began. "Even our orgasms are a performance."

A sharp radar for male bristling, Sara didn't miss Callum squirm at Allyson's assessment.

"Patriarchy, blah, blah, blah."

Allyson scoffed, but Sara let him go on, partly out of curiosity and partly to allow him to dig himself a hole so Allyson could rip his head off and shove him in it.

"Stop to consider that every society is patriarchal. There might be something more to this, beyond your perception of men having an insatiable desire for world domination."

"This *is* a women's studies seminar, Callum," Allyson spat. "So, I think you mean an insatiable desire for *cunt* domination."

Callum smiled, and the class exploded into chatter. Sara felt the urge to play with her hair. She had to work hard not to in these instances. She settled on examining her nails, then playing with her bottom lip. Biding her time before pulling them back in. Sara did have an agenda—her syllabus—and although Allyson's tirades often led them astray, it was a women's studies seminar and Sara felt it her duty as a lecturer of such a class to allow Allyson the freedom of expression and, from time to time, derail her planned agenda. It was a hidden part of the curriculum to let the women in the class have a place to raise their voices, a closeted goal. Today, however, Sara wanted to keep her careful planning on track and didn't let the discussion carry on as long as she usually would have.

Taking a huge gulp of coffee to stave off her hunger, she jumped back in. "Back to our focus on sexual agency." She picked up the text. "The band last night was proclaiming an alternative community of sexuality. What does that *actually* look like, and how does it connect with Stoltenberg?"

Allyson launched in immediately.

Sara shot a look at Seth, who was listening attentively, then at Callum, making sure he was listening. He was doodling.

Sara cleared her throat, trying to wake Callum up to the importance of the point Allyson was trying to make, countering the argument with an assessment of the hegemonic elements within this community. The Bacchantes embodied her utopia, eschewing all traditional expectations for women and men, blurring gender lines, and turning conventional wisdom on its head. They gave feminists permission to be fully sexual beings with agency of desires and explore freely the cultural notions of sexual identity and behavior.

"Taylor Swift, Britney, Lady GaGa," Callum said. "They're counter hegemonic. Giving the finger to the notion that a girl should be sweet and nice."

"Unarguably sexually audacious, yes." Sara folded her arms to finish it off. "But that's not sexual agency. That's performance, all about epitomizing hegemonic male desire."

She snuck a quick glance in Seth's direction; perched forward in his seat, frantically taking notes, riveted. Sara suppressed a smile at his interest. "It fits squarely within the hegemonic definition of feminine sexuality. Within mainstream record labels, these performers are unwittingly buying into the entire value of female as commodity."

Allyson piped in on the tail end. "A hulking chunk of the backbone that supports patriarchy."

"But guys, too," Seth spoke up. "Stoltenberg says guys' sexuality is co-opted by the porn industry."

"What?" Callum threw in derisively.

"Did you read it, Callum?" Sara asked.

"No."

Seth continued. "He says that since the porn industry defines sex for men as penetration of dick into pussy, and everything else is *not* sex, men have very limited agency too."

Sara's arousal at knowing he had read Stoltenberg so carefully, even employing his colloquialisms, flustered her. She'd never felt like *that* in class before.

Callum emitted a half laugh, leaning back in his chair, hands locked at the back of his head. "Well, yeah, the porn industry's right, Coles."

Seth shook his head side-to-side, but so slightly it was probably only Sara who noticed, watching him intently out of the corner of her eye as she was.

"Dude," Callum started again, "we both know blow jobs are ace, but getting your dick in is *it*." Undeterred by the plethora of groaning from the rest of the class, Callum leaned forward again in his chair, hands locked in supplication, looking ready to finish it off. "That's no limiting of my agency."

"Are you for fucking real, Callum?" Allyson yelled. "Do you honestly think you had a choice about your sexuality? You don't think the porn industry shaped your sexual desire and who you want to fuck and how you want to fuck them? You overestimate your role in—"

Callum cut her off. "I love pussy. That's *my* choice." He casually released his locked hands to resume his doodling.

"Exactly," Allyson said, clearly feeling like he was making her point for her. "But is your desire authentic, or is it the porn industry's doing?"

"Is my desire authentic?" he said, mimicking her voice and taking a moment to look away from his doodling. "Fuck me. It's not that the porn industry told me to like pussy. The idea of sucking dick is just..."

Sara looked around the class and her eyes fell on Lisaly, a student who never said much in class. Sara often found herself trying to gauge what she might be thinking. Lisaly was listening, it seemed, and it perplexed Sara that she looked so indifferent.

Seth shot around to confront Callum. "Everyone can hear your fucking hate, Cal. Shut up, you fucking homophobe."

"What? You're gay now?" Callum charged back.

Seth delighted the girls when he simply shrugged; even Lisaly reacted, biting on her bottom lip to suck in a grin.

"Nah, I don't think so. Pussy whipped is what you want to be."

"What does this reading add to this discussion?" Sara raised the textbook again, a novel that presented a story of a young woman who was beaten on her wedding night after the groom discovered that he wasn't her first. The husband was addicted to porn and so it made a nice segue back to the syllabus. "Did you read this, Callum?" she asked, singling him out.

"Yes," he said, too proudly.

"What happens to the bride after the beating?" she asked, hoping to keep them focused for the last few minutes of the seminar, when Lisaly spoke up.

"Who cares? Seriously. Who the fuck cares?"

Allyson, eager to appear supportive, swiveled around to face her with such speed that her chair slipped off its hinge. Everyone was momentarily sidetracked with the concern of the broken chair and Allyson nearly landing on the floor.

Once she was righted, Sara held up a hand to silence the class and turned to address Lisaly directly. "You were saying?" The customarily quiet Lisaly would need some encouragement to continue.

Lisaly sighed, looking around at her classmates. "As the lone brown girl here, I'd like to say maybe it's actually a privilege to care about porn addictions when crimes against Brown and Black women are ignored by the criminal justice system."

Allyson's alert face said, "Teach us, sister." Sara was embarrassed. The Brown student was being called upon to educate her White friends, again. In one breath, Lisaly had said more than Sara had been able to express in the last two weeks of her painstakingly prepared seminar notes, and probably more than the entire 600-page text she had so carefully selected.

For once, Callum listened intently, but they were over their classroom time, and students for the next class were starting to fog up the glass in the door with impatience on waiting.

"Sorry," Lisaly threw in. "I know we've moved on from porn to bride burning."

Sara heard her emphasis on those topic choices and felt the weight of her fatigue. "No, no. Let's pick that up next time." She would have to figure out how to draw this out of Lisaly without turning her into Sojourner Truth.

* * *

While everyone filed out and Sara busied herself shoving everything back into her bag, Seth walked to her desk.

"Sorry I got off track with Cal," he offered, handing in his weekly journal.

"Don't worry about it." She put his journal on the pile and walked toward the door with Seth in tow. "It's understandable. He's provocative."

They stood outside the door as Sara put her bag down to try to squeeze the journals in. She prattled on. "But you should know," she said, busily keeping her attention on the contents of her bag and away from his gorgeous smile, "I think his jocular provocations are deliberate." She'd seen Callum's work, after all. He was making an effort and starting to develop a nuanced understanding of the material.

Seth was too close to her.

"You're shorter than I thought." It thrilled her that he'd also noticed this.

"I was wearing heels last night," she said, thinking about how inappropriately she had behaved with him at the club. "You're shorter than I thought, too."

"You stood next to me for a while last night. You didn't notice then how tall I am?" Had she really been that drunk?

Sara's admiration of him was always at a distance: across a desk in seminar, in her office, or skateboarding across the campus. Standing with him there, she noticed he constantly played with the end of his mechanical pencil, how he stood too close to her asking questions, how she liked the smell of him, that his eyes were blue, and he needed a shave. After the sexual fantasies she'd had about him, his closeness unnerved her.

"I encourage you to journal about your confrontations with Callum and Michael, or…" she stammered, grasping for what to say. "The Men's Circle. That too."

To distract herself from her thoughts, she barraged him with questions about Marco's circle.

"How's it going there? Do you like it? Is it helpful with the readings in the seminar?" She should shut up and give him a chance to speak, but she didn't want to make her attraction obvious. Even after he started to nod and open his mouth to speak, she prattled on, desperate to mask how flushed she felt. "Marco told me you've been in the circle a few times."

More nodding, more intense fidgeting with the mechanical pencil.

"Amazing group," she said, wondering how she could make him so nervous.

At a lull of the incessant chatter, he jumped in. "Are you still having office hours on Friday?"

She tried to look indifferent, hoping to give him a look that did not yell *Friday? Yes! In fact, I'm on the edge of my seat to show you just what a brilliant professor I really am.*

"You wanted me to explain the difference between historical versus material Marxism, didn't you? Sure. Friday, then." She resisted the urge to continue. "Well, I have to get this to my office." She motioned to the journals and papers spilling out of her bag.

"I'm going that way." He picked up his skateboard. "I'll help you carry all this."

On the way there, they fell into an uncomfortable silence. She hoped it wasn't obvious that she liked him. In a poor attempt to deflect, she offered inane chitchat about the weather and price of coffee compared from one end of the campus to the other. In her office, they continued to chat about nothing for so long that it grew dark outside. She wanted to get to know him; it appeared that was what he wanted too. Purposely, she kept conversation light, and she got the sense that he was working hard to do the same.

chapter three

Seth sat in her office that Friday, taking notes as she expertly answered his questions. Sara felt she'd redeemed herself as a scholarly figure. Afterwards, she casually asked how often his band played at the club.

"I get free meals when we play, so as often as they'll have us. I've been playing there since I was seventeen." He said "seventeen" like it was a million years ago.

"How old are you?" she asked.

"Twenty-seven. You?"

Sara was disgusted, both with her immediate reaction to say *only five years older than you,* and the hope that he was asking because he was *interested.* The eek-eek of the creak as she adjusted herself in the rickety wooden chair was deafening. She took this opportunity to dutifully remind herself that she was with Tom. Picking up the book he had returned, she ordered her brain to think of something to say about it. She cleared her throat.

"We toured last year."

Her eyebrows raised with interest, partly because she was relieved he had shifted the conversation.

"It was a crap tour. The only bright spot to it was playing to genuinely enthusiastic audiences. You know, people really living it."

"I'd love to hear some of your music."

Seth smiled broadly and fidgeted in his seat."Do you actually listen to this music or just research it?"

"Both. I'm fascinated with how musicians utilize music as a resistance to culture." The opportunity to talk about it excited Sara. "Sometimes forcing change, sometimes reflecting it." Her momentum faltered as she waved her hand over the tome on her desk. "I'm trying to find a publisher for my book on the feminist music scene."

Seth's eyes widened. Sara took some pleasure in the fact he seemed impressed.

"Hopefully it will make a little way toward exposing the weight of being a woman." She flipped through the pages. "That's all I've ever really want to do, so my interest in the music scene is about trying to improve women's lives through exposing the inequities we have to endure."

"What's the book?" He hitched even more forward in his seat. "Is it a radical theory-based thesis?"

Sara shrugged.

His mouth opened slightly at the intellectual foreplay. She knew she shouldn't, but she went on. Sara upheaved words that described the institutions that had hollowed her out: capitalism, patriarchy, and their corollaries—gender, sexism—while Seth bandied about even sexier words, such as hegemony and deconstruction. Their meanings carried the full weight of her anger, and she hurled them with abandon in her lectures, like weapons against the oppressor. His ability to use them—and in full sentences too—made Sara almost swoon. There was nothing sexier than someone who was a fine thinker.

"I'm reading at the Black Hole tonight," he told her. "I'd love to hear what you think, if you can come, I mean." He started to trail off.

"Right! Yes, I'll think about it. I mean, I probably can. Sure."

After he left, she practically ran to Marco's office. "Tell me about his writing," she said as she busted through the door, thrusting a caramel cappuccino into Marco's face. She breathlessly pulled off her coat and scarf and slumped onto the edge of his desk.

Marco, known to become dreamy-eyed over his musings on Poetry Boy, was thrilled to be engaged. "He not only knows how to craft a good simile, break a line, and write effortless metaphors with effective imagery, but he also tackles fresh subjects. It's just beautiful, edgy."

Her interested piqued. "He told me he's reading at the Black Hole Poetry Club tonight. He said he'd like to know what I think."

"Let's both go!" Marco screeched.

Sara choked on her coffee. "Should we? Really?"

"We should. I'll pick you up."

Sara nodded numbly, wondering if she should go, especially since she would now have to make her excuses to Tom. They were supposed to be having dinner at a posh new bistro. She considered how very grown up that was compared to a dive poetry club. An ironic last thought, especially when Marco added, "I'll offer to pick Seth up too, because he only has a skateboard, the sexy thing."

* * *

To get Seth's attention after the poetry reading, Marco flapped his hands around in the air.

Seth joined them on the long, wide lunchroom-styled table, purposely designed for *community*. At that distance, she could barely hear him, let alone see him in the dim light. When he told them he was starving and needed to order food because he was leaving early to play with the Bacchantes, Marco barraged him with questions.

"You know about Sara's research? On women's music?"

"Just the one band," Sara interjected. "My manuscript you saw earlier, it's an observation study with the Anoraks."

Seth nodded in recognition. "Great band lyrically, especially the songs written by Clair and Tara."

Sara beamed. "You know Clair?" She patted the seat beside her.

"Evidently," said Marco, as Seth accepted Sara's invitation to the seat beside her. "Where the fuck is that cute waiter with the goatee?"

Sara and Seth were too engrossed to notice.

"It concerns me that the guys from the band write most of the lyrics," he said.

"I feel exactly the same way."

"Clair and Tara's voices are really powerful. They should be more up front."

Sara was vibrant in her agreement, but then, seeing Marco all churlish with the time she was getting with *his* Poetry Boy, she backed off, smiling.

"And what a name...the *Anoraks*. Where do they get these ugly names?" Marco was adept at disdain.

"Anorak means raincoat in the UK," Sara explained, "but it's also code for boring and condom."

"Ironic." Marco laughed. Seth curled his lips in a smile, making Sara literally ache to put her mouth hard over his. She looked quickly away, knowing this was not helping her cultivate the impression of a Wellesley scholar.

Still waiting for a waiter, Seth left for the bathroom, giving Sara a moment alone with Marco to ask about Seth's other fresh subjects. Marco disclosed that he'd written extensively about a girlfriend's rape, referring to them as the "Shame" and "Boy" poems, leaving Sara even more intrigued.

"*Shame*? About what?"

"It would be a shorter list for me to tell you what he doesn't feel shame about. Let's see, *shame* about being a man when men do such things; *shame* about his culpability for her rape, since society is organized to privilege him and victimize her; *shame* over his sexual frustration, because apparently, she wouldn't have sex with him for a long time after her rape; and on and on."

Sara's eyes settled on Seth as he returned into view, watching as he made his way back to the table.

Marco took a double take at her ogling. "Hot in a rough way, isn't he?"

Attempting to feign indifference, Sara offered a pert smile and shrugged. "He has a good mind. One of the best students I've ever had." He fell silent on her, and she babbled on, giving herself away completely. "I find him intriguing."

"Don't fuck with me. You're blushing. You want him."

Startled to hear it said out loud, Sara went into a temporary deep denial, scoffing.

"Uh-huh, yes. Stating the obvious here, but he is your student."

"I just think he's cute, for God's sake," she snapped back.

They both watched as Seth was intercepted and chatted up by

their waiter. Sara blathered off platitudes: *I'm only human. You can't help who you're attracted to…*

"And anyway," she said, still watching Seth politely navigate the waiter's flirtations, "it doesn't mean I'm going to sleep with him."

"Great to know, because if you did, you could kiss Wellesley goodbye."

* * *

As Seth approached their table, waiter in tow, she blurted quickly to Marco, "Please don't tell him."

"Of course, I won't fucking tell him. That'd be mad. I don't want to get you fired or have him think he could fuck you for an A."

"Shh. He'll hear you," Sara hissed.

"I found our waiter," Seth announced as he positioned himself beside Sara once more.

Sara, utterly discomposed, jumped right in with her order.

"I'll have the kale salad without the nuts or the goat cheese, please."

"Don't you want to look at a menu?" Seth asked.

"She read it online already," Marco explained, cocking an eyebrow.

Sara, wanting Marco to shut up, looked at Seth, who was giving nothing away in his expression.

She tried to sound playful. "You make it sound weird when you put it like that, Marco."

Marco shrugged, smirking back at her. He motioned to the waiter. "Let the man do his job."

The waiter turned a big, flirty smile to Marco.

"I don't think she's done," Marco told him.

"Actually…" Sara had already started to say.

"Here we go. It's going to be another one of your complicated orders, isn't it?"

Ignoring him, she smiled at the waiter, who smiled back weakly. "If I could get the dressing on the side, that'd be great."

"No problem." He turned back to Marco, then promptly back to Sara, who was still speaking.

"I'll get the apple on the side, too. And how many grapes are in it?"

This question ended both the waiter's note-taking and his patience. "Five. Approximately. Give or take."

"I'll just have two."

He didn't write it down, he just stared back at her. "Okay then."

"Because that's a sane request, isn't it? Two fucking grapes," Marco piped in.

"On the side, too." She was being deliberately provocative now.

With a hint of irritation, the waiter repeated her order. "So that's kale, everything on the side?" As if deliberately trying to make his night more difficult, he then told her about the bread choices that came with the kale (hold-everything) salad. "We have a choice of demi baguette…"

Sara thought about that—a day's worth of calories, at least.

"Or the granary loaf."

"I'll get a quarter of the demi baguette."

"A quarter?" Marco cried. "You want a piece off the end?"

Sara continued to ignore him and the waiter's aggravated expression. Marco laughed. Seth looked utterly bemused.

The waiter walked off after taking the remaining simple orders—quinoa burger for Seth and veggie lamb chop for Marco—but didn't get far before Sara called out in panic.

"Excuse me." She tried not to sound too desperate as she waved a hand to get the waiter's attention. "I'm really sorry. I know I have a difficult order, but forget the bread. I'll have an Americano with fat-free milk instead."

Feeling more drunk than starved, she'd made a snap decision. Coffee killed hunger and, hopefully, would also sober her up a bit. Plus, as she only just achieved squeezing into her in-between pair of jeans, she really couldn't afford to add the bread.

"Do you want the milk on the side?" the waiter asked, a tad acerbically.

Sara smiled back at Seth's confusion, while Marco explained, "She has a lot of rituals around food."

"What?" Although she tried to sound light, she was growing weary of Marco's humor. The daily questions about her food intake and his perception of what it all meant were becoming irksome.

"You don't have to explain my order, Marco," she said before turning to Seth. "I don't have any such rituals. I'm just very food conscious."

Silence.

"I took a nutrition course in college, and since then I've been very—"

"Fucked up about food?" Marco suggested.

Sara looked sadly at him. This was just going too far.

"It's true. You are very careful about what you eat."

She was grateful he got the hint and backed down, even backpedaled.

Marco turned to Seth. "She eats almost exclusively organic foods. You can bet that kale is organic. She'd have researched that. Right, Sara?"

She smiled at his attempt to make amends and got up to leave for the bathroom, where she could take a few bites of the protein bar tucked in her bag because it was only just 8pm and she thought she might keel over before that kale arrived. She kissed Marco on the lips for his efforts before she went.

* * *

Back at the table, she seized the Americano the waiter had delivered, but not before noticing that Marco and Seth were engaged in a deep conversation.

"It takes trauma to write like that," Marco was saying, referring to Seth's earlier reading.

Hearing her cue, Sara lit up. "Absolutely. Rape. That's worth writing about."

Marco nodded. "Yes. I was just saying to Seth that I think the most effective writing is derived from trauma."

"Like my rape."

The word stopped Seth, midstream, from taking a gulp of his iced tea.

"That can produce enough rage to fuel a revolution."

Accustomed to men squirming at this word, yet another typical reaction came with disappointment.

"Sorry." Seth sucked in his lower lip.

She hated that response. It was a sign of discomfort and a way to shut down any meaningful conversation. "Typical" wasn't what she expected from him.

He swiveled to Marco. Looking for guidance, she suspected. After her date rape at the age of sixteen, she had rarely encountered a straight man who could tolerate the word without flinching. It seemed they preferred to keep it quiet, hidden behind therapists' doors, while Sara aimed to demystify it—to *out* it.

She sighed heavily, about to jump into her usual speech.

"What do you make of Catherine MacKinnon's thesis?"

Momentarily struck dumb, Seth's awareness of such a major theorist on the social causes of rape didn't give her time to respond before their meals arrived.

They busied themselves for a few minutes, preparing to eat. Sara moved the grapes around her plate, munching ravenously on a few pieces of kale. Out of the corner of her eye, she watched Seth, mystified by him, both because he was taking huge, thousand-calorie bites of his burger and because he'd stunned her into silence.

When Sara finally recovered, she resumed the conversation. "MacKinnon. Interesting choice." Although bristling at his choice in naming a theorist she happened to disagree with, she was impressed with the reference.

"I know, it's not your go-to theory for explaining anything," he said, seeming to anticipate her criticism. "Especially given that you're a survivor."

They held each other's gaze. A slight shame creeping in from becoming aroused in Marco's company. Thankfully, Marco's voice roused her from that antithetical pedagogical thought. "You know what, I think we're going to have to get this to-go. Your order took up most of the evening, after all." He motioned to his plate while shooting her a look of caution that made her clamp her legs tightly together and rein in her arousal. He nodded toward Seth, who also seemed distracted. "I'll drop you at the train."

"We only just got our food," Sara tried coaxing, but quickly backed off at the wary look that said, *I'm saving you from yourself. Let's get out of here before you tell him you want to fuck his brains out.* Sara nodded in compliance. "Sorry I took up so much time."

Marco jumped up. "Just going to go get that waiter's phone

number first." He picked up the bill. "Be right back." He leaned in to whisper a caution. "Keep your pants on while I'm gone."

This remark alarmed her enough that she jumped up with him. "Yeah. We should get going."

"Do you want to take that with you?" Seth pointed at her barely eaten salad.

"Nah, she won't eat it. A to-go cup for the wine, though, now that she might do."

Marco would have been slapped for that, if he wasn't already across the room—and if he wasn't right.

* * *

After Marco dropped Seth at the station, he drove Sara home in virtual silence. While she was surprised Marco didn't immediately set into reprimanding her for flirting, the quiet was a relief. A post-mortem on her behavior was something she could do without. It was downright ridiculous, she thought, to usher them out of the restaurant for flirting. After all, it wasn't like she was going to act on her lusty thoughts.

In the refuge of her cozy apartment, she curled up on her couch with Seth's course assignment journal.

Knowing he was a musician and poet, and given his quiet calm in the seminar, Sara had expected to read beautiful imagery, but she almost choked on the first poem's opening line. Angry and loud, he took on the first person with a female-identified voice.

"(His) blood on milky fluids."

His blood? Sara wondered if it was a reference to S&M.

"(her) wail, (his) smile, coming when (her) screams finally hurt (him)"

While she'd certainly heard the edginess in his readings at the Black Hole, it wasn't Maplethorpe-esque stuff like this. Some of the other boys in her seminar journaled angry poems too, but predictably, they were angry at women for being angry at them. Sara was concerned by the visceral, angry images in Seth's poem and was troubled by the references to drug-induced sexual experimentations his journal writing explored.

With deeply personal responses to the material, he wrote about his father, who left when he was ten. How he saw him only a handful of times. How his mother's depression and complete indifference to raising him provoked him, at sixteen, to ask to move in with his father. His father had frowned, Seth wrote, seeming to be put off by the very sight of him. He'd guessed it was the shock of having not seen him for six years. Completely transformed from the skinny, freckled boy his father had known into a petulant, sullen, emotionally volatile teenager with a propensity for soft porn, whose changing body and cracking voice seemed to repel his father. "Probably because I just reminded him of his own youth and all his infractions." The maturity of the line and its depth of understanding touched Sara.

Seth's journal revealed the cultivation of a White, male, heterosexual guilt, a sense of unearned privilege. This alone might earn him an A. Certainly it tipped him even further along as a favored student.

Sara climbed into bed to read some more and fell asleep. Her dreams were about him. When she woke, she couldn't remember what she'd dreamed, only that he'd filled her head all night.

chapter four

Another manuscript rejection letter and Seth's CD sat on her desk. Sara tried to throw the letter across the room. It wasn't satisfying. No matter how hard you hurl it, paper just doesn't travel very far. She plunked her head in her hands and began spiraling into self-doubt.

She started with a mental list of all the bad reviews and rejection letters, remembering with impressive accuracy the details of each, and then she considered her waste of time and money. She felt a lump thicken in her throat.

About to drown in an overwhelming surge of self-pity, she lowered her head onto the desk and cried. Self-pity soon gave way to feelings of helplessness, hopelessness, and loss of control. Feelings all too familiar since the rape, which had rendered her unable to take even the slightest of knocks with any degree of balance. In fact, feelings so familiar, she was oddly comforted by them, as if they were her most reliable friends, wrapping her up in their arms, coming to her rescue. She gave into the abandon and sobbed uncontrollably into her shirt sleeve.

After a while, with her face blotchy, nose running, eyes burning and dry, Sara sat silently, pondering the next submission of her manuscript. Finally, she got herself together for the trek across campus to meet her seminar students at the Tin Palace.

When Sara arrived, several of the students were already gathered around a table. Although they were in mid-discussion about

Callum's decision not to vote, they all stopped to greet her, with Allyson jumping up to hug her on her way to the bar.

Sara was deflated by Seth's absence; she wanted to settle her eyes on something beautiful. The ugly debate between Allyson and Callum on the personal as political wasn't helping her mood.

Allyson returned with Sara's glass of wine and a huge pizza to share. Settling into the wine and ignoring the pizza, she listened without interest as Allyson attempted to lecture, cajole, and finally harass Callum into voting.

Callum laughed. "If I vote, will you fuck me?"

"Sure, but can you arrange it for me to fuck your hottie roommate first?" Allyson fired back.

Michael laughed uproariously. Callum smiled and shook his head, accepting his defeat.

Sara needed this sort of banter today, and to be lightly drunk as soon as possible. Within ten minutes of arriving, she was already on her second glass of wine when she spotted Seth through the window. He'd never joined them at the Tin Palace before; the fact it had taken a direct invitation from her to get him to come wasn't lost on her.

Slipping in, smiling at Sara, he effortlessly became a quiet but attentive member.

"Have some pizza." Allyson handed Sara a plate, watching her carefully. Irritated, Sara smiled politely. "No thanks, I'm fine."

Sara turned away and noticed that Seth was watching her. Motioning with her hands, she mouthed, "Come over here."

Bringing his tea with him, Seth pulled up a chair so close that their knees touched. He didn't motion to move from the contact and Sara wondered if he had sensory issues. She pulled his CD out from her bag and admitted she'd only had the chance to read rather than listen to the lyrics. Still, he was clearly eager for her opinion.

"Not enough political subject and too much personal," she told him. "You write about a breakup, but there's politics in that, right?" He nodded, a rapturously captivated student. "Her neediness, that's political because girls are raised to see themselves in terms of their relationships. Bring that up front. And then there's the voice." She shook her head, frustrated. "If you want to write about women's experience, then do it from your perspective, a male perspective."

He looked like he was straining to understand. "Tell us what patriarchy, sex, rape feel like to you." She paused, searching for the perfect punctuation to her lecture. "You're already doing this in your shame poems."

A momentary look of confusion crossed his face, followed by a nod of recognition when Sara added, "Marco told me about them. They sound amazing. I'd love to read them."

He gazed at her, a look that indicated he was pleased by her interest in his work. He turned bashful, averting his eyes, and began to play with the handle of his mug.

"You're clever with turning personal into political in your poetry, so why not sing it? Sing about shame."

His eyes were on her again, making her feel unbearably self-conscious. It was sexy to be around a man who wrote poetry about violence against women. Inwardly, she rolled her eyes at that thought. Knowing she should be more guarded with him, she attempted to mentally reign herself in, hoping she hadn't given too much away.

Seth lit up, shifting himself to the edge of his chair, smiling so animatedly his eyes were almost slits. Apparently, she hadn't deflated him or given herself away at all. Sara hoped he'd race home and write, forging ahead with the feminist perspective he had within him. And then Tom was there, inserting himself by her side, towering over them with a proprietary boyfriend stance, stalling Seth's race home to create.

Tom's arm wrapped around the back of her chair and Sara felt his weight lean against her shoulder. Irritated at the interruption, Sara said his name as if it was a question before she remembered they'd planned a date to watch Bill Mahr. Curiously, she neither felt badly about forgetting about their date nor was she sad that the chance to curl up on the couch together had been missed. After all, she was out in the trenches doing the real work of a professor— building relationships with students and encouraging them in their work—while Tom had likely just dragged himself away from fine tuning another one of his pointless research papers that no one read.

Gathering herself, Sara made the introductions, observing Tom's disinterest as she did so. He'd told her, on more than one occasion, that her fraternizing with students was not only strange, but also bound to lead to catastrophes.

As she prepared herself to leave with Tom, Sara briefly bade her farewells, making a point to tell Seth that she was eager to listen to the CD.

Sara leaned in toward Seth, her head motioning toward Allyson, who was sitting on Callum's lap. "Too much beer there," she whispered to him. "Help her, would you?"

Seth smiled. "I hear she promised to fuck him if he votes."

Sara mocked irritation. "But he hasn't voted yet."

Seth winked at her. "He's doing some groundwork."

Seth's gaze moved to Tom. Sara followed suit. Tom looked incredulous. Taking his arm, she spoke in his ear. "Mirth, Tom."

As they walked across the parking lot, Sara cuddled up against him for warmth, Tom expressing his concern, again, with her pedagogical approach.

"It's a pedagogy of the oppressed, Tom," she tried to explain, sincerely wanting him to understand and embrace it. "We are avoiding ranking knowledge in a hierarchy. Students' knowledge and experiences are just as valuable as the professor's."

From Tom's perspective, professors and students required a traditional relationship for the appropriate degree of impartial perspective to be maintained. Sara objected to every aspect of his position and struggled to reconcile their differences. Her training had exposed her to new-age teaching workshops, while Tom's had prepared him to see students as the curse of academia. So, when he said, "Ridiculous. They're in the academy to learn the scholarship of their discipline. They can't get it through osmosis," rather than lambaste him, Sara only sighed.

There could still be hope for him if I can ever get him to actively listen.

By the time they got to Tom's apartment, he was sensing the tension on the subject and relented.

"Your students are lucky to have you, Sara." He turned off the car and looked at her. "I just worry about you. Be careful not to get suckered. That's all I'm saying."

It was a sweet sentiment. She kissed him, calling a truce for the night.

chapter five

With the pile of publishers' rejection letters multiplying on her desk and her inbox clogged with unsuccessful labels, the call from the Dean of Students' office was welcome. After people playfully calling the Promoting Diversity on Campus Award the "Sara Wolfe Award" on account of the fact she had won it three years running, she was still cheered by the news she'd won again. As it was student elected, it meant a lot to her to receive.

Two local newspapers called for interviews, pleasing her only because she thought the press might provide a platform to promote her research, and perhaps even help with her Wellesley fellowship application.

Excited for any excuse to celebrate, Sara called Jane and Marco. Within an hour, they arrived together, laden with food and alcohol.

"Congratulations!" Marco squealed, beaming at Sara as they plowed into her office, locking the door behind them.

Sara jumped up to hug them. "You do know that alcohol is illegal on campus, right?"

"It's wine," Marco rebutted.

Sara watched nervously as Jane started pulling out containers of food from her bag, mildly relieved as some fruit was produced.

Aware of the looks her friends exchanged between them, she took a grape.

"Eat, drink," Marco ordered as he took a piece of cheese,

watching Sara like she was a specimen as she savored her singular grape.

The three hundred or so liquid grapes she poured into her mug she did not restrain herself with. *Thank god they'd brought wine*, Sara thought, taking a slug.

"Please eat, Sara. It's lunch time," Jane said, plumping the sagging couch cushions and avoiding eye contact.

Looking over the selection of food again, Sara felt uneasy. They knew she didn't eat any of this stuff. She sighed, irked by this tiresome focus on food. She redirected the discussion. "Let's talk about the award."

On cue, Marco became swept up in excitement. Having finished his teacup of wine (a hundred and fifty liquid grapes), he fired off questions, asking about the press calls, the dinner for the awards' recipients, the status of the Wellesley application...

Jane was not so easily distracted. Her interest was a pretense. The polite smile on her face didn't succeed in hiding that she was worried about Sara. Jane's eyes kept darting to the nibbled grape in Sara's hand, the mug of wine, and the spread of food as she flipped busily through the student journals that cluttered the floor by the couch. Sara noticed how hard Jane focused to not react every time she took a nibble from a die-sized cube of cheese.

Abandoning her charade of indifference, Jane gave up the game. "Sara, we need to talk about the way you eat."

Marco stopped everything and sighed heavily. "The ruse is up," he announced, flinging his hands in the air before fixing his look on Sara. "This is an intervention."

Sara burst out laughing, which set Marco off too.

"This is serious, Marco," Jane snapped. While she could be quite pithy, she was earnestness itself when it came to her vocation.

"Why?" Sara was still laughing and didn't really care about the answer. "And anyway, I can't do an intervention right now," she quipped, attempting to sound casual instead of aggravated. "I have to get ready for a lecture." She gathered up her books, papers, and lecture notes, pretending she couldn't see Jane slowly shaking her head at Sara's dismissal of the situation. Sara stopped to consider the offer of another mug of wine from Marco while trying to ignore Jane's tutting and shaking of her head. "Oh, go on,

I am celebrating, after all." He slugged the contents of the bottle into her mug (two hundred liquid grapes). "Whoa. I have class, you know."

Jane snapped. "Marco," she beseeched him, flashing her eyes back and forth between him and Sara.

"Marco," Sara echoed, mocking Jane's admonishing voice.

Jane returned to therapy-voice. Slower, softer, and oozing empathy while still managing to clip her speech so that every word landed punchy, announcing, *I'm not messing. Get serious. Listen up.* Of course, well trained in this herself, Sara could hear a thought-through attempt was underway.

"You know as well as I do that when women have restricting issues, they become experts at hiding the fact that they don't eat— making light of it with humor, *racing off to class.*"

A hot flush of irritation crept up Sara's neck.

Jane continued to press her. "Tell me, do you have any rituals around food?"

Sara had counseled enough women with, as Jane framed it, "restricting issues" to know that ritual is a big part of food for them. Sara had heard them all: prepare food so you can touch it, smell it, then watch others eat it, chew certain foods for ten seconds, then spit it out, go to a restaurant to watch people eat while you drink. She was only a tiny bit weirded out that she seemed to have some rituals that no one else had ever mentioned to her before. She exhaled so heavily she could've caused a draft.

"I'll reframe this for you. Everyone has learned habits around food. Weird little hang-ups, picky ways, but that's not it with me."

Marco and Jane simultaneously raised their eyebrows and glanced at each other.

True to her therapy persona, Jane probed further. "Do you only eat alone? Or only in public? Or...?"

"No," Sara fired back, bored with the badgering.

"Do you buy food to look at, but not eat?" Jane was quick to respond.

"No," she said, exhausted.

"Do you only eat certain types of food? Allow yourself only so many bites? Chew food, but not swallow?"

Sara tightened, gripping the handle of her mug, and she

wondered how she was going to escape Jane's intrusive way of framing everyone as broken, like a walking trauma radar.

Marco sensed Sara's weakening and jumped in. "Do you plan ahead, read the menu before you go to restaurants?"

How dare he? Now she really felt ganged up on. When Jane nodded encouragingly at Marco, obviously pleased to have him return to performing his role as intervention buddy, Sara had a hunch he'd told her about the dinner-order debacle.

"Do you take twenty minutes to place an order at a restaurant?" he continued, with more nodding from Jane.

"Oh Marco, you were the one who made that bizarre. No one would've noticed if you hadn't been all hyper-vigilant and, well, plain weird."

"No, you were the weird one," Marco said directly, no ounce of pity or concern.

Sara scoffed, unable to read whether he was serious or just being funny.

"Reflect on your conversation with that waiter, take out all my teasing, and you still came across as slightly insane, Sara."

Ah, so not funny, Sara reconsidered.

Jane frowned. "Let's not use labels like insane. Not helpful."

"Nuts, then. Completely mad. *Sick.*" Marco laughed.

Jane cocked her head at him. Sara paced.

He dropped his voice to a mumble, trying to get serious. "You have an eating disorder, Sara."

Beginning to hyperventilate, Sara managed to say between gasps, "Those...are...your...words."

Jane frantically rummaged in her intervention kit bag, and landing on a paper bag, emptied its contents and assisted Sara with shallow breathing exercises.

Marco took a deep breath as he watched Sara's breathing, aided by the paper bag, returning to normal. He started again, his voice soft. "Seth noticed," he said, almost inaudibly. "He asked me outright if you had an eating disorder."

Sara tore the paper bag away from her face and began to knot a loose piece of hair around her finger. "And you told him I do?" she said, gasping, then between breaths, "Marco? No! Why?"

Jane raised her voice with concern. "Stay calm. Breathe," she advised, lowering Sara's hand away from her obsessive hair twisting and shooting a look at Marco, her lips in a tight, straight line, head shaking warily. "Marco, is this helpful?"

Silence followed, broken only by Sara's shallow breaths into the little paper bag.

"Sara." Marco said her name softly, taking Jane's calm lead. "Of course I didn't tell him. Give me some credit. I may consider him my friend, but you're his professor, and my dearest friend in the world."

Sara put the bag down. "So, what *did* you say?"

"I managed to evade it, but it was difficult. Uncomfortable."

Jane looked smug, clearly feeling good about what Marco's observations exposed. "See? It's not just us noticing. It's the skateboard guy too."

Sara cringed with the mention of his skateboard. "You're all utterly paranoid. Or suffering from over-zealous trauma-dar," she snapped. "You have this all wrong." She stalled for the right words. "I'm embarrassed to say it because it makes me sound like an unenlightened scholar, especially in light of this gorgeous award." She fingered her award plaque.

"This?" Jane bleated worriedly.

"Dieting. There. I admit it," she announced, like she was courageous.

Looking relieved, Jane patted the couch seat next to her, beckoning Sara over.

Sara didn't budge. "But it's not an ED," she asserted, using the colloquial expression for eating disorder; partly to impress Jane with her knowledge, partly because she couldn't bring herself to say the words. "It's a VST problem."

"A what?" Jane looked perplexed.

"I know. I get it," Sara went on. "Not the paragon of scholarly intellectualism, am I? Given all my failings, I mean." Then, getting completely carried away in her descent into self-indulgent pity, she threw in, "We can write down all my failings if you like, and post them around the campus. They'd probably take away my gorgeous award, and rightly so."

Jane, accepting it for the spiral that it was, turned to Marco. "VST?"

"Visual small talk."

Jane raised her eyebrows, more than exasperated. "Whatever. Listen, you need to get to class. Let's stop here for now. Can we pick this up later? Tonight?"

"Did you hear a word I said?" Sara's jaw slackened. "This is *not* an issue," she belted.

Jane backed down. "Can we just talk then? Maybe just help with this *VST* problem?"

"Not tonight," Marco blurted.

Jane looked at him with dismay.

"I have a date."

Slamming both her hands into the couch, Jane chided him. "Marco!"

Seeing her chance, Sara clamored toward the door, relieved to be saved from wasting an evening with intervention talk. "I'll probably be busy anyway. With Tom or something," she said as she gathered her things.

Jane locked pleading eyes on Marco. "I thought you were here to help."

"There's not much we can do, is there?" Marco turned to Sara. "Just know we're onto you."

With her hand on the door, she turned to look at them squarely. "Listen. I know this is coming from concern and it hasn't really been your deliberate mission to piss me off for the past month or so by patronizingly conflating my VST with an ED, but please, give me some credit."

* * *

By 9pm, not counting drinks, Sara calculated that she'd consumed around five grams of fat and seven hundred calories. Plus, she guessed, around a hundred calories and two grams of fat for dinner. Not bad. Despite that, she was still unable to bring herself to eat dessert, so she settled for watching Tom eat his instead.

Beside the fireplace at their favorite campus coffee shop, watching Tom scoff down a fruit torte, Sara was in the middle of explaining, yet again, the finer points of her pedagogical approach, when Seth and Eyva walked in.

Greeting them warmly, Sara enthusiastically reintroduced them to Tom, who shook Seth's hand and, with a patronizing smile, corrected Sara's introduction. *"Professor* Tom Stafford." *So much for trying to influence his attitude toward students.*

Ignoring Tom's plaintive plea as he looked at his watch, Sara invited Eyva and Seth to join them. Eyva immediately launched into telling Sara about the weekend-long anti-fashion workshop she was running. Tom awkwardly turned to Seth and asked him about the Rock Against Rape concert Sara had told him about.

When Tom laughed at the idea of a concert *"for* rape," as he called it, Sara noticed Seth's brow furrowed and his lips set in a tight, straight line. Jumping in, she tried to save Tom from further embarrassing himself.

"The idea is to raise money for counseling centers. Just like the Take Back the Night rally I host every spring," she said, patting his hand in a gesture of "silly, you know this." Tom rolled his eyes. Sara responded by firing off a plethora of inane comments, babbling on about the weather, campus bus plans, the spring course schedule… She talked on and on, hoping to salvage the miserable interaction and, most importantly, Seth's perception of her.

Anxiety gripped her at the thought that his perception of her might be irreparably bifurcated—a leftie cultural activist exposed as a poser with an anti-feminist boyfriend. His perception of her was the only one out of this painful little gathering she actively cared about, and this troubled her. Deeply. She had to exit, fast, or risk hyperventilating.

Eyva dove in before she could manage a polite escape route. "What are you teaching in the spring, Sara?"

Every time Eyva used her name, Sara saw Tom bristle. Recovering enough to engage in conversation, Sara inquired about Eyva's own plans for the season.

"We're touring to promote our new record," Eyva declared proudly.

Sara whipped her head between Eyva and Seth and back again, flooded with questions. "When's the tour? Are you going, Seth?"

Tom fidgeted; bored or annoyed, or both.

"Yes," Eyva said, answering for Seth. "He's a solid member of the band now."

Sara watched Seth's gaze move to Tom, who had picked up a newspaper and was shaking it out, loudly. Seth caught her watching him. They smiled at each other, eyes locking, lingering a little too long as Eyva went on.

"Still trying to choose between the mainstream label or the indie," Eyva said.

Sara snapped her eyes away. "Mainstream?" she repeated, a tinge of disgust. Mainstream meant being *in* with "the man."

"We're still arguing about that. Right, Seth?"

Sara checked his reaction. Eyes downcast, Seth looked uncomfortable. Sara couldn't believe he was selling out. She wanted to press it, but Tom's patience had been tested enough already.

* * *

After they left the coffee shop and made their way to Tom's car, Sara turned angrily to him and demanded to know why he'd been so rude.

Tom laughed. "You have a peculiar relationship with them."

Freezing, Sara stood by his car. More for entertainment's sake than anything else—because what could Mr. Hegemonic Pedagogy say to enlighten *her* on student-professor relationships—she asked him to elaborate.

"The inappropriate conversations you have, like that night at the Tin Palace. I cannot believe the way you actually talk to him." He seemed unable to bring himself to say Seth's name. "Stop pretending like it's an equal relationship."

While Sara tried again to explain her pedagogy to him, Tom interrupted. "That rocker boy's just an anarchist with no direction, Sara."

Sara tried not to show her hurt and feigned a small laugh. "You sound like Marco." Tom didn't like Marco and Sara knew he'd be offended.

"Exactly how?" Tom was predictably irritated.

"Take me home," she said flatly. She was mad. Not only had he been rude to her students, but he'd poked her fears about Seth and helped to cement her already nagging doubt about Rocker Boy's emotional stability.

In fact, Tom's appraisal had made her wonder why she was still having sexual fantasies about Seth, which aggravated her further because she was enjoying having lusty thoughts about him.

When Tom tried to kiss her, she pulled away. It was his usual way of dismissing what she cared about. Suggestively, he wrapped an arm around her waist and dropped his voice into a sulky, sexy tone, urging: "Come on, kiss me goodnight." Her resolve weakened. She was, after all, still a little buzzed from the two bottles of wine at dinner.

Still parked in front of her apartment building with the car running to keep them warm, she climbed onto his lap. As she kissed him, he slipped his hand under her shirt to unhook her bra, but she was finding it a challenge to push past how he had behaved with Eyva and Seth. Taking one last stab at compartmentalizing her thoughts—placing drunken arousal ahead of principles—she began to rifle through their layers of clothing searching for his zipper.

The thought of car sex in New England, virtually impossible between October and May, brought her back to her complete irritation with his behavior. She abruptly withdrew, climbed off his lap, and adjusted her bra. "Let's just leave it there tonight." As flatly as if she were telling a waiter she didn't want to see a dessert menu.

"What? Why?" Tom said breathily.

Not wanting another drawn-out discussion, Sara told him a half truth about needing to get ready for an early morning seminar and climbed out of the car as aggressively as she'd climbed onto his lap just minutes before.

* * *

She stewed about whether she should break up with him all night and didn't sleep well. The next morning, Tom appeared in her office, humbly apologizing for being a jerk.

"I think I've probably been very, well, unaccepting of your way with students. Everything, really." He paused, waiting for a response. Caught off guard, Sara didn't know what he expected her to say. "I obviously don't understand it," he continued, "but I can and should respect that you just have a different approach. I hope you can do the same with me?"

When she still didn't say anything, a look of concern creased his face. Conflicted, Sara felt like the judge at a tribunal, weighing up his fate. She knew he felt on trial too. It wasn't just about the night before either. When she stopped to think about it, she'd been withdrawing her interest in him for a while now and he must have noticed.

Tom's mouth opened slightly and closed again. He swallowed. She watched his Adam's apple jutting in and out in distress. These slight indications of increased affliction could only express one thing —his investment in her. These thoughts, his GQ looks, and beseeching apology made Sara begin to bend toward him again.

"Oh, another thing." He had a broad smile on his face, indicating his pleasure in his pending announcement. The effort he was making was touching, and Sara couldn't help smiling encouragingly at him. "I realize my attitude has probably left you thinking that I'm disinterested in your work, but that's not true. I'd like to better understand what it is you do."

Dumbstruck, Sara nodded. His exhibition of interest in absorbing her life into his own and his shift in trying to understand her way, offered her renewed hope. He was actively trying to please her.

"For a start, how's the application to Wellesley going?" he asked, demonstrating he was willing to act on his pledge to understand her.

Wellesley, however, was the one part of her work that Tom did bring up, and a lot. Yes, she wanted that fellowship, but it felt like Tom *needed* her to get it.

"It's a fantastic opportunity," he said, beginning to rattle on about it.

She wondered if his interest in Wellesley derived from his embarrassment that her position at the university was not tenured. The fellowship was a prestigious opportunity to work alongside top scholars, but it was also insurance. It almost guaranteed a tenured faculty position, and at one of the best universities.

"I do other things besides my fellowship application, like my book about the feminist music scene, remember?" She wondered if he actually did. She challenged him. "If you really want to understand my work, come and hear some of that music with me."

"If it will help me understand what you do, absolutely," he said without hesitation. "Is this part of the work you want to do at Wellesley?"

She suppressed an eye roll and nodded instead, then put him to the acid test. "How's next Friday?"

Moving himself over to her, he picked up both her hands, holding them against his chest. Pausing between slow, teasing little kisses, he huskily said, "I think that'll work."

Sara kissed him hard on the lips, thinking maybe the condoms in her desk might come in handy after all. Abruptly, he pulled away from her. Flushed from a kiss that should have led to locking her office door, he looked at her sheepishly.

"What?" Sara leaned in to plant soft kisses on his mouth.

"I should say this too."

Sara was the one who looked concerned now.

"I think some of my rudeness, as you perceived it, with that student...what's his name?"

"Seth?"

"That one. Yes. Well, to be completely honest, I'm a little jealous of him." He cleared his throat. "Of the Rocker Boy."

Touched by his vulnerability, she was also unnerved. His concerns were legitimate, and she wondered if it was that blindingly obvious that she was smitten with Seth.

"First of all," she said playfully, shaking off her paranoia, "Marco would just call him 'Rocker Boy.' Secondly, why are you jealous?"

Tom picked up one of her hands again and skirted the floor with his eyes. "I think he likes you. And..." He looked straight back at her. "I think you like him."

Momentarily, her mouth dropped open. She leaped to defend herself, desperate to cover the truth under the pure shock of the suggestion. "He's my student, Tom. You may think my boundaries with my students are unconventional, but I am a professional and couldn't overstep that kind of boundary." That was the truth, although she knew the only reason she couldn't was to save her job.

Tom dropped his eyes. "That's good, because..." He dragged his eyes back to her before he continued, and she could feel the weight of what he was about to say. "Not only could you forget about securing tenure anywhere, but you'd lose your position altogether if you were to…" They both knew what he was going to say, and the sentence hung there, unfinished.

It was just a harmless crush. The questioning made her mad and his warning boiled her, especially considering all the male professors who had propositioned her as a student, smattering sexual insinuations like it was their given right as a man. *Those* professors got tenure. The gravity of Tom's warning sunk in, and despite her anger, it chilled her.

Sara hurtled down imaginary paths of certain doom for her career. Her career had been anything but illustrious thus far, but as she dug deeper into her misery, she concluded that if she could just abstain from sex with a student, there was still hope for the career she dreamed of, and Wellesley.

"What concerns me most," said Tom, pulling her back from thoughts of self-deprecation, "is that you haven't said you don't like him."

Simultaneously amused and moved by this retro, patrilineal display of mated ownership, Sara kissed him. She didn't believe relationships should hold expectations of binding people to be sexually exclusive, but that discussion would undoubtedly lead to another argument. Besides, this protective and vulnerable display was arousing and, ultimately, she wanted sex. Bringing up non-monogamy would defeat that objective, so she decided to humor him and drop it, as well as his pants later tonight.

chapter six

Tom had been hanging out in Sara's office every day since they'd made up. She was joking with him that he was there to soak up all the atmosphere of feminist philosophy that essentially dripped from the walls when their kissing was interrupted by Marco.

"Sara, there's a rape survivor here to see you," Marco announced, standing at her office door.

Tom pulled away, smoothing his shirt.

"Just kidding. But I bet that took care of that boner. Right, Tom?"

Sara giggled, nudging Tom to lighten up. This was not a gargantuan effort, for a change, and the kissing seemed to pacify him, making him amiable even toward Marco.

"Hi, Tom." He pranced across the room, touching Tom's arm effeminately in his flirtiest manner before swinging a leg high in the air as he sat down. "So, you're coming to see the band tonight?" Marco asked, flapping his arms girlishly.

The Friday night gig she'd contracted Tom into had arrived. She hoped he wouldn't hate it.

Nodding, Tom excused himself, Marco's campy display of hegemonic femininity clearly making him more uncomfortable than he could bear.

The second Tom left, Marco groaned. "He's *so* Retro Boy."

Sara was unsure if her sudden feeling of defensiveness was for Tom or herself.

A coy smile on her lips, still flushed from how lovely Tom had been in bed with her the night before, she said, "He may be a Retro Boy, but he is trying. And at least a hottie Retro Boy."

Marco beamed. "Did I interrupt something? Were you finally getting your office sex?"

Sara smiled. "No, but I think it's likely to be soon." Marco looked unconvinced. "Pretty nice sex."

The assurance of good sex could explain most shortcomings from the profane to the sacred for Marco, so surely it could explain one little women's activist having it off with an apolitical, barely leftist guy, and especially one who'd just made the decision to appreciate her activist lifestyle. As she predicted, Marco nodded understandingly.

"Still, there are *some* nice political-activist type boys. You don't *have* to be stuck fucking Retro Boy."

"Go. Get lost," she said playfully. "I have to get ready for the club."

"You can't get a coffee? I have to tell you about a guy I met."

Sara shook her head. "Tell me later?"

"Let's get dinner before the club then," Marco called as he headed out.

The mention of food reminded her she should weigh herself.

"That would've been lovely, Marco, but I'm having dinner with Tom," she lied.

* * *

Back at her apartment, Sara stood on the scale, inching the weight along the notches, barely able to look as she slid it first past 109 pounds, then 106, finally arriving at 104.5. Good. A smile spread broadly across Sara's face. Less than forty bottles of wine in weight; she knew because she'd been Googling the weight of all kinds of animals and inanimate objects lately and was surprised to learn that she was about the weight of a toilet or a Bernese mountain dog. She estimated it would be only another week or two before she could squeeze into her new jeans.

Sara decided she could afford some dinner after all.

She scoffed at Marco's accusation of an unvaried diet, consisting of raw vegetables, protein bars, and yogurt only. This dinner proved her point that she was only conscious about how she ate, not weird about it. Dinner was one half cup of fat-free cottage cheese, two cups of spinach, and four cherry tomatoes. *Take that for variety, Marco!*

After mixing herself another a dirty martini with the Anoraks blaring through her earbuds, she raced to get ready. Since she remained hungry, and would be drinking more at the club, she threw a protein bar in her bag before heading out the door.

* * *

Sara was impressed with Tom. He was outside of his comfort zone in the club; there only for her, trying on her life to see how it fit. It pleased her to see.

The close proximity of all the people, including her graduate students, and noise notably displeased Tom. Sara, wanting to be closer to the stage, tried to coax him to join her, thinking he might at least find it entertaining.

Tom shook his head. "It's already loud enough here." In response to her concerned frown, he pecked her on the cheek. "Go and have fun. I'll be here," he said, picking up his glass of wine.

Within ten minutes of arriving, Sara had taken advantage of Tom's instruction and abandoned him for Marco and the stage.

Marco excitedly nodded to Sara as Seth's band took to the stage, screaming above the noise, "Are you ready for this?"

Sara nodded her head side-to-side. Since Marco had claimed the band was a phenomenon, destined for success greater than regional accolades, she knew she was about to see something special, and she wasn't sure she was ready. However, also knowing that Marco was both smitten with Seth and generally had a higher level of enthusiasm than a cheerleader, she wasn't exactly sure what she should be prepared for.

With the crowd's sudden rush to the stage, she thought about Tom. A mild guilt snuck over her for having left him alone. For him, this might as well have been an alien planet! She gave a cursory look toward the bar, but the crowd was so thick she couldn't recognize anyone. As guilt turned to consummation, Seth's deafening opening chords overwhelmed her voice.

"I hope Tom's okay."

Marco shook his head, indicating he couldn't hear her, then pointed to the stage and to Seth. She refocused, understanding instantly what Marco had been talking about.

Though the crowd sang along with Seth, whose mesmerizing voice alternated between soft and screaming, Sara found his stage presence unnerving. One minute he was calm and collected, almost serene, and the next he was a degenerate who hurled himself around the stage, smashing into everything and everyone. At one point he even landed on the drum kit and drummer. She wondered if it was part of an alter-ego stage performance, which admittedly troubled her just as much as the idea that this risky behavior was genuinely an aspect of himself.

Despite the partly dilapidated drums, they managed to play five songs back-to-back before Seth killed the skins altogether by hurling his guitar with force into the kit. Sara worried he might injure their new drummer, Caleb.

After an enthusiastic applause, Seth, mild mannered once again, picked up an acoustic guitar.

"This song's called 'Shame.'"

Sara caught her breath. He was doing as she'd instructed— singing the Shame poems. Since she couldn't understand the words he screamed into the microphone, she had to trust him when he told the audience it was a song about homophobia.

When anger gripped his face toward the end of that song and he began kicking one of the speakers, the audience charged the stage.

A dozen crowd members joined him, variously dancing or aiding him in the wanton destruction of anything not permanently nailed down. Seth threw himself to the floor with an audible thud. He remained there, prostrate, as the participating stage-crowd continued with their antics of dance or destruction. Sara kept her sights on Seth as the storming of the stage continued. Getting to his knees, he keeled over and buried his head into his arms while the homophobia song came to an end.

Marco laughed gleefully. "Angry boy, isn't he?"

Seth peeled himself from the floor and picked up his guitar. She was relieved watching him approach the microphone again. "Eyva Carter."

A deafening applause exploded as Eyva took the microphone.

"Capitalism leads to patriarchy, patriarchy leads to sexism, sexism leads to violence against women." She paused for effect. "Fuck Capitalism," she spat before bursting into song.

Eyva credited the song to Seth at the end and introduced the next one as his too.

"It's about a boy trying to cope with his girlfriend's rape. It's called 'Boy.'"

It was exciting how beautifully he married the personal and the political in the song and that he'd even given Eyva the spotlight to present it. The depth of his thinking, his authentically considered perspective, affected Sara in the same way the base guitar vibrated in her chest.

Seth was almost motionless, staring into space as he played his guitar, giving all the spotlight to Eyva, standing resplendent in a lacy black bra and bovver boots—she had turned slut on its head with her repurposed uniform. The words she sung were breathless, building into a screamy finale.

As the song finished and the band took a break, Sara returned her attention to a radiant and bouncing-with-excitement Marco.

"Good, aren't they?"

Sara nodded, too much absorbed in the energy of what she'd experienced to vocalize her thoughts or feelings.

She watched Seth maneuver around the stage. He removed his guitar and dismantled a few things here and there. She noticed the intimate way he spoke with Eyva, his sometimes girlfriend, how close he stood and where his body slightly touched hers.

Back at the bar, Tom had a wine waiting for her. Marco, Allyson, and her casual girlfriend Deb joined them.

Sara sipped on her third glass of wine, lazily letting her arms and shoulder bush against him as she drank. "What did you think?" she asked him, holding her breath for his answer.

Tom shrugged. "Didn't see very much from where I was standing. Seemed like a crowd riot. And so loud." They both laughed.

"But did you like the music?"

Tom shook his head side-to-side, noncommittal. "It's an acquired taste, I think, but what about the message?" He looked nonplussed.

"The message?" Sara sighed. "What he's forecasting? Demanding?"

Tom looked amused. "I couldn't understand a word."

Sara was deflated but undeterred. "I'll get you the lyrics to read. It's revolutionary stuff." She would teach him about it, ease him in; maybe he'd even enjoy it next time.

Tom raised his eyebrows, about to say something more, when Seth and Eyva joined them.

Eyva hugged her warmly. Sara noticed Seth slip a hand into Marco's and hug him. Displays of affection like this between men always made Sara happy. She had a fleeting wish for Callum to be here to see it.

When Seth caught her watching them, she felt herself blush and looked away, although not so quickly that she didn't see him smile and slip his hand from Marco's to join her.

Tom on one side of her, Seth slid to the other. The awkwardness was palpable. In a rush to clear it, Sara made comment on his display with Marco.

"I like seeing that kind of gentleness between guys."

Tom's arm slipped proprietarily around her waist, and she watched Seth follow the message. Tom, not unlike an ape beating his chest, glared at Seth, who frowned slightly and turned to Sara.

The response pleased her. Rather than select from the two basic options primitive creatures are wont to do in the face of a challenge from another male for the attention of a female—beating a path in the other direction or fighting for access to her—Seth chose the option available only to creatures with a larger cerebral cortex.

"It's how the Circle is," he explained. "It's how we'll learn to become authentic nurturing boys."

Sara deciphered for Tom. "Marco calls the guys in the Men's Circle his Nurture Boys. He encourages them to be affectionate. Sweeter, really."

Tom looked increasingly awkward. Thinking it might be a good opportunity for a learning curve, Sara went on.

"The idea is to guide the boys through hegemonic gender traps and encourage them to embrace both their masculine and feminine sides." Sara stopped to share a joke with Seth. "Although Marco does unapologetically admit to being trapped in the latter, right?"

Seth grinned.

"But then again, I've never attended a circle meeting, I only understand the theory. Could you fill Tom in on anything else, Seth?"

Seth hesitated. "I think you said it nicely."

"Come on, you're a student of the Men's Circle. It's an opportunity to share what you have been learning." Sara thought Tom might appreciate a remark that highlighted their roles, defining their social dynamics and putting everyone in their respective places.

Silence.

The look of unease exponentially increased on both their faces. Sara was too drunk to figure out how to redirect the conversation and she wanted to slink away. Knowing there was no chance for that, she opted instead for lecture. In tone, mannerisms, and volume, Sara performed "Professor Wolfe."

"The agenda in the Men's Circle is a fourfold raising of consciousness. First, recognizing what the gendered identities are. Second, understanding how these were organized by the patriarchy's agendas—that is, the cultural hegemony of gender. Third, recognizing that creating and enforcing the stereotypes of gender benefits only the patriarchy, notwithstanding the fact that men have unearned privileges in that society. And finally..." She stalled, too drunk to remember. She looked to Seth. "Do you know what the fourth point is?"

"Consequences?" he offered.

"Yes. Good," Sara said, thankful he remembered. "Could I get a glass of water?" she asked of no one in particular.

While Tom beckoned a bartender to get Sara some water, she continued to update him. "There are social and personal consequences of patriarchy. In the Circle, Marco gets the boys to focus on the personal, but here's the cream, Tom."

Seth smiled at her. At least *he* seemed to be appreciating the lecture.

Tom handed her a glass of water. She slugged at it, wishing it could instantly sober her.

"The *personal* consequences are reflected in the violence men do to women, even to each other. Even within the violent terms for masturbation that men often use, like choking the chicken..."

Tom frowned, halting the litany of expressions she had accumulated to support the point. "No need to list them all here," he suggested.

"These personal consequences are then embedded into society." She paused for her big ta-da moment. "The personal *is* political."

Tom didn't look as impressed as she'd hoped; he probably just didn't get it.

"They are enmeshed. Fucking each other." From the look on Tom's face, Sara knew she must have slipped her decorum from professor to drunk. "Sorry I slipped into lecture mode."

Tom pulled her toward him by her waist. "It's okay. I'm having a hard time hearing much of what you're saying anyway."

Seth turned to Tom. "Have you considered the Men's Circle?"

The suggestion was so unpresented to Tom that he had to recover from the question a moment. He laughed, shaking his head an unnecessary number of times. "I don't think it'd be for me."

"No? Why not?" Seth was baiting him.

Sara held her breath, willing Tom to say the right thing.

"I'd rather spend my time doing something more *productive*."

Sara was flabbergasted. Had he really just called the study of patriarchy unproductive? And after his apology too, with his plea to understand *her way*. Her head reeling, she didn't hear the rest. Rattling her head, trying to bring herself back into the room instead of spiraling down a rabbit hole, she managed to catch the last half of what Tom was saying.

"…a slumber party with a bunch of guys in their underwear, being *sweet* to each other?" He smirked at Seth, dismissively turning his back on him.

Sara didn't dare look at Seth. Tom had not only dismissed Seth and Marco—her community—he'd shunned her entire *raison d'etre*.

Calmly, Tom suggested she leave with him. Embarrassed, Sara agreed, bidding only a brief farewell.

* * *

The argument between them in the parking lot was the worst of their relationship.

"I can't believe what you just said in there, Tom."

"I don't like the idea of the Men's Circle," he said casually, dismissing the validity of Sara's distress.

"Fine, but it's the *reason* you don't like it that disturbs me. Your disdain sounds homophobic. *And* you think it's a waste of time to talk about patriarchy?"

Tom sighed, tapping his foot impatiently and looking off to the side.

"Being a feminist—it's my life. And you mocked it. I thought you wanted to understand my community, maybe even be a part of it."

Tom interrupted. "I did *not* say that."

Sara retracted and made a double take at him, stunned.

"You misunderstood, Sara. In apologizing, I was only acknowledging...accepting our differences."

Sara felt ridiculous.

"We have very different training," he went on. "I could never have your ardor for students. I don't even *like* teaching. It's the absolute worst part of my job. I only accept it because it's part of the umbrage of being a professor, a necessary evil so that I can study macroeconomics."

The association of words like "umbrage" and "evil" with teaching made Sara feel physically sick.

"And your fervor for changing the world? Well, it's not my way. My discipline is not activist oriented, like *women's studies* is." His emphasis was patronizing. "In Macro Economics..." He pronounced it in capital letters, accentuating its value and importance. "We just want to understand world economies, not change them."

That did it. Significant world economies were the very agents of patriarchy! Sara's life was about changing those agents.

"May I speak?" she snapped.

Tom nodded, looking at her pitifully.

"I take it back, I'm not fine with you not liking the Men's Circle. I'm not fine with anything about you." Her contempt for him was utterly overwhelming.

Tom looked like he'd been slapped.

Shaking all over, her heart pounding hard in her chest, she gave him her ultimate slur. "You, are the Whitest guy I've ever known."

"What does *that* mean?"

Tom didn't tolerate name-calling, swearing, or childish insults, so she hurled it at him. "You, Tom, are an unfeeling, unthinking asshole. I am completely unable to comprehend your narcissistic worldview! It's all about you, you, you. You're a jerk."

"Grow up, Sara." He turned his back on her and walked away.

"We're through, Tom!" she bellowed, as if it needed to be said.

Storming back to the club, Sara heard his car door open at the same time as she opened the door to the club. She felt nothing but relief.

Marco was immediately by her side as she stepped in. "Seth filled me in on Tom's little homophobic outburst." He hugged her and led her back to the bar where everyone still congregated.

"I didn't expect to see you again tonight. Can I buy you a drink?" Seth asked her.

Between the two glasses of water she'd knocked back during her mini lecture, the icy blast of air in the parking lot, and the blow-up with Tom, she was feeling slightly more sober. Certainly, another drink was warranted.

While Sara settled into her fourth glass of wine of the night, Seth began to apologize.

"I should have thought more before I suggested that. He doesn't seem like the kind of guy who would ever join the Circle."

She tried not to give too much thought to what the comment implied. She felt sick at the realization that she, Sara Wolfe, had been dating a man who was not a feminist, did not ever intend to become one, was not even remotely interested in it, and believed it was, in fact, unproductive.

Still, she congratulated herself for having broken up with such a man. With that mess out of the way, she decided to get to work on all her other messes—like her VST, her drinking, and her fresh concern that, if he was attractive enough, she might hop into bed with another misogynistic homophobe…

Right now, she recognized she was too drunk to clean up the wreckage she'd identified. So alternatively, she decided she quite liked pretending that her life was going well and would continue to ride that broomstick.

She turned to Seth. "I like the songs."

He grinned. "Thanks. I'm glad. You probably noticed it's a pretty personal project, so it's nice to find an accepting audience." After a big slug of tea, he quickly added, "I followed your advice."

"So, are you going to keep touring? Make another record?"

He fired back with a question of his own. "What about you? Are you going to publish your book?"

"Yes. Maybe. If anyone ever says it's good. Which, to date, no one has. And your record?"

"We're working on a contract..." His brow furrowed as he paused and ran a hand nervously through his hair. "Eyva was telling you a bit about it the other night, if you remember?"

Sara nodded, remembering it well.

"The issue is, do we want to go mainstream? We're getting a lot of college radio airplay, and that's just with the indie label. I don't know. We'll see."

With *Don't do it! Don't sell out!* screaming in her head, Sara said, "I'd like to talk with you about that choice, but in a quieter venue because I have a lot to say, of course." *That*, she thought, *and your worrying stage persona.*

Seth looked unsure. "I'd appreciate it. I'd like to hear what you think."

Sara cocked her eyebrows. "Warning: I'm not sure you'll like it."

"Go easy on me. Remember, we haven't made a decision yet." He shifted gears, closing that part of the conversation, and switched positions. "Can I read your stuff?"

"It's not published yet." She felt his eyes on her.

"You've read my unpublished stuff."

Sara wanted the conversation to keep going, even if it was bordering on inappropriate. "I'm your professor." Reminding herself more than him. "It's different. Maybe...when the course is over."

She caught herself sounding just like Tom, and a silence fell between them.

He spoke first. "Didn't we just finish a section on Foucault?"

Citing the theory emphasizing a re-examination of established knowledge and student-professor relationships was calling her bluff. Her whole approach was guided by this re-evaluation of power dynamics.

She was flustered. "So?"

"So? Why do we need to have a social relationship that is based on principles that we both discount as…"

Sara interjected defensively. "Principles we *both* discount?" Suddenly afraid she heard Tom's repeated warnings about crossing boundaries echoing in her head, she cut Seth off before he could respond. "We do have to have a culturally proscribed relationship. My career and, by extension, my role in improving women's social status, depends on me occasionally following the prescribed rules. Unlike you, we can't all take the risk to change things by living entirely outside of a system and shirking every cultural norm."

He furrowed his brow and cocked his head awkwardly to one side, but then Allyson was grabbing him by the arm to introduce him to someone. Before walking away, Seth leaned in close to her. Feeling his breath on her ear, she erupted in goosebumps.

"By the way, congratulations on the award, Professor."

A gaggle of people were crowding him, and she realized she'd been monopolizing his attention, though he seemed disinterested in the local fan posse that surrounded him.

Sara, unclear about why he was emphasizing her title, gave him a questioning look. He held her gaze flatly. His little fan posse was waiting for him, hanging on to his next move, and Marco was making leaving noises, saying his goodbyes to men he'd been flirting with all night. Slowly, she removed her gaze from Seth's, racked with sadness at the idea of leaving without making it all better.

Sara's first-name policy with students was an effort to rip away the social distance a title fostered, and she knew Seth understood this. With the caustic mention of her title, she guessed he might be calling her on her postmodern—or PoMo, as Sara and Marco liked to say—slip and, ironically, erecting the barrier that she had been calling for in her speech.

Irritation crept over her as she put on her coat, contemplating why she'd just championed an anti-Foucauldian position she didn't believe in. Recoiling with the thought, she blamed Tom. It was his influence creeping in. She shook all over with anger at Tom, but a little truth seeped in. It was more than Tom. It was her crush on Seth too. She knew that her testiness and sensitivity to the issue was more connected to her feelings for him than any fear of losing the appropriate degree of social distance associated with traditional pedagogy. She was continually self-aware around him, terrified of giving herself away.

Finishing with her hurried goodbyes, Sara aimed a quick look in his direction, wanting to catch his eye and gain some clue as to where they stood with each other before she left. Seth, engulfed in the excited fan posse, looked right back at her.

She raised her hand to say goodbye. He nodded, offering a tentative smile. Of all the emotional tumult of the night, it was the one between her and Seth she cared about the most.

* * *

Once in the car, Marco turned on her. "Why was Seth looking so crestfallen?"

"I don't want to talk about it right now."

"Speaking while drunk again?" Marco smirked.

"I needed to talk with him, but I got caught up with lecturing him instead."

"What did you want to talk to him about?" Marco asked. "The intrigue."

She shrugged, sullen with the question because it only reminded her that she hadn't talked with him about anything that mattered. Instead, she'd forced a barrier between them and could only hope that it hadn't been permanently cemented. "His performance. His motivation on stage."

Marco looked confused.

"What is his stage persona about? I know he's genuinely vexed about everything, but I can't tell if it's an artifice or a righteous indignation."

"For fuck's sake. Of course it's righteous indignation. What else would it be?"

Sara shrugged, unsure. "There are more effective ways to do it. Maybe it's something...meaner than just righteous indignation?"

Having read his journal and witnessed his thinly veiled anger toward Callum, it seemed there was a strong argument for mean after seeing his performance tonight. He did have a rough history, which signaled a bad outcome for a man.

"Mean? Seth? He's one of my Nurture Boys," Marco said, as if that explained everything about him.

"He's not Nurture Boy out there, is he?"

Taking both arms off the steering wheel, Marco momentarily waved them around in the air. "It's art."

Sara felt deflated. "So, it is an artifice? I never took him for being disingenuous. That's horrid."

"No. He is an angry boy, all right. It's just he's also an artist, so he expresses his anger in this particular way. Not everyone does it your way, Sara."

"Only juvenile delinquents go around destroying property and harming themselves."

"Please. This is fucking ridiculous coming from you."

"What?" Sara shrieked in genuine exasperation.

"Physician, heal thy fucking self. You starve yourself, drink to get drunk—so what's all that, if not self-harming?"

"Self-harming," she sneered. "How can you compare a bit of dieting and drinking to that?" She crossed her arms over her chest in a huff. "Stick to the subject. Let's not turn this into another intervention, please."

Marco rolled his eyes.

"Listen, I know stuff about this boy that I can't share with you because the Men's Circle is a safe place for them to talk confidentially. Tonight, he looked like a whacked out, smackhead juvie delinquent, but that's how he used to be all the time. Now he reserves that behavior for the stage."

Sara let her arms fall, acknowledging some sense in what Marco was saying.

"Fuck. I just can't stand it when you're so critical, so judgmental, especially about someone as sweet and sensitive as him." Marco fell uncharacteristically silent before he added, with a hint of sharpness, "You and your powerful moral purpose, Sara."

The sting of this on top of everything else in her evening had pricked her eyes. "I'm an activist. By definition, I *have* to have a powerful moral purpose."

Marco sighed, relenting. He rubbed her leg. "You're right." She could feel his lingering irritation in his firm pressure on her thigh.

"Just don't go calling him a juvenile delinquent. You're not perfect either."

She pushed his hand away. "You think I believe I am? Tomorrow, I have to start working on all my own problems, beginning with the fact that I'm a feminist who has been regularly fucking a misogynist."

"Tom's not a misogynist," Marco said definitively. "It's just that, at this school, his behavior makes him look…"

Sara found the words for him. "Like the straightest guy ever."

"That's about it. A *very* hot one who, by your standards, which are pitiful, is a decent fuck."

Sara hung her head. "Great. I don't have to worry about a thing after all. No standards. I'll fuck anyone if they're hot enough."

Marco laughed while Sara threw her head in her hands. "I broke up with him."

"Good."

"I think maybe too cruelly."

"Whatever. Look, what he said to Seth about the Circle… Contemptible asshole. He's not a part of our community. It's a fucking good thing you dumped him."

"Thanks. Very supportive."

"Now you get to turn your sights on a boy like Seth."

"A delinquent? Yes, much better choice."

"First of all, I was not suggesting you make him your boyfriend. I think we've already established my feelings on that."

"Mine too."

"I meant—a similarly minded activist boy. And second, you have some nerve calling him that. I've seen you be juvenile." Before she could jump in, he conceded, "*And* me too. You should've seen me today with that boy from the coffee shop. He smiled at me, and I literally giggled like a school-boy-girl."

Sara allowed his hand back on her knee. This time it was soft and affectionate.

She risked elevating the conversation again. "Was he a smack-head as a kid?"

"No more information. I'm cutting you off. You know I'll tell everything if you torture me. I'm too fragile. Plus, I have a date with the cutest boy on campus. I came by to tell you about it earlier, remember? And I'll tell you everything you want to know just so I can live to kiss him."

Sara swayed into the conversation shift. "Who is it?"

"Drew Parker. He's a professor in the Economics Department."

"I've met him. Tom doesn't like him."

"There's a mark in his favor already then," Marco said distractedly. "Just go easy on Seth. Despite what you're thinking of his behavior on stage tonight, he's one of the gentlest boys in the group. And..."

"Are you, Marco Gonzalves, struggling with how to say something?" she asked, smirking.

"Frankly," he said, finally finding the words, "*you* are his feminist guru. He thinks you're utterly brilliant."

A grin spread across Sara's face and she blushed.

"I knew you'd like that. I bet you've always wanted to be someone's feminist guru."

"I can't say that I've been living for the day, but now it's here—wow." After basking in the glory for a moment, she cracked. "I wonder where that would fit on my vitae?"

chapter seven

Sara was too distracted to give her full attention to Allyson reading her poem: *Feminists are the Best Fucks.* She held back a smile as she thought about the events right before the seminar.

She'd received a call from the Boston NPR station, asking for an interview about both her research and the diversity award. Only hours earlier, she'd had a similar request from a newspaper. Of course, it wasn't an offer of publication or a fellowship to Wellesley, but after receiving two more rejection letters in the last week, the fact that anyone held a glimmer of interest in her research was nothing less than thrilling.

Also contributing to her mood was Seth, who'd finally shown up at the seminar after a two-week absence following their exchange at the club.

After Allyson read her poem, Callum silenced everyone when he said it reminded him of a poem he'd come across in an anthology of women's studies. Everyone moaned, thinking he was joking. His usual smirk was absent. He remained serious, explaining that the anthology had been required reading.

After a long pause, Callum revealed he'd taken the Sexualities in Poetry seminar the previous semester.

Sara asked, "Was this the course with Professor Marco Gonzalves?"

Callum nodded, looking embarrassed.

Trying not to adorn a completely shocked expression that

captured the way this struck her, Sara went on. "Specifically, how does it remind you of Allyson's poem?"

"The metaphors for both the female anatomy and orgasm. The myriad similes. It's gorgeous stuff." Callum flipped open his notebook. "I wrote some things down here. Some notes on Allyson's poem."

Sara was open-mouthed with astonishment. The class had fallen silent too.

Allyson laughed nervously. "I think we all need a drink after hearing Callum reference feminist poetry."

"I need a drink after hearing you use the word 'pussy,'" he shot back.

As everyone began to file out, Sara purposely walked over to Seth. While usually he was the one to approach her in class, Sara knew she had repair work to do so went to him for a change. She wondered what she could do or say to convince him that Foucault was back in.

"We've missed you." *I've missed you.*

His smile was warm. "I've missed you too." He meant the collective you of the class, of course, but she let herself briefly indulge the thought that he meant he'd missed her.

She handed him his journal. "It's very good. Nice voice. Read my comments."

"I will." He smiled. "Are you going over to the Tin Palace?"

Sara nodded eagerly, trying to convince herself that her aim was to talk with him about the sell-out and what she perceived was his volatile behavior on stage, but she knew it was mostly just a chance to be around him again.

"Want to walk over together? I mean, if you're going now. Or maybe you just want to meet us all there…"

With his rambling, Sara could see the damage she'd done.

She motioned to the pile of books and papers on her desk. "I have to unload this first."

Before that exchange in the club, he would have offered to help her, but not tonight.

* * *

Once at the Tin Palace, Sara heard Allyson telling the assembled group that she always falls in love with a person, so their gender identity didn't matter.

"How about you, Callum?" Allyson inquired, as if the question needed asking.

Sara didn't listen for his answer; instead she pulled her chair toward Seth, taking her opportunity to reconnect with him.

"Allyson was telling everyone at WRC today that you're getting some air play on college radio stations across the country."

He nodded, responding to the silence between them by looking directly at her for an uncomfortably long time.

Sara rushed to fill the void. "You've missed the seminar a few times. Everything okay?"

"I've been writing," he said perfunctorily.

Getting him to talk was like a visit to the dentist, something taxing. Painful.

When he didn't go on, Sara did something unthinkable. She rubbed her hand over his back. His body stiffened against her touch, but she didn't stop. "What's going on?"

"Pressure in the band. Tense stuff," he said, going on to explain there was disagreement over signing with mainstream record labels.

Shocked to hear he was still considering going mainstream, Sara raised her eyebrows and stopped rubbing his back. She tried to hold back, waiting for him to make the offer of saying more.

"I know we'd be selling out."

"Is there really a choice then?" she said, hoping to both draw him in and make him reflect.

With a great earnestness, Seth looked into her eyes. In her present state of mild inebriation, Sara found this unnerving.

"I'm so fucking sick of being poor."

Sara gave a teasing gasp and playfully threw a line from *The Communist Manifesto* at him. "You have nothing to lose but your chains if you stick with the minor label."

He laughed at her reference to *The Communist Manifesto*, and Sara, unable to help herself, slid into lecture mode.

"Going mainstream will alienate you from your performances, your music, and most importantly, you'll be in bed with The Man."

She admonished herself for lecturing and fell silent, watching him digest what she'd said.

"Okay, one last attempt to convince you that I should go to work for The Man." He paused to sigh heavily. "You said in a seminar you thought it was culture work to filter feminist ideas into the mainstream. You called it 'admirable work.'"

"You listen well."

"Of course I do."

She had to squash the urge to say, *Of course, because I'm your feminist guru.*

"Turning Audre Lorde on her head," Seth said, summing it up in the words she sometimes used in seminar, letting her know that he hung on her every word. "Dismantling the master's house using the master's tools...Maybe I can do that. Work from within?"

While Sara was about to respond, intrigued with his spin on it, she was interrupted by Callum collecting dinner and drink orders.

Sara declined to add to the food order. Allyson was about to say something, but Seth jumped in.

"You're not going to eat anything?" Concern was evident on both his and Allyson's faces.

"I ate earlier," she lied. "And I don't feel much like eating since I've now been rejected by almost every publisher, so my research will end up in some obscure journal."

Sara winced, realizing she'd landed on the very topic that had alienated Seth at the club: her unpublished work. She cast a sheepish look at Seth to gauge his reaction. He looked like a lightbulb, bright with something to say.

"You should go mainstream with it. Get the word out to real people."

She smiled.

"Maybe a magazine like *Allies* would pick it up."

It was a brilliant solution, certainly one consistent with her activism goals. Plus, she liked the idea of people talking about and applying feminist philosophy over a cup of coffee, not just regurgitating it in esoteric fashion to students or plebeian, disinterested audiences as she did now.

Seth put down his cup of tea to assist Callum, who promptly appeared in front of them carrying a huge drink-laden tray.

As he unburdened Callum, his sleeves slipped up, exposing partly healed cuts on the inside of both his forearms.

Sara knew a self-harming cut when she saw it.

He sat down beside her and asked if she'd heard that the Anoraks were playing with the Bacchantes at the Rock Against Rape concert in Boston.

Sara tried to focus on what he was saying but struggled to dispel what she had just seen. Speaking in great dollops, and twisting her hair around her finger too tightly, as she often did when she was upset or nervous, she told him that she would try to be there.

"I hope so," he said.

Rattled, for a moment she had no idea what it was he was hoping for. She must have given herself away too, because she saw a flicker of confusion in his face.

Sara gathered herself. "I organize the Take Back the Night Rally for the women's studies department every spring. It would be great if you could play that."

He agreed immediately.

"Really?" she said, astonished that he would agree so readily. "Shouldn't you talk with the rest of the band?"

"We only ever really want to do this kind of thing. And we'll do it, but only if you promise to come and see us at the RAR show."

Sara agreed and saw her chance to bring up her concerns. "I find it scary to watch you. It looks like you're getting hurt out there."

Seth's eyes widened and he broke eye contact, shifting in his seat uncomfortably.

Maybe too far, she wondered.

"That behavior was," he hesitated before adding, "a regular part of my life once."

"Was? Seems like it still is," she said, considering whether to mention she'd just seen his arms.

He was looking at her as if he wanted to say something but was unsure if he should. He shook his head, wary about taking a chance so soon after the scolding at the club. "Are we back to deconstructing the nature of the student-professor relationship?"

Sara nodded, then put her hand on top of his in a gesture of atonement. "If I ever forget again, you can call me on it."

Seth leaned back into the booth, looked her straight in the eye, and very quietly asked her, "Are you trying to disappear?"

Sara felt her face burning. He was calling her out about her dieting. They were not only crossing boundaries she shouldn't bridge, they were also momentarily changing places.

Not knowing what to do or say, she stared him down. It took Allyson's voice to snap her out of it.

"Hello," Allyson said cheerily.

Sara shot a look at her, then back to Seth. He was still looking at her. Feeling discomposed, she leaped up.

"Gosh, it's so late. I better get going."

She made hurried leaving noises and headed for the door. Quick footsteps followed behind her.

"I overstepped." His face crumpled in worry. "Again."

"You didn't." Sara shot a look over his shoulder, seeing they had the entire class as their audience. They couldn't hear anything from where they were, but this must have looked suspicious.

He looked doubtful. "I shouldn't have said that. It was inappropriate. Not my place."

"You can talk to me about anything. Really." An image of his arms flashed in her head again. She paused to express the gravity of what she was about to say. "And to answer your question, I do not want to, as you say, *disappear*. I do not have an eating disorder. Let's drop that right now."

He nodded so frantically she thought he would do anything to please her at that moment—even drink a few beers. The thought made her smile, glad to know she still had her sense of humor about her.

* * *

As soon as she reached the safety of her car, Sara called Marco. He was not pleased with the interruption to his evening at 11pm.

"What is it?" he shout-whispered down the phone. "I have my date, remember?"

"Right. Bye then."

"Hang on," Marco moaned. "What's up? Are you okay?"

"He's cutting."

As it turned out, this was not news to Marco.

She raised her voice. "We need a plan to help him."

Marco shushed her, reassuring her that Seth had been confronted in the Men's Circle and so she shouldn't worry.

"Don't worry?" she yelled. "When you worry so much about me for something not nearly as significant?"

Marco sighed heavily. "Actually, Sara, I try not to worry too much about you, either. I know you'll both get help when you're ready."

She was about to pick a fight with him, both for saying she needed help and for drawing parallels between her behavior and Seth's—there was a chasm of difference between dieting and cutting. However, she was too concerned for Seth at that moment to be bothered redirecting the argument.

"There's a lot to his cutting. It's mostly about self-harming, but there's an S&M component, I think." Sara expressed her shock, and Marco batted her down.

"Aw, I probably do some things in my bedroom that would shock you beyond this. It's sexual experimentation."

Sara scoffed down the phone.

"What? You just do the traditional fucking thing? Boring," Marco mocked.

She let him get back to his date, suddenly feeling more of an affinity with Tom—very straight, so White, and she didn't like the feeling. After all, wasn't she supposed to be a radical?

All night long she reflected on the sexual side of Seth's cutting. She was repelled by it and yet, she had to admit, it also intrigued her.

She drifted off to sleep with thoughts of Seth, naked, with no cuts and engaging in the less conventional sex she thought Seth might like. She guessed the version in her head was lame, more a role-modeling of S&M than the real thing.

* * *

Brandishing two coffees, Sara ran over to Marco's office early the next morning to try to convince him that they needed to intervene with Seth. When she got there, it was Jane who greeted her at the door. Immediately, she saw the gathering for what it was.

"Is that your intervention kit, Jane?" She waved her hand at the fruits and croissants crowding Marco's desk. Neither Jane nor Marco looked amused.

Sara sat bolt upright on the couch with her coffee, as far away from the food as she could possibly place herself. "Ironically, I came over here to suggest we plan an intervention for Seth."

"I know. Marco called me last night to tell me about that, but we're not here to talk about Seth." Jane was in business mode.

Marco averted his eyes, looking guilty for enticing her to another one of these shows.

Sara feigned despair. "I thought an intervention was supposed to be with all the people who love you. I have two people in the whole world who show up for my intervention. Pathetic."

"Two people who love you more than the breath in our bodies."

She jumped up to kiss Marco for that comment, while Jane took more things out of her bag, including some fancily wrapped cheese, pâté, and capturing Sara's interest and raising suspicion, a bottle of Veuve Clicquot.

"Are we celebrating my intervention?"

Jane shook her head, but also managed a smile.

"Is there an intervention manual that says bring cheese and wine?" Sara asked.

"You do throw the nicest intervention parties, Jane." Marco's comment elicited a stern look of reproof from Jane, clearly as a warning to him that while she might tolerate a bit of humor from Sara, he was part of the intervention team and must behave more appropriately. Marco winked at Sara as she went to open the champagne, but Jane stopped her.

"Let's just wait on this a minute," she said as the warning looks continued.

Sara guessed that Marco had probably been given a severe telling off after his flippant behavior at the last intervention.

Jane immediately got down to business. "Did you know that even your students have noticed that you don't eat?"

Sara drew her breath in sharply and gave Jane a look that said, *What the fuck did you just say?* The humor dropped from the room like a lump of heavy, wet snow on a tiny tree branch. Sara's thoughts went straight to Seth.

"We've talked about that night at Black Hole already."

"I'm not talking about Seth. Allyson says she never sees you eat."

Sara threw her hands up in the air. First Seth with the disappearing comment, and now Allyson.

"Again, another person with trauma-dar. It's just like when cops see everyone through a crime lens. You all have trauma lenses. Maddeningly hyper-focused on it."

"So, in addition to us being delusional, Allyson is too? There's getting to be quite an army of people who are delusional then."

Sara fell silent. She knew she couldn't convince them of how ridiculous they were being.

"Allyson says you have perpetual excuses—not hungry, have eaten, will eat later, have indigestion, don't feel well…"

"Seth's brought it up in the Men's Circle," Marco said quietly, supporting Jane.

"How on earth did that come up?" Sara said, expressing her poleax with wide eyes.

Marco only sighed, dropping his eyes like someone who was withholding information. Sara stared back, not budging.

"You know I can't tell you that."

Jane shook her head. "Will it help to tell her?"

Marco paused for a moment, then said, "I don't know what's going to help, except that she needs to recognize she's starving herself, drinking too much, and is going to kill herself if she doesn't stop it eventually."

"Jesus Christ. All this drama over a diet? I'm not even that thin. And I mostly drink on the weekends."

Jane and Marco rolled their eyes. Sara ignored them, droning on about how good she felt. Never better.

Jane finally interrupted. "Please, just stop it. Even you don't believe any of this."

Sara did believe it. The accusation bewildered her.

"You counsel women every day with these issues, so you tell me, which approach should I take? Should I reprimand you for being a bad role model to your female students, to the women that walk through this office every day?"

"I don't think this tack is helping, Jane," Marco interjected. "She doesn't get it."

Sara had had enough. "Stop talking about me like I'm not here."

They both settled their eyes on her, as though suddenly remembering she was there.

"I ate a sandwich yesterday."

Marco was thrilled. "That's great. Right, Jane?"

Jane narrowed her eyes as she scanned Sara from neck to waist, as if attempting to develop x-ray vision and see the aforementioned sandwich making its way through the digestive system.

"I have no witnesses though. Sorry. Next time I'll make sure to get some."

Jane, ignoring her humor, badgered her further. "And the rest of the day?"

Sara didn't need to think about that. She always knew precisely every single calorie that went into her body.

"I had a yogurt, an apple, carrot sticks. Hardly starving myself, right?"

"The fact that you have it itemized in your head is a bad sign. I bet you can tell us how many calories and grams of fat, too."

Sara winced.

"Are you hungry right now?"

Sara shot pleading eyes at Marco, but he looked away promptly, clearly having decided to obey Jane and her intervention agenda. Sara was on her own then.

"Yes, I'm hungry..." She pulled out a zip-lock bag of Kamut cereal from her bag.

Jane almost screamed. "We. Have. Food."

Clearly uncomfortable, Marco suddenly broke ranks with both Jane and Sara, offering a bone from the Men's Circle, maybe as an effort to divert things. Sara couldn't tell for sure.

"I can tell you one thing about Poetry Boy," he said. "He's very angry about rape."

Jane threw her arms in the air. "What?"

Marco waved her down. "Seth talks a lot about the readings you give him, especially the stuff that draws parallels between sexism and rape, and the thread that explains it."

"Thread?" Sara was swayed.

Jane was obviously frustrated by the direction of the conversation. "Is this helpful? Am I missing something?"

Marco had Sara's rapt attention. "He says, according to you, the thread is The Man."

Sara now understood Seth's reluctance to talk with her at the Tin Palace about the record deal and tour. "I just chewed him out last week when he told me he was considering signing with a major record label."

"On an up note, you've got him writing some incredible stuff based on that conversation about selling out, the thread that connects The Man with eating disorders."

"Finally," Jane exploded. "We come back to that."

Since neither Marco nor Sara wanted to return to that topic, they continued.

"Come to the concert tonight and hear some of it."

Of course, Sara was drawn in. "What concert is that?"

"They're playing a gay pride concert." He flashed his backstage necklace. "I'm with the band."

Having already committed to answering the phones at the Women's Resource Center, Sara couldn't go. She regretted missing the chance to hear the poems sung, to see him perform, but as the image of his self-destructive stage persona leaped into her head, it was probably for the best that she was missing it.

When Marco told her he'd brought her a copy of the "Thread" poem, Jane dropped her shoulders, accepting that the intervention was officially over. Sara grabbed the poem from him and, idly promising them that she would eat lunch, dove into it while Jane's voice droned on in the background.

Although it was written in a poetry code she couldn't fully comprehend, she understood that it was about a girl who was starving herself. The thread for understanding her self-loathing behavior was a sexist society, one that rapes its girls in the hopes that, in their attempts to cope, they will slowly disappear through starvation.

She paused on the word "disappear." It gave her chills reading the word that he'd said to her.

Moments into her reading, Jane tapped her on the shoulder, beaming, and brandishing a fat manila envelope. "This doesn't look like a rejection."

Sara gingerly took the envelope.

It was from Wellesley.

With Jane still prattling on in the background, opening the Veuve Clicquot and explaining that the letter had been sent to WRC by mistake as often happened with Sara's university mail, Sara finally shut her out. She opened the letter. It *was* an acceptance letter.

"I'm being handed an opportunity to improve women's lives," Sara said, shaking all over.

Marco, who'd been reading the fine print of the contract, suddenly exclaimed, "There's a decency clause. God fucking help you."

chapter eight

The past week had been a good one. Not only was she preparing for a visit to Wellesley, but her paper had also been accepted for presentation at one of the most prestigious women's studies conferences, and she'd been given the singular honor of moderator for the panel.

When Marco knocked on her door towing coffee, she was glad to see him. She'd seen him a few nights before at the crowded celebration dinner that Jane had organized for her fellowship acceptance, but they hadn't had the chance to chat.

She threw her arms around his wet, snowy shoulders and hugged him.

"The first snow of the winter," he declared, with enough happiness to raise suspicion as he flopped down on the sofa in her office. "It makes me want to do something romantic."

"You always want to do something romantic."

"Speaking of romance." He shot that Poly Styrene's "SR Way" smile at her.

"Your date at the concert with the cutest guy on campus went well, then?"

Marco answered her by swooning, then giggling.

Sara was pleased to see him like this. Marco was the kind of romantic who was constantly falling in love, getting hurt, and breaking up. He spent more days depressed than happy.

After he told her all about their gay pride concert date (it was amazing. Seth was fantastic), Sara anticipated a full account of the after-date sex. Instead, Marco plunged into an anatomy of the show, raving about the songs and the audience's exuberant response. Sara waited until an appropriate moment to address what interested her most.

"How was Seth?"

Marco sighed heavily. "Pretty whacked out."

Knowing that Marco had been to over a dozen of Seth's shows, this sounded ominous.

"More whacked out than when I saw him at the club?"

"Actually, the night you saw him he was quite tame."

Sara couldn't imagine what "whacked out" looked like, and decided she never wanted to.

"Enough of that. Tell me about the date."

Marco beamed. "Drew didn't take his blue eyes off me all night. Of course, because I was busy with Drew, Seth had to fend for himself."

"Fend for himself?"

"He always hangs out with me. Despite all those girls that fawn all over him, even when he was still with Eyva, he…"

"He's not with Eyva anymore?"

Marco waved his hand around. "That's been off for a few months, at least. Probably since around the time he started taking your seminar."

Sara's face grew hot as she descended into girlhood-crush mode, making her feel distinctly un-professorial as her heart rapidly beat at the thought of an available Seth.

Appalled by this quick descent, she tried to get a hold of herself. It was one thing to have the fantasy of a one-night stand with Poetry Boy, and quite another to consider making it reality. Almost involuntarily, her daydreams rearranged themselves to accommodate the reality of it. The semester was almost over—three weeks and two days, to be specific. She certainly wasn't interested in anything more than one night; not with someone so angry, volatile, and self-destructive. Then, of course, there was the skateboard issue. *But one night? Lovely.*

Marco was still talking. Wondering if one night with Seth would violate the decency clause in her Wellesley contract, she had no idea what she'd missed. Sara refocused.

"…I've come to expect it so much that when I'm handing out condoms to Caleb, Jeff, and Eyva, I don't even bother to offer one to Seth anymore. I know he's not leaving my side."

Sara asked why Seth might shirk the opportunity to choose from a bunch of girls making themselves sexually available to him, but Marco averted his eyes and sipped his coffee.

"I've got some ideas, but I can't talk about stuff from the Circle."

Sara knew her face showed irritation.

"If he didn't hang out with you and Drew after the show, who did he hang out with?"

Marco pursed his lips before tackling what was the comical tragedy of events that followed.

"Well, he was with a girl that night."

Jealousy stabbed at her.

"And that was unexpected, but I was more relieved than anything. I could focus on Drew. When I saw him leaving with her, I just thought, not tonight. I have one fucking condom left, and I'm saving it for myself, not giving it to you."

Sara giggled at the image of him wringing his hands over the ethical implications of such a quandary, so typical for Marco.

He stopped as if to quiet her, give her some idea of the magnitude of the situation for him. "I had to run after him. As much as you can run in a place like that. Plus, it was my super girly run, you know, extra camped-up for Drew's benefit, so it took me a while to catch up with them. I grabbed him by the arm and asked him if he had a condom. That riled him, but he managed to gather himself enough to gloomily shake his head."

He paused long enough to create suspense. Overcome with envy, Sara squirmed and wasn't sure she wanted to hear more.

"And then he said: 'Don't worry about it' and looked at me with this blank expression and walked out with her. Just walked out. I was stricken with worry."

Marco made it sound like the outbreak of war instead of a haggle over a condom. He could infuse drama into anything. "You won't like what happened next, but just remember, it's very rock and roll."

Given the difference in their opinion on what constituted acceptable behavior and what was depraved, Sara wondered if he might be about to tell her that the girl cut him up badly, that he'd been rushed to the hospital. When Marco asked her if she really wanted to hear it, her mind started hurtling to worse places, though for her, what he told her was the worst.

"He came back utterly wasted. I asked him if he'd used a condom and he laughed at me." He took on Seth's drawly voiced inflections. "'We were just getting high'—while this girl's climbing back into her underwear right in front of me. Fucking audacity to say that to me, of all people."

Sara was flooded with contrary feelings. Envy was quickly replaced with worrying visions of Seth high, but she also felt amused, managing a weak smile as she listened to Marco's clever Seth imitation.

Marco told her that the girl settled his mind. "To be precise, she said, 'Don't worry, Bitch. I didn't fuck your boyfriend.'"

Sara smiled at this, despite being worried and unsettled by Seth's drug use.

"Can you believe it? I mean what was with the underwear, then?"

The grin on his face told her Marco had some idea, but not one he was going to give away. Sara decided she would have to ponder on that one herself.

* * *

The whole thing had left her feeling flat with worry for several days. There was some relief that Seth had Marco to watch over him. She kept busy, taking up Seth's suggestion to pitch her research to popular presses. She'd worked tirelessly, trying to find the right fit, and it was Saturday again before she knew it.

While Sara and Jane usually dug around the clubs where girl bands were playing, on this particular Saturday night they were in the mood for a dance atmosphere. The gay club that Marco frequented was the only club free from unwanted male harassment and attention.

Screaming like a little child, Marco beckoned them over through the packed venue.

"I thought you were with the Men's Circle tonight?" Sara yelled over the noise.

"I am. We're all here."

Sara scanned the bar for Seth. It was another hour of drinking and dancing before she spotted him.

It slayed her to see him. Preoccupied as they'd both been, it had been almost two weeks since she'd laid eyes on him. Sara, busy with her hunt for a popular press, had missed a few nights at the Tin Palace, and Seth missed a few seminars because of out-of-state shows. Marco had gone to another show since the gay pride concert and, while he'd tried to tell her about it, she'd stopped him. She really didn't want to hear about Seth's volatile behavior anymore, and especially didn't want to know about any other girls adjusting their underwear after getting high with him.

She watched him as he listened intently to a person whose lips and eyebrows were so expertly penciled and shaped that Sara wondered if they did it professionally. The fem-identified person was talking animatedly and couldn't keep their hands to themselves.

Tom had been the first boyfriend with whom she'd been monogamous. Before Tom, she would act on any surge in her libido when she saw a man she liked. Flirting shamelessly, she'd end up in bed with whoever caught her interest. As a result, watching them with Seth and knowing the pattern as well as she did, Sara was riveted, both by the game itself and with Seth's response. Not only was Seth aware he was being flirted with, but he didn't seem to mind.

The flirting escalated by the minute, and she watched them wrap a forearm provocatively around Seth's neck, lean in closer, and whisper suggestively in his ear. Seth, clearly straining to hear them, also leaned in closer.

Seth's behavior was interpreted as encouragement, and they suggestively kissed him on the cheek. It made her catch her breath, wishing, in her drunken state, that she could be the one doing that to him.

Seth's response to the kiss warmed her heart. He was a good man, she thought as she watched him smile. Despite that, when they caressed Seth's leg and moved their hand to his butt, he promptly but gently removed it. Simultaneously, Sara observed Seth whisper something in his companion's ear. They looked crestfallen. Seth continued talking, touching their arm as he did so. The alluring smile returned in response to whatever Seth was saying. And then they walked away.

Sara took the opportunity to go over to him.

He beamed to see her.

"Gagging for a drink," she told him.

"Here." He offered his beer while she waited for assistance at the bar. "Share this with me."

Having never seen him drink alcohol before, Sara questioned him about the beer.

"I bought one for someone, and I got one for company." He handed it to her. "Have this one while you wait, or you'll die of thirst. They're really slow tonight." Sara accepted. "Congratulations on the Wellesley news, by the way."

"Thank you. And thanks for your suggestion on the mainstream presses. It's a good approach."

The delight that crossed his face made her smile.

"What? You didn't think I'd take a student's advice?" She took a playful swig of beer.

Sara was next to order at the bar when Jane burst in, pleading with Sara to dance with her to Hot Chocolate's "You Sexy Thing."

Sara hesitated.

Seth gave her a little shove. "Go dance. I want to see this."

First, she knocked back the quick chaser that the bartender handed her, motioning with his head to a guy who was grinning at her from a booth. "From an admirer."

Seth raised his eyebrows. "You have a lot of admirers at this club?"

Sara shrugged, the alcohol working its way in, loosening her words. "There are some hot men here, don't you think?"

Her ratio of alcohol to food was off balance, otherwise she would have kept quiet.

He simply smiled. "Aren't these hot men of a persuasion that would preclude them from being available to you?"

Marco joined Seth at the bar as Jane dragged her to the dance floor. Sara looked over her shoulder, smiling at him as she went.

Every time she looked in their direction, she noticed that Seth barely took his eyes off her. Jane and Sara danced their way through the song with several of the men and then with each other. After two more songs, they left the dance floor in need of a drink.

Before taking her beer from Seth, Sara was aware of how closely he watched her as she knocked back another chaser, this one bought for her by Marco. More animated and lively, certainly louder, Sara was drawing more attention than usual from Seth.

"That was interesting."

Sara laughed, sipped her beer, and uncharacteristically bopped her head back and forth to yet another gay anthem.

"It's one of our songs, mine and Jane's," she said, explaining her interest in dancing to Donna Sommer's "I Feel Love."

He gestured toward her sipping.

"Slowing down for the night," she explained.

"Too much already?"

She nodded, giggling loudly.

"You're drunk," he said, but he smiled, making her think he'd probably seen worse at rock shows. It made her care a little less about being conspicuously drunk in front of him.

"Do you maybe want to eat something?" he asked her. "Soak it up?"

"No, I don't want to eat anything, silly."

She leaned into him, pressing her hands flirtingly against his chest, declaring, deadpan, "You all think I have an eating disorder, don't you?" She laughed out loud to communicate the ridiculousness of the notion before leaning in so closely to him that her lips almost touched his. "An eating disorder? Me? Ha!"

Staring back at her with a stony expression on his face, Sara felt his hand on the small of her back, steadying her.

A ripple of sense hit her. "Sober me up?" she pleaded.

"How should I do that?"

"I don't know. Tell me about your record deal. I'm sure that'll make me sober."

He dropped his eyes. "We signed with the major label."

"Sell-out." Sara smiled, but he didn't see it with his eyes still skirting the floor.

The smile wasn't a performance for him. It was an effort to lighten the mood when all she wanted to do was scream at him. Even drunk, she knew the inappropriateness of that choice.

He was speechless, entrenched in his silence.

Sara interpreted his catatonic pose as spineless, but maybe it was self-doubt. Hadn't she tried to encourage him to reflect on the impact of the choice? Pointing out it rejected not only the DIY politics they both shared, but also denied the violence done to women through the patriarchy?

She put a hand gently under his chin, shifting him to face her, forcing him to look her in the eye. She never would have touched him in such a way if she were sober.

"Shame on you," she said softly, almost inaudibly.

The music was so loud, Sara didn't know if he heard her, but her eyes were boring through him.

Decoding his eye-lock as contrition rather than confrontation, she managed a slight smile. And this time it was for him—Sara's attempt to throw him a lifeline.

The alcohol washed back over her and her playfulness with it. "Now you'll have to fuck me for that A grade." Before she even saw his half-hearted attempt to collect himself from the shock of what she'd just said, she buried her face in her hands in panic. "Oh God. Did I just say that out loud?"

She was so lightheaded. Four hundred calories in food and seven thousand in alcohol swam in her body. She didn't even notice Marco standing beside her.

"Yeah, you did. It's a good thing for you that I'm not on the university ethics committee."

Marco was trying to inject some humor into the situation, but Seth turned and walked away from them both, registering the wordless look of concern on Marco's face.

"What the fuck are you doing?" he practically spat, raising his eyebrows and shoulders at the same time. "Blatantly flirting, then saying that to him."

"Obviously I was only joking." She knew that wasn't entirely true.

Marco looked at her squarely. "It was a fucking stupid, very bad joke that you wouldn't have made sober. Not to mention that you almost certainly just violated the decency clause in your Wellesley contract."

The next ten minutes Sara spent in the bathroom, attempting to sober up by washing her face.

When she reappeared, Seth was there, brandishing an apple. "I bet you can eat this."

Sara smiled appreciatively at him for the effort, probably feeling as equally uncomfortable as her. "Yes, I can eat that."

Her feeble little bites, however, reflected her uncertainty about whether she could afford the eighty-five calories. "Of course, it won't soak up the alcohol. I just want to go home."

Seth offered to drive her. Eager to redeem herself as a model professor, she saw this as an opportunity and accepted.

Marco pulled her aside, glowering and shaking his head. "Are you mad? Wait and let me take you."

She gave his hand a reassuring pat as she handed Seth her keys.

Once in the car, Seth's stony silence, periodically interrupted by nervous conversation, told Sara that it wasn't just Marco that was worried about the situation.

A la Goffman, the absence of the equipment symbolically defining her as professor—the other students, the seminar room, her office, the campus—it was almost impossible to carry out that role sitting beside Seth in her car. The setting didn't just transform the roles, it tore them down. Driving her home, at night, drunk; he was now just a man on whom she had a significant crush. The situation was fraught with sexual tension.

A little well of despair pooled in her mind, threatening to drown her if she didn't figure out how she was going to salvage the situation.

When Seth pulled into the carport at her apartment, Sara leaped out, announcing as briskly as she could, "Thanks for driving. You can take my car to get yourself home. Drop it off on campus tomorrow, please." She charged off in the direction of her apartment.

She heard his door open and slam. When he called out to her, she turned, waiting for him to catch up. She knew he was offering protection. "Funny that I need a man to deliver me to my door to protect me from other men."

"Yeah, sorry about that. Think of it as the buddy system."

"Really? So, who will be your buddy on the way back to the car?" Sara answered for him. "Patriarchy. Got to admire its ideological brilliance, right?" When he didn't say anything, she told him, "It's a question."

"Admire its brilliance?" he repeated. "Brilliantly spans time and place. I mean, it's sad, but brilliant."

"And?" Sara asked.

"And?"

"And it convinces the group it oppresses that the system is good for them. Do you have any idea how many of my female students have to think about it when I ask them if they'd rather have a boy pay for dinner or have equal pay? They say in this whiny voice, 'Why can't we have both?' I tell them separate but equal was found to be unconstitutional."

Sara shivered as they reached her door. Seth stood facing her, inches from her body. He reached out both his hands to rub her arms, attempting to warm her up, which only made her shiver even more with his touch.

"You're cold."

With his hands on her, they'd both stiffened. He removed them quickly, dropping them awkwardly to his side.

Sara attempted to neutralize the situation as they both fell into silence again. "Not too cold. I'm okay."

"Thanks to the alcohol," Seth said, jumping in.

"Which I really shouldn't do because I'm so bad with it. As you saw tonight."

"On smack?" He smirked at her, quick with a comeback.

Was that supposed to be funny? "Smack? Funny. Ha ha. Not funny." She rocked her head side-to-side, but drunk and aroused by his closeness, she found she was able to ignore the creep of concern in her head with the mention of drugs.

He was smiling at her, seeming to Sara to be waiting for some encouragement or approval to kiss her.

"He's your student" and "decency clause" hurtled through her head as she drew on the pause and found a few words to throw together instead.

"I flirt shamefully when I drink. I can't tell you how many gay men I flirted with tonight."

"Me too."

She giggled.

They fell silent, holding each other's gaze. It was Sara who tore herself away first.

"Fuck. Now I'm flirting with one of my students."

"I've never heard you say 'fuck' before, and now I've heard you say it twice in one night."

He grinned at her uncontrollable giggles, but she was grateful that he helped her out, dropping the flirting by not holding her gaze that time.

She shivered again. "I lied. I'm freezing. I'd better go in."

"You're so thin. That's why you're cold."

Sara saw him wince immediately, and she wondered if he suddenly remembered her warning to him at the Tin Palace. Seth raced a hand up to cover his mouth. She could see his idle words were giving him worry.

"Listen, I know you're a man who wants to do the right thing, so do it. Your place is to listen, not challenge. Don't you dare challenge me or any woman about the motivations for our behavior or make assumptions about our bodies."

Seeing his nervousness was hitting a breaking point, she invited him in for a cup of tea, trying to lighten the mood.

She unlocked the door, and they walked in together. "Or would you rather have coffee?"

He paused in thought, then asked with deadpan humor, "Got any smack?"

She went with the banter. She put the kettle on and rifled through the cupboards. "Sorry, no smack. Hot chocolate?"

Seth nodded. "That's good. I want to be up all night writing."

As she made the hot chocolate, she reflected on how often he'd mentioned smack over the course of the semester, all Marco's references about Seth's past drug use, and then, of course, there was the incident with the girl at the gay pride concert. Handing him the mug, she fished: "Hot chocolate will keep you up?"

Her apartment was freezing, so she understood why he was holding the mug so close to his face, almost hiding, his eyes and hands fixed over the warmth of it. He nodded.

"Like smack?" Sara pressed. "Smack keeps you up too?"

His eyes fixed on the mug. "It used to."

She decided against prying further, despite the cagey answer holding multiple possible meanings. It might mean that it used to keep him up all night when he used it, or maybe he still used it, but it was no longer effective at keeping him awake. There were probably more options too, but she was too tired to think.

Sara was determined to have him stay long enough for her to recover her image, and after about half an hour of demonstrating that she knew how to be both a grown-up and a professor simultaneously, she let him go.

"Be careful, because while there's nothing out there that'll hurt you, there might be the odd bear going through the trash bins."

chapter nine

Waking up hungover and plagued by an incessant, obnoxious noise in her ear, which she finally registered as the phone ringing, Sara glanced at the clock: 5am.

"Sorry, its early," Jane's voice came through the phone. "But I have to go and get Allyson at the police station. She's been arrested, and I..."

Sara was upright. Apparently, *Playboy* had sent representatives to recruit bunny co-eds, and Allyson, who'd been at the protest rally, was arrested for resisting arrest. Jane felt she should be there for Allyson and needed Sara to be at WRC for her.

Once she pulled herself out of bed, the pain in Sara's side was so intense she keeled over, barely able to walk.

Weighing in this week at a hundred pounds, she felt like a little feather that could be blown away from all existence at any moment. But squeezing herself into the new jeans, she knew she still had work to do; hunger pains were worth it.

To sustain herself slightly, she bought the biggest cup of coffee she could at the local bakery and, after marveling with disgust at the amount of food people were eating, headed for the WRC.

The twenty-five calories from the milk in the coffee made her feel better, even though she was angry with her body for needing so much food.

After a while at the office, Marco arrived, then Jane not far behind him.

"Oh no, it's my intervention team," Sara cracked, but she was the only one who enjoyed the joke. Jane just shook her head and looked at her disapprovingly, while Marco uncharacteristically ignored the chance for a laugh.

After explaining that they'd taken a very tearful Allyson home to bed because apparently spending the night in a jail cell could shake even her, Jane turned to Sara with an expression of directed earnestness.

"Marco told me you propositioned Seth Coles."

Marco's lecture on the topic the night before still fresh in her mind, Sara sighed heavily. "He's exaggerating."

"And he drove you home?"

Sara was glib. "I'm deconstructing hegemonic student-professor relationships."

Jane shook her head. "That doesn't mean sleeping with your students."

Agitated both by Jane's tone and the apparent accusation of stupidity, Sara decided to revel in their anticipatory expressions.

"I invited him in too." It was a coy comment, provoking Marco and Jane to start talking simultaneously, heat rising on their stricken little faces.

"We're worried—" Marco broke off. Being a poet, he was a stickler for finding the right words, structured just so.

Sara batted them down with her hands. "We had hot chocolate together. Honestly. Who are you people?"

Jane turned to Marco as if she expected him to handle this one.

Sara had never seen Marco squirm before. It wasn't easy watching him grapple for the right phrasing.

"You're not just his feminist guru, he...admires you, shall we say."

Jane jumped in. "That's a different way to put it."

"An awful lot," Marco added uselessly.

Sara began to wave her hands in a circular motion, indicating for him to hurry it along, dying to hear more about this plethora of admiration.

He buried his face in his hands. "It's not right that I'm telling you this—it's from the Men's Circle—but he's writing poems and songs about you."

Sara blushed with pleasure. "That's nice, isn't it? So what?"

Marco looked at Jane. "I told you it wouldn't bother her."

Jane shook her head. "Well, it should."

Sara, dismissing Jane's overreaction, turned to Marco. "What's he saying about me then?"

"Sara!" Jane snapped.

Marco put a hand up, quelling the brewing row, and raised his voice for attention. "To be fair, it's not technically sexual."

Sara's face fell in mock disappointment as she declared directly toward Jane, "That's too bad. I was hoping it would be something carnal…filthy, even."

After Marco and Sara recovered from giggling, Jane spoke. "If they're not sexual, what are they? What's he saying that made you tell me you were concerned about them being alone together?"

Marco, falling serious, nodded at Jane. "They're what I would characterize as intimacy poems."

Jane lowered her eyebrows at this. "Really? Intimacy?"

A flurry of emotions tore through Sara. Deflated that they were not sexy songs about his desire for her and simultaneously horrified by her disappointment that they weren't. Shouldn't she be pleased his songs were exposing the ills of patriarchy and not about sexual desire for a woman?

She chastised herself for her stupid crush.

"And what does that mean?"

"Sara wants sex from men, not intimacy," Marco said. "Whereas Seth wants intimacy, not so much sex."

While Sara was bothered by this habit they'd developed of discussing her as if she weren't in the room, she let it go. "Do you think that's maybe why he didn't have sex with that girl at the gay pride concert?" Sara said, proud to have made the connection.

Jane's face contorted in confusion. "What girl?"

Marco nodded. "Yeah. And I think that's why he has no interest in the girls hanging around him after shows. What they're after, he's just not interested in."

Even Jane raised an eyebrow and lifted her chin, her interest piqued.

"Can you imagine? It's certainly what interests me."

"*That* is exactly what concerns me for him. You."

Sara fired back. "He's a big boy, Marco."

"Frankly, it's not just sex you need to worry about. It's this close-ness you've developed with him."

Feeling the gravity of his ridiculous Tom-like warning, she folded her arms and stiffened her posture.

"This suggestion that I should be more traditional with students sounds wrong coming from you." Sara reminded him that his peda-gogy was virtually identical to her own.

"You go too far," he charged, cutting her off. "Gazing into each other's eyes like you did last night, having him at your apartment. It would definitely be considered an inappropriate relationship for a professor to have with a student, don't you think?"

That silenced Sara. She couldn't argue with that assessment.

Marco sacked the silence. "That's exactly what I'm talking about. Can the decency clause withstand that much intimacy? If the university knew how you two behave together, you'd lose your job."

Jane nodded in understanding, and Sara, so rattled by Marco's forecast of doom for her career, didn't even object to his anti-post-modern libido comment.

"And Sara…" Marco was hedging again, using her name in a warning tone. "I'm at torn purposes here because I don't want you to hurt him, just as I don't want you to get fired, so," he paused for dramatic effect, "I'm calling you off."

Hurt and too hungover to be anything less than astonished by his characterization of her intentions, she pouted like a child who'd been told to go to their room. "I'm not even on him."

Neither looked swayed by her defense, which only increased her sense of indignation. "And anyway, what's all this about me and my problems? What about him? He's a complete mess. His behavior is repellent. He's volatile. He probably takes drugs. He cuts himself… while he's having sex."

With this last comment, Sara saw Jane look at Marco for confir-mation. "Really?" Marco nodded. Jane looked back at Sara. "Interesting."

Sara, exasperated by their idle curiosity in masochism, noticed Marco stewing. Her remark on Seth was in self-defense, but she guessed her charge sounded too much like those hurled against Marco as an adolescent.

Marco shot a glowering look. "Are you saying he's not worth loving because he cuts himself? You should've seen my cuts when I was a kid. And what about you? Are you not worth knowing just because you self-harm?"

His ferocity was the last straw for Sara. Her tears fell.

Marco's eyes averted to the floor, choking back a sob. Jane eased him down with a "shush" and gentle pats on his back.

"Just please go easy," Marco pleaded softly. "At least until the course is over. And, for his sake," he looked up at her, "don't fuck him, please."

Despite the outrageous comparison made between her dieting and Seth's cutting, she could see it was said under duress. Sara couldn't help it; she had to hug him. Marco, the guy who was able to turn everything on its head and create humor out of the most unlikely topic, was also vulnerable.

Jane broke the emotional tension. "You're his feminist guru. You have a responsibility here as his muse."

"Muse?" Sara said, stiffening. "A muse is an object. I don't want to be anyone's muse."

Marco recovered. "Ease up. What I wouldn't give to be someone's muse. Anyway, you're no object to him. You're his poetic afflatus." As both Sara and Jane rolled their eyes, Marco added tongue-in-cheek melodrama. "You're calling him to the revolutionary ranks."

Sara was exhausted by the rollercoaster of feelings. "Want to hear something completely different?"

"Yes, please," Jane said eagerly.

"I'm hungry."

Marco looked at Jane for direction.

"Let's go and get some breakfast," Jane suggested, not missing a beat, nudging Marco with her elbow to get moving.

* * *

At breakfast, despite Jane's disapproving stare, Sara ate only two bites of toast and half a grapefruit. She calculated the calories almost instinctively. Not too bad, although she felt the toast had been a mistake. After all, she hadn't had time to research the menu and had no idea how many fat grams or carbs were in that particular piece of bread.

By 6pm, she'd added a few more items to her notebook: a protein bar, five carrots (making a mental note to herself to look up the calories in carrots), and three cups of coffee.

She ate pretty much the same thing every day. It was the only way she could be sure of her calorie and fat intake. Today she would allow herself between three and four hundred more calories, but only if she felt faint with hunger.

She thought about food all the time now. In between researching presses, reading scholarly papers, preparing for her National Women's Studies Association conference, food crept in. It was a pleasant distraction, like a game. Her goal was always to feel hungry, otherwise she felt fat in her jeans. So, she worked at achieving a balance between hunger and starvation. That was the game. Doing it at breakfast that morning, she'd had to remind herself not to share this with Jane or Marco, since she knew they'd turn it into another paranoid worry.

As she got ready for the last seminar of the semester, she played the game, considering which to eat: dried apple rings or Kamut cereal? She kept a kitchen measuring cup in the big drawer in her desk and, if she didn't have the dried apple rings, she would allow herself two cups of Kamut a day.

Lately, she'd been learning to recognize the effects of too much hunger. They included a lightheaded dizziness, faintness, and a stitch in her side that sometimes doubled her over with pain.

While she'd been aware of that familiar growing pain in her side for the past half hour or so, she was too busy to eat. Despite it being December and her fellowship not starting until the following fall, a colleague contacted her to suggest she start attending the monthly colloquia series. In addition, she was busy connecting with a few popular-press magazines who had contacted her regarding an interest in her paper.

Lifting her head too suddenly at the knocking on her open office door, the pain in her side became blindingly intense. Before she knew what was happening, she keeled over in her chair.

Seth shot across to her.

"I think I'm going to throw up."

Snatching at the wastepaper basket by her desk, he thrust it toward her.

Softly whimpering, she threw up bile.

"Put your head between your knees." His voice was slow and calm. It sounded like a good idea, but Sara was too dizzy to move. She was relieved when she felt Seth assisting her with the maneuver. And while it certainly helped, Sara knew that what she really needed was food. Fast.

"Are you sick?"

Sara lifted her head as much as she could. "No." She wanted to sound confident, but it came out as a moan because the slight escalation of her head made her feel ill again. "I'm just hungry."

After he watched her eat the two cups of Kamut, she declared she felt considerably better. Well enough at least to walk with him to the seminar room, and certainly good enough to join them for their last semester get-together at the Tin Palace.

* * *

Unable to find a table, they snuggled together at the bar. The place was crowded with undergraduate students.

"Busy for a Thursday," Sara observed. "There's still another week for regular classes."

Allyson shrugged, now fully recovered from her "time in the cell," as Callum had put it during the recounting of her arrest to the seminar group. "Beginning of the weekend, when you consider it's almost the end of the semester, Thursday's close enough."

Sara recognized several of her underage students drinking and leaned over to yell to Seth.

"I'm a bit uncomfortable with this. I've never seen so many drunk eighteen-year-olds in my life."

Seth, looking around at the crowd, asked her if she recognized anyone.

"Yes. And I'm curious to understand why so many of them are my Friday morning women's studies students."

Seth laughed. "Wonder what you should take away from that?"

When they caught each other's gaze and held it, Sara remembered Marco's warning about inappropriate intimacy, but well into her second glass of wine, she struggled to pull it in.

About to tear her eyes away, she was pre-empted by Allyson, who was mouthing to her: "Are you eating?"

Of course she wasn't, especially after that toast at breakfast. After shaking her head at Allyson, who frowned back, Sara squeezed past Callum and positioned herself next to Seth.

"Heard anything from the popular presses yet?"

A good topic. She knew this would keep her infamous pedagogical approach to a minimum.

"Another rejection letter this morning."

"Ouch. Sorry."

She shrugged. Her confidence boosted by Wellesley, it felt like publishing was a matter of time now. "I've been researching one you suggested—*Feministing*?"

He nodded, looking pleased.

Sara had become increasingly convinced that she was better off publishing there now. After Seth had turned the tables and lectured her that night, she was becoming increasingly critical of academics locked in the ivory tower. She saw a growing chasm between what she did and her peers.

"I may have to convince the popular presses that I don't think of my knowledge as superior or above the streets revolutionary agendas."

"It's a sound place for the pedagogy of the oppressed. They'll love that at *Feministing*."

She almost choked on her drink. "You're correct."

"You're shocked?"

"No, I'm pleased," she gushed, overcome by him and his knowledge of the things that mattered most to her. "Pleased by you. I've never had a student like you. You practically recite everything I say and everything I give you to read."

"High praise indeed."

The wine working inside her, Sara had to resist the urge to gaze into his eyes. She tried to regulate the appropriate notch of intimacy, aiming for the Goldilocks of feminist pedagogy—not too much, not too little, just right.

"Of course, the real difference between scholarship and the rest of it is manifested in the goals, right?" she said, filling the excruciatingly high emotional tension between them. "Scholars are invested in knowledge-for-knowledge's sake, rather than in changing policy and improving women's lives. That's where *all* my writing is now."

Seth raised his eyebrows. "All about promoting change?"

She nodded, taking a sip of wine. "How's your writing?"

"If you come to RAR, you'll hear what I'm writing."

She paused to think about the songs he'd supposedly written about her, curious to hear them.

"The Anoraks are going to be there," he added, as if she needed more convincing.

When she was about to tell him that while she wanted to see the Anoraks, she was eager to hear his songs too, she was momentarily distracted by Allyson, who was simultaneously handing a plate to Seth while straddling Callum's lap and feeding him a piece of pizza torn from her own slice. Sara, raising her eyebrows at the scene, turned to Seth for his appraisal. She could barely take her eyes off them, whereas Seth seemed indifferent at best.

"You guessed this then?" she asked, puzzled.

"You didn't see through all that angry banter that there was something else?"

Incredulous, Sara shook her head.

As she watched Callum very slowly slide Allyson off his lap, Allyson slid her hand easily into his, while Callum's free hand moved slowly over the part of Allyson's body where thigh meets the hip. Sara felt a welling desire for Seth to touch her in the same way.

She could feel Seth watching her as she watched them. She turned to meet his gaze. "What about Debs?"

He shrugged. Sara could tell he was about to move the conversation elsewhere, but she was riveted.

"Do you think they are..." She paused, trying to find the right word to use with a student. "Lovers?"

Seth emitted a little laugh, probably at her choice of words. "I don't know."

Mesmerized, Sara paid particular attention to Allyson's experience as Callum's hands moved over Allyson's butt, then back to her hips and up to the high part of her waist, close enough to her breasts that he was almost touching them.

It'd been weeks since Sara was touched like that, and she was jealous. She wanted all of that. Right now. It was time to go home and give Tom a call.

* * *

It was close to midnight when she got home, but since it was final exam week for undergraduate classes, she knew that Tom would still be awake.

When he answered the phone, she launched in, saying in her most practiced sexy, soft voice that she missed him. He said he missed her too. Forced, polite conversation followed about the end of the semester while Sara wondered how she could contrive a way to get him over to her apartment and into her bed.

"I hate this time of year. I have three huge boxes of grading."

"Poor you," she said sympathetically. She had four, but she had to be nice if she wanted sex.

"And two exams to write. I was doing that when you called. And every student coming out of the woodwork with excuses. I've heard a few new ones this year. They're getting more conniving."

She knew this would inevitably lead to talk about leaving academia for good. At the end of every semester, Tom would talk about how he could make more money doing something else anyway.

"It makes me want to leave academia," he said, making Sara smile at his predictability.

She saw her opening. "Come over for some company then. It's a lonely time of year for you."

"Do you mean now?"

"I know it's horribly late, but yes, now. I'd love to see you, Tom."

Half an hour later, she was in bed with him. Lying beside Tom, she did feel especially good to be held, but her thoughts were on Seth.

For the first time that night, she wondered why he'd come to her office moments before the seminar. Obviously, her being sick in the wastepaper bin had thrown him off his purpose for visiting, hurling him instead into a Florence Nightingale role, which he played adeptly. She'd email him in the morning.

Feeling sober, her eyelids finally growing heavy, she smiled to herself at the thought of emailing with Seth tomorrow. Then the smile fell as she was engulfed by waves of shock and disgust at what she had just done.

chapter ten

She'd used Tom. She felt terrible, and worse still to be ignoring his calls for the past four days since they'd spent the night together. She hoped he'd come to see it as nothing but a bit of fun. It wasn't just that she felt badly about the way she'd treated him, she was embarrassed by it, knowing that she'd behaved that way precisely because she was drunk.

For all these reasons, the idea of a confrontation about it was too stressful to think about. When her phone rang while she was on a call to the registrar's office and she saw that it was him again, she wrapped her hair so tightly around her finger she felt her skin almost break.

She took it out on the registrar, virtually screaming into the phone. "If you can't figure out your computer problems with the grade-submitting system within the next hour, I want someone to walk over to my office to collect my final grades," Sara demanded. She glanced at her phone to see that Tom hadn't left a message this time, and then at the door, where Seth stood, smirking, clearly having heard her rant.

She placed her head on the desk and shook it. "It's a very bad, bad time."

Because she felt so exhausted from her last two nights of all-night grading, she didn't pick her head up immediately. It felt good. In fact, it felt so good she closed her eyes and thought that maybe she would just stay there, take a nap...

Seth's voice stirred her. "I wanted to respond to your email."

At first, she didn't know what email he was referring to, and then she was plunged back to her drunk-sex night. She must have emailed him to follow up about his office visit on the last day of the seminar. She lifted her head, mentally reminding herself to never drink again.

"Most people hit reply."

"I just wanted to see you. Make sure you're coming to RAR tonight."

While she nodded enthusiastically, she didn't mention she was dreading it. While she wanted to hear the new songs, she didn't want to see him bleeding on stage, angry, possibly high, and almost certainly so out of control that she didn't recognize him.

"And I came to see you the other night because I wanted to give you this." He handed her a leather-bound first edition of Simone de Beauvoir's *Second Sex*.

She was speechless.

"Open it."

It was signed. It was priceless. How much money had he made on that sell-out record to be able afford this?

"I can't believe this," she said, fingering the book, her eyes brimming with tears.

He beamed. "It's to say thanks. For the seminar. It was amazing," he stammered. "You are amazing. Lucky Wellesley."

She dared to look him in the eye.

"I thought it'd have you bouncing off the walls."

"And what you saw instead was me throwing up."

"Yeah, not what I was expecting." His mouth held a teasing smile.

She held the book up. "This gives me chills." And so did he. Not only was she now in possession of something extremely precious to her, but he was the one who had gifted it.

"And congratulations on getting published with *B!tch*."

That bit of news had wilted and withered almost as soon as she got the call, drowned out by how troubled she'd been by her behavior the night before when she'd flirted with Seth.

"I have a lot of editing to do for the *B!tch* piece," she said as someone from the registrar's office appeared at her door.

Seth left her to it, but not before nervously asking if she'd meet up with him after the show. She nodded but couldn't help wondering how she'd explain this one to Marco.

* * *

The concert was in the city, and what would normally have been an hour-ish drive turned into three due to a storm that threatened to turn them back.

Drew, who'd bravely offered to do the driving, was fit to be tied when they got there, but that red mood was Marco's fault. Hyperventilating into a brown paper bag for the last hour of the drive, Marco had been absorbed in an anxiety that periodically allowed him enough breath to squeal, "You're going to kill us all," every time Drew edged the speedometer over twenty miles an hour. Sara and Jane, who normally would have enjoyed the display, were grumpy and fed up by the time they arrived at the venue.

As they made their way to the front of the stage, the lights went down and a deafening, thunderous applause arose from the crowd. This was clearly not the usual Bacchantes show. The sheer size of the place and the crowd, the crew, security—it was all new. A very different experience.

Eyva, Jeff, Caleb, and Seth appeared on stage, and Sara felt goosebumps erupt all over her body from the tension in the audience's excitement and at the sight of Seth.

She was struck by how at ease they were in this setting. Pleased for their evident success, she had an uneasy concern for them creep in. Something was happening, and she didn't know if they were in control of whatever the shift was. Now that they were mainstream, she wondered if they had any choice in how their success would proceed.

Seth played the opening chords, and the audience roared approval, charging toward the stage, almost squashing Sara and Jane.

Choosing to watch from the mosh pit was probably not the wisest idea at a show with such a large crowd. Shooting a quick look at Marco, Sara hoped for reassurance that they hadn't survived the icy Massachusetts highways just to be killed at the stadium.

When she saw his happy, smiling face and his bopping body as he held hands with Drew, singing along like everyone else, she assumed the craziness was normal and that they'd probably live through it.

After the first few chords died away, the audience erupted into applause. Sara rolled her eyes at the ridiculous level of adoration. Seth didn't need to do anything to win their approval. She suspected that he could just stand there all night, barely playing a note, and the audience would still love him.

Based on the audience's a cappella version of the first verse sans Seth, she gathered that their excitement was precipitated by the recognition of the song. Finishing the verse, the audience fell silent, reverently waiting for Seth to take over. He offered them a taunting smile, and the frenzied crowd cried out for him to play. Sara realized Seth knew exactly how far he could take the audience in their lunacy. Just when she believed there might be a riot if he didn't resume playing, Seth looked over at Eyva, who, clearly taking it as a cue, burst in with Seth, Caleb, and Jeff.

It was an orgasmic moment for the audience, who, now pacified by attention from their leader and breathless from both the ecstasy and relief of it, sang along.

Seth was complete ferocity, thrashing around with utter abandon, bleeding down both arms. It was depraved, but she understood their enthusiasm. He was mesmerizing, although she couldn't help but think of neck injuries, sutures, and infections the whole time she watched him.

Toward the end, now completely gripped by his anger, he gave up playing altogether, forcing Eyva to take over on guitar. Sara began to suppose that's why Eyva was there in the first place—to take over for Seth when he could no longer control himself.

At one point, he took a stab at playing again, but quickly changed his mind, hurling himself into the drum kit instead. Sara was thinking about the poor drummer when Seth finally whipped off the guitar and, with the angriest expression, hurled it into the audience as hard and fast as he could. Immediately, he fell flat on his back to the floor.

Sara's first thought was for Seth's wellbeing, but quickly turned into mortified horror as she was convinced someone in the audience would get killed by the airborne guitar. Despite her fears, the audience, including Marco, went wild with applause and some lucky person reveled in the victory of taking home Seth's guitar.

As the drum kit was reassembled, a sad young man checked on a bleeding Seth and a bloody-nosed Caleb. Someone else cleaned up the stage debris that had been flung around by the audience; ostensibly with love, but still dangerous, Sara thought.

"What's happening?" Jane asked Marco, as they were unable to fully assess the commotion on the stage. "Is someone sweeping up? Why?"

"Probably lethally slippery with blood," Drew offered, scaring Jane, and forcing Sara to explain he was joking. There wasn't any blood on the stage that she could see. It was all over Seth and Caleb.

When they started playing again, the audience erupted at such volume that Sara's ears rang. Feeling like she couldn't manage much more of this, she looked over at Drew, who was tugging her arm, indicating with his hands that she should make eye contact with Marco.

"For you," Marco mouthed and motioned to the stage.

Sara felt uncomfortable. She was still conflicted about being cast as Seth's muse. After all, he was not the first tortured poet to write a song about a woman. All the same, she was flattered by the compliment, and her school-girl crush was all the more excited by it.

She strained to listen but much of it was completely unintelligible to her. She got the general message though, as Seth sang the entire song with his eyes closed, more subdued. He didn't smash a thing.

The set ended to more loud applause. Seth, striding over to their side of the stage, was followed by fans striving to be as near to him as they possibly could. The surge to the left was like a stampede, crushing Sara so badly she thought she'd be trampled to death.

In a moment of pure alarming terror, Sara felt someone grip hold of her among the sea of bodies surrounding her. She began to yell. When she identified it was a burly security man with arms almost the width of her body, she had already been pulled over the barricade and now only gawked like a goldfish. Standing there on the stage, she looked up to see Seth pointing at another security guard and back to Marco. In teen-girl mode, Marco rushed toward the security guard, who assisted him with a little more effort than he had with Sara. The audience's frenzy seeing Seth hand pick members of the crowd made Sara doubly glad to be out of the mosh pit. With slightly more effort on the security guards' end as they battled off eager fans, Drew and Jane soon joined them over the barricade.

Seth gave Sara one of his sexy grins, causing a familiar tingling feeling to stir deep between her legs.

Promptly, they were all escorted off to the bar, where they were given backstage passes by the same scared young man who had assisted Seth and Caleb on the stage.

"What do we need these for?"

"They'll be mobbed here, so we'll meet them in a private room," Marco explained.

Sara dropped her shoulders and cocked her head.

When Seth had asked her to meet him after the show, she thought he'd meant in the bar, or maybe a coffee shop. Meeting up with him this way made her feel twitchy, like she was playing groupie to a local rock star rather than being a friend or a feminist guru.

"I don't think so. You and Drew go. Jane and I'll stay here." She turned away to order a drink.

Marco insisted. "He needs your support."

"If he really needs my support, he can get it in the bar."

Marco shook his head at her, exasperated. "Have you been listening to a fucking word I said? He can't come down here."

It was surreal that only hours earlier he was still just a student in her office, checking on his grade, picking up his papers. Sara, unfamiliar with this new world Seth had chosen to be a part of, begrudgingly relented.

Backstage was mayhem, with at least a hundred people milling around. After waiting over half an hour, they were finally escorted to another room where they found Seth, Eyva, Caleb, and Jeff, along with a throng of people vying for their attention.

While she could see Seth watching her the entire time, he was surrounded by a small posse trying to entertain him, wanting to be near him, and he couldn't seem to get away. Disgusted by the display, Sara informed Marco she would meet him at the coffee shop across the street when he was ready to leave and sharply turned to make her way down the hallway.

A call came from behind her. "Where are you going?" It was Seth, who'd broken away to follow her.

"Going out for coffee." She kept her tone neutral, casual.

"There's a nor'easter out there."

As if to say that a little storm didn't deter her from getting an espresso, Sara shook her head. "It's too crowded in there. And I don't like the groupie atmosphere."

"Is it okay if I come with you then?"

* * *

Despite being in the city, the snow made everything quiet, and the Christmas lights only added to the surreal atmosphere. While they weren't dressed for it, they decided to walk the deserted streets, neither of them particularly caring that they were cold and wet within minutes.

The grades submitted, Sara was finally freed from the constraints of her role as professor. Believing she could afford to be as friendly as she really wanted to be with him, Sara reached out to hold his hand. He hesitated. She stopped and turned to look at him. They stood there gazing at each other for a while, his eyes searching hers, calculating. Finally, he picked up her hand and slipped it comfortably into his own.

They continued to walk for a while longer. Sara didn't want it to end; she assumed he didn't either, but once completely soaked and freezing, they had made their way to the coffee shop across from the stadium.

Over her coffee and his tea, she made him laugh as she recounted the drive down to the concert. Seth texted Marco, suggesting they all stay at the hotel for the night since the weather was so bad. He grinned as he quipped that he didn't think Drew would survive driving Marco on a long car ride twice in one day and didn't want Jane or Sara caught in the crossfire. As it turned out, Allyson and Callum had also traveled down together and had met up with the others at the bar.

"Why are you so taken with them?" Seth asked as Sara gasped at the news.

Sara shrugged, considering being disingenuous. Should she offer the small-talk version of her interest, telling him that she was just surprised by that particular pairing of activist and jock, or the bare, deconstructed truth?

"Those lascivious gazes between them, all that erotic behavior… it's sexy to watch, don't you think?"

"I hadn't thought about it like that, but, yeah, I suppose."

Sara averted her eyes toward their entwined hands. Her hand looked so tiny in his. Even that felt sexy.

Unable to reign herself in, Sara leaned over to playfully stroke his cheek with a finger, and Seth took hold of that hand too. With both her hands in his, they talked at length over their free refills until one of the two baristas approached them.

"Sorry Seth, closing for the night."

Seth nodded.

Sara watched the barista curiously as he walked away. "Do you know him?"

Seth only shrugged and looked embarrassed, leaving Sara wondering, *what does that mean?*

As they stood piling on their too-skimpy-for-the-weather clothing that had finally dried off, thanks to the assistance of the baristas who had kindly offered to layer their jackets and sweaters over the heating vents in the back of the shop, they were approached again.

"Um, would you mind signing this?" the barista said, brandishing Seth's empty mug and a black sharpie pen.

Sara's eyes gaped. Seth shuffled his feet, digging his hands further into his pockets. He looked like he wanted to coil himself up and crawl back into his abusive mother's womb, but he nodded, taking the cup and the sharpie.

They stepped out onto the snow-covered pavement, hearing the door close and lock behind them. On the other side, sounds of hooting and hollering muffled through—presumably at their excitement at having met *Seth Coles.*

"Don't say anything." Seth reached for her hand. "I'm embarrassed enough already."

"Now all the free refills and the courtesy of drying our clothes makes sense. I just assumed everyone got that treatment here."

Seth dropped her hand to check his phone. "Marco got a room with Drew. He wants to know if you're okay sharing a room with Jane and Eyva."

He picked up her hand to go, but she stopped him.

"Can't I stay with you?"

His eyes blinked rapidly, processing the request. She couldn't tell if it was in a positive way or not.

After a painfully long pause, his voice shook in response. "Of course. There are two beds. You can have one. I can share with Jeff."

"Or I could share with you."

Seth stopped stock-still in the snowy street to look at her intently. "Really?"

"I'm not with Tom anymore." She knew that was suggestive, implying she really wanted to be with him, but she didn't mind him knowing that either.

"I know."

She squinted at him, a silent question; the answer should have been obvious.

"Marco told me."

It seemed there was nothing Marco kept from Seth about her. Although he had no problem holding things from her about Seth. The excuse was always the confidentiality of the Men's Circle.

He offered his hand again. "Let's sort it out at the hotel."

Taking his hand, they resumed walking.

* * *

The sorting out of rooms was a logistical nightmare. While Jane and Eyva were happy with Sara's suggestion that they have the room to themselves, and she bunk with the boys, there were protests to the idea.

"It doesn't make sense," Jeff said sullenly. "We'd have to share."

Seth sighed heavily and flopped down on one of the beds.

Since Jeff was threatening to foil her plan, Sara decided to present her idea blatantly. "I'll share with Seth. Caleb could go in with Jane and Eyva."

While everyone, bar the intervention team, accepted this scenario immediately, Jane folded her arms and made a single cluck with her tongue. Marco stalked over to Sara, hissing, "Come with me" as he pulled her away by the elbow.

They heard Jane making an announcement to the remaining assembled group behind them. "Okay, I have another idea," which was met with a loud groan from everyone.

"He's not my student anymore," Sara exclaimed the moment they were locked in the privacy of the bathroom.

"His seat is barely cold in your classroom. This must have been a tough semester for you, having to wait so long to fuck him."

Sara raised her voice. "Stop worrying about us."

"I'm not worried about you. I'm worried about *him*. Don't you make it just for fun. Not with him."

Sara felt like an especially despicable human being hearing those words. It made her think of Tom. It was one thing to turn hegemonic ideas of feminine sexuality on their head and get sex whenever she wanted it, but it was another to use someone. She knew the difference, even if only when she was sober.

"Jeff will be in the room," she announced, closing the lid on further resistance from Marco. She could neither seduce nor be seduced if they had Jeff as a chaperone.

When they emerged from the bathroom, Jane filled them in on the latest grievances. Apparently, while Jane, likely against her better judgment, had defended Sara's wish to stay with Seth, suggesting that none of the boys would have to share together because her and Eyva were fine, Jeff was fixated on his own idea.

"No, we have two rooms. Three girls and three boys. The girls should all stay together, and the boys should have their own room."

"Jeff," Seth practically barked. "What's the fucking problem? You can have your own bed, stay with Eyva and Jane or…"

Jeff cut him off. "I'll have my own bed if I stay in my *own* room."

"Fucking hell! No one is saying you can't have your own bed, Jeff!" Making a final appeal, he got Caleb's attention and empathy. "Do you care if you share a room with Eyva and Jane? No? Great! I'm sharing with Sara, and we are all sorted."

Jeff put his hands over his face, exasperated, but he shrugged, muttering under his breath about everyone making it so complicated.

Once everything was settled and after Seth lent her the only clean T-shirt he had left, they went to bed—Jeff content to have his own bed, and Sara joining Seth in the other.

Since she only ever intended to have sex when she climbed into bed with a man, she didn't know what to do and was relieved when Seth started a whispered conversation.

He told her Jeff had a huge crush on Marco. Since they knew that Marco had expressed his admiration for Jeff's beautiful long hair, this made Sara giggle.

Jeff shushed them both.

Sara continued in even quieter whispered tones. "Too bad he's with Drew now. We could've fixed them up."

"Drew's good though, isn't he?"

After reassuring him that he was, they both fell silent again until Sara, barely audible, said, "Give me your hand."

Slowly, she slid his hand into hers, holding it at first, then gently and with complete silence between them, began stroking it. When he opened his hand, as if to invite her to continue on the inside of his fingers and palm, she stroked each finger over and over, and then he began to do the same to her.

Sara found the sensory experience and suggestiveness of the stroking very sexy.

However, with Jeff only feet away, she knew they could do no more than this, and she felt the anticipation of what was being denied to her welling into frustration.

"Would you hold me?" Sara whispered, turning herself so they lay spoon-like together. They settled in this position, with his arm wrapped around her, his hand resting on her stomach.

"Are you hungry?" he asked. "Because I am."

Sara laughed softly at this; she was always hungry. "Not too hungry. I have a protein bar, if you'd like it."

"I'll be okay," he said sleepily.

And then she felt his breath on her neck, and she knew he'd fallen asleep.

Distracted by her sexual frustration, her mind was restless most of the night. When they woke in the morning, they'd barely moved from the position in which they'd fallen asleep. The familiar hunger pain in her side mounted as Seth, leaning over her body, gently placed his lips to her cheek, lingering long enough that she almost forgot about the pain. Before she was too tempted to turn her face and discover what his lips tasted like, he climbed out of bed.

Sara lay there marveling at this strange new experience of *sleeping* with a man. Frustration combined with a strange sense of satisfaction and a giddy-schoolgirl joy washed through her. She understood frustration, but she'd never felt this level of satisfaction and joy after waking up next to someone, especially after not having sex. The intimacy of just sleeping with him, the way they had whispered together, touched each other, and lay holding each other close all night was new to her.

Jane and Marco had accused her of not wanting any intimacy with men. Wait until they heard about this!

After gloating on it for a moment, watching Seth as he stood in front of her, rubbing his hair dry from the shower, she remembered Tom and all the missed calls, and all her good feelings dissipated. How long could she evade that confrontation?

chapter eleven

Seth left that morning for the band's mid-Atlantic states tour, but not before telling her he'd be returning to play at a private New Year's Eve party as a favor to Marco. After Sara promised she'd be there, she left for home with Marco and Drew.

Sara was struck with a little fear at just how much she missed Seth after only a week. The time had flown by, partially because preparations for the NWSA were going well. Additionally, Seth called her every day, keeping her amused and making her laugh with stories of the band's life on the road, including the dullness of interviewers, ridiculous photo shoots, and Eyva's new puppy.

After a few more calls over as many days, Tom finally got the message and stopped calling. The dreaded confrontation was avoided.

The New Year's Eve party hosted by Marco's very rich ex-boyfriend, Dougal, arrived before she knew it. The event was so big it had a name: "Have a Gay New Year."

Seth and the rest of the band, who'd just finished playing a set in one of the ballroom-style rooms in the house, a rarefied setting of decadent opulence, were finally on break at 2am.

While the band's unique sound and performance were unchanged, she got a sense Seth was restraining himself. Probably, Sara thought, because he didn't want to get blood on the walls.

When she overheard Dougal declare to Marco, "Seth is depravity itself, Marco. I love him, but I thought you said there would be blood," she giggled and considered telling Seth as he made his way over to her. Worrying it might incite in him a license to unleash his destructive self, she decided against sharing the comment.

They hugged, holding on to each other for long enough that Sara wanted to take him straight back to her hotel room.

"How's the paper coming along today?" he said as she pulled away first, worried she might do more than hug if she didn't.

"It's been all good today." He'd been receiving daily updates on the ups and downs of her preparations for the NWSA conference. She was becoming a perfectionist now that she was about to be a Wellesley fellow.

"So glad the conference is happening when we're there for a show," he said, reminding her of the plan they'd made to meet up in D.C.

Sara finished her drink and grabbed another as a waiter walked by with a tray of martinis. "I'll only have a few hours to get away. I'm moderating, presenting, and chairing something else."

The ever-dramatic Marco slumped down next to Sara on the sofa and declared, "Coffee is my most consistent lover."

Sara, resisting the urge to groan, patted his hand instead. She knew it was the same lament—Drew. Owing to the fact that Drew was her ride to the conference, and he and Marco were having constant spats lately—a big part of which was due to Marco's plan to spend New Year's Eve at a party given by his ex-boyfriend—Sara was starting to despair at making it there at all.

Behind them, a commotion grabbed their attention, and Sara caught sight of police officers. Apparently, they were there in response to a complaint from a nosey neighbor on this leafy suburban street. Nevertheless, since Dougal was so welcoming, rather than bust up the party, the police joined the revelry, smiling broadly and wishing everyone a happy new year, oblivious to the fact that they were being wished a "gay new year" in return. That is, until one of them discovered a syringe and tourniquet in the bathroom. The whole party fell apart, Sara included.

"Ridiculous. Heads are going to roll over a bit of smack on New Year's Eve," Marco exclaimed.

Sara completely lost her temper with Marco.

"For goodness' sake, what did you expect? Cocoa and knitting needles?" he said.

She ignored the weak attempt at a pun, replacing the sticky brown of smack for cocoa and knitting instead of intravenous needles, and shivered all over with worry for Seth.

She still didn't understand anything about his drug use and hadn't stopped wondering about it since that night when he'd told her that smack didn't get him to sleep anymore.

Seth, whom Sara suspected was the owner of the equipment in the bathroom, tried to help calm her down. "Let me give you and Jane a ride back to the hotel."

Instead, she grabbed Jane's arm and raced them out of the house at four in the morning.

A cab was called, but they were still waiting in front of Dougal's gated estate when Seth emerged.

"Get in the car, Sara. It's freezing."

"I'm not getting in any car with you." Her speech was slurred from four glasses of wine and the martini. "Whose car is it, anyway? Did you steal it or something?"

"I'm too cold to stand out here," Jane said as she got in the car, infuriating Sara enough to lunge into a rant.

"You...you are a depraved lunatic," she stammered, emotionally shaken, but mostly drunk. "With too many transgressions to mention." She started to list them in her head, but the alcohol wouldn't let her hold her thoughts, so she gave up before vocalizing any of them.

Seth got out of the car, attempting to coax her in. At the sight of him approaching, she offered her final slur, trying to echo Marco's clever street talk. "I'm a university professor, for God's sake. Not some girl who hangs with smacked-out juvie delinquents."

It didn't achieve the result she was expecting, as Seth, smirking, inquired: "Where'd you learn to talk like that?"

As he closed in on her, Sara tried to run away, but Seth was too sober for her. He grabbed her with both arms right before she collapsed, sobbing. He held her for a moment and, despite her attack on his character, kissed her forehead.

"I'm sorry," Sara cried more softly. "I would never defame your character like that sober."

Seth laughed. "Let's get you sobered up then."

"Yes," she said feebly as he helped her into the front seat next to him. "You scare me," she told him, and he looked at her gravely for a moment before driving past the gates of Dougal's estate.

Drunk as she was, Sara knew she was more terrified of her feelings for him than of all his transgressions. In fact, Sara was overcome with how much she liked him. She smiled, sitting there beside him. Then severely began to reproach herself for caring so much about someone with so very many problems.

Seth didn't try to make conversation with her and, knowing she was too drunk to trust herself to say another word, especially with Jane in the back, Sara was grateful for it. The three of them drove in silence back to the hotel.

While she'd hoped they'd spend the night together, she now decided against it. Not only was she so drunk that she felt unwell, but she was still shaken by the incident at Dougal's. Sara didn't know how to manage the awkwardness when Seth walked with her to her room, but he handled it with aplomb.

"Get some rest."

Sara nodded.

"I leave tomorrow."

More nodding. She knew he was leaving to re-join the tour in New York.

"Let's meet up in D.C.?" he said, reminding her yet again of the plan. When she didn't respond, he placed a hand under her chin, lifting her to face to him. Keeping his hand there, he gazed at her. "Yes?" he asked, all uncertainty.

Gazing back at him, she took his hand from under her chin and kissed it, a silent confirmation that she wouldn't let the chance to see him again in D.C. escape her.

"Sorry I don't feel well," she told him, and went inside alone.

* * *

After weeks of tweaking her presentation, she was standing in her hotel lobby in D.C., waiting for a ride from Seth. They locked eyes immediately when he entered with the rest of the band, joined by a small gaggle of people that Sara didn't recognize.

Eyva caught Sara in a big hug. Sara watched Seth get snapped up by Drew, who was hugging him while he kept his eye on Marco, already flirting with Jeff.

Sara looked on with admiration as she watched Seth expertly redirect Drew's attention from Marco's gratuitous display over Jeff.

They'd talked on the phone regularly, but Sara was still unsure how to act with Seth after her behavior on New Year's. She'd asked Marco about the paraphernalia in one of Dougal's eight bathrooms and Marco didn't think it belonged to Seth's, but Sara still had nagging doubts. She couldn't bring herself to confront Seth about it on the phone, not when he sounded so flat and tired all the time.

When Seth looked over to her again, she made her approach. Drew slunk away as soon as she came near, giving them space. "I honestly didn't know if you'd show." Seth never minced words. Sara waved her hand around at the crowd he'd brought with him. "Be nice if we could really talk, but this…?"

"I'm sorry. Everyone wanted to see you."

"And who are these people?" Sara motioned with her head to four complete strangers: two burly security-looking types, another in a suit, and one with massive sunglasses and wearing jeans and a bright purple oversized sweater.

He looked nervously at the entourage.

"It's okay. You can tell me about your new friends while we walk around the museum," she told him, trying to get him to relax.

With only a few hours free, Seth had asked her what she wanted to do when they met up. Sara, thinking it might break the tension after New Year's Eve, suggested the National Gallery. She was having second thoughts about that now, wishing she'd suggested they talk alone in the hotel room instead. She thought he could use the break too. According to Marco, who apparently knew Seth's every move these days, the band was fed up and exhausted with a relentless schedule of performing, recording, and interviewing.

He became energized when Sara asked him how it was going, appearing relieved that Sara had broken the tension. The familiar giddy feeling she got when she was around him swept over her and she suspected that his uncharacteristic bubbliness was also attributable to seeing her. The stiffness between them was slipping away as they stepped out onto the sidewalk and toward two very smart looking cars with drivers waiting. Seth directed the seating arrangements. Marco, Drew, and one of the burly guys shared the car with them. Sara was snuggled up so closely to Seth that he had to wrap an arm around her shoulders to save them from being crushed. It made her skin feel goosey being so close to him, and she relaxed.

* * *

Standing in the National Gallery, Sara watched Marco and Drew remove candy from the Féliz González-Torres piece of modern art depicting the wasting away of his boyfriend, Ross, from AIDS. The candy art, all one hundred and seventy-five pounds of it in Jolly Ranchers, was intended to represent Ross's healthy weight before his deterioration. As each visitor took a piece of candy, the idea was to virtually watch Ross disappear, just as he did in life.

Marco and Drew were moved to silence by the exhibit, and Sara felt close to tears while she pondered the calories in a Jolly Rancher.

"Just eat it," Seth said to her, sucking noisily on his watermelon pick.

Sara pulled out cherry.

Her selection gave Marco endless fodder for his seemingly insatiable enjoyment of bawdy virgin jokes. Marco was behaving badly all around, in fact.

"It's this weather. It makes him crazy," Sara told Seth as they stood in a corner together, trying to secure a modicum of privacy.

Touching each other's hands, they looked over to Marco flirting unabashedly with Jeff again. He'd literally sat on Jeff's lap in the car on the way over to the gallery, playing with his hair, whipping Drew into a jealous rage.

"Does it make him crazy or horny?"

Like her, Seth was having a hard time not alluding to sex every time he spoke.

"You should've seen him last night at the club," he said, referring to their night out at a local gay bar. Sara, who hadn't gone because she was moderating a panel at the conference, listened with rapt attention as Seth described Marco's suggestive dancing. It was an uncomfortable amount of arousal in such a public place.

"How'd Drew handle it?

"Well, when he kissed Jeff's neck..." Seth started to say in her ear with breathy suggestiveness.

Sara caught her breath, imagining kissing Seth. Then, thinking they should get a grip or a room, she tried to reign it in. "I think his behavior's more about making Drew jealous than a full-on attempt to seduce Jeff."

Right now, Drew, clearly distressed by the display, vacillated his response between humor and disregard.

"Let's try to cheer him up," Sara said.

It hadn't been lost on Sara that, when he wasn't glued to her, Seth was spending his time with Drew, which she considered very thoughtful.

As they joined Drew and Eyva with her new boyfriend, Bass, Sara was pondering both why the burly guys and the suited one were making themselves conspicuously absent and whether or not to eat her cherry-flavored Jolly Rancher.

"Do you know how many calories are in one of these?" she inquired of Eyva.

Eyva laughed at first, but when Sara waited earnestly, Eyva became incredulous.

"Are you serious?"

Sara was struck by thoughts that felt like they weighed as much as the universe in its infiniteness. First, she realized she'd purposely tried to sound casual with the question, which sent her hurtling to another realization: it's not okay to care about a few little calories, especially when you're starving hungry.

With these thoughts causing all sorts of chaos inside her psyche, Sara was acutely aware of the disbelieving stares from Drew, Eyva, and Bass.

Sara started stumbling for the right words when Seth jumped in with the wrong ones. "Oh, she's serious."

This was not the support she was expecting, and it momentarily derailed her. Irritated by their implication that there was something abnormal in her inquiry, Sara popped the candy in her mouth as a statement that there was absolutely nothing wrong with her. She wasn't going to give them the chance to shine a white-hot light on that ridiculous eating disorder accusation again. She'd show them that she could be reckless and eat candy, just like everybody else. Of course, she would have to skip all edible substances until dinner now, but that was beside the point. Damned that she was going to eat these extra calories without everyone knowing it, without them seeing how completely *normal* she really was, Sara drew attention by ceremoniously unwrapping yet another candy.

"God, this is so good." When none of this got her the attention she needed, she began to suck noisily and commented expressively on the flavor, the texture, even the bright hue, which finally drew Eyva's attention.

"You don't get out much, do you, Sara?"

Sara's efforts to refute their perception of her as "ill" had backfired. She felt exhausted with the performance because she'd just perforated a hole the size of the Ganges in it.

Sara caught Seth watching her just as Marco joined them. No doubt he'd picked up the whiff of drama emanating from their little circle and had come to break the tension.

Seth didn't break eye contact with her as they all listened to Marco reeling off another one of his porn cherry jokes.

This was a moment of reckoning none of them knew about. Sara had caught herself, mid act, in her own lie of being "okay."

Drew shot a look at Marco, then turned to Sara and Eyva, apologizing on behalf of Marco. "He can't help himself. He has a Ph.D. in poetry, you see."

For the first time since they'd left for the trip, Marco warmed and blew Drew a kiss. Sara, following the invisible kiss, noticed two young female museum goers approaching Seth for a selfie. One of the burly guys immediately hovered at Seth's side.

Sara turned to Marco. "Who on earth are these people?" she said, motioning to the suited man and the burly guys.

Seth shot Sara a pained look as she watched him with the giggling girls, thanking him so profusely that you'd think he'd saved their lives.

"They're not very friendly," Sara continued. "And no one's even talking to them." While pondering how odd they were as she watched them flanking Seth's side, it dawned on her that they were Seth's bodyguards.

"This is your life? Reduced to Famous Boy?'" she whispered in Seth's ear as she reached him.

He flinched.

"It's amazing that I was able to capture your interest at all in the seminar, given this sort of attention," she teased.

Seth smirked, clearly relieved. She smirked back at him. While she forgave him in that moment for being famous, she would need some time to think about how she really felt about hanging out with someone who was likely going to appear in magazines she wanted to burn rather than read.

She had to get going, her paper presentation was that afternoon. It was bad timing, and they were leaving each other awkwardly again. He took her hand, waving away the bodyguard.

"I know you must think I deserve all this because of the sell-out."

They headed for the exit with the entourage at enough of a distance that they had some privacy.

Sara shook her head, deciding to reserve that discussion for another time.

"I'll be at your presentation. And without them." He motioned to the burleys.

"You won't need them anyway. No one will recognize you there. You see, the NWSA doesn't keep up with celebrity magazines." She punched his arm playfully.

As they arrived at the front steps to say their goodbyes, he turned to her. "Are you okay?"

Furrowing her brow, thinking she had big enough problems of her own now, such as learning how to eat again, Sara motioned to their posse of friends, the entourage, to the steps of the public building where they stood, as if to say, "We can't really talk about anything here."

He started playing distractedly with a button on his jacket. She'd flustered him. "I'm coming up for your birthday." He took a step closer to her so that their bodies were almost touching.

They stood together, hands shoved into pockets, shivering with cold, not wanting to leave each other. They both jumped when Eyva spoke.

"Seth, get a move on."

Sara stood on her tiptoes to wrap her arms around his neck and hug him tightly. And then they left each other.

chapter twelve

As a child, Sara had raised monarch butterflies. She was amazed at the process. Where there had once been nothing but a cocoon, a full and complete life emerged. Black and orange, earnest and excited with enthusiasm; uncertain of its wings, but clear in its purpose. This described her today, on her birthday. It was a good day all around.

She was reeling from the response to her paper presentation at the NWSA conference. She'd received calls from several superstar feminists, all telling her how much they appreciated her work. Having received two more rejection letters on her manuscript that morning, the phone calls had come on the right day too.

Marco had tried to reassure her. "Plenty more obscure presses out there. Have you tried Vulva Press in Reykjavic yet?"

Nothing could deter her happy optimism today. Her party was just hours away and Marco was taking her out to lunch. Of course, since she would be drinking rather than actually eating anything, "lunch" was a bit of a misnomer. Despite having seen a doctor earlier in the day, it *was* her birthday, and surely, she could put off dealing with medical actions at least until tomorrow.

As they entered the restaurant, Sara was talking to Marco over her shoulder when a far-off look of trepidation masked his face. Turning to see the cause of such a reaction from the usually unflappable Marco, Sara saw Tom. Or rather, she slammed into him.

It was mutually cringy and uncomfortable.

Hugging awkwardly, pleasantries passed between them like they had been neighbors instead of year-long lovers, as if she hadn't used him for sex and then never returned his calls. They both made attempts to be friendly. Feeling like the injuring party, she over-stepped, touching his arm, effusive with warmth for fear that he might confront her on why she'd been avoiding him. "So sorry I haven't been in touch."

"I'll get us a booth." Marco excused himself from the situation.

Sara continued, "I've been busy. I suppose the same for you?"

"Sure." Tom nodded in a way that indicated he was going to assist her in framing this encounter as pleasant.

"The beginning of the semester is such a drag, right?" She resorted to inane small talk to fill the split-second silence. "All those whiny students begging to be added to the class." She tutted, then imitated their whining, stopping abruptly when she realized she sounded like Tom in one of his rants about the woes of dealing with the student body.

Sara did loath this time of the semester, but for very different reasons than Tom. She felt wistful saying goodbye to students to whom she'd become attached and was rattled by the transitions of endings, the terrifying prospect of the unknown looming in the distance of "next semester."

Tom helped her out. "I hate the beginning and the ending."

"And what about the weather?" she said, wondering when it would be polite to extricate herself. "A time when otherwise intelli-gent people become bewitched with the hideous notion of moving to Florida."

It was true, but ridiculous to mention. Anyway, a move to Florida made all the sense in the world right then, even if for no other reason than to avoid Tom for the rest of her career.

"I hear it's been one of the snowiest winters in Massachusetts for a long time."

Tom checked his watch.

"Since 1066, I think they said." She was in jest, but Tom didn't seem to get it. She just wanted him to go.

"I just got back from NWSA," Sara said, landing on another topic that would fill the unbearably pregnant pause.

"Is that a conference?" Tom asked, revealing the depth of his ignorance about her field. "How'd that go?"

"Great."

"Good."

Jane entered the restaurant, Marco reappearing by their side. Jane, looking a little wary at seeing Sara with Tom, exchanged a greeting with him and managed a much better small-talk conversation than the one Sara had just mangled.

Marco cut to the chase. "Let's sit down. I'm going to get a drink. Do you want one, Jane?"

Sara jumped in. "I do."

"I know you want one!" he said. "How about you, Tom?"

"Yes, have a drink with us," Sara gushed again, inwardly crying *"No! No! No!"*

Tom read her mind. "I've got a class."

Thank God. Bye, Tom. Bye forever.

And then he slayed her. "Before I go, I should say happy birthday."

He remembered my birthday? At that moment, Sara thought no punishment could be too cruel or unusual for her.

"Thank you," she said, becoming more convinced with every nanosecond that she was the worst, most pernicious, unfeeling person ever born in the history of humankind. She thought of all the ways that she should be destroyed, both in mind and body.

"Marco's planned this last-minute party for me," she lied. The party had been planned for months, even before she'd even broken it off with Tom, but she obviously couldn't tell him that. "It's tonight. Please come." Sara was conflicted about his answer. It would be easier if he said no, although there was a part of her that wanted him to say yes, so that she could be especially nice to him for one night and alleviate some guilt.

"Okay. Yes. I will," he said immediately.

"I'll text you the details," she said overenthusiastically.

Tom left and Jane accompanied Sara to the booth. Sara's pallor rose an eyebrow from Marco, and Jane took it upon herself to explain Sara's latest blunder. "Why'd you have to ask Politically-Pasty Boy?"

Sara threw her arms in the air dramatically. "I slept with him."

"What?" Marco practically yelled. "Again?"

Jane was calmer. "You slept with him? When did this happen?"

"I don't know. A couple of weeks ago. Maybe three."

They stared back at her.

"I'm sorry I didn't mention it before. I was just…well, embarrassed. I was so drunk at the time. I completely regretted it when I woke up."

Marco began to laugh.

Sara lowered her voice. "It'd been weeks since I'd had sex. Weeks."

Marco looked unimpressed. "You're impossible. Worse than me."

Jane's eyebrows raised in agreement with Marco.

"After all you went through making that decision to dump Mr. Hegemonic. And now you're back with him. Oh, Ms. Wellesley, you do disappoint."

"I'm not back with him!"

"Really?" Jane said sarcastically. "Does Tom know that? Because with that invitation to your party, I think he may not fully understand." The waiter, who was delivering another round of drinks, appeared just as Jane declared, "And now you're what? *Polyamorous*?"

Sara shot back. "I haven't even had sex with Seth." Without missing a beat, she turned to the waiter, asking to see the wine list.

"But you'd have him, given the chance," Marco interjected.

Sara sipped her cocktail and perused the wine list, irked with them for not sharing her understanding of the situation.

"Which, by the way, I'm not okay with," Marco went on. "Whether you're with Tom or not, Seth can't be just for fun, remember?"

Too afraid to admit the depth of her feelings for Seth even to herself, and taken up with the hegemonic leanings in the conversation, she leaped on the chance to respond to the political undertone in Marco's accusation.

"First of all, even if I were with Seth, I don't even believe in monogamy. It's the cornerstone of patriarchy."

Jane pursed her lips. "It's more than that, surely."

Sara felt like Jane might as well have punched her in the face.

"No. Actually, it's not. Gender norms are the support system of the patriarchy, and they're used to justify social arrangements that are oppressive to women like—*ta-da*—monogamy. Don't tell me my business, Jane." Sara paused mid-lecture to turn to Marco. "Would you mind telling the waiter we'll have this bottle?" She pointed to the wine she'd selected from the menu. "The service is so slow here."

Marco whined. "Okay, birthday girl, but don't say anything until I get back."

Sara didn't plan to wait for Marco but Jane, pre-empting the dialogue, cut Sara off before she could start. "Okay, you have me with all the theory, but consider the person, not just the political. What about love and commitment?"

"Blah, blah, blah." Sara rolled her head dramatically.

Jane raised her hand to protest, making Sara speak faster, trying to squeeze in a little more before her friend reached a breaking point. "Monogamy is relatively new in the history of humankind, you know," she said as Marco returned to the table.

"The wine is on the way. What did I miss?"

Jane didn't bother to explain and only continued to disagree with Sara.

Marco gasped, drawing their attention. "Uh-oh. Speaking of monogamy..." Following his gaze, they saw Drew standing at the restaurant entrance. "Drop it, please? We can't talk monogamy around Drew right now. He's convinced I'm sexting with Jeff."

Sara waved at Drew to catch his attention. "Are you?"

Marco batted her hand down and jumped to his feet, diverting Drew to the bar.

Sara watched them. Judging by their earnest expressions, it looked like a heavy conversation.

"I can't believe he's being silly, flirting so much with Jeff," Sara whispered to Jane as a sharp-faced Marco returned to the table with a sullen-looking Drew.

"I'm sorry, Sara, I can't stay, but I wanted to say happy birthday before I left." Drew paused, offering a sympathetic smile Sara didn't understand, then rushed off.

"Are you two fighting again?" Sara enquired, guessing the

sympathetic look meant that Drew didn't want to leave but Marco was forcing him out.

Sighing heavily, Marco looked to Jane, and then back to Sara. "Haven't had an intervention in a while."

Sara laughed. "Ah, that's why you had Drew leave. Bring him back, please."

Jane spoke over her jollity. "A check-in."

"I'm too hungry to talk about my eating."

Marco raised his eyebrows, all business.

"It was a joke," Sara said. She grew weary when he didn't offer a pithy comeback. "This is not okay. I'm not having an intervention birthday lunch. Let's do it tomorrow. Or never."

Marco and Jane stared back at her.

Sara filled the awkwardness. "That was a joke too."

"We're concerned..." Marco surveyed her waifish frame. "Do you even get your period anymore?"

Sara's mouth dropped open at his gall. "First of all, I prefer the term 'bleeding' to 'period,' and second of all, I'm not talking to you about this."

It was true. She had stopped bleeding, and much as she would like to have been able to fathom another excuse for it, she knew the only explanation was excessive and sudden weight loss. Her doctor had given her some medicine to kick-start her bleeding, although it came with a warning that it was pointless if Sara continued to restrict. Eating disorder language was not new to Sara, but the doctor using the terms to refer to her own behavior made her feel ashamed. As if she couldn't feel more patronized by it all, as she was leaving the clinic the doctor gave her the number of an eating disorder specialist. Sara sneered, *I'm already an eating disorder specialist*, but she knew she'd caught herself in her own trap as she uncoiled the comment. Yes, she was the expert, but was she referring to her expertise in restricting or to her knowledge on why women do this to themselves?

Despite the fact that she had not planned it, and resented having to do it on her birthday, she gave them a sneak peek of her new life.

"Remember the Jolly Rancher candies in the Félix González-Torres exhibit?"

Marco looked exasperated, as if he thought she was about to crack another joke about her eating issues.

Jane was stupefied. "What was that about?"

After Sara told them everything, including losing her period and her willingness to go into treatment, Jane handed Marco a tissue to blot his teary eyes, then adopted her therapy gaze.

"Please. Not now. Let me just enjoy my birthday. No talk about restricting. No vigilance. Today I'm still Eating Disorder Girl, but take comfort in knowing that I do know this is more than a VST issue."

Jane doubled down. "It's never a good time. We have to start today."

"I have a lot to do today," she stammered. "I'm picking Seth up at the airport. And then I have to go...somewhere. And somewhere else after that, but I can't remember where right now because I'm just that busy."

Marco was softly crying, all drama. "Don't be so self-destructive. What on earth are we going to do with you?"

Sara considered defending this attack on her sanity but decided against it. Instead, she waved the wine waiter over.

Marco looked to Jane for the verdict. She patted his leg. "Okay. Tomorrow then."

"And I'm going to eat, but I've lost my appetite anyway. After all, Tom is coming to my party tonight."

"Did you even look at the menu?" Jane said, shoving it in her hand.

Marco slumped into the booth. "Fuck. Please say you looked at it online already, because we don't have an hour to order."

chapter thirteen

Seth's birthday gift to Sara was the Anoraks.

As they took to the stage, Sara's eyes were on the lead singer, Clair. She was audacious in knee-high bovver boots and black leather miniskirt with long john's cut-off at the knee. "Fuck" was written across her chest and "Patriarchy" down her left arm. Sara loved the optimism, the verve.

Drawn from the authentic girl power revolution, it was a serious questioning of the status quo that had laid the foundation for female singers like Britney Spears, Miley Cyrus, and Taylor Swift, among others. Unfortunately, those girls had misplaced the most exigent message of that revolution—"I'm coming through. Get the fuck out of my way"—replacing it with their sad, insecure little declaration —"Look at me, I'm hot." The "hottie mystique," as Stephanie Coontz called it. Sara shook her head, wondering why women were constantly fucking things up for themselves.

At the same time, she was overwhelmed by Seth's understanding of what would make her happy tonight. When she scanned the room for him, finally locating him in the foyer chatting with Allyson, Callum, and Eyva, all eyes turned to Sara, including Seth's.

Making eye contact with him, she patted her heart in a gesture of swooning for the band, mouthing, "Thank you."

After the "happy birthdays" had died away, Sara made her way over to Seth.

Reaching up on tiptoes, she kissed his cheek. "I like your T-shirt."

The shirt, which had "Loser" emblazoned across the chest, was discussed at length. Allyson was especially keen, wanting to know where she could get one for Callum. When Allyson and Eyva began to talk animatedly about which of their boyfriends had been the most talented at oral sex, Seth frowned disapprovingly before turning to Sara.

He leaned toward her. "I've missed you."

She beamed back at him, pleased to know it and glad to be pulled away from the conversation. She couldn't help but wonder if Eyva was thinking about Seth. Images of them together kept popping into her head.

And then, Tom joined them. They exchanged an awkward greeting; Tom too breezy and Seth noticeably flinching but quickly gathering himself for a perfunctory nod.

Tom, finished with Seth, looked at Sara. "Come and get some birthday cake with me?"

Seth shot a quick look first to her, then to Tom. She guessed he was wondering if Tom had any clue about what she would and wouldn't eat.

"I'm fine, but you go ahead."

"Do you want to get some real food then?" Tom asked.

"No. I'm feeling a bit bloated, actually. Ate already, so I'll pass for now." She was doing the eating disorder show, but now recognized it for the performance it was. One she was going to start working on. Tomorrow.

"Don't you dare say anything," she said to Seth within earshot of Tom. "I've already had Marco lecturing me today about food."

As she had expected, a protracted silence fell between them. Tom was clueless, and Seth had been issued fair warning not to challenge her on it, plus he didn't yet know that she had outed herself as a food restrictor.

She couldn't stand the strain and blurted out, "I'm getting some help. Therapy, in fact."

Seth, momentarily taken aback by the revelation, quickly nodded in understanding.

Tom looked utterly lost. "Therapy? For what?"

"For my food restricting. I have an eating disorder. I starve myself."

"I suspected as much." Tom looked smug, as if he had known all along. Stepping back to peruse her body like she was a specimen, he shook his head. "I see it's helping," he said facetiously, taking a sip of wine.

Out of the corner of her eye, she saw Seth's look of horror, his mouth opened and closed, as if he was about to say something to save her. Sara swooped in herself, neither wanting nor needing his assistance. She put her hand on Seth's arm to stall him and glowered at Tom, prepared to admonish him for being unspeakably horrid, belittling her and not understanding that she needed help. However, knowing the tears in her eyes would ruin the effect, she instead simpered off, mumbling something about needing to find Jane.

Jane was standing against the kitchen doors on the other side of the room, and Sara took her time to work the room on her way over. When she joined her, she heard Clair announcing that the next song was written by Seth Coles.

"It's for Sara," she added. "It's called 'Binary.'"

Hearing this, Sara turned around to see Seth on the stage, strapping on a guitar and speaking with Clair.

The song was classic Seth, with the usual raucous drum and guitar rhythm, followed by softer moments. Sara liked the way Seth hung back in the band, subdued by the girl energy.

Tom, who must have heard that Seth had written this song for Sara, quickly appeared by her side, just in time to hear Sara idly ask Eyva what it was about.

"I don't know, binary oppositions, maybe? Binary codes?"

"What does that mean?" Tom asked Eyva, who motioned with her hand to Sara, the expert.

Sara just waved her hand at him, as if to tell him to forget it. She knew he didn't really care to understand. Then, she had second thoughts. She could have fun with this. She'd planned to be kind to him tonight, but now, feeling free from that constraint and with three glasses of wine sloshing inside the rangy frame that he'd just callously appraised, she let loose.

"It's a language I expect my students to use when they're talking about patriarchy."

"We call them her culture war words," Eyva said excitedly to Tom.

And while she guessed he wouldn't realize she was making a dig at him, she finished him off. "And its consequences, such as rape, sex work, substance abuse, and, of course, eating disorders."

Sara was thinking about Seth, and how very gratifying it was to be around a man who was compelled by the subject of gender and how thrilling she found it.

Finally looking at Tom for a reaction and seeing nothing, she turned to look at Seth on the makeshift stage. She watched him put down the guitar, carefully for a change, while Eyva began to elaborate on the meaning of the song. "I'm guessing this is another homage song to you, Sara."

Tom immediately quizzed her. "Why's he writing songs about Sara?"

Eyva looked sheepish.

"Apparently I'm his feminist guru."

"His what?"

Sara knew this explanation sounded ridiculous to someone like Tom, but her ratio of alcohol to food was so off balance that she felt a bit dizzy, a lot nauseous, and all her interest in explaining quickly evaporated.

"Just let it go," she ordered. "You don't really care to know, and I don't really care to tell."

Just as the conversation reached its peak of complication, Seth joined them. Her stupidity increased exponentially with her overindulgence and, hoping Tom would get the message that they were through, Sara hugged Seth a little too long. When she withdrew, after adding a slow, suggestive kiss to Seth's cheek, she noticed the look of disapproval on Tom's face.

"Don't be like this on my birthday, Tom."

Seth tried to back away, but Sara grabbed his arm, pulling him back.

If Seth was beginning to feel sorry for Tom, Sara knew this would be short-lived as Tom spied Drew and Marco kissing in a darkened corner of the foyer. Tom being Tom couldn't help himself and began to provide commentary that stank of homophobia.

Sara mustered the strength to speak up, although not as politically or effectively as she would have liked. Keeping her remarks snappy on account of her own awareness that the food to alcohol ratio was soon to upturn her stomach, she provoked Tom.

"I was going to get you one of these T-shirts." She touched Seth's chest slowly, suggestively. "I was just wondering which would suit you better. A big L or a little L? Frankly, I think you could pull off the big L."

Tom looked irritated. "You're being childish and not very funny."

Too drunk for reason and glad for it, Sara pushed it further. "Fair comment, but don't you dare accuse me of not being funny." She touched Seth again. "He knows I'm funny. Right, Seth? Tell Tom that I'm quite funny sometimes." Her hands lingered on Seth's arm.

Seth was unable to respond. Instead, he kept his eyes firmly fixed on Tom. Sara began to giggle. Tom stormed off.

After he left, Sara and Seth stood there together in silence while the rest of the house buzzed with noise.

"Why's Tom here tonight?" His voice faltered as he asked.

"As a friend. A guest. Nothing else." She hoped he would read the subtext that was she was really saying was *"I'm only interested in you."*

His facial expression gave nothing away.

The alternative DJ who'd been spinning discs since the Anoraks had finished their set was blaring a playlist of Sara's all-time favorites. To break the silence and change the subject, Seth asked her about the song that was playing.

"The Slits. The song's 'Typical Girl,'" she managed to blurt out before racing for the bathroom.

While she was throwing up, the DJ played Sleater Kinney's "Modern Girl." It felt appropriate, especially when Carrie Brownstein sang the line about hunger making her modern at the very moment she was dry heaving into the toilet. She'd never be able to listen to that song again without associating it with vomiting. Sad.

Emerging from the bathroom, softly singing along with the next song, Sara was startled to find Seth standing there.

"Feel better?"

She shushed him, indicating with her finger that she was

listening to the music. Sara listened, leaning against the wall for support. "No. I don't feel better. Not really. I need to go home."

"It's your party. You can't leave."

"Get me out of here, please. I'm so dizzy. I feel like I'm going to faint."

Seth went into action. Telling her to sit down and not to move with a promise that he'd be right back, he raced off and returned a few minutes later, holding her coat.

On the way to her car, they were chased down by Marco and Jane.

"Where are you taking her?"

Jane followed up with, "Get her home, then call me to let me know she's all right. She's drunk, so don't do anything silly, okay?"

Seth's face contorted, perplexed at what Jane might mean.

Marco deciphered. "I think she's trying to say, 'Don't fuck her in this state.'"

Seth looked mortified. Sara giggled. With a kiss from Jane followed by a hug from Marco, which included a pleading whisper of "Be nice to him" in her ear, they left.

Once they were on the road, Sara finally closed the window against the cold. "The fresh air makes me feel alive again."

Seth took his eyes off the road to give her one of his grins. "Yeah, negative five degrees will do that for you."

It was freezing in Sara's apartment. Not knowing how to be alone with Seth, but too exhausted to care, she practically crawled to the couch and lay down, asking him to adjust the thermostat on the way.

He adjusted the heat and covered her with the blanket laying on the back of the couch. "Do you want me to leave, or should I make you a cup of tea or something?"

"Tea would be nice."

Wearily she called out where everything was as she heard him crashing around her kitchen. He didn't speak to her while he was busy clanking mugs together, filling the kettle, ripping open tea bags, and then made some other strange noises that sounded like packets being opened, kitchen gadgetry, plates. Sara moaned, realizing he was probably getting some food for her. When he appeared in front of her with a steaming cup of tea and a piece of toast, she felt immense relief, even happy, although still weak as water.

She smiled at the non-buttered toast. "This I can eat."

He looked pensive. "Can we talk? About this." He motioned to the toast. "Eating disorders?" He said the words a little warily.

She nodded unenthusiastically because she'd planned to have that discussion after her birthday, but seeing it as a segue to talking about all his issues, she thought it could serve her purpose.

"I saw your pocket-sized Weight Watchers nutrition book on your desk once at the very beginning of the semester. I knew you were using it to help you restrict. And then I started wondering what happened to you to do that to yourself. I knew it had to be something horrific. I knew you weren't just caving to cultural pressure to be thin. Then, when you told me about your…"

She knew he was choking on the word "rape."

"Can we talk about your stuff, too?"

He looked at her quizzically.

"Was that your stuff at Dougal's house? And…" She paused, wondering if she should dredge up her litany of questions, especially since he looked rattled by the first one. "And…I was wondering what you meant when you told me smack doesn't keep you awake anymore."

Seth stared back at her for a long time. It frustrated her that he wasn't answering the question, stalling maybe, while he prepared a passable answer. She was also frustrated that, even though they'd had a roommate on that snowy night in Boston, he hadn't even tried to have quiet sex with her.

She realized her last thought was a little misplaced, but at least it meant she must be feeling better. She sat upright to stare him down. "Do you not want to answer the question? Is that it?"

When he simply nodded, she felt her heart pound in her chest. *He is a junkie? I want to fuck a junkie. I'm a junkie lover now?* She sank into her new status.

"How are you feeling?" Seth conveniently returned the subject back to her.

Her feelings? Nothing, except for what he had *not* said.

Sara shrugged defensively. "Fine." Why should she talk about her problems when he was holding his so close?

"Marco told me you're worried about my cutting."

She nodded, pleased he was willing to discuss at least one of his problems.

"I only do it in the context of the shows. That's where I channel anger."

Marco had also explained that some of it was sexual, but she didn't think she could broach his sex life right now.

"But you hurt yourself. You could get an infection."

He laughed.

"Are you talking to anyone about it?"

"Marco."

"Well, he's a poet. He'll see the romantic side of what you're doing. It's all art to him—"

"And I'm in treatment with a psychologist. One of the Men's Circle organizers."

"Perfect," Sara said, satisfied. "Someone who'll understand the hegemonic masculinity slash male childhood issues."

"How about you? You're getting treatment now?"

"Starting tomorrow. We're a mess, aren't we?"

Seth simply nodded.

With the realization of their mutual messes, another question suddenly came to her. "Do you know why you cut?" She was unprepared for Seth's stinging comeback.

"Do you know why you starve yourself and drink so much? I imagine you do it for the same reasons as me. It makes you feel better."

A silence fell between them that Sara was too emotionally and physically fragile to manage. She shifted the energy by asking if he could make her another piece of toast.

He made no comments about her request. He just filled the order and sat back on the floor beside the couch, sipped his tea, and talked with her.

Sara's blood ran cold with the recognition that they were hurting themselves to feel better.

Just days before, Sara had counseled a rape survivor who was restricting and had told Sara precisely that same thing—that it made her feel better, gave her a feeling that she was in control. Sara understood that restricting was the opposite of control. When you did that, it was the eating disorder, or "Ed," as they called it, that had all the control. Intellectually, Sara knew she had no control, knew she couldn't stop, because every time she considered it, Ed would talk her out of it with ideas that haunt women and threaten to destroy their only access to status in society—as a sexual commodity.

"You'll get fat," Ed would say. "If you eat that, you'll feel awful. Don't eat that. You don't need it." And for Sara, the most effective of all: "You don't deserve it." Though she was an activist and scholar of women's studies, a soon-to-be fellow at Wellesley, she would always be just another rape survivor who was trying to cope in a misogynist society.

She wanted to disappear, and she wasn't doing it fast enough. Damn that toast. It made her feel out of control, fat, lousy. She didn't need it, didn't deserve it. With those thoughts screaming through her head, thoughts of the sell-out and its connection with the system that got women raped settled uncomfortably in her mind, she blurted out: "I've been thinking about the sell-out." Though it made him frown, she continued. "I see another outcome of it that directly affects you. Fame."

She'd teased him about it in Boston and then again at the gallery, but since they were airing out everything tonight, now seemed like the time to express herself seriously. "None of the outcomes seem good. Then again, maybe the outcomes can be good for creating change by working from within, like you were suggesting when we talked about it at the Tin Palace." She raised her hand to quell the happy curiosity on his face, because she was skeptical.

"Audre Lorde didn't think it was possible, so I need to give that some more thought. In the meantime, you could use it as a platform to say something overtly critical of social arrangements." Looking directly at him she added, like it was an order and the only way to be saved, "Be revolutionary. You have to redeem yourself for selling out."

She stopped to sip from her tea. Seth was holding his cup to his face to keep warm. She reached for his hand. He shifted himself from his cross-legged sitting position on the floor to take it.

Looking at their hands, he stroked her thumb with his. "I *am* doing that. A lot of what I've been writing reflects my experiences in the seminar, the Men's Circle. It's been..." He cut himself off when he looked at her face. "You're tired. I should leave so you can go to bed."

She was about to blurt out, "Why don't you come to bed with me?" Disgraceful, under the circumstances. After all, she was still a little nauseous, ready to faint from the combination of hunger and too much alcohol. Yet, in the face of him, her shame apparently had no impact on her libido at all.

While libidinous thoughts were charging through her head, Sara heard the front door open and someone step into the hallway. They shot apart from each other like two teenagers who'd been caught making out.

Jane stood in the doorway.

Claiming that she'd come to check on the patient, Jane said with more gravity than the situation warranted, "I was really worried about you."

Sara guessed that Jane was worried about her having sex while drunk again and had probably raced over to her apartment with foreboding thoughts about the scene that would greet her. Sara figured Jane thought she'd saved the day.

All in all, the whole scene looked pretty innocuous—teacups, plates of half-eaten snacks, and Sara cozily wrapped in a blanket, still fully clothed.

"You look better," she said before turning to Seth. "Eyva is apparently waiting for you to go back to New York. She asked me to have you call her."

Sara was distressed. "You're going back tonight? You only just got here this afternoon."

Seth nodded and took his cell phone out to dial. "We have an interview tomorrow at nine. Now what stupid journalist schedules an interview with a rock band in the morning?"

Sara blurted out with more earnestness than she expected, "Don't go. Stay here." She could see by the way he looked at her that he was considering it, but Eyva picked up and Sara's heart sank because she realized she'd said it too late.

Once he left the room to talk with Eyva, Jane looked at her and asked, in hushed tones, "What's going on?"

"Nothing, unfortunately."

Even Jane managed to laugh at this.

Just then Seth returned. "Eyva wants to go back, but I'll stay, if that's okay?"

After a fair amount of commotion, it was decided that Eyva would drive Jeff's car back to New York. Having agreed to let Jeff keep his car in one of her two carports while they toured, Marco and Drew brought Eyva to Sara's apartment to retrieve the car.

Since she was nervous about driving so late at night, and to New York City no less, Eyva had to be given copious amounts of tea to calm her nerves. At one point, Marco tried to talk her out of it, and only Sara was relieved when Eyva insisted she had to be there. Apparently Eyva's motives were mercenary, since she really wanted to meet this particular music journalist because he was, in Eyva's words, "hot."

"Eyva, you'll be fine," Marco reassured her. "Sara's not feeling well. We should let her get to bed."

Just as suddenly as all the commotion had ended, it began again, with everyone immediately bundling up and making leaving noises. And before they knew it, Sara was closing the door, but not before Marco grabbed her in a hug that said, *I'm worried you will seduce my precious boy.* While she couldn't promise anything, Sara tried to reassure him with a weak smile as she closed the door.

And then it was just the two of them again.

Once all alone in her bed, the house silent, she felt desperately lonely. She called out to Seth, and within moments he appeared at the door to her room. She could just make out his figure in the doorway and noticed that he still wore his clothes.

"Would you get in and cuddle with me, just like when we were in Boston?"

He didn't say a word, just stood in the doorway, his still shadow motionless. Slowly, he made up his mind and stepped into the room. He lay beside her under the covers, propped up on one elbow, facing her in the gloom.

"How are you?" he asked her.

Sara, shaking her head to express *meh*, snuggled up against him. "This is nice, right?" she said. Her eyes already adjusted to the darkness, she could just make out a nod.

"When I was a little girl, I used to think if you held a boy's hand while you were in bed, you got a baby. Can you remember being that young?"

"Not really."

"It bothered me." Sara frowned at the feeling of the memory. "Because, while I liked this one boy a lot, his name was Patrick, I didn't like the idea of sleeping in the same bed with anyone, not even my mother. Then one day I came upon a solution—we could get bunk beds. And if we wanted a baby, we could just hold hands over the sides! I was thinking about contraception at age nine. Amazing, really." They both laughed.

"And I got it all, the boy I wanted and the bunk beds and, with my ingenious contraception idea, well, it all worked out. Then, when I found out how it really all worked, I was devastated and in complete denial. I said, 'That's ridiculous. Who would do that?'"

Laughing together over that lovely innocence, she told him more.

"All the girls were mad because Patrick liked me best. And it wasn't that I was the prettiest. It was because I stood out from the other girls in the town. I was the girl everyone remembered. I never tried to pass as a nice, good girl with all the right opinions and no questions. And when Patrick told me that he liked me best because of that, it made me like him even more. Patrick was my click moment as a feminist. I know it's not a great click moment," Sara said, "because it involves a boy helping me make that connection, but—"

She broke off, thinking about how this had been the story of her life, one boy after another.

Seth encouraged her to continue. "I like the sound of Patrick."

She could almost feel him making the decision whether or not to continue.

"Tom's different."

Sara saw him wince with immediate regret for saying it. She knew that he didn't like Tom, but also recognized this criticism revealed perhaps more about his feelings for her than for Tom.

"Sorry. I shouldn't have said that."

"It's fine," she assured him, but he still insisted that it was inappropriate.

"Tom wouldn't be my choice, but I'm sure that if you're with him, there must be something amazing about him, something I'm just missing. "

Sara cringed at the false impression he had of her as a person of great substance, when in fact she was base. After all, there were only two reasons that she could think of to explain why she'd dated Tom, and neither of them were noble. Reflecting on that and on his elevation of her in general despite the eating disorder and her unabashed flirting with him when he was still her student, she felt supremely shallow. A fraud against her scholar/activist front. Falling silent, she rolled over onto her back and stared at the ceiling.

Seth responded to her, wrapping an arm around her and pulling her close into him. She noticed with pleasure that his breath was slightly heavier. Smiling at this, she encouraged him by snuggling against him even more. Too tired and weak to really respond beyond this, she fell asleep almost immediately, but not before noticing his restlessness and trembling so close to her.

chapter fourteen

The morning after the party, Sara and Seth were both still sleeping, coiled up together, when a cough startled them awake.

Marco stood at the foot of the bed.

"It's time to go, Lover Boy."

While Seth was in the shower, Sara made the coffee. Marco wouldn't stop staring at her. She tried to avert the criticism she expected from him, ever protective of Seth.

"We didn't have sex, so get your mind out of my undies."

"It's not my mind that's been there all night."

"You're wrong. Honest."

Marco laughed. "I know."

Sara paused her coffee preparations to eye him, perplexed by his solid assumption that they hadn't had sex when all the evidence suggested it. Piquing her curiosity even more, Marco looked suddenly on guard, lost for words.

He flustered. "I'm just teasing. I don't know what you did or didn't do together."

He was plainly trying to talk his way out of something. Sara stood stationary, staring at him expectantly, letting him know he was bagged and she was waiting for him to divulge something. When Seth walked into the kitchen at just that moment, Marco leaped on the distraction by changing the subject to coffee.

Noting Marco's relief at escaping the cornering, she wagged her head at him before she turned to Seth, already pouring milk into his coffee.

Sara wasn't prepared for the colossal wave of sadness that swept over her when Seth was ready for Marco to take him to the station. Lingering next to her at the door, Seth stalled. Marco, vigilantly observant where imminent romance was concerned, quickly exited to give them privacy.

"I'll miss you," Sara said, feeling ridiculous.

"Marco and Drew are coming down. Maybe you could come with them or on your own." She could see he thought he'd been too forward. "If you had the time," he waffled, utterly mangling his thoughts with nervousness. Sara found it endearing.

She reached her arms around his neck to hug him tightly. They stood holding each other for several minutes before she pulled away and, after kissing him suggestively on the cheek, they said goodbye.

She sighed heavily. Her next stop was Jane, and the beginning of therapy.

* * *

Jane had told her to prepare a food journal. It wasn't challenging homework. In fact, it was something she did every day anyway.

When Sara handed it to her, Jane looked at it for a few minutes before lifting her head up. "How do you feel physically on 815 calories a day?" she said, shifting forward in her seat, lowering both her elbows onto her knees, head tilted, waiting.

Sara sank into her chair. "Don't do that look at me," she said, waving a finger at Jane.

"What look?" Jane didn't move from her position.

Sara's finger circled the air around Jane's face. "That one. The therapy gaze. It won't work on me."

"Humor me, would you?" Jane sat back, slumped in her chair, matching Sara's posture. "How do you feel on that many calories a day?"

"Depends. Sometimes I feel like I'm going to pass out, so I'll eat just enough to keep me going. Other days I feel like I could get by on even fewer calories." She shrugged, so lethargic with boredom she wanted to leave.

Sara couldn't concentrate. It was pointless to be talking about calories. She thought about pretty much nothing else most of the day anyway, and since she had so many other things she needed to be doing, the conversation frustrated her.

Jane knew her too well not to notice Sara's distraction. "I really need your active listening, or there really is no point. You can't be thinking about grading, or calories, or Seth. What happened there, by the way?"

A smile spread wide over her face. Jane's eyes widened. Laughing, Sara waved her arms in protest at the assumption.

"Nothing happened. Unfortunately."

Jane put her notepad down and frowned. "Do you see how your behavior there is connected to your eating disorder, which is connected to your rape?"

In between sips of her coffee, casually and with little interest, Sara repeated, "My behavior there? Meaning?"

"Promiscuity—" Jane broke off to correct the diagnosis. "Sorry. Hypersexuality."

Sara jumped in. "What I know is words like 'promiscuity,' just like 'slut' and 'whore,' are labels used to control women in a patriarchal society."

"Sara, I know you think I'm a prude. That's not it. I'm just trying to get you to see that your need to always have sex lined up and avoid intimacy…it's all connected to your rape." Sara folded her arms and set her mouth into a tight line. Sighing, Jane charged on. "Intellectually, you know very well that survivors often obsess with control issues. It's usually self-destructive, right?"

"And promiscuity? You're suggesting that's part of the fallout?"

Jane, apparently unaware that Sara was being derisive, nodded sympathetically. "Hypersexuality," she corrected.

Rubbing her hands over her face, Sara wanted to get this over with. Of course, intellectually, she understood what Jane was saying. With the survivors at WRC, Sara was able to solidly situate the eating disorders, drinking, and dysfunctional relationships with men in the assault that had torn more than their skin. After she listened to a stony-faced girl who described her rape with such distance you would think she was telling you how to boil an egg,

Sara would tell her that her behaviors were punishments for misplaced shame, a sense of worthlessness and self-hatred.

While she was working daily to help these women, she couldn't actually figure it out for herself. Her inability to articulate why she restricted, drank, and would have sex with any man who even slightly caught her attention, or how to stop, defied her. Sara felt herself unraveling. She turned Jane in.

"I agree that patriarchy is an oppressive system. Vile. Base," Jane was saying.

Sara sensed a philosophical discourse emerging, even though Jane's plea to "connect the dots" and "accept" were challenging her; she really didn't get how to do that, but she wanted to let Jane know she really was trying.

"I'm actively listening. Go on."

"Humor me for a few seconds here. Forget patriarchy for a moment..."

Sara frowned at the suggestion. Jane nodded her head appreciatively, acknowledging Sara's active restraint to not to jump in.

"I want you to consider whether your need for constant sexual attention should be understood more in the context of your assault instead of the patriarchy."

Sara sighed begrudgingly, recognizing the beginning of an effective, clever argument when she heard one.

"Meaning, promiscuity is damaging you further." Jane began to encourage Sara to think a little more about this alien concept of intimacy. "Do you remember that one-night stand you had after an Anorak show? It was right before you met Tom, remember?" Sara recalled it vividly. "Did that feel different than the two nights you spent with Seth?"

"Of course. There was no sex with Seth."

Jane looked crestfallen, which only made Sara defensive.

"Judging by your utter shock, maybe I need even more help than you thought. Maybe my intimacy deficit disorder, as you see it, is more because of a missing intimacy gene than it is due to my assault. Help."

"How did it feel when you woke up with Seth?"

"It was amazing, actually."

"Listen to the difference. Relief with sex but amazing with intimacy."

Sara nodded, acknowledging the difference, even if she wasn't clear on why it was important. She guessed Jane was satisfied to have her listening at last.

"I've never known you to have intimacy with a man like you seem to be experiencing with Seth. You need that. And only that."

It was hard not to see the truth in that. Jane was telling her to take a break from men.

* * *

Just hours after that first session with Jane, Seth contacted her again about a visit. And then every few days after that too. It was too tempting, like an alcoholic finally joining AA only to have her best drinking friend invite her to the best party in town. In this delicate stage of recovery, she knew that Jane would likely disapprove, so she tried to cooperate with the proscription.

The excuses were so prepared and becoming increasingly more asinine with every request, she imagined he wouldn't be surprised if she resorted to the excuse of needing to wash her hair. He didn't know that she was grappling with a newly forming consciousness.

Against Jane's advice, Sara finally gave in to Seth's request to visit. Despite those therapy sessions that threatened to destroy her sex life, Sara was able to reason her way into it. She told Jane that, since she was still a student of intimacy, there was surely a learning curve, so she couldn't possibly get it right away and be cured instantly. In fact, since her case was so serious, she thought it might take years, so just a few small, controlled exposures to Seth would probably be okay.

Of course, she knew these excuses were pathetic and disingenuous. Her joking about it was irking Jane. In spite of that, since she was driven to distraction by her lusty thoughts for Seth, she'd begun to think it might be bad for her food issues if she was to attempt to squelch all her wrenching desire as well.

On the day she was leaving, Marco dropped by to give his perspective too. Jane was giving Sara a ride to the airport and looked genuinely elated to see him. While Sara finished packing, Jane took him aside.

Their whispered voices unintelligible for the most part, Sara kept latching onto key phrases such as, "contribute to her therapy" and "I wouldn't worry."

Feeling patronized, Sara popped her head into her kitchen. "I am here, you know. And I can hear most of what you're saying."

Jane stopped making tea to offer one last appeal. "How could one night of sex help you?"

"Don't worry about *that*," Marco said.

"Why? Why shouldn't I worry about her having sex with him?"

He stalled, stumbling for words. Again, just as the morning after her party, Sara sensed immediately that Marco believed he'd said too much but was clearly unwilling to say more.

"I just want you to be good to him. Kind." It sounded more cryptic than revelatory.

"Why? What's the worry? That she'll seduce him? Poor Seth," Jane chimed in.

Sara was enjoying this now.

Marco countered. "I'm not worried about his virtue, Jane. I'm worried about his heart."

chapter fifteen

Seth struck up the first few chords of their radio hit "Disappear," and the audience drowned him out with their approving applause and screams. Sara was glad that she'd taken his advice and stayed backstage to watch the show on the big TV screen.

Seth stalled, playing the same few opening chords over and over, apparently waiting for them to quiet down before he continued. When they finally settled down, he closed his eyes and sang a few lines. When the audience joined in with him, he backed away from the microphone and, opening his eyes, smiled at them, playing the accompaniment to their voices. They erupted in gratitude of the attention he gave them.

All angsty at the end of the song, Seth whipped off his guitar and began smashing it into one of the speakers, stopping briefly to indicate to stage security to permit a group of fans over the barricade. The crowd went berserk.

The hand-picked group joined Seth in his destruction of equipment and gear, with one fan plowing into him, knocking them both off their feet and into the drum kit. As Sara fully expected, when the three of them were pulled from the wreckage, the only person bleeding was poor Caleb.

It didn't slow Seth down. Next, he hurled himself into a set of speakers. Satisfied with the body-speaker hurling, he stopped and leaped into the crowd. He was returned to the stage by a security guard, minus his guitar. *A risk you took,* Sara thought, *if you were crazy enough to engage in crowd surfing.*

Back on the stage, he fell to the floor on his knees, rocking back and forth. The band started playing again and he plied himself up from the floor just as a man appeared from backstage brandishing an intact instrument. Taking the guitar, he approached the microphone to thunderous applause.

Their devotion to him was overwhelming. Sara hadn't been following their success into the mainstream observantly, or even at all. RAR had been big before, but now they had become so huge it made Sara wonder about the feasibility of putting on their show for the Take Back the Night rally in April. The sheer size of their audience and the need for thirty or more security men were downright scary to her. *How would this translate in Amherst?* She doubted it even could.

With his lips firmly planted on the microphone, eyes closed, stony in his posture, Seth sang "Energy." Sara caught her breath, bewitched along with the audience who'd grown quiet again to listen. That voice had become not only recognizable, but infinitely more amazing with all the practice.

This song was one of her favorites, despite her misgivings about the buzz around it being yet another homage to her. On the one hand, she was all gushy and flattered, and on the other, she was uncertain about being mused or doted on in this way by a man who was writing love songs about her.

She thought it was hauntingly beautiful, and while most of the lyrics were straightforward, there were also some esoteric lines that troubled her. In particular, she had been especially bothered by lyrical references to doll's heads and dogs. She'd even confronted Seth about it. When he'd only responded non-verbally, blushing crimson, she'd rushed to Marco for explanation.

Marco, ever the poetic-imagery genius, had explained to her that these were sexual images. "Dolls," he explained, "can be thought of as either a child- or a feminine-identified image. On the other hand, dogs are a male-identified image." As if this explained everything, he added, "Voila. I think you can probably figure it out now."

"No clue. Esoteric sexual imagery in poetry is beyond my abilities. Totally challenged there."

He shook his head and laughed at her, as if doubting anyone could actually be that stupid. "Let me put it this way. I wish a guy would write songs with images like that about me."

This wasn't reassuring at all. "Given how depraved you are, that still doesn't tell me whether it's a compliment or not."

Now, as she watched Seth finish the show with this song, she blushed, thinking about those sexual images—the ones Marco practically had to diagram for her to understand. She would be alone with him soon, and they could transition all this to reality.

After the show, they both simply wanted to be alone with each other. First, however, they had to make their way to an East Village restaurant to fill Seth's ravenous appetite. It was midnight when they finally arrived, and while Sara picked at a bare mesclun salad, because despite being in treatment she was still clinging to her no-food-after-eight rule, she watched with wonder as Seth ate rapaciously.

She had her wine, of course, but she decided to stop drinking midway through her third glass. She wanted to be awake enough to entwine her body with Seth's all night and so settled for watching Seth finish eating, commenting on his lithe body against all those calories.

His appearance had changed. It bothered her. Designed to give a naturally unkempt impression, his image was manufactured to the highest degree, probably requiring a team of professionals to achieve. It was a disingenuous, carefully crafted impression of anti-fashion. All performance, no longer the real thing but so cleverly produced it fooled even the most discriminating eye.

The shirt he was wearing, while it looked worn and thrown on without a care after spending weeks at the bottom of his luggage, was probably outrageously expensive vintage fashion, clothing that he couldn't have afforded six months ago. Although it made her happy to see the hemp string that he still used as a belt, she guessed that the faded, torn jeans that he wore with his twelve-hundred-dollar custom-made sneakers were more of the same façade.

The look, the videos, appearances on TV chat shows, features on the cover of *Rolling Stone*—they had sell-out written all over them, and as his friend, she had to let him know what she saw.

"Look at you," she said with concern in her voice. More and

more, her worry was for the impact of the sell-out on Seth. Could he survive and come out the other end as the politically righteous person she had met last fall? "You're even starting to look like a sell-out in your pricey clothes, with your grunge-pretty hair, and what's this?" she said, rubbing her hand against the stubble on his face. "You're a corporate commodity now. How's that feel?"

"Remember, I'm trying out this idea of working from within."

She nodded. "I remember."

"You still haven't told me what you think about that. Your lens on it really matters to me."

"I'm still thinking. First, answer my question, how's it affecting you, your music? It's certainly shaping your impression management." She motioned to his clothes again.

"It's going great. I love it."

Sara sat in silence, observing his flat affect, the derisive tone, softening because she was encouraged by it, believing it to mean he wasn't lost forever.

"You're experiencing what is known as 'anomie.'" She waited for his response, wondering if he was familiar with the concept.

"Alienated. Fucked," he said, not disappointing.

They both knew he had to decide how far he wanted to go with that experience.

Seeming to look for some reassurance that she hadn't given up on him altogether, he reached a hand to her, and she took it. She looked down at the big fingers entwining her tiny ones, then back up to him.

"Aren't you going to eat anything at all?"

Sara pointed to her half-eaten salad. "What do you think I've been doing?"

Seth fell silent, looking at her with that expression she knew all too well. She shook her head at him. "Leave it. I'm good. Not too hungry. Let's get going." And he knew to drop it.

Despite being February, and in the early hours of the morning, they decided to walk the five blocks back to the hotel. Since they both wanted to spend as much of this one night and two days together as possible, there was no rush to get back.

As they walked, she slipped her hand into his. Seth looked at her curiously.

"What's that look for?"

"Are you a one-man woman, Sara?"

At first, not realizing that his query was serious, Sara laughed at the antiquated expression.

"I thought not," he said, matter-of-factly. "I suppose you don't believe in monogamy."

Sara immediately reflected on her lecture to Jane on the subject. Looking him in the eye, she shook her head: no.

"Does Tom know that?"

The question disarmed her. Sara stopped and turned to him. "Why would that matter? As I told you, I'm not with him anymore."

Sara watched a tidal wave of confusion on his face, but Sara didn't know what more she could add to help him out or fill the lull, except to try to get him to explain himself.

Seth became sheepish, dropping his eyes and shifting his feet from side-to-side. "Marco told me you guys reconnected."

Sara was both dumbstruck and furious with Marco.

"He told me that...Tom, at least, thinks he's still in the picture."

"Well, he's not," Sara snapped back, dropping his hand and walking away.

Seth caught up and reached tenderly for her hand again. "I'm just trying to understand," he said, trying to keep up with her fast-clipped pace.

Mad and exasperated, Sara launched back at him. "Regardless of Tom, you must see that this thing between us...well, I have concerns." From the expression on his face, she'd shaken him. "I mean, you're a rock star. And I'm a university professor." Now he was smirking. "I just don't know if this could ever be serious. I'm so much older than you and...you have a few problems that you need to deal with."

Still holding her hand, he stopped stock-still in the street, turning a full and earnest gaze on her. "Like what? What problems?"

"The cutting, to start with." She hesitated before she could force the words from her throat. "And the drug thing." Sara shivered.

He stared at her blankly. "Let's get going. You're freezing."

Given she also had some problems, it was a weak argument. Sara started a little tally of them in her head. The list soon felt endless as she began to unravel a litany of infractions that tainted her character. When he didn't throw them in her face as a defense, his decency was not lost on her. In gratitude to him for not pointing them out, she squeezed his hand a little tighter, hoping to communicate how much she did like him, despite yet another tirade against his character.

Since she was afraid to open her mouth again for fear of saying something else she might regret, she waited for Seth to speak.

"And Tom? No concerns about Tom? You could be serious about him?"

She winced with his emphasis, cringing every time he mentioned Tom's name.

Searching for a way to stall for time, she said, "Tom and I had a lot in common." She scrabbled through her mind, trying to figure out exactly what that was. She settled, blurting out, "We're both academics."

Seth nodded at this while Sara continued to rummage, grasping for any other little thing that might make Tom seem perfect for her, although her only reason for doing so was to avoid making herself ridiculous to Seth.

Eventually landing on *same libido*, she decided to stop there, because obviously she couldn't say that. She fell silent for a moment, dropping her shoulders with a sigh. "I'm a good person, really."

"I know you are. You don't need to convince me, but I'm not such a good person. I've put you on the spot, making you feel like you had to defend yourself. I should also own that I was…fishing for information. I talk to Marco a lot about you."

Sara's anxiety shifted onto new matters: worrying about what information Seth had managed to garner from Marco. She took a quick peek to see if his face revealed anything.

He grinned back at her. "Marco says that Tom had a few things in his favor that made him very appealing to you. Apparently, a couple of redeeming features."

She knew he was trying to settle her mind, thinking she was probably very uncomfortable about his fishing, but this only rattled her more. Her mind reeled as she wondered precisely what Marco had divulged to him, making her increasingly angry at him.

"Marco's very protective of you. He tells you things about me that I don't want anyone, especially you, to know. Yet he doesn't tell me anything about you."

Seth stopped again. Standing in the street, he stepped closer to her, taking both her hands in his. "Why especially not me?"

Sara gave up on any attempt to redeem herself. "I'm trying to preserve my image."

They both laughed and started walking again.

"Don't worry about that," he said.

"But Marco says I'm your feminist guru."

He was quiet. She could sense him blushing, though she couldn't tell for sure in the gloom.

"I clearly have an image to preserve." They walked in silence, holding hands tightly, the hotel now in sight. Sara turned to him. "Even gurus are imperfect. You know that, right?"

Seth nodded and squeezed her hand, seemingly to acknowledge that gurus, like Sara, were still only human.

They climbed the steps of the hotel, where he let go of her hand to pull open the heavy door. She grabbed quickly at his hand as they strode through the lobby.

She turned to him while they waited for the elevator. "What about you? Are you a one-woman kind of man?"

His answer was immediate. "I am."

The ripple of pleasure she felt from knowing it was unsettling. It smacked of an interest in sexual exclusivity, and since she'd neither ever given nor expected that, she didn't know how to feel about this new sensation.

It made her defensive. "Okay, but do you ever see Eyva anymore? Do you believe in monogamy?"

It hit her that she did want Seth to be with her exclusively. What did it mean? Now she wanted what, monogamy? She wasn't sure how to feel about that, and the confronting thought made her squirm.

"No," he said perfunctorily as the elevator arrived and they stepped in.

Sara took her hand out of his and propped herself against the wall, waiting for him to offer more.

"I don't see Eyva. I don't have sex with her or anyone. And..."

He leaned toward her, his voice dropping into a lower, more serious tone. "I do believe in monogamy."

A little shiver trickled through her. She would never have imagined she'd find a phrase so conservative quite so alluring.

Rather than unpack the existential crisis this brought on for her (because, maybe, she wanted that too…) she diverted to humor. "That's only because you're one of those radical theorists." Mocking outrage, she made him laugh. "Honestly. What is it you people don't get about the relationship between monogamy and women's subjugation? It's maddening. Truly it is."

The exchange shifted the energy. Sara relaxed and snuggled up to his arm, feeling herself soften as she complained that she was still frozen from the walk. He wrapped his arms around her, and she leaned into him.

* * *

Once in the hotel room, Sara noticed Seth become shy with her. While they'd snuggled in the elevator, now he was staying as far away from her as possible.

Seth made them both tea and Sara busied herself looking through her backpack. She needed a protein bar to sustain her through the night.

Watching her out of the corner of his eye, Seth asked her if she was hungry.

"We just had dinner."

"No. I had dinner. You drank."

"I had a salad. And I didn't drink much."

"How many calories?"

"About fifty," she said as she took a tiny bite into a 230-calorie, 3 grams of fat protein bar. "And I'm eating now."

He watched her eat. Playfully, she smacked him for it. "Stop watching me eat. It's hard for me to eat around people as it is, let alone have them scoping me out while I'm doing it."

Sara noticed the shift in his face from lively and playful to worry and concern.

Uncomfortable, she filled in the silence. "When I eat in front of people, I think they're judging me." She'd never told anyone that before.

"Do you ever get the comments about your body that restrictors often hear? You know, like the ones you mentioned when you were giving your WRC talk to the university last September?"

Sara recalled the talk. Anyone there that was paying attention would have learned the most effective and ineffective responses in the face of a restrictor. Expressing horror, cajoling, or bargaining were useless and only made the restrictor go underground, to hide it better the next time.

"I do." Sara started to list them. "I wish I was as thin as you. You look so good." That last one always made her the saddest because she always felt so ill. Saying them out loud, but in reference to herself and not at some talk where she was the expert, made her both mad and sad that she didn't see it then.

"How's the therapy going?"

"I'm a savvy patient, of course, so it makes Jane's job easy, I think. How's yours?"

"It's difficult. We're back on tour again in three weeks."

Sara nodded and turned away. She could hear in his response that he was shirking treatment, but she chose to rummage through her backpack instead. After all, she knew that a confrontation would inevitably introduce more tension, and the dose for the night had already reached toxic levels.

Busily spreading the contents of her backpack on the king-sized bed, she invited Seth to join her. "Come and see all my stuff."

Seth read the ingredients on her protein bars, looked through her book selection, read a few of her comments in the blue exam booklets that she'd been grading on the train on her way down to see him. Sara appreciated his interest, especially when he was neither embarrassed by the tampons that lay loosely strewn throughout the mix on the bed, nor did he pretend not to notice them.

The tampons, of course, had only been brought along in hopefulness, because, despite taking the pills the doctor had given her, she was still waiting for her bleeding to start again.

She watched him touch them, pick them up, then push them aside as he peered into her bag, digging deeper into her seemingly bottomless pack in his quest to learn more about Sara through an observation of its contents.

After pulling out a large strip of condoms, his eyes widened. "That's a lot of condoms."

There were a couple more handfuls of loose condoms in the bottom of the bag, and Sara pulled them out, piling them into his hands and laughing at his wide eyes as they spilled out over onto the bed. "They're a gift to Jeff, Eyva, and Caleb from Marco," she explained.

Seth nodded. "I'll pass them on."

Once they'd gathered all the condoms together, Seth handed her a mug of tea, but shaking her head, she said, "Actually, I'm really tired."

His shyness when he asked if she wanted to go to bed returned. Running his hands nervously through his hair, stumbling and waffling over his words, he quickly tried to explain the sleeping arrangement options. He could sleep on the couch, and she could take the bed, or they could sleep together, but this latter option gave him so much anxiety when he suggested it that Sara couldn't help but laugh.

Putting down her tea, she walked over to him and took both his hands. "Of course I want to sleep with you."

He smiled and bent his head to meet hers. She reached her face toward his, opening her mouth slightly, suggestively, inviting a kiss, unable to avoid noticing his nervous gaze. In one deep intake of breath, he withdrew from her suddenly.

"I hope I'm not being presumptuous here, Sara, but just so you know...I don't want to have sex."

Sara was utterly stumped, so taken aback she didn't even notice that her mouth was agape.

"If that's okay," he stammered.

"You don't want to have sex? If that's okay?" Sara remained stony-faced, repeating his words with a degree of horror that might be attendant to something so heinous and depraved that it was beyond human understanding.

Seth was stoic, presumably waiting out her mental processing.

"What if I say it's not okay? Does this have to do with Tom? You know that's done."

He shook his head vigorously at the suggestion, making her reconsider.

"Then what is it?"

Seth became subdued. "I just don't do that. I prefer—"

He broke off. Hanging on his words, Sara wondered exactly what it was he preferred. Her mind racing in a thousand directions, she waited for what seemed like days for him to finish that loaded sentence. *Bondage? S&M? What?*

"I would prefer to just…be close…intimate."

Perplexed, Sara threw up her arms. "I think sex is pretty *close*, pretty *intimate*. Not that I'll ever be doing that with you after this." She winced, regretting it immediately as his face dropped and his eyes momentarily closed with irritation, or hurt—she couldn't tell which.

He gathered himself faster than her, stepping closer but not touching her body with any part of his. This time her closeness didn't provoke that anxious, nervous look he'd shown just moments before. A very slight smile curved the corner of his lips. Pulled back in, Sara was unable to resist the urge to kiss his cheek. It was a very slow, delicate kiss, her lips barely brushing his skin. The attentiveness of it excited her and she brushed her lips lower down to the edge of his lip where she had seen the birth of a smile. She peppered soft kisses on his lips. Seth responded by catching her bottom lip gently with his teeth and drawing her into a slow kiss. Envigored by the invitation after many months of both denying and indulging thoughts about kissing him, Sara's returned kiss was ardent. Abruptly, Seth pulled away from her, searching her face with an expression that looked like "sorry" and dashing her hopes that he'd change his mind just to shut her up.

She withdrew from him with a shrug, upset by this push and pull behavior, settling herself on a good rummage in her backpack, hoping to give the impression she didn't care one way or the other. As she dug around in her bag, she could feel him watching her. Pulling out a toothbrush, she flashed it at him as she stormed past him.

"I'm going to brush my teeth then get some sleep, or grade, or something, whatever."

Sullen expression locked into place, Sara re-entered the room after getting ready in the bathroom and climbed into bed without even looking at him.

Sitting on the pull-out sofa, he watched her. Pertly she asked him, "Would you pass me my tea and those blue books?" intending to ignore him.

"I thought you were tired."

"Suddenly I don't feel that tired."

After handing her the tea and exam books, he left for the bathroom. Rather than grade, Sara sat up in bed, lost in thought about what had just happened.

When he came out of the bathroom, Sara quickly picked up an exam book. He climbed in bed next to her, commenting on her pen. She knew he understood she used purple instead of red because it represented counter hegemony.

Sara could feel him reading the exam over her shoulder. Her assumption was confirmed when he commented, "Wow, did they really blow the answer that badly?"

Slamming the blue book to her chest, Sara scolded. "This is someone's exam. It's confidential. Please don't read over my shoulder."

"Please put the blue book down," he said softly, as though he knew he didn't have any favors left.

Sara hurled the blue book and her purple pen with intense force in the direction of her bag. "Why? What is it?"

His face, full of contrition and concern, only confused her more.

Coaxing her gently down into the bed next to him, she submitted. His breath was warm on her lips as he began to stroke the side of her face with the back of his hand. He brushed her hair back from her face, tracing her features with a purposeful gaze. She was lulled into a gooey softness as he gradually leaned over and kissed her, lightly and leisurely, as if he were savoring each tiny aspect of the sensation between them.

After many minutes, she pulled away from him, noticing his eyes were still closed. When he opened them, his eyes were heavy, the corners of his lips turned upward in a warm, lazy smile.

Despite that kiss, which she was certain had dramatically increased both their heart rates, she knew his resolve about no sex was sticking. Still, she made one last appeal. "This is just crazy."

"What? Agreeing not to have sex?"

She nodded.

They lay there together, Seth stroking her hand. "Sacrifice of present sanity seems worth it."

She didn't know if she could agree with that, so she said nothing, reaching over to pull his arm around her. He slowly began stroking her waist over and over again, and then, slipping his hand into her boy-cut underwear, he did the same to her hip and upper thigh. She lay little kisses on his mouth, then kissed him with such intensity he finally pulled away, telling her he needed to slow it down.

She held his aroused gaze and shook her head at him, sighing heavily with frustration and resigning herself to knowing her only satisfaction was in the effect she was having on him.

Turning her back, she snuggled against him. "Let's go to sleep."

Seth leaned over her to kiss her neck then settled his arm around her, his hand sliding under her shirt to rest just under her breasts.

Almost immediately, Sara recognized the change in his breath. He'd fallen asleep, holding her in his arms.

* * *

The next morning, they lay in bed until eleven, neither of them wanting to get up because they both knew it meant she would be leaving for Boston.

Sara brought up the audience at the show the night before. "They worship you. It's gross, actually. You're going to get a god complex at this rate." She was half-teasing.

Seth smirked but didn't engage her on it. Instead, he pushed back the sheets and gazed at her body.

She pressed him, wanting to talk about the songs he was writing about her. "Is all this affecting what you write? Are you still being political? You should write about the Fair Pay Act. Did you know there's been no movement on pay equity in twenty years?"

Both in their element with this topic, a long political discourse between them began, ending with her criticizing his sexual imagery lyrics, albeit while she was simultaneously enjoying how light his hands felt on her hips.

"Enough of the boy-girl stuff," she said, admonishing him.

He laughed her off. "I write about what's going on for me." He spoke more softly. "About how vulnerable and insecure I feel. About sex, love…"

Sara cut him off. "Extrapolate that to the political. Write about male vulnerability in heterosexual relationships, rather than your personal vulnerability."

He nodded enthusiastically. She felt daring. "You write a lot about me." *He's uncomfortable talking about these songs with me*, she thought, noticing the tension in his shoulders. Moving so close to him that their noses were touching, their lips almost met. "You write about what's going on for you." She pulled away from him slowly, teasingly. "So…am I what's going on for you?"

He nodded, then kissed her.

chapter sixteen

As Marco wandered into her office, Sara started, quickly checking the time on her phone.

"Treatment time with Jane." She was late.

"Sounds so sweet when you put it like that. Like a children's book. I think I might use that line in a poem," he said as she grabbed her things.

"I'm glad you wandered into the women's studies neighborhood because I have to talk to you. Are we still on for dinner?"

Sara had been back from New York for three days, but she'd been so busy catching up, she hadn't had a chance to either confront Marco about what he'd been divulging to Seth or update him about the gorgeous time she'd had with him—sans sex.

"Yes, my place. Seven. And come with all the details."

"You mean you haven't talked to Seth yet?" She knew they talked every day.

"I need both versions."

With Marco right there, she was tempted to confront him, but she had back-to-back lectures, plus treatment with Jane. "Okay, but you tell me his version tonight."

Marco raised his eyebrows.

"I mean it." Sara stood at the door, knowing all this back and forth with Marco was making her even later for her session.

"We'll see. I might."

* * *

It was hard to focus on her session. She hadn't had a minute to deal with anything emotional. The idea of being introspective got no further than dwelling on Seth.

"I want to talk about what happened in New York," Jane began.

"Oh good. Me too." This was more like it, Sara thought as she leaned forward, her willingness for the session now actively apparent.

"We'll get to that in a minute. Let's talk about this first," Jane said, holding up Sara's food journal.

Sara groaned, flopping back into her seat again. She hated that journal, that stupid list of what she ate every day.

"I started bleeding," Sara said with great fanfare, hoping this would divert Jane's interest.

"Just remember," Jane said flatly, deflating Sara's glee, "to keep it, your doctor said you must gain some weight."

Sara nodded soberly, remembering the order.

"What would you agree to gain? You're ninety-eight pounds now, right?"

Confirming this with a nod, Jane had the audacity to suggest that she aim for 105 pounds.

"For goodness' sake, I'm not proposing the unthinkable, like forbidding you to mention the word 'patriarchy' for twenty-four hours." Jane's attempt at humor was met with a gasp of horror. She tried again. "Fine. How about 101?"

If only to shut her up and make the numbers stop stabbing at her head, Sara begrudgingly agreed. She knew her argument that one hundred pounds was the same weight as a baby hippo would only drag out the discussion and hinder her being able to talk about New York.

Jane sighed in relief. "What's the plan, then? How are you going to gain three pounds?"

She waited patiently as Sara sat in thought for several minutes. But her mind was blank. She had no idea how that was even possible, and Ed kept giving her counterproductive suggestions. She was forced to admit she was flummoxed.

Jane confessed she didn't know either but was willing to come up with a reasonable solution. "Once we agree on how many calories you need to add, you must at least promise to try, okay?"

When Sara said she'd try, she got the sense that Jane was resisting the urge to high-five her.

Smugly satisfied with her progress, Jane turned to the other problem, the one Sara was far less resistant to discuss—sex.

"How did things go in New York?"

No surprise to Sara, Jane was elated to know that intimacy had been the prescription of the weekend. After all, it fit Jane's agenda for her recovery ala mission: heal the effects of rape through intimacy.

"He genuinely wants to build intimacy, doesn't he? That's great. I'm so glad he's not diving into sex and letting you persuade him into it."

Sara scowled, not sharing this happy view of it.

"Why do you think it's so bad that I want sex?"

"I don't think it's bad to want sex. It's just that you fuck everything that turns your head."

Jane almost never used profanity. The mix of this and being reminded that she was a nymphomaniac struck Sara hard.

"I never said you were a nymphomaniac," Jane objected. "I said you're hypersexual."

"Semantics."

She patted Sara's hand, obviously sensing the damage. "That's part of the work we're doing here. That and getting you to eat and to stop veritably drowning in alcohol every day." Jane, usually adept at her profession, was mauling this one.

Appalled, Sara exclaimed, "Oh, the litany of problems. You have a lifetime's work ahead of you here. I don't think you can manage the load."

"I'll manage it. One thing at a time."

"Bless your heart," Sara said, rolling her eyes.

Jane smirked.

"Am I really that sick?" Sara demanded.

"You're recovering. Focus on that."

"Cold comfort, indeed."

"Keep wrapping yourself in communities and people that will help you recover. Like WRC."

Sara didn't serve back a cleaver retort this time, as it was finally starting to sound like the truth.

"Seth," Jane proclaimed, using the magic word that lifted Sara's look of dejection into attentiveness. "I think Seth is part of that community that will help you recover."

* * *

When Marco opened the front door, Sara stormed into the kitchen.

"I don't know where to begin," she flustered. "I'm furious with you. *Furious.*"

She noticed the smirk on his face as she went. She'd showed up for dinner earlier than planned; the wait after three days had been bad enough. She just couldn't wait any longer and had rushed through her tasks to arrive as early as possible.

Marco handed her a glass of wine.

"You told Seth about that night I spent with Tom?"

Marco finished his sip of wine before nodding. "You mean the drunk-sex night?"

Sara was frantic. "Why did you tell him about that? Why are you always trying to sabotage this?"

Marco rubbed a hand over his mouth, a distant guilty look on his face. She sucked in her breath. To Sara, this simple gesture was transparent.

"You love him?"

Marco squirmed.

"So that's why you're always protecting him."

He pushed past her empathetic pat to his knee. "Seth didn't buy that you and Tom were just friends. He said Tom seemed proprietary, boyfriend-like at your party. I merely told him why." Marco shrugged.

"Meaning?" she demanded, her empathy decreasing in proportion to her rising anxiety over what details Marco might have divulged.

"I told him you fucked Tom one night when you were drunk, and that, judging by how much Tom was mewing around, it meant something to him. Still."

Sara's mouth fell open. *The nerve!* It took her a while to recover her ability to speak. "Marco, you didn't. He must think I'm *that* person. A nymphomaniac. A drunken nymphomaniac."

"You *are* that person."

Unhelpful, Marco. Sara tried to ignore his comment, too preoccupied with wondering how Seth's impression of his feminist guru had been transformed. She slammed both hands over her mouth in mortification.

"You really care about what he thinks about you." Marco smirked.

"I do. Of course I do."

"Wow." Marco never said "wow." She'd shocked him. He was too literary for trite expressions, unless he was being ironic or edgily current and turning an expression on its head for dramatic effect. Marco was a stickler for the right words, structured in the right way. There was some satisfaction in reducing him to "wow."

"You're falling for Abstinence Boy."

Her initial bewilderment with the comment quickly gave way to astonishment. Suddenly everything made sense—all Marco's warnings, and Seth's behavior with her in Boston and in New York. "He's abstinent?"

With a sympathetic smile, Marco nodded.

"Honestly? Are you sure?" she added, more expression than question. "Why didn't you tell me?"

He spoke quietly and calmly, and Sara felt he was pandering to an impulsive craziness that could emerge from her at any moment. "I couldn't tell you. But I did encourage him to give you a head's up about it."

As if Marco had led her into a lion's den without so much as a "Be careful," she made her attack. "Well, he didn't, and it was a big shock!"

Marco chuckled, refusing to pander to her dramatics.

"Honestly, Sara, it's not like he's dangerous or something. He's abstinent, not a mass murderer. I thought you might be able to handle it. I spoke to him yesterday. He misses you."

"I know that. I speak to him every day too, you know."

"I know."

Sara cocked an eyebrow. "Figured. Is there anything he doesn't tell you?"

"Actually, yes. I asked him how the weekend went with you, and he didn't say much, just sighed."

"Was it a bad sigh or good sigh? Could you tell?"

Marco smiled lewdly. "A good sigh. I teased him about it. I said, 'Are you in love?'"

"Don't be preposterous," she said impulsively, quickly adding with a more coaxing tone, "What did he say?"

"You talk to him every day. You ask him."

"Fuck you."

"Stop worrying. He's so into you."

Focusing on that second part of his comment, she repeated his words. "He's so *into* me?" After New York, she'd learned this, but if Marco had classified information, she thought she surely deserved a glimpse of it at this point in the saga.

Sara waited. Marco poured her another glass of wine. His lips remained pursed.

She pushed him. "Come on."

Marco sipped his wine. Silent. As if the wine, the silence, and Sara's piercing stare was disproportionate to the information, he shrugged, relenting. "I think maybe he loves you, utterly."

Sara didn't care about things like a boy loving her. She was a feminist guru and had far more important things to think about. But there was a sensation in her belly that gave her a giddy feeling and left her fighting back a smile so huge it made her cheeks ache. *Seth loves me? Utterly?* The giddiness might even have been...*joy?*

"There, now you have some inside information."

Sara was still glowing. "That's kind of a big piece of information."

"Not really. It's nothing compared to what he has on you."

Sara felt her heart begin to race. "What does he have on me?"

It didn't slow her heart rate when he took a deep breath, as if angling to set it up. "I want you to understand that I told him these things when I was completely wasted. And, in fairness, I didn't know at the time that he was interested in you, fishing for information. If I'd known, I wouldn't have elaborated the way I did."

Sara's mind reeled. "What did you tell him?"

"He wanted to know if you were in love with Tom."

So sweet, she thought, recognizing that it sounded just like something Seth would want to know. It was completely innocuous. She felt better.

Marco dropped his eyes to his wine glass and blurted, "I told him that, while I was one hundred percent sure that you weren't in love with Tom, you were pretty committed to him."

"That's not so bad."

"Then when he asked why you were with Tom if you didn't love him, I may have pointed out that you thought he was hotter than hell and always available for sex." He continued in a flourish, as though he was hoping she couldn't follow all his words. She heard every single one of them. "I also told him that, despite these two redeeming features about him, you prefer younger guys. I told him I thought it might have something to do with stamina."

Sara felt herself becoming catatonic.

"I also told him that you think Tom's a homophobic asshole and couldn't tell the difference between an intersectional and psychoanalytic philosophy even if there was the promise of head in it for him. And I may have told him that head is something you love to give. Nothing wrong with loving to give head." His humor was infuriating.

Sara, who only really swore when she was seriously mad, distraught, or under intense pressure—or, in this case, all three—threw herself into a profanity-laced meltdown. "I know there's nothing fucking wrong with loving to give head, but if you were a woman, you would understand that you don't tell a straight guy that you like to give head because of the damn fucking gender rules. Straight men are infamously disingenuous about sex. They love all the little gender games. Fuck!"

"That's not fair," Marco charged.

Sara was not having it. Dismissing his support of straight men everywhere with an eye roll, she threw her head into her hands.

Marco leaned forward, rubbing her leg in a gesture of comfort.

She muffled from behind her hands. "You've made me sound like the shallowest thinker in the world." For a moment, her face reappeared. "I'm supposed to be his feminist guru, for God's sake." She flopped back into her palms. "He must be wondering why he ever put me on that pedestal. I should just quit competing with the thought leaders at Wellesley right now. I quit. I just quit."

"There's also the eating disorder. Now that's not a quality you'd expect in a real thought leader, is it?" Marco said, finishing her off.

In normal situations, Sara might appreciate the attempt at humor, but right now it exasperated her. She threw up her arms in despair. "I don't want to hear anymore. You can save the rest for another day. Maybe when I'm at Wellesley around all those great world-esteemed thinkers, then you can blackmail me."

After a flurry of tutting, Marco said, "How can I make you feel better?"

Sara suggested that he tell her something weird or bad, hopefully both, about Seth—or anyone really.

"Do you want to hear about his abstinence kick?"

She took three huge gulps of wine, prompting Marco to push the appetizers closer to her side of the coffee table.

"Will it make me look or feel better?"

Marco teased, "I don't think I can help you there, but I will say that Seth is into some pretty nice stuff, sexually speaking. I think you would love it if you gave it a chance. It'll really get you off, but in a soulful, DIY way."

This was supposed to make her feel better? Sara didn't quite know how to respond. "Try again. This is not helping."

"He's on an intimacy kick."

"What are you talking about?"

"Listen, I tell the straight boys in the Men's Circle to try different stuff. Experiment."

Somewhat familiar with alternative/DIY sexuality culture, Sara began to both worry and wonder in what way Seth was involved in this community. "So, you are the reason he's abstaining?"

"It was more a response to the DIY culture readings," Marco objected. "I only offered some guidance."

Sara nodded and made up her mind. *Blame Marco.*

"He actually asked me to fill you in a bit about the DIY sex stuff."

"Why would he do that?" she asked, fearful of the answers that might come.

"Because he realized it might sound a bit wild to someone like you."

"Someone like me?" Sara was offended by the insinuation that she was not "wild."

"I told him it might seem pretty funky after the sex you were getting with Tom."

Sara, slack-jawed through so much of this conversation, was beginning to get a dry throat.

Just when she thought it couldn't get any worse, he added, "I told him Tom was too quick and didn't like to give cunnilingus."

Sara waved her arms in the air in bewilderment. "What did you say that for? When did I tell you such a thing?"

"After a few glasses of wine, of course."

Sara put her glass down to rub both her templates. "I want to remember this as the moment I swear off alcohol." But then she reached out for the wine bottle. Marco watched her fill her glass to the rim. "But I really need to feel drunk right now." She took a slug, then raised her glass to him. "Cheers to you, Marco." She took another big slug before throwing her head back to speak to the ceiling because she thought she'd slap Marco if she looked at him right then. "I do not fucking believe this." She dropped her eyes to her wine glass. "I'm sure you told him all about my expurgated sex life because you knew I wanted him to know that information. So thoughtful of you. I owe you."

"Actually, I withheld a lot of information."

"Really?" Sara managed to remain composed. She couldn't explain this eerie self-possession, except to say that it was the alternative to screaming.

Marco smirked and got up again to get their dinner. After he retrieved the homemade goat cheese pizza from the oven and grabbed the kale salad that Drew had made the night before, he joined her back at the coffee table.

"Sorry, nothing's on the side," he said, referring to the salad and the pizza.

Sara knew he was trying to be funny. She wouldn't indulge him. Instead, she gulped her wine, not knowing what to respond to first —the fact that he'd told Seth the finer details of her sex life, or the need to inquire about the mysteries of this wild sex she'd been missing out on.

Marco dropped the subject with a heavy sigh. "I guess it was too much information."

"A tinge."

"All right, but it's why he thought an explanation might sound better coming from me. I mean, he knows you're already a bit dismayed by his behavior—the cutting and his Angry Boy shows—and he didn't want to add to that."

Sara shook her head. "Somehow he thought this would sound better coming from you?" She couldn't help but laugh. "You, who could make toasting bread sound like a sexually depraved activity?"

"Ironic, isn't it?"

"It is, but…" She rolled a hand in the air, encouraging him to expound.

While she was eager to understand Seth's abstinence, she wished he'd tell her directly, even if he thought it might scare her off by adding to her belief that he was depraved.

"Tell me about this funky, wild sex that you think I might be too straight for."

It was an apprehensive question, as she was worried that the truth might be so funky that it would give her bad dreams.

Marco's expression was that of someone trying to figure out how to explain a complicated concept to a very dull, stupid child. "It's DIY, experimental sex. There's all kinds of stuff—fetish, BDSM—and then there's the abstinence thing, which is basically the idea of doing everything but fucking. I mean, everything, but penetrative sex."

Sara appreciated Marco's attempt to use direct language, but she wished he'd just keep talking without stopping for her approval.

"The idea is that avoiding penetration will increase intimacy."

Sara looked crestfallen, resigned to her fate with Abstinence Boy. "You said I'd love it. What's to love? Because so far, I'm not getting that part."

"There's lots of looking, stroking." Sara looked hopeful at that one, prompting Marco to say, "Stroking, yes, but not in any places where you might usually go, and always with the lights on. And, of course, kissing." He stopped when Sara gave a little gasp. "Oh," Marco said dramatically, seeming to observe Sara's sudden recognition.

She blushed and Marco laughed.

"Not so wild, huh? It definitely takes some getting used to."

Sara slumped again. "It sounds sexually frustrating." She then gaped at him suddenly, inquiring, "BDSM-ish?"

"You say that like it's a disorder."

"It is a...."

Marco put his hand up to stop her. "No, it's not. It's really not. It's just not what you do."

"Yeah, you're right, I don't do domination with leathers or submission all tied up or any kind of bondage, and I certainly don't *do* not being able to achieve orgasm without pain."

Marco sighed. "Oh so vanilla! There's so much more to it than that. But the point is, Fem-Guru, what if he does?"

"Well, that's nice for him," she declared facetiously.

Marco demonstrated how much of an ass he could be and clapped his hands together, laughing shamelessly at her disapproval. "It is very, very sexy stuff."

All Sara could think was that she was chasing sex with someone who was abstinent and into S&M.

As if to prove his point, he gave her an example. "BDSM was something he explored with Eyva. She got off watching him cut and cutting him."

Sara listened, speechless, her mind reeling with the details. She wondered how he managed to spill the details of Seth's crazy sex life so plainly, as if it was chitchat about the weather.

"Honey, it is about intimacy," Marco said, softening, probably because she looked as peaky as she felt. "Don't get lost in the S&M part of it. The best feeling in the world for him is achieving intimacy, not an orgasm. Does that make sense?"

"No." Sara felt slightly sick.

When Marco attempted another explanation, Sara stopped moving kale around on her plate to wave her arms at him. She had to stop him for fear of throwing up just thinking about it.

Marco put a hand to his mouth as if to silence himself. "You're shocked. You're so sexually dull. You can see why he didn't want to tell you."

They'd finished the bottle of wine, and Marco was trying to convince her to stay the night and to eat something.

"Maybe a banana?" he suggested when she refused any more mouthfuls of kale.

A banana equals 110 calories, she knew, but just to please him, she agreed to eat it. She was struck by his concern, especially considering the pain he must have been in nursing his broken heart.

"Are you okay?"

He looked baffled.

"You know, over Seth?"

A smile spread across his face. He nodded. "I'm over it."

Once she was wrapped up on the couch for the night with a cup of tea and the *New York Times*, he walked away, telling her to read the Arts section first.

She found a review of Seth's show in New York City from the previous weekend. After recovering slightly from the fact that this was just one more piece of evidence confirming their exploding success, she read the review.

The caption read "Got Politics?" In addition to the full spread, there were three pictures of the band. One was a shot of them performing together, the next a close-up of Seth going ballistic at the show, and the third a studio shot of the band's carefully constructed, stony-faced, mean-look publicity image. They looked just like rock stars. She groaned in disapproval but started reading the article. Seth never failed to mention that much of their music was a criticism of gender politics. If he could communicate critical philosophical messages this effectively to such a wide audience, maybe it was a good platform after all.

However, as she read on, her optimism faded. Rather than radicalize the message about women's sexual desire being subsumed by gender politics, the reporter depoliticized it, connecting it instead to Seth's performance on stage.

She'd promised Seth that she'd give some thought to his agenda of being a sell-out that could work from within enemy lines, so she picked up another paper from Marco's stack of Seth Fandom and kept reading the reviews, trying to gauge his effect in the mainstream. And then she came across one in *Rolling Stone*.

Despite its reputation for being a premier music journal, this interview was focusing on questionings aimed at exposing Seth's personal life. The interviewer asked about the rumors that most of the tracks on the new record were inspired by one of his professors. Seth admitted it comfortably, but apparently the reporter was dissatisfied with this. Presumptuously, the next question went even more personal, with the reporter asking if this professor was the same person whom Seth had been romantic with. Sara was appalled. The reporter had the audacity to imply that she'd slept with him, and while she was still his professor.

Seth wouldn't answer the question; she wanted to kiss him for that. The reporter, however, was not dissuaded. Single-minded in his determination to draw out the details of the relationship between them, he wanted to know if this professor was also the inspiration for his love songs. He listed them, ending with "Other Man," and asking Seth if the rumors were true that it was about the intensity of his jealousy toward this professor's husband. She couldn't believe this rubbish!

Now, not only was she a professor who had sex with her students, she was an adulterer too? All this cheap shot reporter wanted was to create a scandalous story. Sara dropped the magazine and sat bolt upright. The decency clause! Who would Wellesley believe? Her or *Rolling Stone*?

Fuming at the tactlessness that could cost her everything, she picked up the magazine and read faster. While the reporter hadn't mentioned her by name, it didn't matter, because if the latest Jesus Christ of rock (Seth) responded positively, she knew thousands of reporters would be working round the clock to unearth her identity.

Seth's response was a relief: "I'm finished commenting on that."

The sell-out just kept getting darker. On the one hand, he had a platform, but since the popular press were persistently depoliticizing his writing and focusing on making him a celebrity, she wondered if the sell-out was worth it. Mostly, she worried about the cost to him. Sara knew he would eventually be repelled by the crazy adoration from his fans and the way the press hung on his every word—if he wasn't already. Knowing how damaged and sensitive he was, she worried how he'd manage everything that was coming his way. Thinking about it led to a sleepless night. She guessed it would be the first of many.

The next morning, when Marco was making coffee, Sara pointed to the reviews. "You think that's a big deal, look at these." He threw a small pile on the table.

Sara's eyes grew big as she glanced over the plethora of reviews, all in national newspapers and magazines.

"They're huge." Adding, after a quick pause for dramatic effect, "Huge sell-outs."

Marco threw the *LA Times* review in front of her. "Not huge sell-outs just yet, but according to this one, the tour will 'solidify their exploding success'…blah, blah, blah."

Sara, began to read the *LA Times* review, but got interrupted by Marco, who'd handed her two more newspaper reviews. "These all say the same thing."

Sara felt the blood drain from her face. "Can I take them home to read?"

* * *

She read them all, several times each, still trying to understand the cost of the sell-out and the efficacy of it all.

Marco was right, they all said the same thing: a politically charged, feminist, queer-identified band destined for greatness. As if to confirm all her fears for Seth, one review gave her chills with its ominous foreboding. "One has to wonder how this young band will manage the excess—money, sex, alcohol, and drugs."

Drugs. It rang in her ears.

She picked up the phone and dialed Marco.

"You said you were wasted when you told Seth all that stuff about Tom and me. You didn't mean drunk, did you? Did you get wasted, with him?"

"It's all very postmodern. You know, experimenting with sex, drugs, uncensored, radical living." He talked almost like it was romantic. Marco tried to change the subject. "Did you read those articles I gave you?"

"Together? Did you get fucked up together?"

"Well, it's no fun alone, is it? So, yes, Sara, I asked him if he could 'turn me on,' if you know what I mean."

Sara coughed nervously into the phone. "And you mean by

that…what? That he was 'turned on' too? What drugs does he do, Marco?"

"You should talk to Seth."

"He won't talk to me about it."

She knew Marco felt protective of her too, and that maybe, if he realized how much this would affect her, she could get the truth out of him. She waited, her breath heavy and irregular.

"Everything," he said solemnly at last. "He does everything and anything he can get—smack, crack, speed. *Everything*."

chapter seventeen

The knocking on Sara's front door was Marco. She hadn't been expecting him and had failed to reach the door before Tom. While she stood quite a distance behind Tom, she could see Marco's face read: *what the fuck?*

"Good morning," Tom said casually, pulling on a sports coat and picking up his bag to leave.

Sara was appalled at the scene. From her position at the end of the hallway, it couldn't have been more obvious. Tom carried the smug air of a man who'd just got laid. Marco, never one to hide his feelings, stood with his mouth agog in utter shock.

"Hello, *Tom.*" He inflected his name to show his disdain and strolled past him, glaring at Sara.

"Bye then," Sara said, waving.

He gave a twitch of a smile at her from the threshold of the open door, lifting a hand to wave back. "See you at seven for dinner?"

Sara nodded.

"What?" Marco screeched before the door was even fully closed. "You fucked him? Again?" He didn't wait for an answer. "What about your other boyfriend?"

"I don't want to talk to him again. Ever," she shot back, shaking.

It had been one week since she'd found out that Seth was doing "everything," and, unbeknownst to anyone else, four days since she'd gotten back together with Tom. Her real boyfriend.

"I know, I know," Macro said slightly more sympathetically as he came to stand beside her. "You're sad, furious. I get it, but at least hear him out."

Sara wiped her tears and runny nose on her hand. "I don't want to. He's too messed up."

"But not you, huh?"

His therapy-like tone irritated Sara. It felt too sympathetic, and in her state of mind she wanted a showdown, to let everyone know the depth of her grief.

Her silence worked.

Marco went from zero to thirty. "No, not you, with your jam-packed schedule of starving and drinking." And then thirty to sixty. "And fucking Tom." Then over the limit. "And, in Jane's opinion, this denial of Seth's existence, while still managing to defame him, is messed up."

"Is that a clinical diagnosis?"

Marco looked ready to smack her. "I think wanting to avoid any confrontation with him as a way of breaking up with him is evidence of your own ever-growing list of self-destructive behaviors. You're blowing it there."

"*I'm* blowing it? Let me see if I'm getting this. You're saying I blew it because I dumped a junkie?" she countered, looking like she might hit him if he made a pro-Seth statement.

"Yes. Think about it. Try to find some itsy-bitsy pocket of reason in your mind."

"Oh, I will. I'll give it some thought. You know, in between running the women's studies program, publishing my book, and presenting colloquia at Wellesley, I'll think about how I let a self-mutilating heroin addict slip through my fingers."

"Have you made a decision to be permanently sardonic?" he asked rhetorically. "I wish you could see how ugly it is."

Sara found one last ounce of energy and threw it. "He's the last person on earth that I'd want to have an intimate relationship with." She'd only said it for effect and, realizing this, Sara slammed her head into her hands, her voice breaking with emotion. "I do know, you know. I know I'm messed up."

The fight gone from him now that Sara had crumpled, Marco mellowed. "Do you own tissues?"

They walked into the kitchen together, Sara located the tissues and curled up in a sobbing heap on the couch.

Marco sat with her. "And your way of dealing with Seth is to fuck Tom?"

"Yes. Since you told me that bit of news that Seth forgot to tell me, despite the fact that I asked him—many times."

Marco gaped. "He never told you *anything*?"

"No. I didn't know he was actively using. And especially not everything."

Marco nodded. "Fair enough. He misled you there. He really should've been upfront with you. Transparent."

Sara sat up, pleased to have him on her side. "And I'm not even going to think about Wellesley. I have a decency clause, for God's sake. And I'm just plain scared of him now." Her emotional steam was gaining momentum again. "I can't be with a scary junkie. His lying about it was just the end."

While she was devastated to learn the extent of Seth's drug problem and felt justified with that alone as reason enough to drop him like a dead sparkler on the fourth of July, what troubled her more was his lack of honesty with her about it. That was what made her stop the daily calls to him and even stopped her listening to any of his messages.

"I'm done."

"Maybe you should tell him that. Or about that," he said, motioning to the door to indicate the elephant that just left the room. "Are you really back with him?" he said in disbelief.

Sara nodded, still shaken by the knowledge that she'd been on the verge of being with a junkie. Tom had taken on a new sheen since. "I even have a UTI from all the make-up sex."

"Ew. What are you doing with him?"

"It's okay that we're not postmodern kindred spirits," she said firmly. Marco scoffed, but she raised a hand to him to let her finish. "Like Tom, I'm being a grown-up now. He's willing to accept my way, so I think I should accept his."

Marco threw his arms up. "I disagree. Completely. Being a grown-up isn't about settling, it's choosing to be with someone who gets the very fucking essence of who you are."

Sara curled a clump of hair around multiple fingers, feeling them slowly turning white with the tension. "I seriously underestimated his understanding of the DIY lifestyle."

Her pretense wasn't lost on him. "No, Sara, you didn't. Tom doesn't get it. Doesn't even want to get it."

She tried to smile at that, because now he was rattling her. While she desperately missed Seth, she did not want to want him. She knew, on the other hand, that Tom was good for her. *He really is good for me*, she told herself, working hard to believe it. She didn't divulge her doubt out loud, knowing Marco would use it to implode the fragile basis of her relationship with Tom.

"He might not be an activist, but as you once pointed out to me, he's not a misogynist either."

"High standards indeed."

Sara raised her voice above his brittle laugher. "He's a liberal. And...stable. He's together." She nodded, as if convincing even herself of her answer.

"Sara, you're Mr. Hegemonic-husband shopping. You want to be Mr. and Mrs. Hegemonic."

Sara returned to her torrent of tears and tried to convince them both. "At least he won't die on me shooting up. At least he has a fucking real job and a car."

Marco cocked an eyebrow. "I get why you're done with Seth, but I don't think fucking Tom—or anyone else, for that matter—is—" he broke off. "Sara, does Jane know about Tom? That you're being hypersexual?"

Sara let out a huge sob. Thinking about any of this or dealing with any of this was too much. She fell into his outstretched arms.

"Oh, look at you." Marco appraised her body. "You look awful. Have you lost more weight?"

She cried until her eyes refused to water.

* * *

After she showered, they left together for campus. Sara made a solemn promise to Marco that, after a quick stop at her office to collect her things for class, she would head straight to the WRC and check in with Jane.

Once in her office, Sara plonked herself down at her desk. It caught her eye immediately. On top of the pile of mail on her desk was a fat envelope from a minor, virtually obscure press that did not look to be a rejection. Instantly, she became flushed with the giddiness of being on the gilded cloud of published dreams, and then, just as suddenly, she felt something else.

She was unable to acknowledge that this great day, a day she'd doubted would ever come, was happening. Here it was. Right in front of her was everything she had been grasping at: Acceptance. Worth. Acknowledgment.

And she felt absolutely nothing.

She was too overwhelmed, too tired, in too much pain from too much sex, and far too hungry to respond...

Then it came. It was the response her body favored lately, heaving sobs.

Still flat with shock from the publisher's letter, she called Jane.

chapter eighteen

Despite checking in with Jane every day for the past week, Sara was feeling more ill than ever. Still mystified by her hollow response to the publishing deal and exhausted with all the organizing involved in the Take Back the Night rally, she'd restricted all week. Today was the worst. The day of the imminent confrontation.

The rally, just two days away, was the university calendar event she felt most passionate about. Her enthusiasm tempered, and all because of a guy. *Pathetic,* she thought, with complete and utter aggravation that a guy could do this to her.

As if she needed any more stressors, the magnitude of the response generated by the national press coverage of the event and the pressure it placed on her as the organizer was even more overwhelming than she'd anticipated months ago when the band was only gaining traction. On top of it, she was inundated with calls from the panicked campus police who, upon hearing that the event would draw tens of thousands, had hysterically demanded more security. Police units from several surrounding towns were commissioned to help cope with the anticipated crowds that had already begun to pour in and camp out on the huge campus field.

Apparently, local hotels had been booked for weeks, and hotels for miles around were filling up to accommodate the throngs of fans descending upon the campus. The buzz was charged, both on the campus and in town, with local businesses excited for the boost an influx of people would bring to the town.

As she expected, the media had been unrelenting for the past few weeks, so much so that she'd been forced to cancel a couple of classes to cope with the demand for interviews marketing the event across New England. Still, she tried to make time for Jane.

"Maybe my flatness on the book offer is just stress from the rally? Hunger?" Sara wondered, sitting in Jane's office at WRC.

"And there's *Tom* too." Jane accentuated his name, which Sara read as a synonym for her other problem: hypersexuality. "You're restricting, binging on sex and alcohol." Jane reached out to touch her arm. "Don't beat yourself up. Symptoms get worse under stress. And not just the rally; you have the shock with Seth too. It's a lot to be dealing with."

"Yes. Our biggest year ever with the rally."

"I want to talk about Tom," Jane said.

"Why overanalyze it?" Although, in the week since her decent into Tom, they had progressed into being very much girlfriend and boyfriend. "I'd rather talk about my restricting, the drinking," she bleated, frustrated.

"How did this even happen? You don't even like him."

"No, I do. I really do. He's been so sweet. When he called the day after I found out about Seth…" She trailed off, not wanting to say it again. "And then he just kept calling, leaving all these nice messages, asking how I was when I was so low."

"Vulnerable is what you were."

"He was worried about me." When Jane remained unmoved, Sara pressed it, trying to convince her by adding with feeling, "He asked over and over: how are you, Sara? How are you?"

"If you recall, I called every day to ask the same question."

Sara implored Jane to understand. "I wanted to cry and tell him everything, but I couldn't think of how to articulate it. I thought, *do I really tell him?* Do I say, 'Oh, you know, I just ended a relationship with that twenty-something, self-mutilating, S&M junkie student.' It all just sounded so mad. It made me sound nuts, stupid. To risk everything for a ridiculous crush."

"A crush? What are you talking about?"

"We didn't even have sex." Sara shrugged, as if that settled it.

"Ah, I see. You think you weren't in a relationship because there was no sex. That doesn't come as news because, after all, you don't do intimacy, do you? You're hypersexual."

Sara met her with a stony silence. Jane sighed.

"You're not fooling me with this cleverly executed show of disdain for Seth. I mean, I understand why you need to do it, Sara. I know you're more afraid of caring for a man than you are of gaining five pounds, but tell me you don't really believe in your own performance?"

"Okay, okay! I know, all right? But it's over. Okay? It has to be over."

"Fine. Good," Jane said abruptly, obviously taken aback by Sara's acknowledgment of the performance. For a moment, Jane's usual flurry of therapy words came to a pause.

"Just know," she said at last, perhaps almost regretfully, "that you can't avoid dealing with it just by minimizing it, Sara."

Sara shook her head with distress. "I wish I was in a Jane Austen novel, then I could avoid all this. I could say, 'Excuse me, Mr. Coles. Good day to you,' and exit to Bath."

"It's hard being a grown-up."

Sara didn't like the insinuation. "I'll tell you who the grown-up is. It's Tom. I wish you and Marco could see that. He's good to me. He makes me feel safe and normal."

Jane lowered her eyebrows. "Really? What about all his comments on your eating? Your body?"

Sara suddenly regretted telling Jane about Tom's positive comments about her body. She knew it wouldn't bode well for him when she divulged that the thinner she became, the more he admired her. To Jane, of course, this had translated to being unsupportive in her therapy.

"What are you suggesting? Tom is all bad, and Seth is all good? You're starting to sound like Marco, who only thinks that because he's a hopeless romantic."

"No. I'm saying you should not want or need either of them. Romanticizing the situation isn't helpful. You should focus on getting better, wanting to get well. Or at least *want* to want to get well."

Sara couldn't help but smile at that—"want to want to get well." *Want to want Tom. Do not want to want Seth.*

"I have to go and deal with the rally now. Off to get Marco, who is not being helpful, just moping around waiting for Seth."

"I'll talk to you later?"

"I'm going to be too busy with the rally."

"Then you must check in with me again tomorrow, okay?"

"I'll try."

Jane stalled her. "I know this is going to be hard to hear, but you need to remove both of these men from your life. Try being alone. And you need to do it today."

Sara cocked her head. "I don't have enough time to count calories, so I'm not sure I can find the time it will take for that today."

*   *   *

She picked Marco up and they headed to the event field, or what everyone on campus called the Spectacle.

Not happy just to participate, the band had arranged for their entire tour to come to campus. This meant that the campus itself was not only besieged by throngs of exuberant fans but was steadily emptying too. Students, staff, and faculty alike disappeared to gaze at the spectacle of the tour.

The Spectacle included three tractor-trailer trucks filled with equipment, a huge crew, a full set that took two days to assemble, and disruptively loud sound checks from the Anoraks and Jane's Malady, the band's support groups for their tour.

Sara stood in a soggy, wet field with Marco, watching the Anoraks run through a sound check. Marco made cartoon-like applause at the sight.

The rally had become the Bacchantes Show. Given the money they were going to rake in for the cause, Sara wasn't complaining. While there was no cover charge, people were asked to donate with a conscience. This year all proceeds were marked for rape-torn war zones in developing and undeveloped countries around the world. With the sheer volume of people in town, Sara suspected the cash generated would be sizable, easily the rally's biggest year.

"What is it with all these double noun name bands?" Marco asked rhetorically. "I mean, have you noticed that so many of them are preceded by the noun 'Jane'? Jane's Disease, Jane's Addiction, Janes'—with a fucking apostrophe after the 'S'—Fucking."

Initially, Sara shrugged a response. She hadn't smiled in about three weeks. Drained from the session with Jane, exhausted from both the planning and anxiety about all the what-if scenarios that were ruminating in her head, propelled forth by the sheer magnitude of the event. She'd definitely not smiled even a little bit since learning about Seth's drug use.

The sensation and sound that began to escape from her throat was unexpected. At first, she thought maybe it was a heart attack, but then she recognized the familiar sound as laughter. It was as if she'd been conserving it.

Almost choking, she spoke unintelligibly through her laughter. "You had a verb in there, Marco. 'Fucking' is a verb, as you well know."

When Marco looked at her with concern, it only made her laugh more. Then, becoming almost euphoric, it all stopped abruptly and was replaced by her normal reaction, great bursting sobs. Marco hugged her, rubbing her back soothingly, shushing her gently. "You're exhausted. Stop worrying."

While he was still hugging her, he motioned with his free arm around the field, the outlay of the organized chaos that was the band's tour, and said, "Look, it's happening. You've done it and it'll be okay."

* * *

When Seth arrived later that day with Eyva, Caleb, and Jeff, there was sudden chaos in Sara's tiny apartment—screams from Marco, hugs, kisses, incessant talking, and Sara trying to hide.

Eyva screamed her name, dragging her out of a corner hiding spot. Seth noticed.

Giving him what she hoped was a dismissive smile and a simple nod of acknowledgment, Sara felt anxiety well in her as she took in his frown. More conciliatory in the face of him, Sara begrudgingly considered that perhaps she did owe him some explanation. However, more as an excuse to avoid a confrontation than anything else, she still harbored a fantasy that he might come to accept that it was over and leave without expecting any explanation at all. Apparently, that fantasy was about to be blown to dust.

Sara straightened as he approached her. Presenting her best let's-keep-this-strictly-business/I'm-not-your-friend demeanor, she spoke quickly, attempting excitement and enthusiasm for the event.

"Did you see this town when you came in? The people?" She overstepped it, gushing too blithely, knowing that any silence would present an opportunity for the confrontation she hoped to avoid. Sara kept going. "It's complete anarchy."

He merely nodded to acknowledge the colossal chaos in the town, then dismissed it as unimportant with a shrug. His reaction silenced her. In that instant, she realized two things. First, avoiding a confrontation was going to be more exhausting than she'd anticipated, and second, while the event was huge for her and the entire community, it was just another day-in-the life for him.

She couldn't imagine the stress he faced, but her feelings of empathy for him were short-lived.

Seth saw the opportunity and grabbed at the silence. "What's going on, Sara? Why won't you talk to me?"

Agitated and stalling for time, Sara looked at him blankly, then began speaking in sound bites. "Nothing's going on. Just busy. Stressed with this rally. Got to get going, actually."

As she headed for the front door, she said to no one in particular, "Shut the door on your way out. I'll see you all later." Since no one except Seth was listening, she shook her head in irritation and put her hand on the doorknob, wiggling it frantically as it always stuck. Seth was in front of her in seconds, just as Sara freed the door open. Holding her by both shoulders, he blocked her escape.

"I have to go." She didn't look him in the eye and did her best to feign control.

"You're coming to the sound check, right?"

She wriggled away from his hold, resorting to sound bites again. "Don't think so. Lots to do. Have a good sound check."

He was standing so close to her, too close given the tension between them. She made the mistake of looking into his face, and his eyes locked on hers, simultaneously moving her heart, chipping away at her pretense of disinterest, and challenging her better judgment in her resolve against him. She could tell he knew he was in serious trouble, and that it was plaguing her.

"I was thinking that maybe we could hang out here together later." He bit his lip. "You know, talk?"

She reminded herself that he was a lying junkie. Tearing her eyes away, she fiddled with the doorknob. "Not tonight."

When she looked back up at him, he wedged himself between the silence again.

"At the fundraiser tonight then?"

When she said she didn't know if she'd be able to make it, Seth screwed up his face in bewilderment. "You're the organizer."

Sara, fumbling around for the right words, reached for her hair, tangling a clump of strands around a finger so tightly she felt a pull on the follicles. Foolishly, she'd left yet another space for him to slip in a final question.

"Did you talk with Marco?"

Thinking quickly, Sara decided that, rather than dredge up the real reason for her hurt, she could use Marco's explanation of Seth's bedroom behavior as a scapegoat to explain her aloofness toward him. She went for it.

"You should've told me about your…weird sexual proclivities yourself."

Code for: *You should have told me about your drug use.*

"You could've been more transparent about it."

Code again: *Transparent about using everything.*

"I suppose it says something about your age, really. You probably just didn't know how to be a big boy about it."

She could see he was numbed, rendered speechless by her acerbic tone. Her own discomfort being so great, Sara didn't even try to make it easy for him. Rather, marveling at her newfound ability to humiliate him with such panache, Sara believed she'd finally bought time to slip away as he reeled from her attack. For some inexplicable reason, however, she forced herself into the silence this time, using the full weight of her anger at him.

"And what made you think it'd sound better coming from Marco? Of all people."

The barbed tone now appeared to have him rooted to the spot, stock-still, ironically now looking like he was the one about to march out the door. He managed to find a voice, although one so soft and broken that it alarmed her.

"I just thought since you trust him and he's the expert on DIY, you'd feel more comfortable, safe to ask all the questions I knew you'd have."

"I don't care," she said unconvincingly, trying to sound more impatient than angry and heartbroken. "I think the DIY stuff is the least of your problems anyway."

"So, what are my bigger problems, then?"

Sara just waved her arm at him, saying with frustration, "If I get chance, I'll talk to you later." And she marched out the door, swinging it closed behind her.

chapter nineteen

As Sara returned to her table with Tom at Marcello's, she was still trying to decide whether to attend the fundraiser or not.

"Are you all right?" Tom asked her, handing her a menu. She took it, although she'd already consulted it online. "You've been to the bathroom twice in the last ten minutes."

"I feel awful," Sara told him, pretending to be interested in the menu. "I should know better than to take antibiotics on an empty stomach."

Tom's apparent oblivion with her eating disorder was impressive. He was either clueless or he just didn't care. Either way, it was refreshing not to be hounded.

He never asked why she had an empty stomach or what she'd eat to feel better. These were the questions she would've expected from Jane, Marco, and Seth, but not Tom.

While Tom ate dinner and Sara drank three glasses of wine paired with a plate full of organic, locally grown spinach, she felt faint. Having increased her restricting in the past few weeks, she felt faint most of the day, every day. The rest of the time she was just hungry. Tonight, it was made worse by the fact she had deliberately not included a power bar in her bag.

"Are we going then?" he'd been asking all night, this time, as they paid the bill at 10pm. She knew he was dreading the fundraiser, and thought it was more than enough that he'd agreed to be at the rally, but he wanted to know the plan, and her ambiguity visibly annoyed him more. When she finally made up her mind to go, Tom grew sullen. While this would usually have bothered her, she reasoned that there were worse things, like being with a junkie.

Sara had accepted that activism was not Tom's method for achieving change. He didn't have enough angst in him. Born into wealth and privilege, he'd never developed an appetite for righteous indignation. His agreement to go despite his lack of interest gave her reason to reward his thoughtfulness and she offered a reprieve from the fundraiser.

"You really don't mind if I don't go?" Tom asked with relief.

Knowing the club would be an affront to Tom, she smiled and shook her head.

The club, with its giant murals of naked men in various stages of sexual arousal, the music, which could always be heard blocks away, and the abundance of gay men doing what gay men do when they're in a safe place, would only add to his dismay over Sara's political agenda.

When the cab pulled up to the club around 10:30, people were still lined up around the corner, trying to pay their $150 donation to get in. Sara was really glad for those three glasses of wine she'd nervously guzzled at dinner. She knew her agitation had not been lost on Tom; his suspicion was aroused but he didn't press it, she supposed out of relief that he could go home and drink one of his single malts or pricey bottles of wine while reading the *Economist*. She kissed Tom distractedly in the cab, dropping her bag twice before struggling, repeatedly, to open the cab door. He withdrew from her.

"What is it about Seth Coles that brings out every ounce of dizzy energy in you?"

She stalled for time, scoffing at the very suggestion. "Don't be so silly," she said, to convince herself as much as Tom that Seth Coles had never brought out any such school-girl nonsense in her comportment. She motioned her hand at him as if she were swatting flies. "I'm just nervous about the event, honest Tom."

She knew she shouldn't try to articulate anything more right now. In her present state of minor drunkenness, if she risked rambling it would prove his anxieties were accurate or, at least, not completely baseless. Then there was the small matter that her attempts to quell Tom's fears would tumble out of her mouth as infeasible lies.

Clearly her response had been convincing enough because Tom was kissing her slowly and holding onto her like he really wanted her to go home to bed with him. However, the combination of the UTI-induced sex embargo and the nervousness Sara was feeling about seeing Seth kept her usually lively libido at bay. She pulled away, saying she really had to make an appearance as the organizer and that she wouldn't be too long. One a.m. at the latest. Given that Tom knew sex was out of the question for the next week, Sara thought his willingness to mew around her bedroom waiting for her to come home was a sweet gesture.

Once inside the club, she scanned the room. Jane was talking with Allyson and Callum at the bar. Before she could reach them, she was intercepted by Marco. He grabbed her by the arm with a bit too much force and, to her horror, steered her away from her friends and straight toward Seth.

Faced with the presence of Seth and all that wine swaying in her, the UTI suddenly had no impact on her libido at all. Her resolve began to blow away like a dandelion clock in a hurricane. Her determination fought to keep firm as she tried to hold onto all the reasons why she wanted to end this with him, although, with her libido and her present state of inebriation, it was a losing fight.

Marco practically tossed her toward Seth. She'd never seen him look so pissed off. "Talk to each other," he demanded over his shoulder as he stomped off.

While Sara was surly about being put in this situation by Marco, she could see that Seth was not happy about it either.

He made a stab at civility, picking up a beer and extending it toward her. "I've got four. Take one, please."

Taking several swigs of the beer to both fill the silence and avoid conversation, the bottle turned out to be a poor occupation as it was almost empty after only a few minutes.

"Why do you have four beers?" Sara asked, stalling with small talk.

"People just keep buying me beer. As you know, I don't really drink, but apparently they don't know that."

Taking one last swig that finished off the beer, Sara said, "I'd better go and mingle, although being social is the last thing I want to do."

"There's a chanting meditation going on upstairs if you'd prefer that. It's Eyva and Caleb's thing now. Chanting."

"I suppose they're doing it to cope with their guilt. You know, from selling out, and all that."

Seth laughed.

She decided, since she was here and drunk-ish, she might as well go for it. "Better than the other escape option, I suppose." She turned her full gaze on him.

"What's that?" From the stony glare he gave her, he'd probably already guessed the answer.

Calmly, Sara put down the empty beer bottle. "The junkie, wasted, druggie option." To send home the point, she locked eyes with him before she walked away, relieved that he didn't follow her.

Marco didn't leave Seth's side all night and actively avoided her. She guessed he was moping because she'd upset his precious boy. She decided not to worry about it. She'd known him long enough that any damage to their relationship was repairable. Marco was sympathetic to her feelings, she knew that, despite the fact he'd chosen to abandon her for this occasion. While she missed his humor in the midst of all the hackneyed mingling, it was a hardship worth enduring if it meant that he kept Seth at a distance from her.

Engaged in banal conversation most of the night, Sara listened with disinterest to the buzz about the band. To her horror, she learned from one source that the band had released three music videos. It made her sad to think that some of the most amazing songs were now immortalized in such a way. And, according to Allyson, they were planning to make more. Allyson began droning on about one song that was soaring up the charts. Sara said she didn't know it.

Falling uncharacteristically quiet, Allyson shot a look at Callum, clearly a shared secret.

"It's a very sexy love song," Allyson offered. "There's all this stuff about how he can't get enough of her head. I bet that's a metaphor." She raised her eyebrows at the innuendo while child-ishly nudging Callum. "And how her radical commitment to social change turns him on. I wonder who he's talking about? Do you know? Hmm? You, maybe?"

Sara mocked humor at Allyson's conclusion. When she opened her mouth to respond, Allyson cut her off, apparently not finished spelling out the details.

Sara's cheeks burned as panic coursed through every cell in her body. Completely rattled, she desperately tried to present herself as only mildly interested in the details. Since faking it appeared to be her forte tonight, she tackled this one with aplomb.

"With references like 'head' and 'turned on,' the song could be just as much about drugs as sex or love," Sara said, adding she thought there was a good chance that they'd misunderstood the song altogether. She went on to tell them that, since they were in love, they subsequently expected the rest of the world to be feeling the same. "It's just a song," she said, although her heart pounded in her chest as she said it. Whether this song was about her or not, it certainly had people suspecting. Callum was a student of hers again this semester, and apparently, he was convinced that she'd seduced a heroin-addicted student. And maybe Wellesley would be convinced of it too. Maybe they would drag Callum to her tribunal, as well as *Rolling Stone*. Sara began to spiral fast and furious, imagining how it would play out in the national press:

> Sara Wolfe, college professor and Wellesley Fellow, loses everything after admitting to engaging in a bizarre sexual tryst with a heroin-addicted former student.

Seth appeared by her side with his shadow, Marco. She wanted to confront him about the song, about how it compromised her, and how mad she was at him for everything. Drawing on any last sober thought she had left, she decided instead to shoot him one of her well-practiced I'm-pissed-with-you-please-leave-me-alone looks.

Judging by his posture and ability to make eye contact with anyone or anything but her, she quickly realized he'd been brought to her side under duress by Marco. But he managed to congratulate her on the book news, still avoiding eye contact and keeping a physical distance. Reeling under the influence of all that wine, two beers, and half a strawberry martini, she couldn't tell if he was being nice or sarcastic.

She mumbled, "Thanks," and they fell into another awkward silence.

Marco broke the silence. "Speaking of drunk..." Which, of course, they weren't, but Sara guessed he was suggesting something about her behavior. She could feel the room spinning.

When Eyva walked up, Seth, seemingly biding his time in Sara's company, took it as his cue to escape. Mumbling something about needing to see Caleb, he trudged off as Eyva loudly proclaimed how "blissed out" she was after chanting and meditating for hours.

Apparently, the noxious noise and the odorous smell of alcohol were interfering with Eyva's *bliss*. Despite this, she soon became engrossed in conversation with Marco. Sara was horrified as she listened to them giggling together about Seth's six-hundred-dollar jeans and one-thousand-dollar sneakers.

"I bought him the jeans for a laugh, really," Eyva said. "You know, just because I could. And he enjoys the irony of wearing them with that hemp-string belt."

While she was afraid to hear any more of this talk about excess, Sara couldn't resist listening.

"And you know those black worn-out laces from his converse sneakers? He wears those with his one-thousand-dollar sneakers to be ironic too." More laughing.

"Disgusting," Sara declared. "All that money on clothes."

Smiling back at her, Marco playfully said, "Shut up, Ms. Designer-fucking-jeans."

Sara felt sadder by the minute, both with Marco's point that she really wasn't one to criticize and because she was feeling very ill from the unbalanced ratio of alcohol to food.

Utterly doused in her bliss, Eyva went on to tell Marco and Sara about the band's sold-out European tour scheduled for September. As if that wasn't enough to convince Sara that they'd all made a pact with the devil, plans were also underway for a world tour that winter. Yet, despite her disgust, Sara still couldn't help but feel concern for Seth. Not unlike the *New York Times* reporter that had interviewed him, she wondered how he would cope with all the excess.

Seeing the opportunity to leave, Sara offered the slightly less blissed-out Eyva her couch for the night.

As soon as Eyva left them to say her goodbyes, Marco made a spectacle of Sara's departure, pulling her aside in full earshot of Seth, who had returned with yet more free drinks in hand.

"Have you eaten anything?" he asked Sara.

When she just shrugged, Marco became irate and grabbed Sara by the arm to put some pressure on a real response. Out of the corner of her eye, she saw Seth's body tighten. It was beyond his comfort too, but as if unable to stop himself, he stepped in.

"Back off, Marco."

"Did you know she's so thin she doesn't get her period anymore?" Marco's face was red with exasperation as he delivered his news like Sara was no longer standing right beside him, despite his hand still gripping her arm.

Seth's countenance remained unchanged. Staring at Marco, hardly believing what she had heard him announce, she barked, "Thanks for sharing that bit of news with the world. Just so you know, I did get my period, as you call it! And you are absolutely, positively no longer an honorary girl."

"What?" Marco's said, perplexed.

Sara was incredulous. "Girls don't talk about their bleeding like that in front of straight men."

"Why not?" Seth injected himself into the conversation.

Sara suddenly recalled his complete comfort in New York with her tampons strewn all around. She hoped he'd forgotten about that because it did ruin her point.

"Take Tom," she said, guessing Marco had already filled him in on that too. "He's completely male about bleeding. He's so uncomfortable with any mention of it." She was about to complain about men in general and Tom in particular, but stopped herself, realizing she'd played right into his hands by saying something negative about Tom.

She quickly corrected her representation in her own head. Dear Tom, who at this very moment was turning down the sheets and drinking tea in her bed while he graded midterm exams and prepared his application for the summer fellowship in Italy. Tom, who raved about her body and, now that she'd lost twenty-five pounds, would have sex with her even when she was bleeding. Even though he did it begrudgingly, it was still sort of sweet. When Sara realized she'd been standing there thinking these thoughts while Marco and Seth patiently looked on, waiting for her to finish her point, she collected herself.

"I've had too much to drink to talk this much. You two carry on."

"My company excluded, right?" Marco said. "I mean, unlike straight men who don't recognize their White privilege, like Tom, I don't find your bleeding icky."

Sara hoped he was done, but she knew he was bitter about her retraction of his honorary girl status.

He stared at her and went on. "We've chatted about your flow. The extent of your cramps."

Sara picked up one of Seth's free drinks and averted her eyes, letting Marco know he should shut up. The drink, which was clear and tasted a little like gin, was putrid.

"What the hell is this?" she asked Seth.

Taking the drink from her, he said he didn't know, so she probably shouldn't drink it. He then dove back to his point. "Why are you encouraging gender games? What other topics can't we talk about together?"

With this, Sara immediately recognized her profound attraction to him. He was irresistible to her precisely because he could walk the talk. She had to work extra hard to disengage from him to resist being pulled in. Her earlier fragment of determination was diminishing into a shadow lurking down a dark corridor, fading away. *He's a junkie*, she reminded herself, but drunk, she added: *a cute, kindred-spirit sort of junkie.*

Of course, Marco knew Seth's mind turned her on, and she could hear his laughter at her speechlessness. She composed herself enough to remind him.

"Privileged, straight men are all about controlling nature, not being connected with it, like women. Different cultures. Different lives."

"Don't be so essentialist. You don't believe that different cultures shit," Seth jeered.

Sara closed her eyes to avoid his because it was interfering with her mantra: *he's a junkie.*

Marco became her unwitting assistant, ending the party when he turned to Seth to ironically say, "Wouldn't you love to see Sara turned on?"

Instinctively, she knew Marco was making a junkie reference, not a sexual one. "Are you wasted, Marco?"

The question rendered Marco speechless. Everyone knew that if Marco was wasted, it reflected on Seth too.

Seth, who had momentarily closed his eyes with Marco's comment to Sara, looked as though he was preparing himself for the fallout. Opening his eyes, he met Sara's glare. He exhaled heavily.

"Are you high too?" she asked him, noticing Marco slink away, leaving them to it. He shook his head.

"Did you get Marco high tonight? Turn him on?" It infuriated her that he just stood frozen to the spot, staring at her. She could see he was calculating his response, planning the damage control, but it was too late for that now.

"You won't answer me?" She shook her head at him. "You've never answered any of my questions about your..." Her voice shaking, she broke off and began to walk away. Before she took two steps, Seth caught her by the arm.

"I did get Marco some...stuff."

"What stuff did you get him?"

When he told her it was heroin, she was startled by the enormity of both her rage and sadness. She charged away from him.

Seth caught up with her before she left the club, and she could see that he was as taken aback at the firmness of his hold on her. It was so insistent, so determined, she couldn't get away from him.

"Let's talk outside."

Noticing the audience they were drawing, Sara consented.

Once outside, she backed away from him and headed for one of the expectantly waiting taxis that were lining the block outside the club.

Catching her by the arm right before she stepped into the cab, he said, "Sara, please. Can we talk?"

As a burst of cold spring air filled her lungs, Sara felt awake.

Exhausted from avoiding the inevitable conversation for so long, she spoke in a flood of emotion.

"Yes, let's talk. I don't appreciate your lack of transparency about your drug use. I don't like that you've been turning on my friends. I don't like that you're writing songs about me that are exposing me to rumors, making me vulnerable. I don't like that you mutilate your body. I don't appreciate that you couldn't talk to me about your sexual...scene. And then..." She looked up at him, breaking off as his eyes fixed on her. She felt herself weaken, so quickly averted her eyes.

She was about to address the one transgression that could never sway her from her purpose. It wasn't that all his other issues were anemic next to it, but rather, like his inability to be open with her about his drug use, this issue was a barrier that was impermeable. Whereas the other problems could be worked through, this could not. "That life you once led before all this rock star crap, before you tethered yourself to capitalism and making a buck..." she began accusingly. "You asked me if you thought you might be able to work from within to create change."

He looked so anxious to hear her verdict that Sara felt wary of heaping one more thing onto him, but she'd already started now.

"I don't think it can work. You're working in a system that, just in order to preserve itself, keeps working to depoliticize your art and reduce you to fame. You owe it to these causes, like the rally, to be involved. You have a responsibility to participate now. All, the same," she said in a flurry, "it's not lost on me the effort it took to get yourselves and all your gear up here. I'm incredibly grateful to you for it, but let's just let things go, okay?"

Seth looked shaken with her final assessment of it. He managed to choke up some words, "Let what go, specifically?"

Sara waved a hand between them. "This. Us. Maybe we can eventually be friends again. Maybe."

Expecting an acknowledgment from him, an acceptance of her assessment of the situation, Sara waited a moment. When she didn't get anything from him, she tried to pull away from his hand, which still held firmly on to her arm.

"Please let me go."

He did so immediately.

She got into the cab. As it pulled away, it struck her that she had forgotten all about Eyva and the offer of her couch for the night.

chapter twenty

Standing backstage with Tom, Sara was struck by the band's comfort with the attention that greeted them as they took to the stage. Even Tom, who sat on the floor with a newspaper, was captivated. From the audience's tremulous applause to the giant-sized cameras maneuvered by small trucks, and handheld cameras with lenses the size of large pot lids carried by overweight men who followed Seth's every move, it was all jaw-dropping stuff.

Gripped as she was by the scene on the stage, Sara tried to resist being introspective, to push from her mind what loomed between them, not to mention the curve ball of Tom being there by her side. She'd planned this event with Seth's band in mind for months, and Tom was the last person with whom she'd expected to be sharing the day with.

The first song over, Seth backed away from the microphone, giving the stage over to Eyva. She was visually enthralling in her frilly nightdress, knee-high bovver boots, teased hair and heavy, smeared make-up. Sara noticed Tom watching her curiously.

"Why does she have the word 'slut' written on her arm?"

Sara was pleased with his interest. "She's being deliberately binary."

Tom shook his head in disbelief, looking at Eyva curiously.

"She's making a statement, Tom. It's clever." Sara tried to help him understand. "She's putting opposites together. Coupling girly sweet with tough, hard, whore-girl edges."

Tom looked at Sara like she was speaking in tongues.

Sara noticed Eyva and Seth were wearing matching bandages on their arms. The sudden stab of jealousy as she wondered if they'd spent the night together disgusted her. After all, Sara had broken up with him. He might be reaching out to Eyva for commiseration. She felt miserable as she worked hard to keep the images of them together from ping-ponging through her mind. They'd probably been doing things together that she did with Tom. That idea was dismissed as quickly as it arrived, however, because she guessed Seth found penetrative sex incredibly dull, passé. And, since Catherine MacKinnon herself had referred to the behavior as an inherently violent act, Sara briefly considered that maybe she should refrain from it too. It was an idle thought, knowing as she did that it was more likely that she'd renounce Catherine MacKinnon before she would become abstinent.

Eyva stood in front of the microphone. "Capitalism leads to patriarchy, which leads to rape." She waited for the din to die down. When it didn't, she turned to Seth, the rock-audience whisperer, motioning for help. After he approached her, whispering something in her ear that made her laugh, she tried again. As if she'd enchanted them now, they quieted down immediately when she spoke.

Speaking with just the perfect hint of anger, Eyva told the audience, "Women around the world have the right to live without fear of violence in their lives. As they walk down the street, as they just simply exist in their own homes."

The crowd, apparently in gratitude at hearing their indignation spoken so prominently in a public place, erupted into applause. When it died down, Eyva went on with her lecture.

"This is especially to the men in the audience and all the men listening and watching on social media. Recognize your role in the oppression of women locally and globally. Think about what you say, what you look at online, in movies, in magazines. Don't be culpable in that oppression."

Sara suspected that the only people applauding at this were women and Marco, but feeling Jane's hand in hers, Sara felt her bottom lip tremble with emotion.

Eyva's own voice broke with feeling as she screamed, "Hey Massachusetts girls! Take back the night!"

At that, Seth's guitar drowned out the applause.

It was all too emotional for Sara and Jane, who cried and hugged. It was apparently all too much for Tom as well. He looked completely stunned by it all. Sara was sure nothing had astounded him more than Eyva's assertion that capitalism was linked to rape.

Seeing the contortion of horror on Tom's face, Sara prepared herself for the full wrath of his indignation, the litany of questions, but instead, she felt his mouth brush suggestively against her ear.

"She sounds just like you," he whispered.

For that, she kissed him slow and long because, not only had he pleasantly surprised her, but he'd also called a truce to their perennial disagreement about the relationship between capitalism and patriarchy. After she withdrew from him, she was mortified to see Seth watching them. He quickly looked away.

While the show was becoming increasingly frantic, it appeared Sara's display brought on Seth's nihilistic abandon just that bit sooner. An angry ferocity gripping his face, Seth whipped off his guitar and, after what could only be described as a simulated fucking between one of the speakers and the neck of his guitar, he hurled it with an almighty thrust into the air. While the audience erupted in their approval of his destruction of somebody else's property, Seth next turned it on himself. Hurling his body around the stage and into equipment, he was lost to everything now, including the cameramen and the microphone, even guitar playing. Since this behavior had also whipped the audience into their own frenzy, Sara was more understanding of the police's concerns about public safety. She fully appreciated why they'd demanded back-up forces, especially now that she believed it might be necessary to help quell the burgeoning riot.

It all looked very rock and roll.

Sara turned to Tom, encouraged by their moment earlier. "Nifty," she said.

Tom shook his head. "You would never guess he had so much angst. He's always been so quiet in all my encounters with him."

"And very sweet too," Sara added, berating herself instantly for both the thought and the comment. She passed it off as a result of the intensity of the moment.

Watching him now, as he directed all his energy into destroying yet another guitar, smashing it over and over again into one of the speakers, Sara rolled her eyes at the stark contradiction with the word "sweet."

With sweat coursing through his hair and down his face, he'd become overheated and removed his T-shirt to wipe his face. His stomach was tracked with gashes. Tom's reaction helped affirm this was not normal.

"This is contrived, right? It's all a performance—part of his act?"

Sara assured him that it wasn't. "It's an experience, not a performance for Seth. And the cuts are real."

Tom looked stunned.

"Marco says it's art," she offered, fishing for Tom's response.

"He would say that."

Trying to convince herself more than Tom, she tried to explain it again, but Tom was completely fixated on Seth, who was pulling himself up from a prostrate position on the stage. Taking a fresh guitar from a crew member, he motioned to Caleb. Eyva and Caleb apparently understood the silent signal; they nodded. Caleb put down his drumsticks and lit a cigarette. Seth began playing acoustic, mellowing. It indicated a transition in the show, and Sara began to anticipate the shift to the ending phenomenon that she'd been reading about.

The press called it "The Bacchantes Finale Phenomenon"—a mini riot unwittingly incited by Seth at the end of each show, apparently the result of his unpredictable behavior. According to all the best music journalists, if Seth became increasingly nihilistic, he tended to take the audience over the edge with him, putting the fear of God into security as the audience staged what the music press were calling a "rock coup d'état."

Sara could sense the building excitement in the audience, and it was making her uneasy, edgy. All the signs were there that Seth was feeling only mildly vexed, but when he suddenly threw himself down on the stage in that knee-thrust motion that always made her wince, they had their answer.

Like a scene from Ancient Rome, a reign of chaos (with all the attendant violence and blood), Seth unleashed himself, concentrating all his energy on self-destruction. With his guitar swung over his back, he climbed onto a high piece of the set. Holding onto a piece of pipe just above his head, Seth smiled down on the wildly excited audience that was now coaxing him to jump. At first, the look on his face was one of assessment, deciding if this was a good idea after all, but then he leaped. While he sailed through the air at speed toward the outstretched arms thirty feet below, Sara held her breath and looked away. When she heard the audience's reaction, Sara allowed herself a peek, figuring he was probably still alive.

As he was carried aloft by the audience in what looked like relative gentleness, security went into action. About half of them dove into the crowd to rescue him. The rest were split between standing there, not quite knowing how to manage the scene, or grabbing and clinging onto any of Seth's reachable limbs.

Sara was struck by Seth's calm, his implicit trust in the fans, who returned him crowd-surfing style to the stage minus his guitar, which had been ripped from his badly groped body. When he waved to the fans and left the stage, Sara thought she'd never seen him so angry or bloody at a show before.

* * *

Lying in bed the next morning with Tom, she felt dizzy, almost faint, and very nauseous.

"Sorry," she managed to mutter to Tom, who was kissing her, his hands between her legs, as she dove out of bed and charged into the bathroom. Despite her valiant effort to get there in time, she missed the toilet and threw up on the bathroom floor.

"Fuck," Sara exclaimed, watching the tiny pool of bile that had been the contents of her stomach seeping into the grout on the tiled floor. Tom's useless inquiry from the bed only added to her irritation, but not even this could interfere with her elevated mood, which Sara attributed to that magical combination of Prozac and the phenomenal success of the rally. Take Back the Night had raked in more money in one day than the combined total of twenty years of the rally's history.

After cleaning the floor, Sara walked into the bedroom

announcing she was hungry. Tom showed himself to be even more useless by asking her how she could be hungry after she just threw up.

She plodded through to the kitchen to look for the lowest calorie, lowest fat food choice she possessed. She stood in the pantry, eyeing the cereal boxes and reading the carbohydrate, calorie, and fat columns like her life depended on them. She once had them memorized, but since she was barely eating anymore, she needed a quick review.

"You'll get fat eating outside of mealtimes. Come back to bed," Tom called.

Sara put the cereal box back on the shelf. Her sides ached so much with hunger, she changed her mind again and guiltily grabbed a small handful.

It was dry and stale. Sara cried while she ate, angry she couldn't control her hunger and sad for her aching body. And then she cried some more, thinking of Seth and his cutting.

Feeling considerably fatter, but better, she climbed back into bed with Tom. No sooner had she snuggled up in his arms, Sara shot out of bed again, this time overcome with the urgency to pee.

"Where are you going now?" Tom sulked.

Sara was in agony. Barely able to make it to the bathroom, her sides were aching with hunger and now whimpering with the pain of trying to pee.

Sitting on the toilet, crying softly, she scolded herself for being so drunk the night before that she'd shirked her doctor's no-sex-for-a-week order. In her drunken state, she'd convinced herself that this piece of medical advice was probably only a recommendation and that four days of antibiotics was surely ample time for recovery and a return to comfortable, pain-free sex. As she cried, it also occurred to her that Tom had not shown any concern or objection as he'd slipped into her.

Barely able to pee without screaming, Sara thought she'd have to see the doctor right away. Since it was Saturday, it would have to be the emergency clinic at the university, which would be packed with panic-stricken students who were there for the morning-after pill after a Friday night's excess. As she began to groan at the thought of spending the entire morning waiting in line, a victim of her own excess, she heard a faint knocking on her front door.

Sara scraped herself out of the bathroom. She thought she could feel her heart giving out at the sight of Seth and Marco just as Tom called out, "How's the peeing working out?"

Rolling her eyes at what they both just heard, Sara reluctantly invited them in.

Unable to think of any reason why Seth would be there after everything between them, Sara couldn't keep the dismay from showing on her face. Marco was clearly pained to be there himself under these circumstances, and Sara observed him register both her discomfort and Seth's as he quickly stumbled over an explanation.

"We'll be quick." He motioned to Seth. "He's got to get to the airport. We're just here to pick up some gear left here the other day."

Marco pushed past her, calling over his shoulder to Seth that he'd help him with the gear. No doubt in haste to avoid being alone with her, Seth took off in a virtual jog after Marco, rounding the corner into her kitchen at such speed that he almost knocked Tom out when he met him coming around the other side.

When Sara observed Seth's sharp intake of breath, she wondered which had provoked it—the body slam or the close proximity of Tom. Seeing them side-by-side, Sara was struck by the physical differences between them. They were both about the same height, but with several days of hair growth on Seth's face, his shoulder-length, unkempt hair, his uniform of jeans with the hemp-string belt, and his baggy, holey T-shirt, Seth was the anti-Tom.

Even though there was every sign that Tom had spent the night with her, from the T-shirt and shorts that he'd clearly slept in, to the bedhead, he still managed to personify GQ Boy. With his clean-shaven face, his clean-cut, almost orderly bedhead, smelling of cologne even at nine in the morning, wearing his fashionable shorts and Harvard University T-shirt, he represented the anti-Seth.

When Tom touched Seth's arm in a manly gesture of apology, Sara could see that the bulk of the discomfort was Seth's. Apologizing profusely but unable to look him in the eye, Seth recoiled from Tom's touch as though he had a fatal communicable disease. Taking a stab at civility, Tom offered everyone coffee, but to Sara's great relief they made their excuses, only hanging around for a few minutes to be sociable.

Having the two of them in the same room together, with Seth actually attempting to respond to Tom's small talk while staring at the floor, was too much for Sara. She shot a beseeching look at Marco, hoping it begged, screamed "save me." Thankfully, Marco noticed her look of desperation and, grabbing Seth's arm, tried to whisk him away. Seth resisted the tug and stood firm to the spot. Sara caught Tom's eye and knew he'd noticed the fleeting look she'd exchanged with Seth.

Still, she had to try to communicate everything in the three-second silence that stood between them before he left. She mouthed, "I'm sorry," and she really was sorry. Sorry, but she couldn't be with a junkie or someone who worked for The Man, mutilated his body, and was into sexualities she didn't understand.

She knew it was particularly cruel to do this to him right in front of Tom. She could see that he resented being put in this situation of pretense. Seth, the antithesis of pretension, tore his gaze away first, responding to her sorry with nothing.

She could see he thought he meant nothing to her and, knowing full well that she was so much to him, she could almost feel the horns growing out of her head. She wished everyone else could see them too because then it would lend visible evidence for her wickedness.

"I can't help it. As you can see from these," she would say, pointing to the horns and giving a helpless shrug, "being malevolent is in my nature."

Sara knew she had every good reason to be doing this, but not knowing when, or even if, they would see each other again, she wanted to just touch him, to hug him before he left. However, he'd already walked off. He was in the car now and driving away. Out of sight. Gone. The look on his face as he left haunted her, leaving Sara with a torturous desolation that ached from her toes to her chest. The pain of the UTI was insignificant to this, comparable to a soothing hot cup of tea by the fire at her favorite café. Yes, given the choice, Sara believed she would welcome a lifetime of painful peeing to spare her this.

Panic engulfed her as she realized she didn't understand this visceral physical reaction. Was this just sadness at having hurt him? Her conscience pricking a nerve? Or despite knowing he was too flawed, was this about him leaving?

As she stood there, frozen to the spot with the door wide open to the rainy, cold spring day, Tom asked her the question that changed things.

"What's going on there?" He nervously rubbed the back of his neck.

Still reeling from everything that had happened in the space of half an hour, she responded absently. "What?"

"You and him. What's going on, Sara?"

Shaking her head resignedly, aware of a hammering ache in the back of her neck signaling an imminent migraine, she told the truth. "Nothing. Nothing anymore."

Sara did consider that it might be important to add that nothing had happened when they were together, but she didn't. After all, she guessed that, since Tom would be so flabbergasted to learn that she'd associated in such a way with someone like Seth, Rocker Boy, he would dump her anyway.

Tom shifted his weight and gave a heavy sigh. "Anymore?"

Now that she'd said it, Sara knew that it was over. This was going to be one of those times she should go back to bed with the intent of staying there for as long as it took for it to be over. She had a clinging hope that, if she slept long enough, she'd be handed a reprieve from wallowing in the mess she'd created—with Tom, with Seth—permitting her to skip the repercussions altogether. No migraine, no involuntary sobbing or encroaching bleak perspective causing her to despise happy people and be apathetic in her personal hygiene, because why clean your teeth just so you can die with a beautiful smile? Especially when Sara knew she'd never smile again anyway.

Tom prompted her again, but this time with more agitation than impatience. "What does that mean?"

"I slept with him a couple of times. That's all," she said too idly, before realizing that she'd misspoken, causing Tom's jaw to become slack with shock. "Not sex. Just sleep. No sex at all." She wobbled her head side-to-side. "And some kissing and..." She trailed off, grasping around in her throbbing head for evidence of intelligent life, but it was pointless. She couldn't even form a word, much less whole sentences, and an explanation was further away than Seth would be by tomorrow.

Overwhelmed with what had transpired in a matter of minutes, first with Seth and now with Tom, Sara felt a few drizzly tears tip from her eyes quickly becoming a deluge, coming down so fast that her hands were operating like inadequate windshield wipers. As Tom stood in front of her, indignation and anger gripping his face, Sara knew this wouldn't clear up. He was not only expecting her to throw together a clump of words, he wanted a clear explanation. And he deserved one.

With her windshield-wiper hands gaining momentum against the storm of tears that smeared her blotchy face, she took a deep breath as she rummaged around her head again for an explanation. Surpassing her own expectations, Sara managed to dig out a few pertinent verbs, careful to avoid any unnecessary adjectives.

"No sex. Just kissing. And a stroking thing he's into, but no sex."

He didn't say anything, but his body language and facial expression were screaming anger and confusion. For fear of saying something even more incriminating, such as "and I think I'm in love with him," she rambled incoherently, repeating the same verbs over and over to fill the excruciating silence.

When Tom finally jumped in, Sara fell silent, grateful for the interruption.

"Stroking what?"

Sara was exhausted with her flailing efforts to communicate anything effectively and feeling terrible because, while she finally admitted to herself that she didn't actually want to want to be with Tom, he wasn't a bad guy.

"Tom, I think I need a break from boyfriends for a little while."

If he'd looked sad, she probably would've reversed her position completely. Instead, he looked utterly pissed as he tore off, collecting all his things from around her apartment. Beginning to rant as he passed her in the hallway, he told her that she was welcome to Rocker Boy, that he would find some gorgeous Italian woman while he was on his fellowship in Italy, and that she'd commiserate with him over having wasted a year of his life with *her*. She could see through the bluster; he was upset. Recognizing this as she did, she really should have kept quiet and let him rage. However, she was in real pain now from the inability to pee, and in response to Tom's disrespect toward her, toward Seth, Jane, and Marco, and as a result of the hammering sensation pulsing through her head, she spoke out of turn.

"You're so…male."

Tom stopped, aghast. "I *am* fucking male. What the fuck am I supposed to be?"

"Less male. That'd be a good start."

Dressed and having gathered his things, Tom stood at the door. "And how should I begin to do that?"

"Be more female. Think about others before yourself. Think about 'taking care of' rather than 'taking from.' Learn to listen."

Without responding, Tom walked out the door, closing it quietly behind him. Sara opened it again and slammed it for effect. Then she sat down on the floor and cried—for Seth, for Tom, for herself. For the first time since she could remember, she was without a boyfriend and, much to her dismay, she was scared.

* * *

"I broke up with him," Sara said into the phone to Jane.

Jane sounded pleased. "Tom? Again?"

Sara was startled to hear Tom's name, because she'd been thinking only of Seth. "Both of them, actually."

Jane was over in fifteen minutes.

"I'm so hungry. I haven't eaten anything except an eggcup full of cereal," Sara told Jane, who busily rummaged around trying to find something in her refrigerator. It was almost bare because what was the point in having food when you didn't eat?

Jane handed her an apple. "Only eighty-five calories and no fat, but seriously, it's one o'clock in the afternoon, so why haven't you eaten anything?"

Sara shrugged. "Seth. Tom."

Knowing Jane wanted her to make a commitment to her no-men-or-sex prescription, Sara paused thoughtfully for a moment, considering the enormity of that particular task while she took a bite of the apple.

Given the current emotional frailty on top of rigid restricting, the drinking, and her latest obsession—editing like a crazed person—the idea of being boyfriend-less was really more than she could manage.

Jane's eye on her, she took another bite of apple, then tossed it into the compost bin. In the midst of her crisis, she knew Jane accepted her unwillingness to bend on her other destructive behaviors right now and especially appreciated it as she considered what she was about to say out loud.

"Marco says I'm a strong woman but deeply flawed."

"He's a strong woman, deeply flawed. Did you mention that to him?"

Sara spoke earnestly, letting Jane know this wasn't a time for joking. "I'd be a little less deeply flawed if I took a break. And that's what I'm going to do. Be by myself. No boyfriends. Officially. On the record." To cover herself, because she didn't know how successful she would be in this endeavor, Sara made the timeline parameters vague. "For a bit, of course. Not forever."

chapter twenty-one

Two weeks into her man embargo, Sara was standing in line for coffee at Wellesley's student union with two acclaimed scholars. Sara caught sight of a student reading a magazine with a picture of Seth emblazoned across the cover. The headline almost stopped her heart.

BACCHANTES FRONT MAN IN STORMY RELATIONSHIP WITH WELLESLEY FELLOW.

Doing a double take, Sara saw there was a picture of her with a caption: "Love in the classroom."

Sara desperately scanned the magazine stand, and there she was again. That one, which featured her showdown with Seth at the taxi stand the night of the fundraiser, was beyond damming. There was no way she could have looked less like a professor—in her sparkly strapless top, designer jeans, and Manolo Blahnik's—and very evidently drunk.

She was stunned. While the news from that night had been gossip fodder around town, it had never even made it into the campus journal. Ironically, however, it had been widely circulated around the world. Sara saw her Wellesley career imploding.

Frozen to the spot, sputtering like an idiot, her turn to be served at the counter had come but, instead of ordering coffee, she blurted, "I don't fucking believe this" within earshot of the two superstar feminists who had accompanied her to get coffee.

One of them responded to her expletive. "Any of it true?" she said, picking up the magazine and beginning to flip through the pages.

Sara recoiled as she watched her rifle through *Hello Magazine*, stopping at a full-page spread with a blow-up picture of that infamous night.

"Is it true he's a heroin addict?"

Sara smacked her hand across her mouth to save a little moan from emanating too loudly, as Icon Feminist Number one tutted with empathy. "Poor sod."

Sara tried to sound blithe. "I suppose this will get me fired."

"What?" Icon Number One looked perplexed with the question. "Why do you say that?"

"The decency clause."

"Oh psh." She laughed, batting her hand at the very idea of it, before she re-joined Icon Number Two in speed-reading the article. "Wellesley seems to attract badass feminists. Take Clara," she said, motioning to Icon Number Two. "She's been before the dean for public drunkenness more than once." The two chortled at this.

Sara reeled with disbelief. *Could this be true?* she thought. *Did one of my idols just say my concerns are immaterial?*

"Great music. The feminist polemics are on point," said Icon Number One, tearing herself away from the article for a second. "And it says here that you nurtured this."

"It says you're his 'feminist guru.' Hysterical," said Clara. "And I quote, 'The most complex woman he's ever known.'"

"It does?" Sara said, trying to read over their shoulders.

"Wonderful stuff. The students here are obsessed with it."

In the whirlwind week of lectures and colloquia, a meet and greet before she would officially join Wellesley in the fall, Sara had noticed Seth-obsessed students everywhere; his music blared from every dorm room window, and student after student wore T-shirts with Seth's face emblazoned across them.

"They were so excited when we hired you. They think you're *awesome*," said Icon Number Two, inflecting on young people's overuse of that word.

Icon Number One chimed in. "We'd have a coup on our hands if we hadn't hired you. And as for the stupid decency clause, the dean would get banished before they'd let her even bring you up on a hearing, let alone fire you."

Icon Number Two concurred. "Truth be told, the faculty loved it too. We wanted to hire a scholar-cum-activist. A PhD, but someone working within the mainstream to promote change. Turning the sell-out on its head. Being all Audre Lorde, using the master's tools and all that. Clever. Inspiring stuff."

The exquisite irony.

Sara walked to her car in a fog, noticing a few students pointing at her. She waved. One of them called out a few lines from Seth's song "Binary" as if it was poetry. As if it was Audre Lorde. Sara continued walking but threw her head over her shoulder to smile at them. They reminded her of Allyson. Full of angst. Enough to be silly and yet believe it revolutionary. She covered her mouth as a little burst of laughter erupted from a happy, joyous place.

She got to her car, then drove to a parking lot off campus and sobbed with exhaustion from the rollercoaster of emotion. Exhaustion from the pressure of Wellesley, wondering if she really was good enough. Exhaustion from her hunger. It was too much irony for one lifetime, let alone ten minutes.

Arriving back home for a dinner out to celebrate her week at Wellesley, Sara felt trepidation at the thought of being around Marco and his incessant chatter about Seth. It was hard enough to be committed to her man embargo, and these near-constant updates about Seth's daily movements only served to impede her from moving on. She wanted so much to tell him about the magazines and the ironic twist, but she held off, knowing it would invite more Seth updates that she wasn't ready to navigate right now.

She settled on her other pressing piece of news—the intellectual and emotional pressure that was Wellesley. Marco responded in his characteristic fem-style speak, encouraged by Drew's presence and complete with squeals of joy, gasps, tag questions, and affirming comments to everything Sara said.

He clapped his hands together. "You belong in that community. They're going to be so glad they took you in."

Anxious at the weighty expectations of everyone, she wrung her hands. "What if they discover I have nothing to say?"

"Sara, they're endorsing you on the strength of the research you did for the book," Jane encouraged while Marco nodded. With the mention of her book jolting her back to her strict editing schedule, Sara panicked at the realization that she hadn't edited in twenty-four hours.

"My editing's ahead of schedule."

"Of course it is," Marco said. "Do you ever do anything else?"

After dumping two men in the space of twenty-four hours, Sara had thrown herself into editing. It served as a respite, keeping her from wallowing in the melancholy of her man embargo. She much preferred editing than turning her purple correction pen on herself, and she approached the task with the same gravitas that she had previously reserved for her eating disorder.

Her other obligations—lecturing, the WRC, her therapy, listening to the Anoraks' latest record on her iPhone at the gym, because ninety-eight pounds just wasn't thin enough anymore—were all just a time sink that she resented.

As usual, she drank more than she ate, and Drew, not having been coached in such matters, confronted her. "That's not dinner. Those are vegetables and alcohol."

When Drew looked confusedly at Jane and her desperate nonverbal signals for him to stop, Sara, attempting to divert his attack, ran off to the loo.

Once safely locked in a bathroom stall, Sara reflected on how lousy she felt. In fact, this described how she'd felt all week. Just a few nights before, suddenly feeling faint from hunger while she was at a party given in her honor, Sara needed to politely extract herself from a gaggle of eminent scholars. One moment she was engrossed in conversation with some of the most inspirational thinkers that would ever be known to humankind, and the next she was sitting on the floor in a public bathroom stall, enveloped by an all-consuming sense of despair that she couldn't explain. Sara had wept and wailed like a veritable banshee, stopping only when a bout of hunger-induced nausea engulfed her completely and she heaved into the toilet bowl.

When she returned, a silence fell over the table. It was obvious they'd been talking about her.

Marco smiled sympathetically and patted the seat beside him. "Come and sit by me."

Just when the atmosphere at the table had shifted away from an energy so negative it could produce a tension headache, Marco brought up the band.

"I spoke to Jeff Evers today."

Despite Jane's penetrating glare, Drew's anxious wriggle at the mention of Jeff, and Sara's heavy sigh, Marco's capacity to turn the conversation toward Seth was unstoppable. While everyone knew about Sara's commitment to her man embargo, her tenacity couldn't have been clearer when she pleaded with Marco.

"Listen, I'll eat dessert *if* we could please not talk about Jeff, *etc...*"

It raised everyone's eyebrows. Sara batted her hand at them like she was swatting a flying bug because they didn't know the truth. They wouldn't be so in awe if they knew that being boyfriend-less felt like an insurmountable task, more painful than cutting back on alcohol and restricting combined.

Marco ignored her request. "I miss Seth," he whined, slumping his chin into both hands. Drew patted his hand in comfort.

Jane immediately picked up the dessert menu, cleared her throat, and started to read aloud.

"These new boys in the Men's Circle...ugh," Marco complained, despite Jane's attempts to swerve the conversation. "Seth set the bar too high and now the Circle is ruined for me forever."

Sara realized Seth had also set the bar too high for Tom or for any man she would date after him. Even thinking of him as a junkie didn't put her back on track or temper her searing regret. No matter how great her efforts to put Seth to the very back of her mind, there was always something—a book, a smell, a place—that brought him racing to her full consciousness.

"I miss him too," Sara said.

Even that night in the bathroom stall at Wellesley, her thoughts had settled on Seth. Sitting on the floor feeling faint, a panic setting in because she didn't have a protein bar, she raked through her list of permitted foods, trying to remember which of these were present on the banquet table in the other room, when she had been flooded with a reluctant memory of Seth helping her through exactly one of these moments.

There she was at Wellesley, in the company of women whose

work she'd been reading and admiring for years, and now they were hanging on *her* words, inviting *her* to speak at their historic symposium, expressing their interest to work alongside *her*. And lying on that bathroom floor, thinking about Seth, all she felt was gutted and raw. Anomie. She'd expected too much from Wellesley, from publishing. Neither would make her well. The instant feelings of glorious happiness she'd expected to obtain were fleeting.

Marco tutted and grasped at a chance to talk about Seth and the band. Drew, wary of any talk that might bring up Jeff's name, bluntly returned to the topic of dessert, coaxing Sara to pick something.

Jane, equally eager to move on, pointed to a dessert on the menu called Chocolate Beast, suggesting with enthusiasm, "I'll split it with you."

Marco continued anyway. "Apparently Eyva is dating the tour manager, who has the unlikely name of Bass and, equally as improbable, he's a Janeist. He has her so blissed out that I'm worried for her. I mean, she's got to be having some serious problems getting angry enough for those shows."

Drew joined in, happy Jeff was no longer the topic of discussion. "I bet she's scrawling 'namaste,' 'blissed out,' and 'goddess' on her body now."

Everyone laughed in all the appropriate places, while Sara considered if she could afford to eat a spoonful of a dessert to please Jane, who eyed her hopefully.

"Remember Clair from the Anoraks?" Marco piped in between the laughing.

Believing the query indicated the tide had turned away from the band, Sara joined in. "Of course," she happily declared. Knowing they were on tour supporting the Bacchantes, she added, "How's the tour going for her?"

Marco looked contemplative for a moment. "Sounds like it's going well. Jeff says that Clair and the drummer from Jane's Malady, ironically also known as Bass—as if there could be two people in the world so disadvantageously named—are doing a pretty good job of getting Seth fucked up every night."

Everyone knew the dinner was over then.

"Okay," Drew started, turning to Marco to speak in a whisper that wasn't audible to Sara.

"Call him," Marco pleaded, obviously satisfied that his dramatic delivery of the information had done its job and clearly not deterred by whatever it was that Drew cautioned.

"He really needs a good friend right now. And he's been a good friend to you."

Sara couldn't deny that. And she almost hated him for it.

chapter twenty-two

Ultimately, Sara agreed with Marco. She did owe Seth something, if for no other reason than to honor the profound friendship they'd fostered. Marco had told her that Seth was impossible to reach by cell, so she should text him, email him, anything but call him. It startled her when he answered on the first ring.

Uncertain how to behave after all that had happened between them, Sara tried to speak to him in pleasantries. He did the same and the conversation was cringingly awkward, coming out in great dollops, then drying up.

"I hope you know I'm your friend," Sara tried.

"Of course. And I'm yours too."

Worried that might open it up to talk about something that really mattered, such as the way she'd treated him, Sara stammered, "I... just want you to know that I'm here for you. As a friend, I mean." She winced at the banal cliché. "That's what friends are for."

They used to talk every day, and it had never been like this. This was painful, and since apparently neither of them knew how to progress the conversation, Sara tried to get off the phone quickly.

Seth finally let her off the hook. "I'll let you get back to it."

Sara was so distraught at how the call had gone so badly, she'd almost hung up without responding.

After saying goodbye, Sara sat for twenty minutes, just staring at the floor. To cheer herself, she threw herself back into her editing.

Three hours later, she was still engrossed, ignoring the ringing phone until she heard Seth's voice on her machine. Almost killing herself sliding across the floor to pick it up, she said breathlessly into the phone, "Seth, I'm here."

"I just talked with Marco, and he's coming on the tour with us for a couple of days, and I was wondering if…as a…good friend, you would want to come too? With Marco?" He dropped his voice to a softer, quieter tone and added, "It'd be really good to see you."

* * *

That night, while Sara made springtime margaritas in her apartment for Marco and Drew, who, she had noticed, were now inseparable, Marco revealed that Seth had called him, completely perplexed and looking for advice after their weird phone conversation.

"I had to do a lot of repair work for you. Apparently, you used the word 'friend' about forty times in the space of five minutes. I had to convince him your intentions were good, that you were reaching out—albeit incredibly ineptly—and he should call you back."

While Drew was laughing at Sara's ineptitude, he was stopped short by the mention again of Jeff Evers's name.

"Jeff called me again today," Marco said. "He's so pleased I'm going out to see them."

Drew demanded to know precisely why Jeff Evers was calling Marco so often, and *why* he was so desperate for him to join them.

Sara knew this was torturing Drew, but she couldn't help herself. "Well, it's spring. The time when the non-DIY sexuality man's fancy turns to fucking."

Marco laughed uproariously. "Your sense of humor about that is coming along nicely. Proud of you."

Sara smiled mordantly, her sex-free existence made all the more miserable by Marco's chock-a-block, sex-full life.

"Come with me?" Marco held his hands in supplication.

Drew was begging too. "And save Marco from himself while you're there."

"I'll need all the help there is."

She knew he said it with the explicit purpose of drawing a groan from Drew, but—with great trepidation and apprehension at the thought of seeing Seth—she agreed to go. How she would feel or behave around him after their last encounter felt like a mystery she wasn't sure she wanted solved.

* * *

Standing in an empty stadium in San Francisco, facing a stage where Seth and the rest of the band were running through a sound check, Sara was still unable to believe she'd acquiesced to join Marco.

Her sense of disquiet was amplified by this unreal world of sensory overload. The sound and light checks, booming disembodied voices speaking directly to Seth about acoustics, volume, vocals, and Seth's voice back to them was intense. When Seth saw them, he interrupted Sara's sensory attack. Grabbing her hand, Marco marched her onto the stage.

Seth hugged him and Sara was overcome with gratification that these two people whom she cared so much for had each other. Tears pricked her eyes. In complete contrast, she was not surprised at Seth's edginess as he greeted her. Hugging her briefly, he moved away so quickly that Sara noticed almost everyone cringe as they tried not to watch, pretending to carry on their respective conversations when they were really all discombobulated by Sara and Seth's graceless display.

Standing around like unwitting voyeurs, checking watches, staring at the floor, orchestrating a cacophony of throat clearing and sudden small talk, the onlookers became an unwilling audience of a poorly staged theater show. Seth turned away from her and busied himself with the repositioning of his guitars. Sara was forgiving; his behavior said much more about his distress in this situation than anything else, but it disconcerted her that Seth didn't take his eyes off her while she chatted with the others.

Sara spied Marco and Jeff hiding at the corner of the stage, practically making out. She shook her head in exasperation. "Drew has charged me with the impossible task of keeping Marco out of Jeff's bed for three whole days."

"Good luck with that," Caleb called out.

Seth smiled as he strolled over. "That's not such a big job. He's a flirt, yeah, but nothing more."

Shooting him a look of incredulity, Eyva offered her support to Sara. "I think you're going to need help. Look at him."

They all looked over at Marco, who was standing in front of Jeff, stroking his chest.

"He's been here five minutes and already he's a cock tease," Eyva declared.

At that, Sara called them over to join the rest of them. Marco and Jeff slowly sauntered over hand-in-hand.

Seth turned to Sara. "He won't fuck up. He's too much in love. He told me as much."

It wasn't an easy conversation, but at least they were speaking.

"But in love with whom?" Eyva called out as Seth grabbed Jeff by the arm and led him away from everyone.

"Drew," Seth and Marco mouthed simultaneously. Sara couldn't help but grin.

Marco fell into easy conversation about dinner with Eyva and Caleb, but Sara watched Seth talking with Jeff off to the side before they joined the rest of the group again.

Sara tried to get out of dinner with her practiced excuses: lack of hunger, jet

lag.

Seth whispered to her. "Just come, you don't have to eat. They won't notice."

She felt a renewed interest in dinner. The company and the wine list would keep her occupied for ages.

When they got there and the waiter appeared, Sara did have a moment's panic. The seating arrangements were unfortunate. For obvious reasons, she'd placed herself between Jeff and Marco, but this made little sense now when she needed an ally who would help her to order nothing without anyone noticing. When Seth motioned to Sara to sit beside him, she was there before he'd finished pulling up a chair for her.

Sara ate a baleful of spinach and drank a bottle of wine. She was relieved to know that Seth had been right that, with the exception of him and Marco, no one noticed that she ate nothing.

After dinner, Sara prepared to attend the show but passed out backstage before it all began. As she came around, pleading with

Marco to keep her collapse a secret from Seth until after the show, Sara was attended to by the tour's physician.

The poor doctor, on tour with a bunch of heroin-abusing rockers, had taken one look at Sara's wasted-looking frame and assumed drug abuse rather than anorexia. Caught in a paradigm warp, unable to see any behavior other than through a druggie lens, she said to Sara, "What did you take and when?"

Sara was relieved when she woke up in her hotel room with Marco by her side. He relayed the entire drama to her with so much expression that even in her weakest condition to date, she found herself smiling.

Apparently, the doctor had wanted Sara admitted for observation. Marco suspected her lucky escape was owing to his suggestion that she slip Sara a few electrolytes instead, which made the doctor perk up, probably with relief to engage in an act that resembled real doctor-like duties rather than all the detox paperwork that had taken up her time on the tour.

After the show, Seth came straight to the room Sara and Marco were sharing. He exhaled heavily when he saw her and flopped down prostrate on Marco's bed.

"We saw some of the show from the room," Sara told him.

Seth didn't seem interested in talking about the show. He rolled onto his side to give her a penetrative once over. "You look a bit peaky, but okay."

Sara couldn't say the same for him. His pallor was almost white. Noticing the fresh bandages on both his arms, she wondered if it might be due to blood loss, exhaustion, drugs, or perhaps the combination of all three.

"Tell me about how the tour's going," she said, returning his shrewd gaze.

"I hate it," he started to say, not moving from his position next to a sleeping Marco. "I've never felt so…"

"Anomie? Fucked?" Sara said understandingly.

They both raised their eyebrows, remembering the same foreboding conversation they'd had in New York.

"You gave me plenty of warning about selling out," he said, acknowledging all her cautioning.

Sara raised a hand to stop him. "Hang on. You're misunderstanding. I'm not asking so I can scold you yet again. I'm asking because I'm concerned about you."

He looked stunned with her shift. Sara tweaked a smile, trying to convince him. Given how harsh she'd been about it in the past, she guessed he neither knew what to make of this turn, nor whether to dare to respond and ruin the effect of what she'd said. This was Seth's life now, only amplified by orders of magnitude. Sara, having been rendered emotionally spastic over the rally, was in awe of his composure in the throes of it all.

Sara, shivering from cold, prompted a shiver in Seth.

"Come over here," she said, patting her bed.

The very suggestion brought a momentary flicker to his face that Sara read as uncertainty.

"I really want to talk with you about this. And you're cold." She patted the bed again. "Get under here and get warm."

Sitting bolt upright in her bed, and as far away from Sara as possible, Seth poured out all his misgivings about the sell-out. With Sara's encouragement, he told her that he hated the audiences' adoration and expectations of him, the impudence of reporters who pried into his personal life, the music press and their depoliticizing of his songs, and the controlling record label encroaching into everything, including the brutal tour schedule.

In mutual agreement, they talked about how contracts with corporations who were only invested in making money rather than supporting art could only serve to disease both the product and the creators. Listening to him talk about the process, about how the show had become a performance, no longer an experience, confirmed what she'd always suspected: excessive profit destroys artistry.

It made her worry for him all the more.

Beginning to feel uncomfortable with the protracted silence that hung between them, she nudged him. "I hope you're not expecting to find a resolution to your existential crisis tonight."

It made him smile slightly. Sara debated where to go next—drugs, self-mutilation, bizarre sexual fixations—none of which were insubstantial topics. Knowing she had to pass gingerly about his alienated, delicate soul, she started with what she thought was an innocuous comment.

"I want to thank you for rescuing Marco from Jeff. What did you say?"

"I told Jeff to back off." Looking straight at her, clearly making a point about fidelity, he added, "And then I told him that Marco's just flirting, not really interested in anything more because he's in love with Drew, so not good company."

"Drew's concerned that Marco'll give into the temptation of Jeff. He thinks he needs to do some bad boy stuff so that he can start writing again," Sara informed him.

Seth shot a look at Sara. "Marco's not writing? He has to write to live."

"I think Drew's worried being in love is ruining his writing."

"Dark, brooding, broken hearts produce the kind of existential angst that can become the basis for the best writing, although not good company."

"I hear Clair's been good company for you."

She honestly hadn't been fishing for information about his love life, just innocently waiting for a prime moment to discuss his drug use and Clair's support of it. *No more, no less*, Sara told herself, while a little voice in her head knew she cared too much for it to be as meaningless as she told herself it was.

Seth was silent.

"Are you...with her?" *All right, maybe a little fishing.*

Seth almost incurred whiplash spinning his head around so fast to glare at her.

Sara shook her head vigorously. "Forget it. Don't answer that," she said before he had enough time to even open his mouth. "None of my business at all," she added, thinking this approach was wrong on account of a couple of truths she had remembered. First, she was taking a break from men, and second, this tack was not the way to be a good friend. A friend who was planning a one-to-one intervention of sorts.

Another heavy silence descended on the room, like a nor'easter before the snow falls. An attempt to regain her image as a "good friend" and not jealous high-school ex-girlfriend, Sara tried again. This time with better intentions and a renewed verve of directness.

"Marco heard that Clair's been, and I'm only quoting here, 'getting you fucked up every night.'"

When she was met with another stony silence, she was infuriated by the stonewall reaction. "If you really want me to be your friend...you absolutely must talk to me."

Seth rubbed his face with his hands, hiding.

"I've asked so many questions, so many times, and you've managed to evade everyone." Sara noticed her hysterical pitch and her wildly flapping arms as she poured out her litany of worries. Exhausted from animating her anger and worry so physically, she was somewhat relieved when Seth grabbed at her flailing arms and, holding them down, made soothing noises.

Seth spoke nervously. "I'll answer your questions."

Sara had never seen him so tense. Unable to look at her, he fixed his gaze on his hands, biting at his bottom lip and exhaling heavily at his false starts. Beginning to speak, he'd break off and repeat the whole process again multiple times before finally becoming coherent.

"I take Rohypnol, roofie, after shows as a downer. When we don't have a show, I cook junk. I always have iron." Sara must have looked lost because he stopped to explain the druggy colloquialism. "Sorry, heroin and crack cocaine. And I take a few different amphetamines." He stopped, shook his head side-to-side, clearly considering something. "And sometimes barbiturates, although I rarely do that anymore, and so they don't really count, but in the interest of full disclosure, I thought I should mention that."

Too stunned to speak, Sara was relieved when he continued, working his way through the year of unanswered questions. The list was so ridiculously long, she couldn't even remember most of the drugs he'd mentioned. His matter-of-fact manner, as if he were telling her about his favorite ice-cream flavors, distressed her.

"The New Year's Eve party? No, not mine." After exhaling heavily yet again, he was finally able to look at her. "What else was it? How often, how much, right?"

Sara nodded, and he returned his gaze to his hands.

"Every day," he said. "As much as it takes."

When he looked at her again, as if to confirm he was done, it was Sara's turn to look away. She was revolted and scared by the image of him with a tourniquet wrapped taut around his arm as he tried to locate a nice vein or being so wasted he was unconscious. She considered that, since this was as much a part of his persona as the part he'd exposed to her, she barely knew him at all. She was paralyzed by a swell of conflicting feelings. Terror and fear were replaced with an all-encompassing sense of sadness and protectiveness.

Staggered momentarily, she didn't realize that a flood of tears was blinding her, forcing her to mop at her face with her shirt sleeves. To her horror, Sara felt her nose was running liberally too. Seth handed her a box of hotel tissues, but he still didn't speak. They both knew that anything he said at this point would be cold comfort.

Fuck the tissues. Instead, Sara wiped away at the extremely unattractive mess on her face with her hands. She recognized the spiral into misery, and she willingly climbed into that well that stripped her of all sense of proportion. Her ability to reason, to speak, let alone describe how she was feeling, were all drowning with her.

Her capacity for resignation and apathy about the human condition increased exponentially as she considered, since there were more questions about the origins of the universe than could be answered in the time that was left for human life on earth, that they were all going to die anyway, that all life on earth would eventually dry up, in the scheme of things, why even bother with tissues? Did snot really matter?

Seth's voice shook her from her thoughts. "What are you thinking?"

In the middle of her misery spiral, Sara was struck by his concern for her. He'd asked about her wellbeing when she thought the concern should all be for him. A dawning lucid moment amidst all this incoherence stirred in her, and she saw with clarity what Jane and Marco had seen all along.

Her problems were no different than Seth's.

They were both completely self-destructive, both self-harming. After listening to him describe feelings that she believed to be anomie, she saw herself in that bathroom stall at Wellesley when she'd been drowning in a sense of displacement and alienation. Bottom line, attaining success had no more fulfilled him than it had her.

Sara was moved enough to reach out to hold his hand. Given

that she was still busy wiping her nose on her other hand, hooked up to an IV, fully clothed and sitting several feet away from him, it seemed like a safe, non-romantic move that solidified her offer of friendship. While resting his head against the headboard, Seth turned to look at her for a moment before taking her offered hand.

"Okay?" he asked.

She wasn't okay at all, of course, but she knew his query was only a cursory check-in, intended to ensure that she was still breathing.

* * *

They must have finally fallen asleep while still holding hands because, when Sara awoke, it was morning and Marco and the tour doctor were standing over them. Seth shot out of her bed fast, as though he'd just learned it was infested.

While the doctor examined Sara, adding yet another bag of electrolytes to the IV tube, she watched Marco studying Seth's discomposure, his smirk signaling he presumed Seth's twitchy nervousness was an attempt to mask libidinal energy. Sara watched the slow drip of the IV fluid, thinking: *As if, in our state.*

"How are your arms, Seth?" Sara asked. As she hoped, the doctor insisted on looking at them, despite Seth's objections. His arms were a mess, the worst Sara had ever seen them.

The doctor bandaged his arms again. "Remember, no heroin when you're taking antibiotics."

Seth nodded, his face turning crimson from the mention of heroin in front of her, or so Sara assumed. The doctor said she would check in later and left.

Marco, observing Seth bandaged up like a mummy and Sara pasty pale, hooked up to her IV, declared loudly, "What a mess." He then further traumatized Sara when he looked straight at her to add, "Time to eat. Again."

* * *

Agonizing over how to navigate the next meal with everyone, Sara placed herself between Seth and Caleb. She was relieved to see that it was just the band and Marco this morning. Unlike last night, there was no entourage from the record label and no Anoraks girls present.

Given her new knowledge about Seth's other self, a doppel-gänger that was completely unknown to her, she was amazed at how good she was feeling. She guessed it might be attributable to the constant dripping bag of electrolytes or maybe even the energy radiating from the perpetually blissed-out Eyva, mixed with her feeling of relief at Seth's openness.

Sara knew from her twelve years studying human behavior for her Ph.D that honesty is virtually a human right. No matter the incomprehensible, horrific, visceral agony of it, everyone expects and deserves it.

You shall know the truth, and the truth shall set you free. *Was that the Bible or Karl Marx?* she pondered, moving three pieces of cantaloupe around on her plate. To conflate Marx and the Bible was ironic, she thought, allowing the distraction to keep her occupied while everyone talked about food.

As lost in her own thoughts as she was, it took the mention of the word *drugs*, so laden for her now, to rouse her from her thoughts. While it was evident to Sara that she'd entered the conver-sation midway through, she re-entered just in time to hear Eyva declare, "Who needs drugs when you can be blissed out?"

Sara snapped her head around to look at Seth, checking for his reaction to this news, but didn't notice any shift in his behavior. Everything he tasted or looked at, anything he said or did was viewed through the prism of a diagnosis—druggie. She watched Seth notice her hypervigilance. From his glare, she could see he knew precisely why she was watching him.

When Eyva got up to leave, saying she'd been invited to a chant downtown, and Caleb asked some esoteric questions about it that Sara didn't understand, Marco proposed the idea that Sara give a little seminar to those who weren't going to the chant.

Jeff received this idea with great enthusiasm. "You should join us on the tour. Teach us how to politicize our personal experiences."

Sara laughed at the excited chatter, enjoying this representation of herself as a feminist-to-go, but mostly she remained distracted by Seth's every move. When Marco suggested that she could be the tour's feminist guru, Sara noticed Seth bristle. Since his behaviors were always so understated, the reaction would have easily slipped by if she wasn't so focused on her scrutiny of him. Sara hadn't overlooked a blink without making note of it, let alone this display of irritation.

Eyva and Caleb said their goodbyes, and Sara managed to keep her eye on Seth, wondering about his umbrage over the guru comment.

When he looked over at her, catching her watching him again, he leaned over and whispered in her ear. "What's up?"

In the interest of privacy, Sara leaned over to him, feeling him shiver as she unwittingly brushed her mouth against his ear. "Are you on anything right now?"

Seth huffed with intense irritation at the question, settling his gaze on his hands in his lap. "When I'm around you, no, never. I couldn't manage to speed or be narcoleptic on rophy and be with you at the same time." He looked right at her. "Can you stop checking me every five fucking seconds for signs of shivering or whatever else it is you're looking for?"

Sara could only manage a nod of compliance because that sudden truth had left her embarrassed. She hadn't been consciously aware that she was dissecting Seth's every move for evidence of drug use, and yet the same scrutiny of her behaviors around food infuriated her. It was patronizing when people analyzed her restricting. These people, who thought they were superior to her, to Seth, preoccupied themselves with condescending questions: *Is she hungry? Will she or won't she eat? Should I tell her to eat or just suggest she eat? Should I tell her she's too thin?* Unlike everyone else, Seth did not see her through the prism of her diagnosis, so she made up her mind not see him through the lens of his.

Marco and Jeff stared at Sara and Seth from the other end of the table, observing their hushed voices.

"Do you two want to hang out with us? Or do you have other plans?" Marco said loudly, startling them out of their private conversation.

Sara shrugged begrudgingly. Her chaperoning gig was exhausting, and all she really wanted was some time alone with her editing.

Seeming to read her mind, Seth offered to go along instead so she could work. "You should get some rest, too," he suggested. "That way, maybe you can make it to one of our shows before you leave."

* * *

Under doctor's orders, Sara went to bed for more rest instead of the show. After it, Seth and Marco came to join her. While Sara worked her way through the fantastic bottle of wine Seth had bought for her while he'd been chaperoning Marco and Jeff downtown, he asked her how her editing was going. Marco, still in writer's block, decided he couldn't listen, let alone participate in that conversation.

"I'll just take a walk and see if Jeff wants to do something."

Not wanting to be alone with Seth, and suspecting Marco would end up in Jeff's bed, Sara changed course. "It's one a.m. What are you planning to do with Jeff at this time?"

"It's San Francisco, not Amherst. Maybe a club?"

Since he was now virtually passed out on Marco's bed, Sara had to nudge Seth several times to bring him to a state of semi-alertness. "What do you think? Do we need to go with him?" She really didn't want to go out. She snapped. "I was hooked up to an IV all night."

To her irritation, this only made Marco laugh. Sara was exhausted with managing Marco's libido, especially now that she had no support from Seth, who'd already fallen asleep again.

"Oh, just go."

After spending twenty minutes in the bathroom primping, Marco kissed her and told her he wished she'd come.

Almost asleep herself, she pointed over to the sleeping Seth and said, "I'm fine, really. And when he wakes up, I'll send him back to his room."

Marco shot to the door, glee all over his face. Seeing his eagerness to meet up with Jeff, Sara suddenly thought of Drew.

"Please try not to completely mess everything up for yourself. Just try to be a good boy, for me and for Drew, and yourself."

* * *

When Seth woke at two a.m. to find her reading Judith Lorber, he was clearly disoriented. Sara, riveted by Lorber and finishing her third glass of wine, couldn't sleep and was glad for the company. If she hadn't been in an alcohol-induced state of disinhibition, she would have been much less audacious in her conversation.

"Seth, people think that 'Other Man' is about me." Her voice came out flattered and silly with too much wine.

Seth appeared instantly wide awake. "If you personalize it, it is about you."

"And are you writing songs about Clair now?"

She thought the question was vague enough. It was possible there may have been some motivation behind it that he hadn't fathomed, something much more profound than jealousy. After all, hadn't she read that he'd said in one of those horrid magazines that she was the most complex woman he'd ever known. But subdued by alcohol as she was, Sara hadn't considered that, having asked her similar questions about Tom, Seth knew the smell of jealousy well, and Sara reeked of it.

"Why would I be writing songs about Clair?"

Sara wasn't expecting this. She stalled for time while she desperately looked around the room, as if expecting the appropriate response to appear from her wine glass or the ceiling.

He smirked, rubbing a hand over his chin. "Do you want to know if I'm with Clair?"

She hoped he wouldn't bask too much in the warmth of being on the other side of this with her. Dignity vanishing in her glass of wine, Sara cast her eyes down. "Well, are you?"

Instead of putting her out of her misery, he asked, "How's Tom?" *Ouch. Touché.*

"It's a fair question," she said.

She hadn't told anyone except Jane about her breakup with Tom. It was just too embarrassing. Off, on, off, and then on, off again.

When she sighed, he rescued her. "I shouldn't have asked."

Given he'd been so utterly transparent with her now, she bravely launched in, intending to face her embarrassment. "He's fine," Sara found herself saying instead. She was stumped as to why she'd offered this bit of useless information on Tom, especially since she had no idea how Tom was doing. "He got a fellowship to Italy," she added. "Will you go too?"

"Me? No, no, no, I'm not going to Italy. Funny. Italy. I mean Italian economics is a bit of a misnomer, right?" She smiled too broadly. "Have they ever had a stable economic system?" Sara snorted with laughter to cover her unease, which was already plainly evident.

Grasping around in her head for more information on Tom that she might have read in the campus journal but hadn't bothered to remember, Sara suddenly became excited as she landed on something else to fill the silence. "He's been appointed chair of his department."

She started to fill in, to evade Seth's original question, rambling on, adding that it was unfortunate that Tom's department was essentially a bastion of paternalistic relations and a keen supporter of capitalist theory. Seth looked suspicious. Sara knew he must be guessing there was something that she wasn't telling him, but he didn't interrupt her.

Feeling like she'd exhausted the subject of Tom, she stopped suddenly. "You didn't answer my question."

He paused, making her sweat it out. "No, I'm not with Clair, although she has been great company."

Sara, not knowing how to interpret the company part, waited for him to expound on it.

"Great company while I've been taking care of my broken heart."

That startled her almost sober.

"She understands what I've been going through." He paused as though his next words were the answer to the world's mysteries. "Because, Sara, she was in love with you when you were studying the Anoraks."

She wasn't sure which was the greater revelation, but all she could repeat in her head was: *Seth is in love with me.*

"So, she understands why I'm so fucked up and want to get fucked up, and so we get wasted on junk together."

Before the words *wasted* and *junk* were uttered, Sara had been salivating at the idea of tumbling into bed with him, despite her vow to be between boys. It was as though one minute she was on the French side of the Euro-tunnel track, hurtling so fast toward experimental sex with Seth and so far away from her commitment to being abstinent, and the next moment incurring whiplash as the breaks slammed on at 180 miles per hour.

Flooded with images of taut tourniquets, needles, and cooked junk injected into the veins of Seth and Clair, Sara felt revulsion.

"You're looking at me like that again. Just like you did earlier when you asked if I was on. Just like people look oddly at you when you say: 'I can't eat that.' That's what I do. I experiment with drugs." He looked down. "With sex too. It's not so unlike you. Restricting is your thing, but you know it's not okay with people. That's why you hide it. That's why I hide my stuff from you."

Sara caught herself. She had told herself just the day before not to see him through a druggie lens anymore, and here she was doing it already. "You're right. Our issues are not different, but what you're doing is more dangerous. My issues won't kill me."

"Yes, they will." He sighed as though he wished that was enough of an argument. "I'm sorry to bring this up because I know you don't like straight boys talking about girls' bleeding, but when I asked our doctor about the long-term effects of amenorrhea, she told me it was pretty bad. You're doing irreparable and permanent damage with the laxatives and all the other stuff you do to your body, so don't tell me what you're doing isn't as dangerous."

While intellectually she realized he was right, she started to argue with him again because she could stop if she wanted to. However, even that thought wasted away like a lone leaf trying to grow on a dead tree, as Sara considered that she only wanted to want to get well. She couldn't stop. She'd learned that much about herself in therapy. She was back on the g-force side of the tunnel again, and she needed to get out to feel safe.

"I'm sorry about your broken heart."

chapter twenty-three

Sara fought to prevent her thoughts from drifting to him but had come back from San Francisco with romantic giddiness. She tried to harness it in front of Jane, knowing her goal was to keep Sara focused on her healing mission, which only partly included remaining single and sex-free.

Jane said with a teasing smile, "How big is this crush you have on him?"

Sara buried her face in her hands to hide her grin. Since she was always so effusive about all things, she knew the fact that she'd said nothing about either the trip or Seth gave her away entirely.

"What is wrong with me?" she beseeched of Jane while they were sitting on the lawn in front of the WRC drinking iced coffees. It was such a perfect spring day, but Sara was a picture of distress. "He fills my head up. I don't need this."

Jane was motivating Sara to stick with the staying-single plan but irritating her with the advice. "Accept that you like him," she said, as if it were just that easy. "Be with it."

At this suggestion, Sara's voice rose so high with aggravation that it caught the attention of people passing by. "I don't want to be with it. I can't stop thinking about him. Even when I'm editing, my thoughts drift to him."

"And?"

Sara recognized Jane's therapy techniques. This one was encouraging her to process out loud to better understand herself. Sara's thoughts weren't any deeper than the next words she blurted out. "God, I think he's so lovely."

"Accept that feeling. You don't have to act on it."

Sara got up to go, finally more amused than irritated. "Shut up. And don't ever use the word 'accept' again in my presence," she said.

Jane stalled her. "I know I shouldn't be encouraging this, but did you hear about the interview he did with Terry Gross?"

* * *

Sara looked up the interview in her office and listened to the Terry Gross podcast episode three times. She could've listened ten more times. She still couldn't believe Seth was making radical feminism sound mainstream, making the everyday political. Terry Gross had understood that Seth's songs were politicizing the personal, even the so-called love songs, and she'd given him full reign in the interview to politicize them.

She was supposed to be healing herself, not falling for some guy, and listening to his voice on the radio podcast was not helpful, but it was nothing compared to the visceral impact of looking up and seeing him, in the flesh, standing in her office.

Seth, so sick from exhaustion that the tour physician had ordered a two-week hiatus, had been resting at a friend's house in Atlanta for the past week. Since Marco's birthday was approaching, he'd arranged to come up for five days.

With Marco by his side, Seth stood in front of her, too close as usual. It had been three weeks since she'd seen him in San Francisco, and the very sight of him—that smile, the sound of his voice— was kale to her soul.

She threw her arms around his neck, and the sensory overload was almost more than her poor little libido could bear. It was like an annoying little child who kept pulling on her mother's skirt, demanding, "Gimme, gimme." The smell and touch of him as he hugged her tightly, the way he looked at her as she slowly pulled away, letting her hands drop from his neck to linger on his shoulders, made her goosey all over.

Sara felt like she deserved some sort of recognition for

restraining herself from lingering longer. Her life history had comprised of a commitment to never being without a male sexual companion and that familiarity battled against her new status as "sans men" continually. It left her afraid to think about men at all. Being unfamiliar with the parameters of playing her new role effectively, she often overstepped it, behaving standoffish and disinterested. On top of that, she was afraid she'd give her strong feeling about Seth away.

She gathered herself. "You look tired."

"I am." He looked down at the floor, then back up at her. "It's good to be here. Good to see you."

Still struck by his pretty grooming, Sara playfully teased him, but she could see that he was so pleased to be home again that he barely noticed. There were other changes too, but the carefully crafted anti-fashion impression of the phony rock-star persona was substantially muted.

She scuffed her foot against his old sneakers. "I can see that you're wearing some of your old stuff."

"I'm not letting those fucking executives touch my hair again."

Marco laughed, touching first Seth's hair, then his stubbly cheek, and finally patting his bottom. "Pretty boy without it, don't you agree?"

Sara only grinned. She thought it was safer not to comment; her role as a single woman still so tenuous she knew she didn't have all her lines down.

As they walked into town together, Sara noticed the attention his famous face drew. He was completely indifferent to it as she walked with him to all his favorite places: the Licker Store for coffee; the Bagelry, where Sara ate her usual baleful of spinach with even more copious amounts of coffee; the Tin Palace, where they met Callum and Allyson for a drink; and then on to the Women's Studies department, where the faculty heralded him as a virtual saint after the interview with Terry Gross.

Dinner at Marco's that night also revolved around that interview, much to Seth's annoyance and everyone else's glee. Despite Seth's attempts to steer the conversation away from himself and toward Sara, who had a review coming out in the *Feminist Press Review* that week, everyone was fixated on the topic of Terry Gross's Fresh Air interview with Seth.

"I loved it when you referred to her as 'Terry,'" Marco said.

"What the fuck was I supposed to call her?" Seth said, and they all had to sit and listen to Marco's litany of lewd suggestions.

Everyone moaned at him, and Marco laughed. "What kind of a fem-identified boy would I be if I didn't have this in my arsenal? That being said, I love her so much I could fuck her."

Drew jumped in amidst the groaning that followed the last piece of his comment. "Speaking of love, how come you didn't tell us about Tom, Sara?"

Sara choked on her drink while shooting a look at Jane for guidance. Jane, her only ally, darted her eyes to the floor, her napkin, her fingernails, offering nothing to save Sara.

Seth leaned over the table. "What about Tom, Drew?"

"He's off to Italy for the year. Said he needed to get away." Drew shook his head uncomprehendingly.

Everyone looked to Sara for clarity. She kept her gaze fixed on Drew, wondering what to say.

"He's having to defer the chair position," Drew went on, much to Sara's utter misery. "What I was wondering, Sara, is what man would want to get away when he has a girlfriend of your ilk to keep him here?"

Unsure of what to say, Sara kept silent while trying to look busy pouring herself another drink and shooting a pleading look for help to the dumbstruck Jane.

"Fucking obtuse, straight, White boy," Marco chimed in with an answer.

Just when she'd begun to believe that Jane was not going to rescue her, fiddling as she was with her fork, her bracelet, anything to avoid redirecting this thread of conversation, Jane leaped in. "I love Italy. All that pesto on everything." A feeble attempt to change the subject, which Sara noticed made even Jane roll her eyes.

But it did the trick, as Marco joined in. "All those Italian men." Now Drew was rolling his eyes. "Stop," Marco said to Drew, slapping him playfully on the knee before leaning over to kiss him on the lips. "Haven't I made it clear that you are my kindred spirit? My one true love?" he said dramatically.

Sara was impressed with Jane's clever ploy to shift the focus to travel. It was not enough of a deterrent for Drew, however.

He tore his gaze away from the intensely swooning Marco to say, "I, for one, am glad he's going. As chair, he'd be fearsome, but I expect you know what he's like."

Jane looked at her helplessly. Sara realized she had no choice but to sweat it out, captive to whatever was about to happen.

"I've never known anyone so ambitious, so driven. He just brought in the biggest grant our department has ever seen."

"Too bad that doesn't show up in bed. Right, Sara?"

Sara shot Marco a sharp look. While they were accustomed to talking together about their sex lives, they had a strict, unspoken agreement to talk about it with one another, not in company.

Embarrassed, wondering what Seth was making of all this, Sara looked at him out of the corner of her eye. Mortified that he caught her watching him, she swiftly darted her gaze elsewhere, but not before noticing the smirk brewing on his face.

Jane tried to sway the conversation again. "Well, I just want to say that I can't wait to read your review in the *Feminist Press Review*. Can you believe it?"

It made Sara nervous just thinking about it.

Seth jumped on the new topic. "Have they given you any idea what to expect?"

Sara took several big gulps of her fruity cocktail. "Rumor has it that it's not bad. Anyway, it's only FPR. Not like getting an interview with Terry Gross."

While everyone started talking at once in response to minimizing such a hotly coveted review, Seth summed it up. "I would stab Eyva to death to get reviewed in FPR."

"But Eyva would love that," Marco teased.

Sara knew she was annoying everyone with her inferiority complex, but she pressed her point. "*Terry Gross*, Seth. You interviewed with Terry Gross, not some obscure press."

"I'll admit it's been the absolute highlight. Beyond any amount of pleasure I've gotten on this whole sell-out trip."

Jane, who'd listened to the interview live, said she was so pleased to hear someone talking on the radio about gender and sexuality from a feminist perspective.

"I've had a nineteen-year-old girl in my office every day this week," she said somberly.

Everyone looked at Jane, waiting to be brought to their knees. Jane told them what they all expected to hear—a tragedy.

"She gets drunk, wasted, and she ends up in bed with whomever she was hanging out with that night. Her total value is in who will have sex with her."

Sara, unable to control her feeling of connection with this girl, let out a small guttural moan. "This is a girl without sexual agency," she said, perhaps trying to subconsciously separate herself from the similarities between her and the conversation. "After rape, it's understandable that a girl struggles to know intimacy with anyone who has a penis. Sex with a man becomes something that is hard, fast, mean. With the exception of the great sensation of a cock deep in your cunt, as unfeeling as possible."

After saying it, Sara realized that, except for Jane and Marco who knew her well enough to expect her words, she had stunned everyone into silence.

Seth's mouth was actually agape, Drew looked horrified, but Marco was almost amused. "On the positive side then, there's the cock-in-the-cunt sensation to look forward to. That's something, isn't it?"

When a smile broke out on Sara's face, Seth and Drew joined in. She immediately and completely forgave him for turning a painful topic into satire because, after all, if you didn't laugh, the only other choice was to stab yourself to death.

Sara, knowing any conversation pertaining to sexuality theory intrigued Seth, turned to him in professor mode. "How do you think gender norms are connected with sexuality?"

Seth only shrugged though, suggesting that she was the better person to answer that question on such an obviously sensitive topic.

Sara's voice began a crescendo into lecture pitch. "Living in a culture that operates through hegemonic femininity, women cannot experience sexual agency…"

Sara realized that Seth was the only one really listening, but she went on anyway.

Marco turned to Drew, loudly informing him so that everyone could hear, "This is foreplay for these two."

Seth and Sara shot mutual looks of disapproval.

Marco laughed. "Don't be so fucking disingenuous, you two." Despite Sara's scowl, Marco continued to needle them relentlessly because he was never to be put down by opposition when he knew he had a truth that needed to be told. "You two need to get a room and put everyone out of their misery of having to watch this performance. Do something, Agency Girl," he said playfully, but then threw in for fair warning, "or I'll have to say something that will seriously embarrass the two of you."

"I don't think you could say much more to embarrass us," Seth said bitingly, but playfully.

"Don't challenge him," Sara warned. "You know as well as I do he's not even using his real powers yet."

Marco beamed.

Sara was grateful for Jane's support when she jumped in, swerving the conversation back to the point. "I really like your new song, 'Desire,'" she said to Seth. "Now that's a song about female sexual agency."

When everyone began to ask him what he was writing, Sara noticed Seth shifting in his chair like the seat was covered with sharp objects, completely uncomfortable with all the attention on him.

He shrugged. "Mostly poetry."

Marco immediately took the bait, and a conversation about poetry lasted the rest of the dinner.

* * *

After dinner, sitting on the lawn swatting mosquitos into the early hours of the morning, Drew and Marco said they were going to bed. Sara didn't think anything of this until she noticed a look exchanged between Jane and Marco, and then Jane suddenly claimed to be tired, too.

"Good idea, Jane," Marco said, congratulating her on her wise choice. "After all, we might not get to sleep at all tomorrow night," he added, reminding them all that the following day was his party, when they would all be going to Boston to celebrate at Queer Choice, Marco's favorite gay club.

Not knowing how to handle this abrupt en masse exit that appeared to be contrived, Sara sat stoically on the grass beside Seth while everyone feigned tiredness. When it was just the two of them, Sara, determined not to have it go unnoticed that she'd eaten at least four bites of salmon and three pieces of pasta at dinner, used this to jumpstart conversation away from the rigid quiet between them.

"Did you notice how much I ate at dinner?"

"I think dinner was a bit of a performance, right?"

She waited, sensing there was more.

"It reminded me of the Jolly Rancher incident in D.C. You commented on every nibble. Fish never tasted so incredible. It was like a T.V. commercial for the fish board."

She wanted to crawl away. He was right, but it made her defensive. "I'm under no false impression that eating a few pieces of salmon and pasta make me look normal," she snapped. "But I am trying to get well." Her voice was shaking.

"Is it okay if I go on?" he said softly.

She relaxed, nodding.

He pointed out that it wasn't just her fish board commercial that drew everyone's attention, but also the pure fascination of seeing real food, not just spinach, actually pass her lips. "That was good to see." Seth's voice dropped. "And you deserve to get well. How are you really doing?"

His concern for her, as always, touched her deeply.

"Pretty awful, actually. Hungry." She flopped down prostrate onto the grass next to him, exhausted, feeling like physical hell, a veritable tube of toothpaste squeezed out, then cut at both ends and squeezed some more. Still, she summoned up the energy to say something she'd been meaning to say for a while. "I'm sorry for the way I behaved at the rally."

"You mean when you dumped me?"

Sara sucked in her breath and covered her eyes with both hands, nodding. She sat up, took both his hands in hers, and looked intently at him. He returned the gaze.

"I think my behavior toward you was…ignominious. I was condescending about your age, your DIY sex…stuff."

Seth, smiling at her, questioned, "DIY?"

"Isn't that what it's called? DIY culture? Experimental sex."

He continued to look amused.

"Whatever. You know what I mean. I'm sorry that I was derisive about it."

"Thank you."

She let go of his hands, and he hugged her. Given the way she'd treated him over the last several months, she thought it was brave of him to hold her like that. He seemed to put concern for her above his own feelings.

"I've missed you, Sara."

She was committed to her boy-less, intimacy-building program and she didn't want to mislead him, to inadvertently hurt him again, so she said nothing. Instead, she kissed him on the cheek, hugged him as warmly as she could, and withdrew.

"Goodnight, then," she said, lingering. They went to bed, Seth to Marco's couch and Sara to bed with Jane.

chapter twenty-four

Sara read it again. Her review in the *Feminist Press* was beyond glowing. Unable to bear the weight of the praise or the responsibility it signaled, she took the ten copies she'd bought and hid them under her kitchen sink. FPR, a singularly preeminent review of scholarship and activism, was lauding *her* as a leader in feminist thought.

"Me?" she said to Jane in disbelief. "A thought leader?"

Jane, who'd met Sara at her front door at 9 a.m. with copies of the review, went off to answer the knocking at the door.

It was Seth, brandishing a copy of the review in his hand. "Did you fucking read this?"

Sara, giggling both at his reaction and her own giddy disbelief, hugged him.

Seth and Jane pored over the review, talking incessantly with over-excitement, making Sara even more unsettled. In fact, the review utterly unnerved her. Sara would have been happy with, "Not bad. Good try." This was too much praise, and high expectations were beyond what she could cope with.

Hoping to move beyond this focus on her new status as thought leader, Sara told them they should all get going to Boston.

* * *

Sara couldn't wait to get to the dancefloor once they arrived at Queer Choice. Seth had not only made a private reservation at Queer Choice for Marco's birthday, but he'd booked Queer Division, Marco's favorite queer-identified band. As Sara listened to Queer Division play a song they'd written just for Marco, it wasn't lost on Sara that Seth had done all of this for her best friend.

When Queer Division went on break, a phenomenal alternative DJ blasted an entire set of Marco's favorite alternative and gay-anthem dance songs. The first song was the Jam's "Going Under-ground," dedicated to Seth.

Since it was a song about *not* selling out, she thought it was an ironic choice, but, no doubt, a deliberately provocative one. Marco, who was continually encouraging Seth to think more about every-thing from the imagery in his writing to his sexuality, probably intended it to be a playful poke, a challenge to tear down the preten-sions of the phony rock-star image that constantly threatened to devour him.

Sara's thoughts, meanwhile, were consumed by Seth. His wet hand on hers the other day when she took a sip from his iced tea, the feel of his cheek and body against her when they hugged, the way his mouth moved around her name when he said it, how sexy she found his quietness…

Be with it. She rolled her eyes at the mantra that Jane had suggested she do in those moments when all else failed. She went over the list of distractions she'd given her on the car ride down, which were meant to keep her mind off Seth while she worked on herself.

She now stood in the club listening to the final chords of the Jam, and the beginning of Frankie Goes to Hollywood's "Relax," yet another song dedicated to Seth. This one, with all its references and images of the male orgasm, only hurtled her closer to the abyss. She put namaste on repeat in her head. Believing there was probably nothing that could save her from breaking her vows to heal herself, she was grasping now at any small piece of eastern philosophy that might help her accept her desires while still keeping her libido at bay.

"Ironic song choice," Marco said, holding hands with Drew and laughing at Seth's expense. Sara looked around the club for him, wanting to check his reaction to it. Locating him at the bar, she was appalled to see that he was looking right back at her. She averted her gaze, then dared a dart back. He was grinning back at her, clearly amused by this show.

When Sara heard the start of Kate Bush's "Running Up That Hill," she gave herself permission to let dancing take priority over being revolutionary for at least the next three minutes. Swaying her hips to the thud, thud of the drum resounding in her chest, she comforted herself with the choice to give into the beat and let her body sway more and more wildly. *Dancing to this song is a political choice.* Its message about gender bending guided her rationale. It was a bit of a stretch, more of an alcohol-induced thought, really.

The two margaritas she'd drunk steeling through her, Sara noticed the attention of Seth and Marco as she danced. Both stood at the bar, eyes fixed on her—Marco bopping up and down to the music, Seth stone-faced, and Drew not paying attention at all as he was handing Marco a cocktail and Seth a bottle of water. Sara wished she knew what they were talking about.

While she danced with Roo, a very attractive gay man who did an incredible impersonation of a straight man in the way he was holding her, she recollected with sadness a conversation she'd had with Marco about gay men's ability to camp hegemonic heterosexism. "We learn how to pass for straight," Marco had told her. "Just to avoid getting the shit kicked out of us."

While Sara would never have condoned this behavior in a setting that was not queer supportive, she thought her overt sensuality with Roo was okay because everyone knew they were camping a tired hegemonic script, flipping and mocking it. In fact, Sara thought, as she felt Roo's hands on her butt, they were being politically audacious. With that in mind, she camped it to the hilt while she sang the suggestive lyrics directly to her gay-cum-straight dance partner.

As she headed back to the bar, she met Marco and Drew on their way to the dancefloor with Jane.

"Hey, it's our local thought leader. Nice dancing." Gesturing his head toward Seth, he leaned in toward her ear for a modicum of privacy. "Go and spend some time with Horny Boy."

Drew tugged on Marco's arm, but Sara, choking on what he'd said, grabbed his other arm, insistent. "An explanation?"

"I asked him if he was jealous watching you dance with the only other straight boy in the club, and he said—"

"Roo is straight?" Sara said, cutting him off.

Drew jumped in. "That wasn't obvious?"

Marco laughed. "Exactly what was it about his behavior that led you to believe otherwise? Because it couldn't have been the fact that he barely took his hands off your ass. Or his eyes off your tits."

Sara felt stupid. "It's a gay club." Upset with her own idiocy, she barked at Marco. "And you told me gay boys do straight very effectively."

Marco shook his head. "Not *that* effectively."

Sara entered repair mode after reaching the precipice of hysteria with the knowledge that she'd inadvertently made out with a man in front of Seth, the one person she really wanted to be with. She began to walk away, then stopped herself. Disarmed as she'd been to learn about Roo, she'd forgotten to ask Marco what he was insinuating with the new moniker.

She grabbed his arm again. "He's horny?"

Marco leaned into her ear. "He told me he wasn't jealous, just horny."

When Sara pulled away from Marco to check his face for signs of sarcasm or some other emotion, she saw none.

Sara joined Seth at the bar, immediately ordering another drink.

"Did you put Marco up to the Jam song?" he asked, referring to the song that was playing when she'd arrived at the club.

"It's a classic," Sara said.

"It's a song about selling out," he quickly shot back.

Sara looked at him in mock horror. "Is it?" Though she didn't feel light about the subject at all. She'd been deconstructing it anew in the wake of the events at Wellesley, the Terry Gross interview, and her own review in FPR. It had made her wonder all the more about the effectiveness of her high moral purpose in the land of patriarchy, stuck here in her academic cocoon on the highest, dustiest bookshelf of theory and idealism, preaching to the already converted. It made Seth's forum just a tad more revolutionary—maybe a lot more—than her own.

"It's still a big issue for you, isn't it? My selling out," Seth said, his eyes focused on his hands, placing them on the bar, splaying each finger in and out over and over.

"You know I'm more concerned about the impact of it on you," she said, reminding him of their conversation in San Francisco.

Sara was feeling dizzy—not from a saturation of alcohol, but with a sobering recognition that Seth was the activist, the culture worker, filtering important ideas into a mainstream press that wore hegemonic blinders, disputing and challenging cultural notions of femininity and masculinity one rock show and interview at a time. The sell-out wasn't a sell-out at all.

She was feeling both audacious and excited to tell him her new understanding of it. "You're doing good things. Really working from within. Tearing down the master's house with the master's tools. It's inspiring people. I saw that at Wellesley."

She could see that he was both astounded and pleased to hear it.

"Terry. Fucking. Gross, after all."

He rolled his eyes at the mention of it again. "Feminist. Fucking. Press."

Hot Chocolate's "You Sexy Thing" blasting from the dancefloor, Sara found she couldn't stop herself from giving him one of her flirty smiles. While trying hard to be in control after two margaritas, one glass of wine, and a gin and tonic, she could only hope it was one of her more mildly flirty smiles. Intending to get his attention away from his hands and onto her, Sara leaned across his body to stroke his face.

Seth pulled away from her. "Are you flirting with me?"

Sara hmphed and slumped her body onto the bar. "You're supposed to flirt back."

Seth looked sullen. "I would flirt with you. I really would, if I thought you were sober and if you hadn't just dumped me two months ago. And…if you didn't already have a boyfriend."

That, she considered, and the fact that she'd practically given another man a lap dance on the dancefloor. Too drunk to manage an adequate response to all these fair points he was making, and feeling faint with hunger, Sara darted off in search of the comfort of Jane, but before she took a second step, she felt his hands on her waist, steadying her as she swayed toward the floor, almost collapsing with faint. She was grateful for the silencing.

He held on tightly. "Let me take you back to the hotel."

Mortified by so many mistakes, Sara would have preferred to walk the night streets of Boston than be alone in a cab with Seth, so she told him she was perfectly capable of getting back to the hotel on her own steam. And then she promptly passed out.

She came around in a little, dim-lit make-out booth in a dark corner of the club, Seth leaning over her, quickly removing the offensive smelling salts while simultaneously brushing her hair away from her face with his other hand.

Sara wondered why hell hadn't swallowed her whole yet as she tried to haul herself to a sitting position. Seth protested, and Sara was thinking if she could just know the peace of burning in hell then everything would surely feel so much better. After all, she considered with a nod, eternal hell could only be mildly unpleasant compared to this humiliation, and at least there she would be with her own people.

Except from a few exchanges with the driver, they barely spoke in the un-airconditioned, sweltering car.

Seth finally broke the silence when, once in the hotel elevator, he brought up the subject of her dance partner. "Roo seems nice," he said with a smirk.

She virtually screeched as she tried to defend herself. "I didn't know he was

straight."

"Yeah, I guessed that."

"You guessed? How?" Sara said in half relief, half amazement.

"I knew you wouldn't perform for a straight boy."

"Thank you. It's nice to know that some of my friends haven't despaired of me altogether. On the other hand, Marco thinks I'm the village idiot."

Seth shook his head.

Sara ignored him and asked for the sake of humor, if nothing else, "Is it just you and Marco, or does everyone think I'm stupid? That I can't tell the difference between a gay man and a straight one?"

"I'll admit that Marco did have a lot of fun with it. While you were dancing, he kept saying things like, 'I've been telling people that she's a thought leader, but no one will believe me now.'"

Sara's mouth fell open, but also appreciating the joke, she smiled. "Fuck him."

They stepped out of the elevator a bit lighter. Rather than move on, they both just stood there together watching the doors close. Still not moving from the spot, they watched the elevator move on again and then return. Despite fighting fatigue and hunger, not wanting to let him go, Sara spoke more to stall for time than any desire to continue revisiting the Roo incident.

"I should've guessed about Roo."

"Don't worry about it," Seth interrupted. "I'm much more worried about Tom."

With the mention of his name, Sara observed how swiftly Seth became a portrait in anxiety. With a sharp intake of breath, eyes downcast, both hands shoved into his pockets, and scuffing at the floor with a foot, he went on. "Remember when I asked you about Tom when we were in San Francisco? Well, I wasn't asking about him. I don't give a fuck how he's doing unless it's about how he's doing with you."

"Why do you want to know?" Sara asked, moving to stand directly in front of him in an attempt to get him to look at her.

Biting at his bottom lip, Seth smiled tensely and shrugged. "Not any good reason. Maybe it serves my masochistic tendencies."

Realizing the agony she was putting him through with this protracted silence, she spoke quickly and in great chunks of non-sentences as she always did when she was anxious.

"Here's the deal. Tom and me? Finished. That's it. Nothing else to say really." She only hoped it wouldn't invite any romantic innuendo now he knew Tom was out of the picture, committed as she was to sticking to her man embargo for at least another hour or so.

"I suspected something was up."

Sara felt silly that he'd been guessing as much despite the fact that she'd said nothing. "What made you suspect?"

"When you gave me that odd sort of news report on him in San Francisco, giving me his schedule, and then the other night at Marco's, when Drew was going on about him and you had your mouth wide open in total shock. Jane clearly knew something that the rest of us didn't, and then—"

Sara interrupted him before he could add to what was already an elaborate list of clues. "I should have mentioned it before. To all of you. You're my friends, after all." She looked at the ground.

"Did you break Tom's heart too?"

"Maybe." Sara squirmed, thinking she'd said it too breezily. If she hadn't been so preoccupied with admonishing herself for being so unfeeling, darting her eyes up and down the corridor of the sixteenth floor, wondering if she might be able to scuttle down a nearby vermin hole, she would have noticed that Seth was working hard to stop from laughing.

"Relax. You have enough empathy for women in worlds we don't even know about yet. I know you care."

"Despite all evidence to the contrary, I think Tom's all right. Essentially a good person. And so am I. Really. And I'm working on some pretty big stuff right now, for myself. In between editing my book, chairing, the WRC, I'm trying to get well."

"How's all that going?" His voice was thoughtful, caring. "I mean, today. Because I know from all my own stuff that there are good and bad days."

She paused, wondering how much more information was safe to provide. "It's a mess. Apparently, I don't know how to be without a guy. I've been plowing my way through one relationship after another, overlapping them like pieces of celery on a food platter, with no thought for how it worked. *If* it worked. Just terrified to be alone." She checked his reaction for signs of shock or disgust, then went on. "You and Tom were just the next two pieces of celery to lay on the proverbial platter."

His eyes were fixed on her face. He listened thoughtfully.

"But I want to stop. I really want intimacy over just sex. That would be good for me."

Her admission creating a new tension between them now, Seth nodded and asked her what intimacy involved for her. When she told him it meant that she was between boyfriends for a while, a weighty silence followed, punctuated by Seth taking a breath so deep that Sara wondered if he would ever exhale.

After sharing that, she wondered what she could accomplish in saying the next unexpurgated truth when it was moot anyway, but she was bursting to say it. "Although it's sort of bad timing," Sara said. "Because…"

"What?" he said, taking a step toward her.

She fought to not fall into him. "Well, I'm in love with you." She plowed ahead at top speed. "Of course, I need to pull back on those feelings, right? After all, I'm supposed to be between guys. I need to take care of myself for a bit because, as messed up as I am, I can't be in a relationship." Sara paused, debating whether she was done. "Right now, anyway."

When she finally looked at him, she saw his face transform, and she couldn't decipher whether it was exasperation, disbelief, confusion, or maybe all three. She took his hands and looked into his eyes. Seth nodded his understanding, slowly withdrew his hands from hers, and stepped back toward the elevator. Sara wrung her fingers over her palms and in between her knuckles. Seth tapped his fingers on the elevator call button over and over, keeping his gaze on the floor.

When she began to apologize again, he raised his hand and put one finger very gently on her lips. "Shhhh. It's okay."

She had a choice. She could throw away her boyfriend-less existence by taking his finger from her lips and putting it suggestively in her mouth…but that was just one choice. And she liked to believe that was the old Sara, the one whose understanding of real intimacy stretched to the width of a hair and grabbed onto her libidinal urges like they were a lifeline and she was the drowning victim. She had to admit that even the new Sara hadn't dealt with most, if any, of this yet, but she was trying, and that must count for something. She couldn't give in now.

Seth kissed her cheek. "Get some sleep."

He walked away, leaving her still standing in front of the pinging elevator, questioning whether she would have been strong enough to walk away if he hadn't.

chapter twenty-five

Sara traveled home the next day to return to her editing. In between frenzied bouts of it, Sara also threw herself into cleaning out her office at the university. As she packed books, took down photographs and pictures, boxed other memories, and cleaned out her desk, Sara saw that she'd been so immersed in the excitement of Wellesley she'd not prepared herself for the emotional overhaul of sealing her office. She'd been at this university for ten years and, as the walls emptied and the dust from the bookshelves made her sneeze, Sara felt her bottom lip begin to tremble.

Finally leaving her empty office, she wondered how much finality a person could take all at one time. Later, while shopping for the farewell dinner for Seth that she planned to prepare that night, Sara decided that based on all that she was coping with, it was probably pretty infinite.

Seth, who'd stayed with Marco in Boston after the party for work, was returning that afternoon. Since he was scheduled to turn right around the next day for a chartered flight from Logan to re-join the tour in Arizona, and after enduring a round of interviews with music journalists, Sara couldn't understand why Seth was bothering to travel from Boston to Amherst for a dinner at her house.

When she'd shared this with Marco, he'd laughed at her. "You can't guess, huh?"

She supposed he meant that Seth wanted to see her, but after she'd shot him down yet again, she couldn't understand why he would want to be in her company, despite that she longed to be in his.

She was caught off guard when Seth arrived well before the others. "You look a bit hot," she told him, taking in his sweaty appearance, his shirt clinging to his chest, his hair stuck to his neck.

He followed Sara into the kitchen, going straight to her refrigerator and, opening the door, leaned into it, sighing with relief. "I had to walk half an hour in this fucking heat to get here. If I had a home, I'd buy a car."

While she got him an iced tea, smiling at his attempts to cool himself off by guzzling the tea while fanning himself with the refrigerator door, Sara sympathized, both with his over heatedness and his homeless state.

"It's so fucking hot in here," he moaned.

Sara watched him take in the blasting fans that were perched precariously in several windows, the billions of vegetables crowding the counter and, no doubt making him feel hotter, the shrimp sizzling in the wok. "How come you don't have AC?"

"I can't afford it," she told him as she poured him another iced tea and continued with the veggie chopping. "Neither the units nor the electricity to power them. Your paycheck, on the other hand, could probably power New England."

She saw him cringe a little. It was a glib comment, and she immediately regretted it. She hadn't meant to needle him; she was just struck by the comparison of his wealth and her relative poverty.

She rubbed his arm as a gesture to let him know she was an idiot for saying it and tried to change the subject. "I could've picked you up or you could've come with Marco, you know."

Seth was explaining that Marco was going to be late because he was meeting Drew's parents for the first time, when they both looked up at a rumble of thunder that threatened to shake off the roof. As the summer storm became imminent, darkening the room, Sara and Seth were drawn to the open porch door to observe the colossal rolling bruise that hours earlier had been a cloudless, azure sky. The rumbling, strained groan that emanated from the sore in the sky was punctuated suddenly by a deafening crack of lightning, momentarily illuminating the room before it gave way to teeming rain. Sara and Seth raced around ripping fans out of sockets, closing windows, and wiping wet floors. After their energy was expended in the clean-up, Seth got another huge, ice-filled glass of tea. They stood together, watching the biblical-level downpour.

Dragging themselves away from the spectacle of the storm, Sara returned to the cooking and gasped at the scene that greeted them. Having swallowed the evening summer light whole, the storm had thrust the apartment into a gloaming light now illuminated only by the candles that Sara had been burning in her kitchen-cum-living room space before Seth had even arrived.

The candlelight inevitably created an instant romantic mood, making Sara think on her suspicions that Marco had been trying to get her alone with Seth. But, within half an hour after the storm began, everyone else arrived, which subsequently only made her think she was being paranoid, or maybe worse—equally culpable in contriving these situations.

The storm raged until dinner, making the already blisteringly hot day even steamier and forcing Sara to adapt her hot shrimp dish. With Seth's help, while everyone else drank themselves cooler against the miserable humidity, Sara cooled the shrimp in ice before tossing it with the pasta.

During this little culinary process, over dinner and throughout the evening, Sara kept looking at Seth out of the corner of her eye. He caught her every time. Even more upsetting, each time, he winked, making her blush not unlike a coquette in a Henry James novel. With great satisfaction, there were a few times when Sara caught him looking first. And then, after flashing Seth a smug smile, she had the pleasure of being the one forcing him to avert his eyes, the one to make him blush.

Busy at this game while she listened to Drew bragging about how Marco had won his mother over by admiring her Delftware plates and her Marimekko throw pillows on the couch, and everyone else's chatter, Sara was caught off guard when Jane turned the discussion to Marco's party at Queer Choice.

"Wasn't Queer Division amazing?"

Everyone agreed, but Sara was unprepared for the twist in the conversation. While beginning at what she thought was a fairly high-level assessment of Queer Division's talent, the protracted discussion then shifted to a celebrity magazine-infused conversation about the front man, Shephard Hibbs, and where he was spending all his "sell-out money," as Marco referred to it.

Noticing Seth withdraw, Sara thought more on her earlier comment to him about his wealth and the implicit message that it was ill-gotten sell-out money. When Marco made a comment about the unfortunate coupling of money with fame and how Hibbs was "just asking for an existential crisis," Seth got up from the table.

Protective of his feelings, Sara touched his arm and gave him her most "I am not a part of this let's-trash-rock-stars-for-spending-their-money-on-air-conditioning" looks. Seth only smiled back at her, not seeming upset at all and only motioning with his empty glass that he was off to get more iced tea.

Marco added, "It's sad that Shephard is not putting more of his money into the queer community." Noticing the private exchange between Sara and Seth, he waved a feminine-styled hand at Seth. "You, on the other hand, are Put-Your-Money-Where-Your-Mouth-is Boy. You..."

Sara, shocked by Marco's disregard for Seth's feelings, interrupted him. "Stop it. Why are you calling him that?"

Marco looked aghast at her interruption and waxed esoteric poetry with a smile. "Oh, Ms. Anna Akhmatova. You are a bard, a heaven bird."

"What does that mean?" Sara snapped, not understanding any of it.

While everyone looked astounded at Sara's sharp tone, she tried to look conciliatory, feeling awful as she did for snapping at Marco. She'd initially confronted him to protect Seth, not wanting their last conversation to be about selling out when they'd only just put the topic to bed, but Marco's response had left Sara feeling under attack. While she knew he didn't mean it as such, that it was just clever banter, under the pressure of the unrealistic expectations she imagined would follow her review in FPR and the idea of Seth leaving, she was feeling sorry for herself. Sara could feel the spiral of emotion gaining weight in her almost weightless ninety-two-pound body as she struggled against her little pity party.

Marco continued to sip his drink while he listened, and literally choked on his wine when Sara added that she would appreciate it if he could explain precisely what he meant so that the small, dull child in the room might understand.

"Is that you, then? Are you the small, dull child?"

She knew it was overstating it to call herself that. It was the sadness combined with a near toxic mix of self-deprecating thoughts and pity and, having expressed as much to Marco on the phone the night before, she hoped he would be easy on her.

All eyes turned to Sara.

"You need to reinvent yourself," he said softly. "After all, baby girl, a small, dull child in the back of the room is not a thought leader."

"Don't ever call me that again. The pressure."

Marco swatted her comment away.

She knew he said it to make her feel better, to remind her that some of the best thinkers in the world were heralding her as one of their own. But she really had begun to wonder if she was good enough, especially now Wellesley thought they were getting a brilliant scholar and activist.

While she'd been cleaning out her office, with nothing to do but think, she'd even considered that maybe they got the reviews switched. Maybe her review was really terrible and the *real* thought leader, the one for whom the review was actually written, was wringing her hands at this very moment and wondering what went wrong with her brilliant thesis. In fact, self-deprecation being her second favorite game after restricting, these were thoughts she'd considered constantly since the review broke.

"Get a grip on those nihilistic tendencies," Marco said, rubbing her back as he stood over her, taking his drink from Seth.

"Oh, I'll get to work on the erosion of my ego first thing in the morning. Then again, maybe not first thing, maybe right after I work on the erosion of the ozone. And while I'm at it, all the other eco and social catastrophes, because I have as much chance of solving them as I do my own ego issues."

Everyone laughed except Marco, who was looking like he had an announcement. "Before your little pity party there, you interrupted me."

Sara had not forgotten the sell-out conversation that Marco had been having almost to himself. She shot him a look, and Seth told him to leave it, which made Marco giggle.

"I was in the middle of telling everyone my new moniker for you," he said, wrapping an arm around Seth's shoulder. Put-your-money-where..."

"We remember the moniker. What's your point?" Drew jumped in, as if he was unable to tolerate Seth's squirming.

"Seth has given almost all the proceeds from the tour and the first record to charities he admires."

Everyone spoke at once. Sara felt guilty for the quip about her air conditioning units, which at the time had seemed a worthy cause, but not so much now. Jane told him she hoped he'd saved a little for a car.

As Marco started listing the admired charities and everyone oohed and aahed, Seth acted shy, as if he wanted to move things on. "Listen to the peepers," he said.

The windows wide open to the night and the sound of the peepers deafening their conversation, Sara turned out the lights. They all sat by the candlelight at the kitchen table and counted the fireflies as they came out.

At midnight, when Marco said he had to drag Seth away, Sara felt her tummy tip over and a lump in her throat at the idea of him leaving—and for how long? After all, he had no apartment here now, and with the success of the band, he could live anywhere.

Everyone was milling around, gathering to leave. Sara hugged and kissed them all, saving Seth for last. She sidled over to him for a hug, but instead, on impulse, found herself asking, "Stay?" Thinking he might say no, judging by the nonplussed look on his face, she was relieved when he finally nodded.

Seth, seemingly trying not to draw attention to the fact that he was staying, disappeared into the kitchen, only to have Marco call to him to hurry up. Sara bit at her bottom lip, wondering how to manage the moment because she knew there would be a big reaction from Marco once he discovered that Seth was spending the night with her.

Sara tried to sound as casual as possible. "Seth's staying tonight." Knowing no one could ever make that statement sound casual, she prepared herself for Marco's comments. Instead, she noticed a few looks quickly exchange between Marco, Drew, and Jane.

"Fucking finally. Do you know how many attempts we've made over the last four days to get you two together?"

She did know, and suspected Seth did too.

Seeing Seth leaning against the hall wall, clearly impatient for them all to leave, Marco smiled lasciviously at Sara and left them to be alone.

Sara turned to Seth, taking his hand in hers, the one that was not perpetually holding a glass of iced tea. She led him back into her living room, asking him along the way how he felt about going back to the tour.

"I can deal with it a few more weeks. Not much choice, really."

Following that dismal purview, Sara asked if he thought his conscience was up to it. Could his arms take a few more weeks of abuse? Was he was going to do drugs every night? As she fired her questions at him in succession, Seth stopped to face her.

"Probably and definitely," he said. "Respectively."

Sara nodded, saddened by the recognition that she'd reached a stage of resignation about his drug use. She wanted to support him the way he had her, but she was full of concern.

"I like that you don't get high around me."

Seth dropped her hand, rubbed his face, and sighed heavily before he brought his gaze back to her. "Where's this going? What is it?"

The tiniest breeze was coming in from the open porch door, so she pulled him toward it, and they sat in the darkness of the room, savoring every lick of it. Facing one another, holding hands, she explained to him that she thought his not getting high around her was encouraging.

"I think it indicates that you really do want to get well."

"Do *you* want to get well?"

She shook her head at the question. "I asked first."

"No," he said quickly. "I don't."

Falling silent because she'd been unprepared for that truth, Sara dropped her eyes, watching Seth play with her hands, moving his fingers around hers. After several minutes of this, Seth reminded her to answer the same question.

She shook her head and began to cry softly. "I want to, but I don't seem to be able to."

When Seth leaned forward to kiss her forehead, an act of such empathy that only made her cry more, Sara looked up at him, pleading.

"Do you think you could at least promise to try to want to stop? To think about it?"

Seth, wiping her tears away over and over again with his thumb, made a promise to think about it, but only after the tour was over.

Sara nodded with acceptance. "Will you promise to be careful? Will you try to not kill yourself?"

Seth said he absolutely would do that, if for no other reason than the promise of seeing her again. "I'm in love with you, Sara."

"I know. But I like hearing you say it. It sounds lovely."

"I know you are, as you say, 'between men right now.'" He paused nervously. "I know you want to put all of this off, but I just want to know, if or when you're ready, are there any deal breakers here?"

Sara held onto his hands, examining them in exquisite detail, saying nothing at all.

"The drugs, the sell-out, the self-harming, the experimental sex, or the fact that I won't have sex with you. Are these deal breakers?"

Sara loved this last one in the list of potential deal breakers. Honestly, wouldn't that be a deal breaker for anyone? Starting with the easiest first, she told him, "You've taken care of the sell-out thing. After all, Terry-fucking-Gross."

"Thank-fucking-God I got that interview."

Smiling at him, Sara quickly raised both her hands and placed them firmly on his shoulders, indicating mockingly that he shouldn't consider himself saved, not even by Terry Gross. "Experimental sex? I can deal with that, but not wanting to have sex with me, that's a deal breaker." He smiled at her warily, so she let him off the hook. "No, Seth. No deal breakers here."

Of course, it was all just cold comfort because, as she reminded him, she didn't know how long it would take for her to work on all her issues with intimacy. He lowered his head, focusing his gaze on her fingers as they entwined his.

Sitting there, hanging on to every faint breeze that came through the door, Sara drew away from his hands and touched his arms, tracing some still fresh wounds. As she began to stroke them gently, she heard a quiet moan of what she perceived was pleasure. Looking up to his face, she saw his eyes were closed.

"Do you like that sensation?"

After taking his time to open his eyes, he nodded and smiled at her. Sara asked if it was a DIY thing.

"There's that DIY thing again. You've said that before. What do you mean by that?"

Sara, unsure, embarrassed both by her lack of understanding as well as her uncertainty, shrugged dismissively. "I don't know. Marco said that's what you're into."

"Not sure I like the sound of that. I think of DIY as living outside of hegemonic culture and its fucking gendered, mindless script. So, it means experimenting. With sex."

Relief now flooding her, Sara smiled at him as he explained his response to her touch. "I just enjoy you touching me, that's not a DIY thing. I just love it. That's all."

At that, Sara leaned forward and kissed him for a long time and, finally withdrawing, she asked him if he would go to bed with her.

A puzzled look crossed his face. "I thought you needed to work on all your issues with intimacy."

Sara waved a hand in the air. "I'm a thought leader. If nothing else, surely that means I'm a fast learner?"

Seth, smiling broadly at her attitude shift, shyly looked down at their playing hands again.

"I've always wanted to go to bed with a thought leader."

Remembering to be at least true to her intimacy program, Sara interrupted him. "No sex. Just intimacy." She ran her fingers along his arm again. "I need the practice."

Seth wore one of those jaw-aching smiles. "That's a good thing, because that's all I do."

* * *

Once in the bedroom, Seth turned on the light while Sara turned on two box fans to keep them from expiring in the heat. When she turned around to see Seth watching her, Sara walked over, kissed him, and gave herself up to the utter pleasure of being touched by him.

Despite the intense pleasure of her every nerve being stroked, Sara found her thoughts drifting. Long arms, she observed thoughtfully as he managed to kiss her while stroking the length of her legs at the same time. After a split second of experiencing the pleasure of his hands on her legs, her thoughts flitted again from that sensation to wondering what all this DIY business was about. After Marco's build-up that it would get her off fast, she was certainly eager to learn more.

Maybe she should be trying this stroking thing too. What should she do? What would he like?

Because her thoughts were there a lot, her hand naturally went to his arms. Sara began to trace over the inside of his arm, just as she'd done earlier when they were sitting by the porch door.

Sara felt Seth's breath change as she ran a hand from his arm over to the lower part of his stomach, moving away from kissing his lips to his cheek, then to his neck. She suddenly felt his hand between her legs, slowly stroking the inside of her thighs.

Sara made her way down to his legs, congratulating herself for what she considered to be a noteworthy focus on experience. Of course, with this thought and her attention to precisely how her hand was working over his thigh, she realized she was more focused on performance than experience. Disappointment swamped her.

Utterly exasperated with this infuriating life that was lived exclusively in her mind, Sara worried this inattention to both the physiological and the emotive might indicate adult onset ADD when she suddenly felt Seth's entire body stiffen beneath her hand.

An almost inaudible moan escaped his mouth while their lips were still lightly touching. Sara panicked. Clearly shifting into automatic pilot because she knew the performance so well, Sara had slipped a leg expertly, gently against his groin. Seth pulled away sharply and her education in alternative sexualities really began.

More upset by the interruption than alarmed by her failing attempts at the intimacy program, Sara sighed heavily and whined not unlike a little girl whose toy had been confiscated for naughtiness. "What? Why are we stopping?"

He nodded understandingly. "I'm trying to keep us on track. Focused on intimacy." He searched for her eyes. "Not orgasms."

"I've changed my mind," she said, like it was an epiphany. "I've decided I want an orgasm instead."

"It gets easier." He laughed at the doubtful look that crossed her face. "You'll figure it out."

Getting used to the feeling of sexual frustration was not appealing to Sara. She looked at Seth as though he'd just suggested she would eventually learn to accept patriarchy as an inevitable evolutionary system of human social organization. "But it's masochistic, surely."

"As I think you know, some masochistic behaviors feel good to me."

Sara looked at him with a curious smile instead of horror. In the past, the latter would have been her default response. It felt good to be hearing about it from him instead of Marco.

She laughed, smug in her new knowledge. "Of course, you love the intimacy program; you actually experience sexual frustration as pleasure."

Seth smiled. "So, we're both getting something different out of the intimacy program, as you call it. For me..." he paused, almost blushing, "it's great sex."

She watched his face falter with her quiet.

"Maybe you don't agree...?"

Sara certainly didn't define the intimacy program as either fun or pleasurable, but she had to admit the intense feelings between them, combined with an energy she could probably harness—feeling like she could run a marathon, edit eternally—felt pretty fantastic when she could get out of her head. That thought made her sigh heavily.

"What are you thinking?"

"It's my focus."

"Focus?"

Looking at him, she wondered where to begin. "This takes a lot of focus for a woman. It's ninety percent emotive for us. For men, sexual experience is almost all physiological, right?"

It was a rhetorical point, not a legitimate question, and Sara slipped into professor mode as she pulled herself to a sitting position in the bed. Seth automatically shifted to student mode, repositioning himself so that he was propped up by an elbow, resting his head on his hand, listening intently to her.

"To experience sexual pleasure and not just slip into a performance of the acts, women need to be in a very specific emotional place."

"I do know all this. I was in your seminar, you know, but..." he paused, seemingly to emphasize his disbelief, "this is true even for you?"

"It's not what you'd expect, right?" She nodded with great drama. "Not from a so-called thought leader. It's all of us. *All* women. We just talk, talk, talk to ourselves when we're supposed to be experiencing the pleasure of the physical." Seth took both her hands in his. Sara went on. "Deb Tolman's research on how girl culture affects sexual experience really explains it nicely."

"Tolman? She's at Wellesley, right?"

Despite the interruption, he'd impressed her. He'd been researching Wellesley, investigating the program and the faculty she would be joining.

"My favorite is her interview with a fourteen-year-old girl whose boyfriend wanted her to give him a blow job. Her decision to do it was clearly driven by girl culture, a bunch of social pressures and expectations, such as 'it wouldn't be nice to say no,' but the main point was, when Tolman asked her if she'd enjoyed it, the girl told her there was so much going on—Was she doing it right? How could she get better at it? How long was it going to take?—that she really didn't have time to think about enjoying it. In other words, experiencing it was something she had to remind herself to do. No sexual agency. All performance." Sara shook her head in disgust. "Personal experience can always be explained politically."

Seth smiled at her. "And you can't get much more personal than an orgasm."

She corrected him. "There's not much that's personal in the female orgasm. It's all political, all the result of being raised to think of others first. How long it takes to achieve it, how she feels about the way she achieved it, if she looks okay while he's doing it, how he feels—if he's using his hand, or going down on her, you can bet she's wondering if his neck is getting stiff or his hand aches. If he likes doing it..."

"I agree. I'm sorry. It's a fucking pain."

Sara nodded, pleased with both his apology, which she loved because it acknowledged his culpability in patriarchy, and appraisal of the situation.

"You know, though, Sara," Seth said sheepishly, lowering his gaze. "Men do sometimes have the emotive stuff too."

Sara shook her head in frustration. "Oh please." She cut him off as he tried to object. "Don't tell me about that."

Seth broke in softly. "Oh, I've been all performance before."

"But you're Seth. You're lovely."

After he kissed her for that and before they were both startled by the shock of lightning from yet another burgeoning thunderstorm, Sara noticed him withdraw his gaze from her. She knew he was thinking something that wasn't being said.

"I'm not sure I can handle going back to the tour."

"Only a couple of weeks left." She tried to buoy him, though she was worried. After all, if he knew he couldn't manage the cutting, the drugs, what was he risking? Reassured again when he told her that the worst of re-joining the tour in Arizona was that she wouldn't be there, Sara told him she could meet him.

Listening to the summer thunderstorm rage outside, they curled up together and finally fell asleep.

* * *

Sara woke Seth at five a.m., panting on the floor.

"What the fuck are you doing?" he said, rubbing his eyes, trying to focus on her.

"Sit-ups," she said breathlessly. "I didn't get chance to do them yesterday, so I thought I'd get them in now."

"How many more?"

"You don't want to know."

A million sit-ups later, Sara got up to join him back in bed.

Having adjusted to the light, Sara lingered by the bed, experiencing the pleasure of watching his eyes all over her body. When she finally got into bed, after kissing him for a long time and helping him remove her bra and boy-cut underwear, Sara was glad the lights were on because, after she enjoyed watching him look at her, her eyes got to linger on him too. As Sara did the admiring, slowly looking him over, she realized how much pleasure would have been lost with the lights off.

After feeling his hands on her waist, hips, butt, tummy, thighs, Sara was suddenly alarmed by the sensation of both his hands on her breasts.

"Hang on," she told him, pleased with her sense of presence as she removed his hands.

It was quite a moment for Sara. Despite that every cell in her body was in experience mode now and performance was nowhere on the horizon, that she was in a space of desire that was swelling and spilling like those cliff-side houses in Topanga Canyon during a flood—topple, topple, topple—Sara had stopped him. That, she thought a little too proudly, is how badly she wanted to understand intimacy. To get well.

Seth apologized petulantly, swore under his breath with frustration, and then groaned with disappointment, either at being stopped or with his own ineptness, Sara couldn't tell which.

"I'm just trying to keep us on track," she said, mimicking his earlier advice and voice, making him laugh. She patted his chest. "You'll figure it out."

"Sorry for being patronizing earlier," he said, referencing her mockery.

"Shhh. It's okay," she said, stroking his face. "Unless…"

"Yes?" he beckoned.

"Unless we both agree to move on," Sara suggested.

"What do you want to do? Where are we going with this?"

When Sara replaced his hands on her, he sighed heavily, which she understood as uncertainly rather than desire.

"Only touching," she whispered. "And tasting."

She felt him relax. He lay down to face her and pulled his body flat against hers.

Feeling him against her tummy, his eyes glossy with desire, he was completely lost in experience. She envied him that, especially when she felt herself slipping into performance mode the moment he spoke. When he murmured some barely audible instructions to her, she had to ask him to repeat himself.

Audible in his urgency to let her know what he wanted, he said, "Slowly, okay? And stop a lot. I don't need to come."

Sara, smiling, adjusted accordingly. He kept his eyes fixed on hers as he slipped his hand between her legs.

"Stay focused on how it all feels and tastes. Nothing else," he reminded her.

This was DIY Sex 101, and she had completely missed the course. Sexual agency, conflating with desire and experience, was front and center, and mere performance was unacceptable.

He had to stop her hand on him over and over because, apparently, she neither stopped nor did it slowly enough. When he thought he couldn't risk it anymore, he disappeared under the sheets and between her legs. Tasting herself on his mouth after he resurfaced, she became desperate with desire as she watched his eyes become fixed and intense when she reached down and explored stroking him again.

Afterwards, she folded his arms around her and, despite the summer's heat, Sara shivered, suddenly chilled with just a cotton sheet covering them as the thunderstorm erupted outside.

Seth reached down and pulled up the duvet to cover them both.

"Turn off the light now," she instructed him.

Before he did, Seth looked squarely at her, though playfully. "That was a bit beyond the intimacy program. Sorry if I misled you there."

Sara giggled. "I thought that was your thing. Aren't you supposed to be good at it? I think we can blame it on the sit-ups. Clearly too much for you."

He flipped the lights off. "I'll try harder next time. Like I said, I'm sorry. I lost my focus."

"You were intensely focused. Didn't want to interrupt you. You were having such a nice time."

"Seemed like you were too," Seth said, wrapping an arm around her, pulling her into him.

"You noticed?"

"It helps when the lights are on." After a pause, Seth added, "How was your focus?"

"Pretty perfect."

"I'd expect nothing less from a thought leader."

Since it was their last night together for at least two weeks, they were determined to be awake for as much of it as possible, but exhaustion must have finally overcome them because they both fell asleep.

When Sara awoke, it was beginning to get light, and the thunderstorm that had erupted when they were falling asleep was picking up in intensity. Lightning cracked and thunder echoed through the apartment. Despite this tumult and the intensely sticky heat, Sara felt perfect, snuggled under the duvet with Seth.

chapter twenty-six

It had been a frantic ten days since Seth had left. The last push with edits before the September deadline had kept her busy, and she was relieved to be celebrating with Jane. Two glasses of wine down, they were uproarious as they talked about Wellesley, the WRC staffers, the plans for the summer party that Jane held at her house every year, and Jane's new boyfriend from the physics department.

With slightly slurred speech, Jane leaned against Sara and said, "Guess who thinks she's pregnant?"

Sara, alarmed, but not so much that she couldn't take a sip from her drink, said, "Not you?"

Jane's screwed up face said, "*As if.*" "I haven't even slept with Medium-Energy Boy yet," she said, referring to her boyfriend by the moniker Marco had given him.

Penetrative sex was a preoccupation lately, probably because she wasn't having any. "If I had a boyfriend that would do that to me," she told Jane teasingly, "I wouldn't waste any time at all. In fact, I might not do anything else."

"What about the intimacy program? I thought that was going really well?"

Sara nodded with enthusiasm. "It is."

However, she also had moments of frustration with it, deep enough that she knew she'd likely be begging Seth for the old-fashioned kind of sex when he got back from the tour. He'd permitted the sexy idea of it in their phone conversations, but he'd had to talk her down on the phone a few times, even suggesting she use something if she needed that sensation so badly. One time, Sara scanned the kitchen appliances while on the phone with him. Seth panicked, telling her that vegetables were safer. They both laughed like idiots, but she was serious, and he knew it.

Luckily the phone rang, so she wasn't pressed to reveal details about the trials and tribulations of the intimacy program.

Racing to the phone to hear his voice, knowing that it must be him since he called multiple times a day, she was caught off guard when Marco's voice came through instead.

Without the hysterics he was known for, Marco told her quickly and plainly that Seth was in a coma after an overdose of heroin.

* * *

Looking at him through a window into his fancy private intensive care unit, hooked up to a bunch of ominously beeping machines, and the bustle of nurses, and the seriously anxious faces of his three private physicians, Sara recalled his promise to her the night he left for the tour to stay alive. He barely looked alive.

Not taking her eyes off him, she asked Marco, "Why is he blue? What does that mean?"

Out of the corner of her eye, she saw Marco's shoulders shrug. "The doctors said something to do with a heroin overdose," he said, his voice cracking with emotion. Their companionable silence was punctuated by people in white coats talking about Seth like he was a specimen.

"And is he going to be..." Sara paused before adding, "all right?"

Her stomach lurched when Marco told her, "It's a waiting game, they say."

The next morning, the band arrived. After Eyva saw Seth, Sara watched how she buried her face behind her hands, rocking back and forth on the sofa. An empowered rock-fem icon, now looking so small, so helpless. Caleb and Jeff just looked on, stunned and drained dry.

Nothing. No response. Not for two solid days. On day three, for a few hours there was a small periodic flicker of response. Just as she got hopeful, it vanished. By the evening of day four, she pleaded with his absent bluish face. When she said his name and saw a shift in his eyes, it hardly made her hopeful. This animalistic simple response, after four whole days, while tubes and probes stuck out from almost every hole in his head, still made him seem barely alive. The physicians proclaimed it to be the hope they'd been looking for. "A great sign," they called it.

Barely comforted by their reaction, Sara chilled when one of them told her, "If he's made it this far, he should be okay now." Since she'd never allowed herself to consider that he would be anything other than okay, Sara promptly went into the bathroom and threw up.

As she lay in the bathroom stall, Sara vaguely heard Marco's voice. Scraping her off the floor, ignoring the shrieks and protests from the women in the bathroom, he carried all ninety pounds of her out of there as, coiling herself into him, Sara tried to impersonate Seth and disappear.

She drifted in and out of sleep, curled on the couch adjacent to where Seth lay in semi-consciousness.

"You'll manage all of this a lot better if you fucking eat," Marco said, with hands balled, madder than she'd ever seen him.

Sara had eaten only when Marco had forced her. She'd managed almost a full protein bar each day, and about twenty cups of coffee. That was the best she could do.

She lay on the couch, weaker than she'd ever felt through the whole mess of her eating disorder, and watched them remove every tube from his head. Seth, who hadn't shifted his gaze since opening his eyes just hours before, suddenly turned to look directly at Sara. She held her breath. He faintly smiled at her, then opened his mouth in an attempt to speak but managed only sickly sounds. He fell asleep almost immediately after. Gaining strength from this sight, Sara found enough energy to cry. Her tears were gratitude and relief. Wiping her eyes, she ordered a sandwich.

While Sara sat eating her sandwich, feeling so much better that she was having feelings again, the physicians approached Marco about a medical press conference.

Sara balked at the suggestion. "We're not doing that," she cried. Since day one at the hospital, his fame only added to her distress.

The press literally camped outside, waiting for a scoop on the lurid details. She'd passed them on that first day at the entrance to the hospital, assaulted with flashing cameras and a barrage of lights. Stunned at first because they'd called out to her by name, she'd quickly felt *silly*. *Of course they know my name. My picture has only been on the cover of every magazine.*

The physicians, accustomed to dealing with celebrity patients, had smiled patronizingly at her naivety, insisting that this was the best strategy for getting some relief from the press's "relentless pursuit for information on Mr. Coles' condition." When they went on to explain that the press's interest in his condition was only part of it and that they were also digging for information on why he was there in the first place, Sara became convinced that the physicians probably did know best.

"How you want to handle this is up to you," the team of physicians said. "We won't answer those questions, but we can advise you on how to handle it, or maybe you want to use Mr. Coles' people to advise you."

Sara shot a look at Marco. "Does he have people?"

It turned out he had plenty, including a publicist, a personal assistant, a manager, and a team of attorneys, along with a host of others. Sara's mind boggled.

"Where's his security guy?" Marco asked them.

"He needs them in here?" Sara was incredulous.

The physicians, clearly sensing that Marco and Sara needed a private moment, turned away to talk; even medical professionals deferred to Seth's fame and money.

"Security lies low when you're around. At Seth's request, Sara." Marco tried to make it clear. "After that incident with the security guys in D.C., he worries how it'll look to you. He only does it because the label demands it. 'Protecting their investment,' he told me."

"He must hate that," she trailed off, looking at him lying there barely conscious.

Sara sat dumbfounded, reeling from the knowledge that all these people were working on this problem, spinning a life for Seth as he lay in a semi-conscious state. And then she headed straight for Eyva.

"What can you tell me about this?" Sara asked her as they sat in the hallway outside Seth's room.

Eyva mumbled some sad comments about the consequences of Seth's coma to the band, shrugging as she added that she hoped the fallout would be minimal since there were only two more tour dates.

"Fuck that," Sara told her. "Tell me what happened."

Eyva looked very low. "You should try to get him into detox. We all need the assurance that he'll stop fucking doing this. And not just for the band, but because we fucking love him."

Ignoring her sweet plea, Sara said, "This has happened before?"

Eyva looked squarely at her. "He's OD'd probably three times on this tour alone. Clair probably knows of more."

Silenced by this news, Sara felt goosebumps breaking out all over her as she listened to Eyva elaborate.

"Clair's taken care of him, even resuscitated him on more than one occasion." She picked up Sara's hand. "I've seen him in various stages of junkie trouble, including being blue with cotton fever, unconscious, not breathing, you name it."

Anger welled in her. If she'd only known the extent of his problems, been clear on what there was to be afraid of, she would have been able to avert this altogether. She felt sure she would never have *gone with it, been in the moment, accepted her feelings,* or anything else suggested in Jane's Zen-shit wisdom. The problem was, Sara was in love with him, and while she understood she could save herself from further entanglement in the mess of his life by simply leaving, she knew there would be no escape from grieving him.

* * *

After he was airlifted to a fancy New York City hospital, she stayed with Seth for another week. Another six days in a private room at this hospital, Seth was ready, according to a court-ordered mandate, for a month lockdown in a private detox clinic in the city. While Sara didn't stay as part of his entourage, she got to fly down twice a week.

When he finally became fully cognizant of her presence, he couldn't bring himself to look at her until she climbed into bed with him and kissed him like he was oxygen and she'd been deprived of air. She didn't even remind him that he'd promised to stay alive but had almost not managed that much. She didn't even feel angry with him. Rather, the fault was all hers for having uncharacteristically fooled herself into believing that a boyfriend who was doing "everything" was okay, after making her mind up that she wanted him that night in September at the club. After a month at the clinic, Sara flew down to pick him up and returned home with him to Amherst.

Finally home, sitting there on her bed, he looked full of life again. And after four days of barely leaving her bedroom for ten minutes at a time, Seth to load up on food, Sara to make tea, Sara was considering begging him for sex.

Unlike that last night before Seth had left for the tour, Sara believed they'd stuck to the intimacy-not-orgasms prescription with such diligence in the last four days to qualify for an advanced degree of some sort. While the experience was intense, she believed her level of sexual frustration was reaching the limit, just as it had in those sexy phone conversations with him while he was on tour.

Weakened as she was and recognizing signs of a crumbling in Seth's resolve, Sara took advantage. Playfully propositioning him, reminding Seth to consider her sexual agency, she told him she was getting weary with desire. This perception of the intimacy program was apparently abhorrent to Seth. He recoiled from her, making her burst into hysterical sobs.

"So, are we just never going to do it?" As if she were some kind of animal in heat, she pleaded, "I really need it."

He exhaled. "You like it that much?"

"You don't?" Sara said, petulant and sullen.

Initially worrying her sick as he averted his eyes to her hands, seemingly preparing to offer some revelation that she wasn't likely to accept, he made her grin instead when he queried, "Just to be certain, we are talking about fucking, right?"

After affirming his understanding with a nod, Sara listened as Seth explained himself. "Sure, I like it, but I don't think it's always a good idea. Especially not if you're aiming for the intimacy thing, or something more experimental."

Scrambling to recover her perpetual lapse in memory about the intimacy program, Sara said, "I definitely want that, but I want *that* too. I do. I really do," she said a little desperately.

With sincere amazement at her insistence and apparent need, Seth smirked and asked a question that stalled her. "What's so great about that for you?" Sara's jaw went slack when he shrugged and added, "I mean, the female orgasm is located in the clitoris, so the mouth, hands—that's got to feel the best, right? Better than *that* anyway. So, what is it? Is it just the sensation?"

Sara was perplexed by his amazement, as if she'd just confessed to enjoying the sensation of an ice-cream headache. "You know, I think that's it. What a gnarly thought. I wonder what's wrong with me. What a pervert you must think I am, enjoying heterosexual penetration."

Seth put his hand playfully over her mouth to stop her. "I should have expected this. What was it you said at Marco's that night about the feel of a cock in your cunt?"

"I wasn't talking about mine specifically," Sara said, choking on her tea as she protested indignantly. "I was talking in general. And don't change the subject."

"I'm still talking about fucking. Isn't that the subject?"

Sara's sense of humor was still intact, but her frustration with the direction of the conversation was growing. She knew he could sense it.

"I just want to make sure I'm understanding you. You're making a case for me to fuck you, right?"

"Sort of." She couldn't put her finger on it, but this was a new desire. There was something niggling at her, both about her needs and his understanding of them.

Seth pressed her again. "What do you mean?"

Nodding vigorously because the niggling was starting to become a clarity. Her need for it, this desire to have him so deep inside her, felt different.

"I'm making a different case. I want you to be with me. Deep inside me. Close as you can get." She didn't dare look at his face as she added, almost in a whisper, "To make love to me."

She shot a quick look at him to check his reaction. In less than a split second, she saw he was all softness, but he was silent—and for so long that she went on, filling in the silence, guessing now that the smile meant he was wondering how to let her down lightly.

"I get it. You don't want to," she said, taking both his hands in hers and kissing them. "That's okay for a while, I suppose." As she observed his anxiety, Sara became despondent and stern. "I know I told you there were no deal breakers, but I think you should know that I will need that at least a few times before I die."

"So, this would be bad, huh? You know, going without hetero-sexual penetration between now and when you die?" Looking at her squarely but a little uncertainly, he queried. "The rest of your life? Do you want to spend that time with me? Is that what you're saying?"

Sara nodded, and a smile spread broadly across Seth's face. She straddled his lap to kiss him, almost scalding them both with the hot cup of tea he still clenched in his hand.

With his eyes all glossy with desire, Sara assumed his quiet was due to the distraction she'd created in his lap. And when he seemed to confirm this by wrapping his hands around her hips in apparent encouragement, she thought, who cared about why he was so insistent about the intimacy program when it seemed like he was about to honor her request? All of a sudden, to Sara's utter despair, instead of assisting in a little bit of a lap dance that she thought might warm him up to the idea, Seth hauled her off his lap altogether.

Exasperated, Sara took his face in her hands, forcing him to look at her. When he shook his head, removing her hands from his face and getting up off the bed, Sara didn't even consider trying to make him less uneasy. Fed up and downright irate with his hedging, she demanded to know.

"Tell me what it was about your experience with Eyva that made you want to become abstinent."

He looked stunned, clearly not wanting to be drawn into that conversation. "I didn't say it was Eyva. Once I learned about the alternative sexuality communities, I decided I preferred alternatives anyway."

Sara looked unpacified by this response. "Marco told me that Eyva used to cut you when you were in bed together."

He averted his eyes and bit so intently into his bottom lip that Sara thought he might draw blood. "That's not the problem."

Sara's mind darted around, wondering.

Seth put her out of her misery. "She was very critical of my... stamina." He looked right at her.

"That's not nice." It came out flat and hollow, given what she knew Marco had said to him.

"I think she was probably justified," he said, exasperating her with his defense of Eyva, protesting against her culpability. "Most girls have political reasons to be critical about boys' stamina, I think. Boys are often more concerned about their own orgasm."

"It's just a pacing thing that can be fixed. Taught," Sara said meekly.

"Really?" He seemed intrigued by the suggestion.

Sara nodded vigorously at his curiosity. "I suspect your biggest problem was a combination of the sadistic component and the fact that Eyva was just too young to help you figure it out." She pulled herself back on to his lap. "You're with me now. I can help you with that." She laughed at his reaction as she made him squirm with her next question. "How quick are you anyway?

He put his hands on her hips and leaned into her. "By the way," he said, "I hate that expression 'make love.' Can we say 'fuck'?"

Sara nodded, smiling at this request, and then kissed him slowly.

"You want to teach me how to fuck you...slowly?" he said, still playful.

After they kissed for a long time, Sara resumed her ploy to warm him up to the idea. When he began to expertly pull her across his lap, Sara withdrew from him this time, against both of their libido's will. And, echoing her words from that night in the gay club, she told him, "Of course, if you want me to teach you, you'll have to fuck me for it."

"Seems like that would be part of the deal."

chapter twenty-seven

"I'll be out in a minute," Sara called from the bathroom, responding to the knocking on the door.

Jane's voice came from the other side of the door. "Why are you spending all your time at my party in the bathroom?"

"What do you think I'm doing in here?" she said, opening the door and pushing past Jane, hoping to quickly re-join the others gathered on the lawn rather than have a conversation about her penetrative-sex-induced UTI.

Allyson wandered out to the lawn clutching the biggest bag of soy chips Sara had ever seen. Positioning herself on the grass in between Sara and Jane, she tore into the bag of chips and grabbed a huge handful before offering them around. When she came to Sara, Allyson pulled the bag away.

"That's right. You don't eat."

Sara had been doing so well with her eating since Seth had been committed to rehab, so Allyson's flippancy elicited a wince from Sara and a glower from Seth. Sitting on the lawn together, they all listened to Allyson tell them about Callum's uncanny relationship with her clitoris.

"He could find it with a pine needle."

"Ouch," Jane joked.

Sara noticed Seth watching her.

"He has the best relationship with my clitoris than any boy I've ever known," Allyson went on, while Sara and Seth continued to gaze at each other. "Or any girl, come to that."

Seth was smiling at Sara now.

"Huh, you wouldn't expect that, right?" Eyva weighed in. "You know, since a woman would know the terrain so well."

Allyson nodded. "You would think that, but no," she said, offering the soy chips around, again bypassing Sara.

Seth picked up Sara's hand and squeezed it. This was their first real outing since he'd arrived home three weeks ago. There was no time for anything except just being alone together. Save for Sara's brief trips to Cambridge to decorate her Wellesley-based apartment and the time she spent on her frenzied writing, they were holed up, inseparable.

Sara's need to pee again overcame her and, after announcing she was going to the bathroom, was startled when Eyva grabbed her by the arm.

"UTI, right?" Evya said in front of the growing audience, which included Jane's boyfriend, "Medium- Energy Boy," and a few new WRC staffers that she'd yet to meet.

She was embarrassed it was that obvious. Hoping to slip away with as little fuss as possible, she simply smiled at Eyva. After all, she considered, it's not like they knew why she had a UTI.

"Of course, everyone knows the major reason women get UTIs, right?" Eyva added.

Sara had relaxed too soon. Not wanting to out Seth to the DIY sex community as just another lumpen headed, bougie straight guy who was engaging in something as passé as making love to his girl-friend, she jumped in to offer another plausible explanation. "I've heard swimming pools and ponds are a major culprit."

While Seth smirked back at her, seeming to hold in a laugh, Allyson asked an innocent question. "Have you been doing a lot of that, then?"

She drew her eyes away from Seth and his smirk, which seemed to say, *I don't care what they think*, and back to Allyson, just hoping for someone to say something about pond bacteria.

Seth swooped in, wrapping an arm around her hips. "Drew told me he read in the newspaper that there's a lot of bacteria in the pond behind Marco's house. They've even closed it down to swimming."

Allyson shook her head. "Well, for me it was fucking four times a day. Of course, maybe if I'd just peed after each time, it would've been okay. They say that helps."

Sara was thinking about that. Just four times a day. She looked to Seth to gauge his reaction to that number. He raised his eyebrows at her. She stifled a giggle. If only they'd limited it to that, but as many times as they'd done it—and every day for three whole weeks— well, there was no remedy other than rest and antibiotics for that.

Sara slunk off to the bathroom, wondering when she would learn.

* * *

The next morning, feeling slightly better after a restful night, they were on their way back to Sara's "town dwelling," as she facetiously called her close to Wellesley five-hundred-square-foot Cambridge studio.

Seth was not happy about the move to Cambridge. Unlike in the city, people never bothered him in Amherst. Sara loved how he handled his fame there. While he turned heads and people would stop and say "hi," Seth would just continue walking, but always say "hi" back to them in a pleasant, towny kind of way. At least there he went about his life in relative anonymity. Sara worried for him in Cambridge and felt guilty that she'd dragged him away from what was an almost normal life.

She'd chosen Cambridge because of its metro buzz, for the intellectual, cultural bustle that was so unlike Amherst and soccer-mom-in-her-Mercedes Wellesley. She hadn't given much thought to how it would affect Seth. After all, he was leaving for the European tour in a few weeks, and then a world tour in January. He wouldn't even be living in Cambridge again until next spring, and her fellowship would be over in the summer anyway.

They'd just driven into Harvard Square, only a five-minute walk from her apartment, but Sara, so desperate to pee, had insisted he pull over.

"I can't park here," he said, but Sara was already fidgeting with the door handle while the car was still inching along in traffic.

"Park illegally. Whatever," she said, leaping from the car.

"If we don't soon get some control, we should get stock in cranberry juice," Seth yelled after her.

She would've found it funny under normal circumstances, but she had other more pressing things on her mind to deal with as she shot into the Harvard Coop.

Sara emerged from the bathroom ten painful minutes later. Standing on the third-floor balcony of the Coop, scanning the lower floors for Seth, she suddenly saw a small crowd gathered by the door. To her horror, in the middle of it, she saw Seth, looking sad with the attention.

Sara raced down the stairs and into the posse of fans. Smiling at the gathering crowd, she took one of the coffees Seth was holding, grabbed his other hand, and rushed him out of there.

After grabbing a cab for the five-minute walk back to her apartment because she knew Seth just couldn't get away fast enough, Sara wondered how she was going to move him here at the end of the month.

The studio was on the top floor of a beautiful ten-story mansion house, and today was the hottest day of August in recorded history. Sara was grateful for the AC units that Seth had bought for the apartment. Cloistered there, sighing blissfully with every blast of icy air, they finally spoke.

"Sorry about that," she said.

"I don't want to talk about it."

"I do," Sara said, feeling both bad about what had happened and culpable for his misery, knowing the experience wouldn't have happened in Amherst.

"They'll tow you," he said, seeming to try to change the subject as he referred to her car that they'd ditched in favor of a fast getaway. "I'll obviously pay for that."

"I want to talk about what just happened. I don't like paparazzi taking my picture. I don't like being followed."

Seth looked at her, all sadness. "Then don't be seen with me."

Silence fell between them.

"Are you okay?" Sara finally spoke.

"No, I'm not." Seth angrily shook his head. "I won't live like a fucking rock star, besieged by admirers and paparazzi. I want to stay in Amherst."

Sara was stunned. "This is ironic. I used to think I couldn't be with you because your life would be too hard for me, but now you're saying my life is too hard for you. My ordinary, everyday life."

Seth started to talk over her, unleashing the depth of his existential nihilism, explaining to her that it wasn't her life that he couldn't handle, it was his. He was pissed—with the industry, with the performance...even with the fans.

Unprepared for the torrent of feelings from the usually quiet, calm Seth, Sara listened while he rattled on and on.

"This fucking industry has molded and manipulated this band into something unrecognizable to me. It's become even worse since San Francisco."

Next, he turned his fury on the entourage: the physicians, therapists, publicists, personal assistants and managers, the legal crew. In a long stream of profanity, the fans took it next. "Our political mission is not only lost on the new fans, but they're completely unconnected with any alternative community."

He gathered himself and began to both thank her for hearing him out and apologize profusely for losing it.

"Your indignation is righteous," Sara said, letting him know she understood his outburst. "I know all too well how difficult it is to be around people who're jarringly dismissive or even outright rejecting of the truth when your whole point of existence is to communicate the personal as political. God, just think about Callum at the start of the semester."

"My celebrity status is messing with that," Seth told her. "What I'm trying to say is that I can't live here as a rock star. I want to quit."

"Seriously?" Sara was stunned.

Seth kissed her in a way that said he wanted to move on to other things, but even that slow kiss couldn't distract her. While he'd clearly been giving this some thought, Sara needed some details.

"Can you do that?" She pulled away from his kiss. "Just *quit*?" Sara was giddy with the idea. "I once said I was going to quit being scholar-cum-activist because I don't think I'm very good at it."

"That's not the same. Fighting for women is in your nature. You can't quit. You've got to keep the battle up against patriarchy and hegemony—that's in your DNA."

"You just turned me on," Sara said, only half playfully.

"I'm serious," he said as she helped him off with his T-shirt.

"Then do it," Sara challenged him.

He looked quizzically at her as she tugged at the hemp string on his jeans. "I thought you didn't feel well?"

She flashed him a lascivious smile.

"I have a boner for virtue," he said, taking her hand off his groin. "Don't get so happy because it's not all good news. I have a contract, after all."

"A contract for a world tour. And it's a sell-out," she added teasingly, eliciting a playful slap on her butt from Seth. "That means you can't quit, right?"

"I don't know." He pulled her back close to him. "All I really want to do is stay here with you. And get stock in cranberry juice."

Sara pulled away. "I've learned my lesson there. From now on, I'll remember to pee every single time after we make love." She used an expression that she knew made him cringe, insisting as he did that, except for uncool gynecologists, no one actually dared to say that anymore. "And, for the sake of the intimacy program, I suppose we should cut back. I bet you'd love that."

He nodded, but Sara saw his brow furrow. She suspected he was concerned she was making a "too-big-to-bear" concession to be with him, Intimacy Boy. Sara wondered if they could make a deal. "I'll agree to divide our time, so long as you agree to replace one form of masochism for another."

Seth cocked a questioning eyebrow.

"If you can replace self-mutilating with the intimacy program, then, yes, I'll agree to that," Sara clarified.

Seth looked down at the mess of scars on his arms and nodded. "As long as the intimacy program can be a big part of what we do."

Sara agreed happily, hornily.

chapter twenty-eight

When they weren't in bed practicing the intimacy program, they were writing and transitioning—Sara to Wellesley, Seth to life in Cambridge. Since officially starting at Wellesley the week before, she was overwhelmed with exhaustion. Nevertheless, that was nothing new at the beginning of the semester; she bristled against change even under the best circumstances. What was new, however, was her inability to manage it.

Sara prepared to head into Wellesley for a seminar, dragging her tired body around the studio, trying to find her umbrella in one of the boxes that had yet to be unpacked. Finally locating the umbrella under a purple mohair wrap, she grabbed that too, both for comfort and warmth. It was only just September, but the weather was already cooler. More change. She felt her eyes become moist with sadness at the idea of this shift in the weather. Berating herself to get it together, she neither understood her emotional reaction to everything, nor her inability to get into her role as a Wellesley fellow without collapsing into self-debasing sobs every few hours.

Heading out the door for another round of self-doubt, she called out to Seth sitting on the bed playing his guitar. "Off to perform as thought leader again."

He got off the bed to see her off. "That's okay. I'm performing as a rock star in a couple of weeks."

Sara, cracking again under the pressure of Wellesley and then her guilt over what Seth was forced to live with in Cambridge, burst into tears. "I'm so sorry," she wailed.

Accosted daily as he was on the streets for autographs and photos, he was getting a head start on the rock-star role. At first, perturbed by his lack of anonymity in Cambridge, he'd taken to wearing disguises. Quickly becoming tired and fed up with the effort, in disgust he resigned himself to staying in the apartment and never leaving. Holed up all day, he passed his time writing and playing guitar. Yet, even bearing this heavy burden, he still took the time to comfort her.

"What on earth's going on? You've been a wreck since we got here."

That was an understatement. On top of the general malaise and doubts about her abilities, she'd been feeling ill too. Even after the fever of the UTI had long since left and her fainting episode from hunger after being too busy keeping up at Wellesley to eat, the persistent nausea that refused to leave was not helping. For added comfort, she wrapped the mohair a little tighter around herself as she added the loss of her support system to the list. Jane and Marco may as well have been a million miles away, and Seth was off to brave a European tour, ostensibly drug free. One by one, the people she spent all her time with were being snatched away like the leaves on the maples in front of her apartment building.

She tried to sum all of that up. "What if they figure out I'm not a thought leader after all?"

"It's a lot more fucking pressure than being a rock star, isn't it?" Seth declared, not helping.

Sara hurled her head into her hands, beseeching. "Help me. I can't do this. I'm not good enough."

"Why would you doubt yourself? They don't. Just accept that they accept you."

Sara grimaced, recoiling from the Zen part of his statement.

Seth reminded her of all the credits that justified her new position. "You're teaching the seminar they specifically reserve for feminist superstars, am I right? The other teachers were who? Remind me?" He started a list, not waiting for an answer. "How's that feel?"

She was feeling like she was anything other than a superstar and much more like a physical mess and poor excuse for a human being.

Seeing her paste pale, Seth looked alarmed, grabbing her by both arms right before she collapsed.

Despite the fainting spell, Sara insisted that she couldn't miss the department colloquia and left for Wellesley, but not until Seth had coaxed her into eating something.

* * *

Sara drove home early, exhausted. The last thing she expected to see waiting for her was Allyson, and it was especially surprising because she was also crying on Seth's shoulder. Sara, assuming the worst and thinking it was probably to do with Callum, said, "Stay for dinner."

Seth shot her a wide-eyed look as he shook his head, mouthing "no." However, it was too late as Allyson was already accepting the invitation.

"You're tired, Sara," Seth said.

"Jane's coming for the weekend anyway. And I had a nap in my office."

Sara's puzzlement deepened when she observed Seth's disapproving look as she handed Allyson a huge margarita.

"No, you should go and meet Callum," Seth said emphatically, slugging at his iced tea. "You two need to talk." Sara shot a look at Seth, hoping it would communicate her irritation with the mystery just as Allyson began heaving hysterical sobs at Seth's suggestion.

Sidetracked, Sara moved away from inquisitor role to comforter. Making soothing noises, she protested. "You can't go like this. You're too upset." A look of self-satisfaction crossed her face as she settled on what she thought was the perfect solution. "Call Callum. Invite him for dinner." Observing Seth's open-mouthed horror at this suggestion, Sara shrugged back at him, mouthing "what?" as she hugged Allyson, comfortingly shushing her sobs.

Thirty minutes later, amidst a lot of tutting from Seth and without Sara having gained more understanding of the situation, Callum stood in her kitchen. Chatting with Jane about her failing attempts to grow an herb garden, Callum was finishing Allyson's margarita after she'd declared it was making her feel nauseous because she hadn't eaten anything in hours. With everything seeming to go perfectly between Allyson and Callum, Sara was feeling smug when she felt Seth's hands slide around her hips as she prepared dinner.

"What's up there?" she whispered, motioning with her head in the direction of Allyson and taking a big gulp from his iced tea.

Seth looked at her quizzically as she held his glass, taking another drink before handing it back to him. "You're not drinking?"

"I don't feel that well." Sara returned his curious gaze. "Why? You want me to drink?" She knew what he was getting at, but since she wanted to faint, puke, or both every time she drank, she hadn't even sipped anything alcoholic in the last two weeks.

"What's wrong?"

"I've been ill," she reminded him, bothered by his badgering, and kissing him to shift his worry.

He'd been worrying about her a lot, it seemed. She guessed it was because of how sick she'd been with the UTI, and all her lunatic-level moments of nihilism since the move, and because he was anxious about leaving her in twelve days. She thought there was nothing to really worry about. After all, between Wellesley, her concern for Seth's comfort, and the nausea she'd endured from the first two rounds of antibiotics, who could drink?

"I think I might've picked up the flu. There's a lot going around, but what's going on with Allyson?"

Callum interrupted them before he had chance to respond. "Let's feed Allyson before she keels over."

Allyson positioned herself next to Seth, as far away from Callum as possible, and Sara felt her vainglorious satisfaction with her matchmaking arrangements begin to deteriorate. Sensing the tension between Callum and Allyson growing more palpable with every second, Sara tried to shift both the energy and the food on her plate.

"How're the first few weeks of the semester, Callum?" Sara asked, chewing occasionally on the odd grain of rice, unable to eat because she was feeling nauseous again. This time the trigger was the stress of leaving Wellesley early when she should have been there for an evening reading.

Seth was watching her, so Sara put a piece of tofu on her fork while Callum talked enthusiastically about his new program at

Boston University, seeming relieved for the distraction from Allyson's scowling.

For the fifth time, Allyson snapped at him. Callum offered a conciliatory smile, what looked to Sara like a white flag. Allyson remained entrenched against him and shot back a pout that would rival any six-year-old. Doubling down his efforts, Callum leaned over to affectionately stroke her arm. At his touch, Allyson burst into sobs.

Everyone fell silent. All the faces in the room were awash with a combination of bemusement and worry as Allyson wailed, not unlike a dying animal. All except Seth's, Sara observed. As she pondered Seth's lack of reaction, Allyson turned her outburst onto Sara.

"Eat something, will you? You're so fucking thin."

"Shut the fuck up," Seth threw back at Allyson.

Ignoring his order, Allyson dove back in. "I can't eat because I feel sick to my fucking stomach, what's your fucking excuse? You're not fucking pregnant."

Before the question could settle, Sara was struck dumb—less by the news than the delivery. At first, amused by the impressive amount of profanity that Allyson had squeezed into her lashing, Sara quickly shifted to become hurt by Allyson's rage toward her. Sara was quick to forgive as she remembered Jane's warning that night. *So, this is who Jane had warned me about being pregnant the night Seth became so sick.* However, the smile that tweaked at her upper lip withered just as quickly as a new thought struck her. Symptoms that she'd attributed to stress or to the after-effects of all those rounds of antibiotics, perhaps even the actual flu, which as she'd told Seth just moments ago was going around campus, began to develop into a new hypothesis.

Sara retreated to her head while everyone else was busy pandering to Allyson's hysteria. The room closed in, heavier than a black hole, as she fought desperately to remember when she'd last bled. It had been at least six weeks, maybe more if Sara dared to be honest with herself. Her previously happy thoughts of what she'd be doing with Seth later were shredded.

Gripped by the gravity of worry, she went into full drama mode. The need to duck and cover until the mushroom cloud had settled made her want to hide under the bed. But even then, she'd still have to breathe in the choking ash and invisible gas, and that would be enough to cause final annihilation. She felt the blood drain from her face and nausea settle in. Since all eyes were still on Allyson, Sara wondered if anyone would notice if she threw up in the skillet, handily within arm's reach.

Gathering herself and daring to try to lighten the mood, Sara quipped back at Allyson's mean retort instead. "No, Allyson, just an eating disorder, but thanks for your understanding."

Allyson, crying softly now, pleaded with Sara. "I'm so fucking sorry. You have to forgive me. I'm on an emotional fucking roller-coaster right now. I barely fucking recognize myself."

That sounded familiar.

Sara took her first look at Seth since the mushroom-cloud realization moment and saw that he focused on Callum. It occurred to Sara that Allyson must have told him she was pregnant, and now he was looking for the potential father's reaction. This would also explain all of Seth's behavior since she'd found Allyson crying on his shoulder.

Abruptly, Seth averted his eyes to his plate, seemingly acknowledging the moment between them should be private. He flicked a look to Sara before looking back at Callum with a troubled gaze that said, *What a mess.*

chapter twenty-nine

Barely able to confront the truth behind her symptoms herself, let alone talk to Seth about them, she'd managed to divert him another week, staving him off by simply looking busy and muttering dismissive clichés. She was relieved when it was Saturday again, and she could rest.

"A reprieve from being a thought leader for two whole days," she sighed to Seth as they lay in bed together. He made no response.

Seth had been quieter than usual for the past day or two. Whether this was because of his imminent departure for the tour or his concerns about her behavior, Sara didn't know. Since she still wasn't entirely convinced that she didn't just have the flu, she didn't want to ruin their last few days together by talking about idle worries.

Later in the morning, Seth confronted her, ranting about eating disorders and *not* babies. Sara was relieved. In an attempt to get her to eat something, he'd made toast.

"You could eat it dry," he suggested.

Under threat of puking, Sara refused, and Seth exploded.

"Fuck, Sara. You're throwing up, losing weight. And I think you've stopped drinking to compensate for the extra calories you've been eating. What's going on?"

He was right—she had increased her daily calorie intake and stopped drinking. Despite filling her ravenous appetite, the nausea-induced vomiting throughout the day attributed to her steady weight loss.

The doorbell rang, rescuing her from having to provide yet another weak explanation.

Seth's look of exasperation prompted her to offer the same suggestion she had every time he'd asked this question lately. "Can we talk about this later? There's a lot going around, flu and stuff." She charged off toward the door.

Jane, Marco, and Drew had arrived for the weekend. Boisterous embraces were exchanged all around, and in the middle of all the commotion, Sara exchanged a look with Seth. His decidedly unhappy expression remained as he sullenly propped himself against the arch into the kitchen. Marco's attention settled on Seth, ever sensitive to the energy in a room. Sara was pleased he marched right over to him.

Jane, who'd secured a grant, pulled out her phone to show Sara and Drew the pictures of the office space the university had seen fit to give them as a result. Sara wasn't paying much attention, distracted by Seth and Marco's earnest looking conversation.

Jane tutted. "You're not even looking."

Sara looked back at Jane with tears in her eyes.

She hadn't intended to let them know about her worries before she'd spoken to Seth, but Marco and Jane ambushed her into a confession the minute Seth left to take a shower. Having heard about her odd behavior, Marco asked her outright if she was pregnant. Drew didn't look at all surprised by this line of questioning.

So he is in on it too.

Panicking, she tried to avoid answering. "There's a lot going around," tumbled involuntarily from her mouth.

"Well, I certainly hope that's it. I mean, only stupid women get pregnant by accident," Jane said.

"Not thought leaders, for sure," Marco added. "That'd be embarrassing to explain to all your friends at Wellesley, right? 'I got knocked up because, despite being renowned as a great thinker, I didn't think to use a condom.' That would just slay you, right?"

Drew shook his head at Marco. *Too much.*

Sara, turning crimson, hissed at Marco to keep his voice down. Under the peril of Seth hearing, she blurted out, "I don't think that's very fucking fair. It happens. I mean, Allyson is a very smart girl, and she got fucking pregnant by fucking accident."

Sara rarely swore, and never in a stream of profanity, not unless under extreme duress. Marco and Jane, knowing they'd cornered her into an inadvertent confession, pressed further.

"But Allyson has a latex allergy," Jane said unhelpfully. "She can't use condoms."

Weakened, Sara scrambled for a defense. "There's the birth control pill." She looked to Drew to see if he could throw her a life-line, but his face said, *Keep me out of this.*

Marco nodded. "True, but Jane told me Allyson can't use the pill because of a family blood clotting issue, or something like that," he said, helping to push the argument in support of Sara's stupidity.

"Yes, and she's tried all kinds of new-fangled devices. Everything."

Marco tutted. "Sounds like she worked really hard not to get pregnant."

Sara rubbed her forehead. "What are you trying to say, that I'm stupid?"

Mouths agape in astonishment, their suspicions confirmed by this apparent admission, Jane snipped, "Frankly, yes."

Resentfully, Sara nodded her agreement. "Yes, given your fucking rigid definition of stupidity, I suppose I fall somewhere along the continuum, but while I might know for certain that I am indeed stupid, I don't know for certain that I'm pregnant."

Sara stared at all three of their stunned little faces, their focus fixed behind her. Between Marco's warningly raised eyebrows, Jane's wide-eyed sucked in expression, and Drew running a flat hand over the top of his head, Sara had all the confirmation she needed that Seth was in the room and must have heard that last comment, at least the very last word.

Fucking great, she thought as she turned to look at Seth, who, without taking his eyes off Sara, said softly, "Would you mind leaving us alone for a bit?"

For a brief moment, Sara thought he meant her and was flooded with relief, but of course, he didn't mean her.

Drew jumped into action first and began to haul Marco to his feet, firmly shushing him every time he attempted to open his mouth. Jane hurriedly grabbed her things and was close behind them. At the door Marco and Drew had already bolted past, Sara caught Jane's eye as she held it open.

Sara's face crumpled to say, *Do you really think I'm stupid? Please don't hate me for this, I know you think this is terrible.* Jane's face sternly but compassionately said, *Go and deal with this*, then she left, closing the door quietly behind her.

Left standing alone with Seth in their one-room apartment, Sara stared at the closed door, wishing she could be on the other side of it with Jane and Marco.

"Fuck," Sara lamented, bagged and cornered.

Seth jumped in with a warning. "Don't you fucking dare say there's a lot going around or can we talk about it later. Why are you talking to Marco and Jane and not me?"

Sara turned to look at him, quickly explaining that Marco and Jane had caught her at a propitious moment.

"Propitious for me. Were you planning on talking to me before I leave in three fucking days? I don't think so, right?" Seth fell silent. Dropping his head, he bit his bottom lip, tears welling in his eyes.

Sara sank further into her denial as she interpreted his melancholy, attributing it to the threat of impending parenthood and not to her lack of transparency with him. "I really think it could be the flu. It might be. Maybe. I don't know."

"I know you haven't bled in two months, Sara."

Sara's mouth gaped, shocked at his insight. "How would you know that?"

"Because I'm fucking paying attention," he snapped. "Kind of reckless not to, the way we…" He looked down at the floor as he trailed off.

"The way we what?"

"We haven't been careful every time, right?" he said, looking right at her. "We've been careless. Stupid."

Exasperated at hearing the word used twice in reference to herself in the space of ten minutes, Sara just stared back at him. It was one of the most uncomfortable silences she'd ever created. It settled over the room.

Seth, at last, exhaled so heavily that it startled her. "Just tell me. Are you pregnant?"

Flustered, Sara began waving her arms around as if she were groping for the right words to suddenly appear out of thin air. Finally, she had to admit the inevitable had caught up with her and began to cry. "I think so, yes," she whispered meekly.

* * *

After the allotted three minutes had passed, Seth insisted that she check the pregnancy test. Unable to see the truth glaring nakedly up at her and preferring instead to figuratively, as well as literally, pull it into view gradually, Sara had hidden the test under the bed.

The bed, as she approached it, was only about ten feet from anywhere else in the apartment and looked lurid to her now. It felt like ten minutes to span the five paces to the bed. Seth, unable to bear the suspense, got up to put the kettle on.

Getting up from her crouching position on the floor, Sara pulled the test into full view. She tried to do it without being noticed, not wanting to distract Seth from his kettle minding. At that moment, all she wanted was some privacy to register what she'd learned. The hush in the room was as loud as a baby's scream, and she knew he was watching her as she turned, with ominous quiet, and walked into the bathroom.

Once in the bathroom, Sara loudly exclaimed a stream of profanity, then began to softly sob.

Sara heard Seth knock lightly on the door and then the sound of his head gently resting against it. His voice was muffled through the door.

"Good news then?"

Sara was in no mood to respond to his efforts to lighten the situation.

Once he'd managed to talk Sara out of the bathroom, she sat down on the couch next to him. Virtually catatonic, her eyes red and bulging with a perpetually runny nose, Seth handed her tissue after tissue. Sara dismissed each one, her sleeve epitomized her despair better, highlighting her sense of isolation and her anger with her body.

"It was just a couple of times that we messed up."

"Apparently that was enough. And anyway, I don't really know what all this is about. We fucked up. I assumed we were taking chances because you didn't mind the potential outcome. This outcome."

Sara looked at Seth like he'd just said something so utterly ridiculous that she was shocked into silence. "The few times when we, as you say, 'fucked up,' were, as I recall, after I'd had a few glasses of wine. *You* should have been more responsible."

Seth looked stung. "That's not fair, and you know it. Honestly, does it even matter now?" He saw Sara's resigned look and proceeded more softly. "We need to move into what we do now. How do you want to take care of it?"

Sara gasped, then shrieked. "What?!" Clasping both hands over her mouth, she cried with dramatic disdain over his choice of words. "How do I want to *take care of it*? Like some 1950's back-street abortion!"

Falling silent for a moment, Seth watched as Sara frantically twisted strands of hair around her fingers. "I take that reaction to mean you don't want to have an abortion," he said calmly. "Fine."

Sara shot a look of disgust at Seth and leaped off the couch for dramatic effect. Her pregnant body protested the movement and a dizzy faintness gripped her. Alarmed by her sudden pasty pallor and unsteadiness, Seth jumped up to catch her right before she hit the floor.

Shrugging off his firm hold on her, Sara continued to try to make her point. Hoping to communicate the depth of her indignation with what she perceived as his flippancy, she paced. Moving quickly at first, she soon gave up, forced to slow down because the whip of the turn started to make her feel faint again and she had to slow down. Unable to release her emotions with movement, she resumed the frantic twirling of hair tightly around a finger, pulling hard enough at the follicle for strands to pop free.

"You want me to have an abortion?"

"I didn't say that. It's up to you. I defer to your decision, Sara."

The platitudes infuriated her. But her own drama and the constant drip from her nose and eyes that now required constant wiping was getting exhausting. She threw all the weight she could throw into barking at him.

"Of course I'm fucking pro-abortion, for fuck's sake. In addition to escorting scores of women through those throngs outside of clinics, I've had one myself." With the fight all gone from her, she collapsed back onto the couch. Taking deep, cleansing breaths, both to calm herself and to avoid throwing up, she added, "I just don't want one this time."

Seth nodded, the face of composure against her rattled nerves. To warm them against the shock, he made them both a cup of tea.

"I'll admit I'm scared," she offered, trying to coax a word out of him. Seth sat in a somber silence, sipping from his tea. "I don't know why, but I just feel differently about this pregnancy." She raised both her arms in the air, spilling some of her tea as she did. "I don't even know why, but I do." She looked at Seth again for some reaction. More tea sipping commenced. He wasn't even looking at her now. She tried again. "In a way, I get why you're not saying anything. You probably don't know what to think or feel." She put her tea onto the table and reached out to touch his knee, wanting some contact with him because right now his silence and averted eyes made it feel like he was so far away from her. "It's not happening to you, is it?" she offered, pointing a finger at her flat belly, indicating there was something nefarious going on inside her. "Of course, I'm saying all this in real time. I'm still processing it." Deciding to blurt it all out at once but knowing it was about to utterly discompose him, she didn't dare look at him as she asked, "And, I just need to know, how do you feel? I mean, do you want to have a baby? With me, I mean?"

Once the words were out, she fixed her gaze on him. The look on Seth's face was so stripped bare that for one awful moment Sara expected a loud groan to emanate from his mouth before he threw some of his sell-out money at her and walked away. When the silence became unbearable, visions of having to sue him for child support and moving in with Marco and Drew, sobbing and destitute with a bundle of baby in her arms, filled her head.

"Fuck. I don't know," he declared as his face blanched.

Sara, beginning to hyperventilate with all the emotional tumult, suffered a fresh wave of nausea in her newly fragile body that forced her to charge into the bathroom, yelling behind her, "Fuck you, then!" before promptly throwing up.

Once she'd finished throwing up, Sara was mortified that she hadn't closed the door behind her. Seth stood in the doorway, watching her spitting the last few bits into the bowl and wiping her mouth on the hand towel. She leaned against the wall of the bathroom, resigned.

Seth joined her on the bathroom floor. Picking up her hand, he said, "I'm just in shock. You've had a hunch about this for some time, whereas I'm just hearing about it now."

She nodded in understanding. Hoping for more clarification, she waited.

"This is lousy timing."

She had to agree with that.

"But if this is what you want, then okay, of course."

Sara no more knew that this is what she wanted than she understood how to dismantle patriarchy. It was simply a visceral reaction.

* * *

Somehow Marco understood both sides perfectly. Around eight p.m., he returned, this time minus Drew, giving a little tentative knock on the door to her apartment and sheepishly slinking in, asking if he was needed for anything. Sara fell into his arms.

Before Seth left for tour, Marco lovingly spent the next three days trying to explain Sara's perspective to him. At the end of it, Seth still looked utterly blank.

Marco changed tack, causing Sara's jaw to slacken when he shrugged and said directly to Seth, "And, anyway, while you're figuring this out, what I want to know is how the fuck this happened in the first place, Abstinence Boy. When did everyone stop sharing their truth?"

Eating crackers to stave off her near-constant nausea, Sara listened to Marco rant.

"And you," he said directly to her. "How did you manage to fuck up on such a colossal scale?"

At that, Sara buried her face in her knees after brushing cracker crumbs off her shirt. "I just ate two hundred calories in carbs. Leave me alone," she said, beginning to cry softly, sick to her stomach both with the binge eating and with Seth's imminent departure.

chapter thirty

Less than twenty-four hours after he'd left to join the tour in Paris, Seth left a message on her answering machine: "Hey Sara, just wanted to let you know that I'm still, as you like to say, processing and…well, just call me. I miss you. And I really miss fucking you."

Coming from the person previously known as Abstinence Boy, she beamed.

She dialed. He answered immediately, begging her to let him pay for her to fly out so they could be together for the weekend. As soon as her Wellesley schedule would allow it, she flew out, which ended up being three weeks after his first plea.

He picked her up at the airport with his bodyguard/driver in tow, making Sara raise her eyebrows questioningly, gesturing to the "heavy" they'd brought along as protection for Seth.

"Can't we just take a cab?"

Seth, rolling his eyes with disdain for the bodyguard, explained that the tour reps had insisted on security. "But I have some good news on that," he said cryptically. "I don't think they can force that on me for much longer."

While Sara wondered what he meant as they drove across London to the hotel, the state of his arms was a bigger concern. Judging by the bandages, it appeared his self-harming had increased. Given that they talked every day, and she knew it wasn't going well for him, at least this time she had expected it.

After a long time kissing in the back of the car, Sara fell silent.

She felt his eyes on her as she traced his arms, knowing he understood her concern. He'd told her everything in those phone calls from various hotel rooms throughout Europe.

"How is everything else going today?" She was talking about his drug use. While she could deal with the cutting, three days ago Sara had hung up the phone on him when, in confessional style, Seth had told her that he'd been using again.

With all the physical changes in her body, she couldn't manage it. The combination of her burgeoning protective feelings for the baby, not to mention her fragile emotional wellbeing as she prepared herself for the reality that her whole life was about to be transformed, Sara was feeling vulnerable and not at all inclined to be sympathetic. Seth had called back repeatedly and left four messages that same day. When he called repeatedly the next day, on hearing the panic in his voice at the thought of losing her, her resolve snapped, and she'd picked up the phone.

Seth seemed to be sensing all her anxiety again. "I know what you're thinking. I seriously fucked up. I'm sorry for it."

With their bodies squashed hard against each other in the car, unable to get close enough after being separated for weeks, he spoke at speed. "I've been checking in every day with my psychiatrist. In fact, she's coming out to join the tour. I demanded they pay for her to be part of my official entourage."

"Is there anything they won't do for you?" Sara threw up her arms, marveling at their agreement to his demands, making him laugh sardonically.

"Our music is just a commodity to them, making them all rich. You bet your fucking life they agreed to it."

Seth told her that the tour reps had been nervous, worried sick by his threat to leave if they didn't do this, but also pissed, confronting him on it. He said they'd snapped at him, saying they were having a difficult time understanding precisely why, in addition to his professional and personal entourage, he wanted more.

Seth mimicked the tour reps. "You want us to pay for a psychiatrist to help you with your drug habit?"

At the mention of his drug habit again, Sara stopped laughing and fell silent.

"Just remember, Sara, I don't have a drug habit anymore. It's touring that makes me vulnerable, but I'm working on it. Just like I know you're working on your stuff. And I'm doing well. For the most part anyway."

Like Sara, he was in traditional treatment programs now, though they both considered the intimacy program an ad-hoc sort of therapy.

"I really want to get well…" He'd told her this many times in the last few weeks before leaving for the tour, and it had inspired her to want that for herself. Sort of.

Sara, crumbling at the sight of his anxious brow and his worried taut lips, pulled his gaze on her when she shushed him, her lips brushing his.

The polite kissing in the car was replaced by ravenous making out before the door even closed on their hotel room. He'd come right there, barely into the room, leaning against the open door while she simultaneously undressed and kissed him.

"Hey," Sara exclaimed. "What are you doing?"

While Seth claimed to be just as surprised as her, Sara giggled at his relieved smile. "Yeah, right."

After he'd reciprocated the favor and, to please her, submitted to the pacing regimen, he literally begged her for the intimacy program. It concerned her, believing that such a need for sexual frustration was just more evidence of his increasing need for pain.

After they couldn't stand any more intimacy for fear of orgasms occurring yet again, Sara suggested that he might want to talk to his psychiatrist about increasing his medication dosage.

"I have, and she is, but just to warn you, you'll likely be seeing more of this at the show tonight." His eyes closed with exhaustion.

It made her shiver to think about the show, to see more masochism all over

him, but it was Wembley Arena. "It's special. Please come," he'd begged.

Suddenly remembering the good news he'd alluded to in the car, Sara made a mental note to ask him about it.

When she woke up, Seth leaned over her, smiling, telling her someone would pick her up in an hour to take her to the show.

* * *

Seth hung back, giving the stage to Eyva at London's 90,000-seat Wembley Arena. Sara felt chilled all over as she stood backstage and listened to Eyva chant the opening to "The Communist Manifesto."

"The history of all hitherto existing societies has been a history of class struggle." Then, taking liberties with Karl Marx's definition of class, she added, "Women and men, black and white, rich and poor, gay and straight, you have nothing to lose but your chains. Nothing to lose but your chains."

In the middle of the last chant, the audience erupted with applause at the deafeningly loud wailing from Seth's guitar as he opened with the first few chords of "Radical."

Despite Seth's cynicism and exhaustion, watching the show, Sara saw nothing except the powerful energy that had put Seth and the band in the spotlight in the first place. She empathized with his disdain for what their shows had become—contrived. A performance rather than an experience. The damage this spectacle was creating in him was evident to her. Where was the good news in this for him?

As they entered the middle part of the show and the intensity picked up, Sara observed Seth begin to lose himself to the experience. Thrashing his body around the stage with such abandon, it was only a matter of time before he'd be scarred in some way. He almost knocked himself out climbing and falling from a very tall speaker. Hitting his head on the way down, Seth went on to play through two more songs, completely undaunted by the probable concussion he'd incurred.

Wondering when Caleb would be the next target of Seth's single-minded intent to harm himself, Sara began to anticipate the moment, wincing every time he looked anywhere near the vicinity of the drum kit. What had now become a natural consequence finally happened, and Seth ended the intense middle period of the show by jumping into Caleb's kit. While Caleb escaped just in time, the drum kit, along with Seth's guitar, did not.

As Seth hammered his guitar again and again into Caleb's kit, destroying both instruments in his angst, the band was forced to take a break while the crew located another drum kit and guitar.

Seth left the stage and headed straight for Sara. When he reached her, he kissed her so intensely that she pulled away from him.

"I'm so fucking in love with you," he said, pulling her body back to him.

Querying the intensity of their kissing and his evident arousal in the presence of an uncomfortably close crew, she stopped him again. He took her hand and put it on his groin.

"Seriously?" Sara said, although she was immediately excited. "Here? Now?" she questioned, already scoping out a darker corner.

As if that wasn't enough to make her completely aroused, he sent her straight to ten when he began to plead. Leading him to a black spot in the recesses of the backstage, Sara laughed as she shared her observation that they'd never done it in the dark before.

"Kind of have to when it's public, don't you think?" Seth acknowledged with a smirk, putting his hand up her skirt while she worked to undo his hemp-string belt, saying, "Now here's a sweet little story for the pregnancy memory book."

He stopped her in a sudden breathy whisper to give her instructions. "Just nice and slow. Remember, I don't want to come."

Sara whispered back, "Okay, but just remember—I do. I'm not a masochist."

After kissing her long and hard before he returned to the reassembled set, she noted how he was yet again blissfully happy in his sexual frustration.

Seth readjusted himself, then put his hand on the lowest part of her belly and asked her how she was feeling, how the processing was going.

When Sara told him her due date, he had his answer.

"You really want this, don't you?" he said.

Her nod was as firm as the hand he held to her belly. "And you?"

He removed his hand from her belly to place both hands behind his head, as if he didn't know what to do with these strange appendages hanging off his arms. Hands still cradling the back of his head, he stretched, then looked at her, shaking his head. *Not there.*

Sara understood. She wasn't worried about his lag behind her, or if he'd ever catch up, but just glad for his frankness, his transparency about everything.

"I talked with Callum. He's actually excited about Allyson being pregnant," he said, dropping his hands to his guitar, fiddling with a tiny scratch.

"I think Allyson is too, now the shock's gone and they're talking..." Sara reached out to touch his fiddling fingers.

He enveloped his hand around hers. "You know I'm not there, but I do know I want you. I think anything would be good with you."

She'd never before known a man who could behave like such a big boy. While the shock of her pregnancy had put them both in a spot, it was her decision to change both their lives forever, and she thought he was handling it with a self-possession rarely seen in grown-ups far older.

Thinking about that as she watched him end the show, mellow this time and without further self-mutilation, she couldn't wait to get him back to their hotel room. Or, if they were unable to wait until then, Sara wondered if maybe the green room would be empty.

* * *

The next morning, after several hours of the intimacy program, Sara suggested they ditch the security and drive somewhere out of London so they could be normal. While the bodyguard was hesitant, Seth was able to battle through the pushback to convince him that it was a private thing.

After the rental car was arranged and the bodyguard looked the other way, they drove off together. Aimlessly driving around, pregnancy hunger suddenly overcame Sara. And, accompanied as it always was by nausea and dizziness, she told him they had to stop.

They ended up in a perfect spot: a tea house converted from an orchard, replete with deck chairs and tables amidst the apple trees. While Sara salivated at the sight of the food, Seth looked on, amazed, because he'd never really seen her eat a meal before.

"Can you believe this?" She was amazed herself at her newly found appetite. "I have no choice. I literally throw up if I don't eat every couple of hours."

And it was more than that too. Sara finally had her motivation, feeding that ravenous hunger as she'd been doing ever since the doctor told her that she was "dangerously thin. Too thin to deliver a healthy, full-term baby."

Seth watched her feed her motivation. "Is it going to upset you if I tell you you've gained weight?" He leaned in to kiss her. "It's nice."

Sara, curious with this interpretation of her five-pound weight gain, forced him to elaborate as she put another forkful in her mouth.

"I like to know you're okay." Then pausing, he dropped his eyes to her breasts. "Plus, selfishly here I realize, really nice tits."

"You just wait," she said as she joined him in gazing at her breasts. "Apparently, they're going to be bulbous and bursting with veins. And already orgasms feel different."

"They do?" Seth was immediately intrigued. "How?"

"I feel them more in my uterus now. That whole area just rolls and throbs during an orgasm. It's like the baby's participating in it and that thought sort of kills the whole feeling."

He urged her to reconsider the experience. "Lucky. You get to have a different orgasm. I would love that. Maybe a painful one for me would be good."

Not convinced, but listening to his enthusiasm, Sara smiled when he put his hand on her lower belly and dropped his voice.

"When you come, you could think about the good fuck we were having when we did this. That's really sexy when you think about it."

She kissed him, giving him a lascivious smile. "Let's go. I want to test this idea."

With the dual intent of testing Seth's little hypothesis and relishing his chance of being anonymous, they checked into a bed and breakfast. Exhausted from alternately practicing the pacing and intimacy regimens the night before and much of that morning, they both fell asleep almost immediately.

* * *

When they woke up, Seth pleaded for the intimacy regimen, reminding her again of his masochistic tendencies. She withdrew from him.

"What's wrong?" he asked her, becoming exasperated.

"Exactly when are you going to increase your meds again?"

Seth's turn to withdraw. "Why? What's up?"

Taking his face in her hands, Sara forced him to look at her. "I'm just concerned that you seem much more intense in your need for the intimacy program, cutting, drugs—all masochistic needs, right? And the meds are supposed to help you need that less."

While he maintained eye contact with her, he didn't respond, making Sara incredulous. "What are you going to do when I leave? It won't be as easy for me to hop on a plane when you're in Australia and I'm heavily pregnant."

He explained in a whispery voice that the plan was to steadily increase the dosage over the next few weeks. "I'm taking care of it as best I can."

Sara pulled herself flat against his body as they lay in bed together, kissing him to soften the blow of what she was about to say. "I don't think it's going very well."

"I think quitting will be the biggest help, Sara."

She couldn't believe what she was hearing. He'd told her that he couldn't quit because of his contract.

He intercepted her thoughts. "This is just not working for me. I'm a self-destructive, miserable fucking mess."

"You mean because of the tours? The rock star performance?"

Seth nodded. "It's the catalyst for all my stuff. Jessie, the psychiatrist, has helped me to see that the drugs and all the self-harming is made worse by it. An escape from it. I remember shooting up one day because I had an obscenely large professional entourage waiting for me in a hotel lobby. When I told the tour doctor this, rather than recommending I quit, their answer was to get me a psychiatrist who helps celebrities cope with being a celebrity. I don't want to cope with this. You said you considered quitting academia because you didn't think you could ever be as good a thinker as those at Wellesley. And I've thought a lot about that because I never want to be good at this. I never want to be one of the best at being a rock star."

Sara interrupted him. "Didn't you say you can't quit? You have a contract."

Seth smiled. "This is my good news. I have a bunch of lawyers working around the clock getting me out of that very contract. I'm done. And I've been writing on and off for the last year. Poetry, I mean."

Nodding numbly at this, Sara said, "Well good, but can we get back to you quitting?"

"They're sort of related."

"You're quitting? For good?"

He nodded, smiling at the emotional mix of disbelief and joy on her face.

She sputtered in her befuddlement. "Sorry, how does the poetry tie in here? Because you said it did."

"I just got a few poems published. And I'm just going to focus on that." He tried to change the subject. "What do you think? Do you want to go back to the pub?"

She wouldn't allow him to creep out of it. Winkling the whole story out of a modestly blushing Seth, she discovered it was an entire book of poems. And he'd not only secured a top agent and publisher, but also received an embarrassingly large advance and a three-book deal.

"What are you, a creative genius or something?" Sara declared, aghast.

Seth pushed back, scoffing, "Don't be so fucking modest, Ms. Feminist-fucking-Press."

They lay down together. Sara watched him looking at her belly in wonder at what was happening to her body, and a heavy silence fell between them that she interpreted as sleepiness from her jet lag and his tour schedule, but the exhaustion-induced silence that was luring Sara to sleep was anything but sleepy quietness for Seth. Startling her awake with the sound of his voice, Seth said, "How about you and me?" He stopped to clear his throat.

She turned slowly to look at him. "Is there more?"

"We could be sick together."

Sara relaxed the frown on her face. "I think we're broken together."

Seth stared at the ceiling. "Okay. Broken then. But I mean, could you be committed to doing that with me?"

Sara screwed her face up. "It's too late. Go to sleep," she said, peppering kisses on his eyelids.

"Do you still think monogamy is a natural evil? Is it inevitably enslaving to women?"

Sara plumped her pillow. "Didn't we cover this once?"

"Would you consider it with me?"

She stopped plumping to look at him. She knew he knew she couldn't resist the argument, that she'd be drawn in. "Well," she started off in lecture mode, "you know the philosophy of historical materialism and all anthropological research on early humans points to monogamy as possibly the main culprit in the origin of patriarchal control."

Seth grinned. "So, that's a no, right?"

Sara started curling her hair with a finger. "You know, we could work from within, right? Turn Audre Lorde's thesis on its head—use the master's tools to dismantle the master's house. We'll reinvent it, create an unexpurgated, authentic version of monogamy."

Seth grabbed a pen and scrap of paper from the bedside table. "I'll take notes. Carry on."

Sara gave him a playful push. "Stop it."

Seth spoke out loud as he wrote. "Use the master's tools against them." He turned to her, rolling his hand to motion for her to continue.

Sara played along. "We'll own it, take it back, just like *take back the night*."

"Ta-da," Seth sang. "Then we could write a seminal paper, a retort to Audre's."

Sara snuggled into her pillow, her elvish display replaced with a thoughtful quietness. Seth met her there. She kissed him on the lips, soft but ardent, withdrawing to say, "Let's do it. Let's commit to being broken together, maybe forever."

acknowledgments

Thank you to Michelle Lovi for believing in this book in the first place and welcoming me into the "Oddy" family at Odyssey Books. And my heartfelt thanks to my first editor, Jessica McPherson Dainty. I am so grateful for her meticulous editorial attention, guidance, belief in this book and its cast of characters, and decade-long unwavering support. I am also deeply appreciative to Cerid Jones, who worked on the final (year-long) edit. After so many years trying to get this book into the world, her keen editorial eye was inspiring at a time when I needed it most. Many thanks as well to my first readers: Jo Wilson, Nan Hibbs, and Cath Smith.

I have the most beautiful family. All my love and gratitude to Vance and my children, Blythe and Bryony. I lived inside and through the characters in this book for over a decade, and sometimes (and in varying degrees) my family became just as invested and obsessed, such as the time when I picked up Blythe from elementary school and she hopped in the car and said to me, "How's Marco today?"

And finally, thank you to the writing community, literary agents, and generous friends for their support. I am especially indebted to specific people for their guidance, big heartedness, and friendship: Nan Hibbs, Lisa Whitney, Trish Siefer, Rebecca Parker, Deb Newman (a champion for women, as well as my website designer), Rebecca Faith Heyman (for careful reading and feedback on my work, writing workshop, and invaluable podcasts, especially First Line Frenzy!), all the participants from the Works Writers Conference (2019), Aida Lily (literary agent guru #1), Elizabeth Kracht (literary agent guru #2), Ashley Hasty (for featuring me on the Hasty Book List), too-many-people-to-name from the annual writing fest known as NaNoWriMo (and especially the Book Doctors for an early review), the Writing Group at Wellesley Centers for Women, the Best of Women's Fiction Podcast, and the Women's Fiction Writers Group.

about the author

A professor of gender studies and sociology for over 20 years, Judith Jackson-Pomeroy retired her academic regalia to write women's fiction. When she's not writing, she earns her keep working as the Acquisitions Editor for an Academic Press and Research Collaborator at the Justice & Gender-Based Violence Research Initiative at Wellesley Centers for Women, Wellesley College. Her fiction is described as a take on modern womanhood, with themes of sexual politics, mental health, and addiction that pushes back with humor on the redemptive narrative trope, and features tartly funny, unapologetic, complex female protagonists who will make you laugh, facepalm, and cry. This is her debut.

www.jjacksonpomeroy.com